Kali

on a

RAMPAGE

Kali

on a

RAMPAGE

R. D. Cervo

NEW PULP PRESS

Published by New Pulp Press, LLC, 926 Truman Avenue, Key West, Florida 33040, USA.

For information contact:
Publisher@NewPulpPress.com
ISBN-13: 978-0692606186 (New Pulp Press)
ISBN-10: 0692606181

To Catarina and My Brothers

Kali

on a

RAMPAGE

"The ultimate tragedy is not learning from your suffering."

Consider this quote a warning!

ONE

10:30 Saturday evening. Life is difficult when you are age 22 and you have the facial complexion of the late Yasser Arafat and the cauliflower ears of a grappler. Life is even harder when you also have florid schizophrenia. The illness is rearing its ugly head in the mind of Warren Ritchie. He is home again, standing in the downstairs bathroom of his parent's raised-ranch. Some of the original pale-pink tub tiles are missing. Staphylococcus laden black-brown crud is growing in patches on the tropical fish shower curtain. Ancient specks of dried Colgate-spit and little hairs encrust the sink. The grime is exposed in the glare of the overhead light bulb.

What are they doing to me? What could it be? What do they want? Should I just man-up, be stone-cold, grow a bigger set of testicles, forget the cups, and slice off both ears now?

The beads of Super-Glue are now tacky around the rims of the two orange Dixie cups. Warren is staring at his reflection. The toilet water is yellow with pee. There is no thought to flush after being engrossed in examining his body in the bathroom mirror for the last two hours. He had removed all his clothes except for his underwear. Belly flab hangs over the frayed band of his XXL tighty-whities that are not so white but rather blotched with coffee-stain colors. Reaching 6'1 and being wide with big doughy thighs, he has been growing fatter and fatter. Some of his pills caused a relentless craving for sugar. He drank cherry flavored root beer by the gallons.

1

What are they turning me into?

He palms one of his man-boobs. His chest is almost a B in bra size. Tweaking one maroon hairy nipple, a droplet appears. It is watery and milky. A rare side effect of certain anti-psychotic medications is for male patients to lactate. Warren had been taking his pills in a haphazard manner. Most days he skipped; other days he swallowed handfuls. He mixed the old discontinued prescriptions along with the new ones. Little, amber pill bottles with labels like Risperdal, Zyprexa, and Seroquel are lined up on the edge of the sink next to the Dixie cups, the tube of Super-Glue, and the retractable carpet knife.

Oh no! They are trying to turn me into a woman!

He squeezes more fluid out of the other nipple.

Out in the living room, Warren's father lets out a loud popping fart. The sound startles Warren for a moment and he brakes his gaze from the mirror. Mr. Ritchie Senior is in a giant, green vinyl recliner, trance-like in front of the television. He is anemic and small but with a large blockish head and a graying crew cut. The nerd glasses magnify his unblinking, blue eyes to the point of appearing disproportionate and freakish. A Bic ballpoint pen is forever being grinded in his mouth. The news is on. It is always on. There was a detonation in a Hindu temple in New Delhi by al Qaeda. 18 dead. The terrorist used a nail-bomb suicide vest. Video footage of grieving and angry faces flicker on the TV screen and on the lenses of Mr. Ritchie's glasses.

Upstairs, mother is sedated to the world like all the other evenings. She is obese, weighing in at almost 300. She is a mound under the blankets and the musky comforter. Mother had long stopped cooking, dusting, and mopping. Bottles of OxyContin are on the nightstand. She often weeps and says she needs the pills for her bulging discs, bad knees and nerves. "I have to rest, I'm in pain" is her mantra. Mother has not been coming downstairs much anymore.

Warren returns back to his reflection in the mirror. The reason that his ears are gnarled with scar tissue is from his frequent twisting and scratching in a futile attempt to stop the voices. Many times he picked and dug at his ears causing them to bleed and get infected.

If this doesn't stop them from broadcasting into my brain, I swear I'll do the bi-lateral Van Gough!

He picks up one of the Dixie cups and presses it to the side of his head, covering his right ear. Then he does the other side. The Super Glue binds to his skin. Warren looks oddly primitive-extraterrestrial with the two new protrusions added to his features.

This will block the signals for now! But I have to stop them altering my body any further! No way in hell will I let them do this to me! I am not some big fat girl with titties! I'm a big boy! A big dude! A macho-man! A heavyweight contender! Spartacus! Yes, a big-big-big alpha stag that can take a lot of ----------------pain!!!!

With a trembling hand, he fumbles with the slide button on the carpet knife. A thin triangular razorblade is released. It is ultra-sharp and pointy! With a mixture of fear and rage, Warren quickly takes his right thumb and index finger and pinches and stretches out his left nipple like he is trying to remove a piece of old chewing gum from under a desktop. And he...

Swipes with the carpet knife.

"AAAAAAAAHH!!!"

The dirty sink turns red. Bright crimson blood pours down Warren's chest and over his big fishy-white belly. He faints and begins to drop, the slippery severed nipple falling from his fingers. The carpet knife is still in his right grasp. A muffled but resounding thud is heard throughout the house. Mr. Ritchie Senior turns his head while still sitting in the recliner and stares at the bathroom door. On TV, a Hindu mob is chanting "Kali! Kali!" evoking the wrathful goddess of revenge and death. Mr. Ritchie slowly turns his gaze back to the television screen. He bites down harder on the plastic Bic pen and it splinters in his mouth.

11:20 pm, Saturday. The ER at Saint Rose's Hospital in New Haven is hopping. It seems that a horde of city residents decided to have heartaches, strokes, heroin overdoses, car crashes, breach-births, and bullet wounds all at the same time. A gaggle of teen-age girls is brought in after rolling their Mitsubishi Montero. One has a severe intracranial bleed. The whimpering and screaming make strange music. An 85-year-old ambulanced over from a nursing home just went into cardiac arrest. There is shouting and monitors are beeping and buzzing. Added to the mix is a pediatric trauma alert as docs frantically try to remove a large seedless grape that is lodged way down in a toddler's windpipe.

The sliding doors of the ER open again as paramedics wheel in a 22-year-old, obese, white male with a self-inflicted laceration to the pectoral area. Warren Ritchie's nipple had been left back on the bathroom floor like a piece of discarded pepperoni. There would be no hope of reattachment. Warren's mind is in overdrive. Being brought to the hospital fueled the delusion that *they* were to perform surgery that would alter his sexuality. *They're gonna give me tits and hips like Playboy's Miss January!!! Size 36, 28, 32!!! Or maybe size 38, 29, and 30. Or maybe size 35, 30, and 32!!! Or may be...* Warren has an archive of the old Playboy magazines under his bed and in piles in his closets. He has an autistic knack for remembering all of the girl's stats starting with issues from the 1960's.

Warren begins to scream out the numbers, "37, 26, and 35!!! 39, 27, 31!!! 35, 30, 31!!! 36, 28, 33!!! ..."

He struggles against the straps that bind him to the gurney. His chest is taped and the pressure bandages are seeping. The head ER doc barks out orders, "Get that guy quiet! Hit him with a Haldol, Benadryl cocktail! And why the hell does he have paper cups covering his ears?"

In the back of the ER there are a series of beds set aside for psychiatric admissions. The area is usually clogged with frequent flyers coming down from crack binges, smack withdrawals, all night benders, Dust psychosis, benzo delirium, being-stuck-on-stupid from K2, over-heating on Molly.... And the list goes on.

"Who do I have to fuck around here to see a nurse?" Yells out Mattie Gallagher, "My head hurts!" Mattie is old school. Straight alcohol is his game. Smoking Bath Salts is as alien to him as an iPhone. They say if his admissions to the ER were Sky Miles, he could have gone around the world twice, first class. It being Saturday night he is piss drunk again. He is sitting on the edge of his bed in observation room 1050. Dried blood is caked on the side of his face. The police brought him in after they found him on the sidewalk, blitzed, stunned and bleeding. It is unsure if someone popped him in a bar or if he walked into a signpost.

"Mr. Gallagher, please lower your voice and lay down!" said a nurse as she rushes by.

"Why don't you lay down with me! Get one of your nursey friends too! You can sit on my face while she rides my shillelagh!"

Mattie was often viewed as a bad ethnic joke. He is a 100% Irish and comes from a long line of alcoholics. Some say he looks like a sleazy Bing Crosby. He is emaciated and hollow chested with a greasy white comb-back. Even though he never set foot once on a golf course he wears atrocious golf pants and pastel windbreakers. At age 61 he cannot remember a day in his adult life without having a drink in his hand except for those periods of incarceration for driving-while-shit-faced. After the third DUI Mattie lost his license forever but now and again still manages to sneak behind the wheel.

Another vice that Mattie is inflicted with is gambling. He bets on everything from the ponies to the greyhounds. It was a dark day in his life when he was banned from both Indian Casinos in Connecticut after the multiple episodes of public inebriation and fistfights. These days he hangs out at OTB. There are also the usual wads of lottery tickets and scratch-off games stuffed in the pockets of his plaid pants. He believes deeply in his heart that someday his big ship will come in.

11:31 pm. Hospital aides begin to wheel Warren back into the psych area. The plan is to medicate him, put him under, and suture him up. Warren continues to shout out numbers, "37, 28, 30!!! 35, 27, 31!!!" Soon, there are no longer accurate Playboy centerfold measurements but rather numerical gibberish as Warren's thoughts become more loose and disorganized. "50! 312! 9! 5000! 11! 32! 109! 4! 1003!!! 62!!! ...." His sense of panic goes turbo as he feels the nurse's syringe in his thigh. Warren bellows, "DON'T!!!"

Mattie yells back, "Yea, that's right, son! Don't let 'em take ya down easy!"

Within moments Warren experiences an odd sense of detachment as if he were leaving the planet. Tears streak his cheeks and he starts to sob and babble. Then blackness.

"What's with all the numbers?" asks Mattie. "Is he some kind of safe-cracker?"

Nobody answers. Nobody ever pays attention to Mattie.

The sliding doors to the ER open again and there is another stretcher, another person, and another heart in fibrillation.

THREE

Monday morning, 8:30 a.m. The Elm City Behavioral Health Center opens its doors. It is one of New Haven's over-burdened, outpatient psychiatric clinics located smack-dab in the hood. From the front, one can see a three-story façade of old brick tagged with graffiti. The upper office windows have the shades pulled for confidentiality. Inside, a small team of docs, social workers, addiction counselors and nurses do their best to serve over three thousand people with mental health issues that live in the community. The waiting room is often packed with those just willing to get their prescriptions refilled. Part of the mission statement at the Elm City Behavioral Health Center is to promote quality of life.

Peter Fray is the only psychologist presently working at the facility and on Monday mornings he often questions his quality of life as he sees the enormous stack of referrals and consults on his desk. A blissful weekend just ended which involved him mostly spooning in bed with his girlfriend, eating Indian food and listening to tacky new age instrumentals.

Off to the races again.

Peter has the cliché psychologist look. He is 54, graying a bit in the beard and in his uncombed, frizzy hair. He likes corduroy and tweed even in the summer and wears wire-rimmed glasses. On the walls of his small, windowless office there are various diplomas and certifications. Peter worked as a clinician in state hospitals in the early years before the movement against institutionalization. On the prodding of his ex-wife, he attempted his own private practice but was never much of a businessman and it all fell apart. Publishing was the next trial. He tried writing a self-help book but could not help himself to finish it. The Elm City Behavioral Health Center was waiting for him. The money was poor compared to other opportunities and the workload daunting but he took the position. The reason involved a common insecurity for some people with big diplomas.

I really don't know what the hell I'm doing.

Peter periodically has the fear that he is highly inadequate and can never truly help another human being.

I'm a shithead. Therapeutically impotent.

It is recommended that a clinical psychologist also be receiving therapy in order to deal with the work related distress and burnout. Peter had been receiving informal counseling from an old classmate some years ago but it all went bad when his chum lost his license for accepting a blowjob from a female client who was in the midst of a manic, hypersexual episode. Peter often wonders who is counseling his friend.

Peter takes a swig of his coffee and reaches for the first file from the stack before him. The typed label reads – RITCHIE, WARREN. Peter opens it. A procedure at the clinic is to take a photo of the client when he or she enrolls in the treatment program. The front desk clerical staff does it during the initial intake. The photo was paper clipped inside on the first page of the file. Peter stares at it and sees a familiar facial expression. It is the blunted, flat affect of a person with schizophrenia. Distant. Vacant. Peter wonders how the young man must have felt to be photographed.

He mumbles, "It surely doesn't help the paranoia."

A week ago, the client had come to the first

appointment and met with one of the psychiatrists for a medication consult. This morning, the client was supposed to return to meet with Peter for a behavioral screening. Peter read through the enclosed psychosocial report. He learned that Warren had been an accounting student at the University of Connecticut. During last spring he had his first major psychotic break. Campus security found Warren hiding in a janitorial storage area, ears bleeding, and his sweat-pants soaked with urine. He had stopped going to classes. Delusions involving his dorm room being bugged and fitted with surveillance cameras were noted. Warren had believed that his professors and the Dean of Academic Affairs had him on a web-cam.

"Poor kid," Peter utters.

From April to the beginning of October, Warren had been hospitalized in a psychiatric unit up near Storrs, three times. Stabilization had been rocky due to typical, non-medication compliance. Warren was recently released to return home to West Haven to live with his parents.

Peter turns to the next page on the report and speaks aloud some of the salient points. "No brothers or sisters. Only child. Mother has a history of clinical depression with psychotic features. Nothing about the dad."

Looking back at Warren's photo, Peter re-examines the bloated features and patchy stubble.

"His ears looked deformed?" Peter says. "Dating must have been tough."

Dr. Fray's assumption is correct. What the report did not tell was that Warren was still a virgin in his senior year at college. He had never cupped a breast through a sweater. There was never a girlfriend. No high school prom. The last time a woman's lips touched his skin was when he was eleven and those cold lips belonged to his mother, which gave no points on the scoreboard of rites of passage. The obesity, the five o'clock shadow and monk bald spot were all like the Mark-of-Caine on campus. Warren chain-smoked. XXL gray sweats appeared to be his everyday attire. None of the contemporary 20ish-year-old hard-bodies with belly-shirts and pierced navels would ever return a smile. What he usually got back from females was the expression of *Ick! Weirdo Alert!*

Warren liked Japanese anime, grandiose-trash-talking professional wrestlers, Star Wars, and math. There were also the old Playboy magazines but he hardly ever masturbated. He found modern Internet porn too intimidating and scary with its infinite sea of writhing variety. Warren's sexual desire was faint. No morning wood. His penis stayed shriveled in the tallow of his groin. During those precious times when his dorm-mate was gone or zonked-out on Jagermeister and weed, Warren would run his hands across the glossy pictorials of the skin mags. With an almost religious dedication, he recited and attempted to remember the various centerfold models' tits, waist, and hips stats. It was his personal bizarro attempt at intimacy.

On most days until closing, Warren haunted the campus library and stayed for hours at the computer center. To his professors, Mr. Ritchie was an identification code and a marginal 2.6 written on a blue exam book. He was usually invisible to the other students except for the occasional ridicule from the mean and immature ones. The Giant Gray Barney was a cruel nickname that stuck.

In his loneliness Warren Ritchie's schizophrenia had festered and erupted.

Peter closes the file. He is ready to meet Warren Ritchie.

"Good morning, Doris," said Peter after pressing the intercom button to the waiting room on the first floor, "Can you send Mr. Ritchie up; I'm ready."

"Sorry Dr. Fray," said the front desk receptionist, "I

was just about to call you. We got word from Saint Rose's. He's been hospitalized on Saturday for trying to harm himself. It's a no show."

"Okay, thank you."

Peter pauses. He puts the file to the side and wonders if he will ever meet the young man in the photo. Over the years Peter has looked into the faces of thousands of people tormented with psychosis and depression. A question many times asked is, how many fall through the cracks? Peter knew the answer, *a lot*. Peter takes another sip of coffee and goes to work on some overdue, billing documentation.

Then there is a voice, "I see you have a cancellation, doctor."

Peter snaps up his head from his notes, startled. He had forgotten to shut the door to his office. Standing in the doorway is Francis LaBoudy.

"I scared you doctor," says LaBoudy with a mean, little titter.

Peter clears his throat and asks, "Francis? Do you have an appointment?"

LaBoudy laughs in a mocking tone, "Oh no Doctor Fray. I don't need your therapy. I never needed it. I just came by to tell you of your defeat."

It had been approximately two months since Peter had seen this client. The last session ended with security being called and LaBoudy being strapped to a gurney and sent off to the hospital. The client has changed his appearance again and Peter notices that he now has an accent. It is sort of haughty-European-ish. LaBoudy is dressed in a stark white shirt and gray dress pants that need to be hemmed. His thin black hair is greased back with Vitalis. It appears that he has been avoiding the sun being so pale. At first glance his physical stature is not that imposing. He is on the small side with thin arms and legs and a bit of a potbelly but his little, tiny brown eyes are so intense that they often cause people to have concern, i.e. ------------ the fucking willies.

"I don't understand, Francis," says Peter in a calm professional voice. "I haven't seen you in some time. What's been happening?"

LaBoudy suddenly steps into the office and stands in front of the desk. Peter stiffens in his chair.

"Don't be so jumpy, doctor," smiles LaBoudy, "I'm leaving in a moment. And of course I don't expect your small intellect to understand. It is my birthday. I just turned 50 years old. This world is going to get a taste of the real me that has been stifled by you fools for so many years! You and all the other charlatans could never fathom my potential."

"I feel uncomfortable, Francis. I'm concerned about you."

"You should be concerned." LaBoudy leans forward and briefly places his hands on the desk.

"How come? What are your plans, Francis?"

"No need to call the security guard, doctor. I'm far from being suicidal. I want to live grandly while the world cries!" LaBoudy tosses back his head in a theatrical manner and laughs louder and harder.

"Okay, Francis," Peter says with a still level tone. "Would you like to sit? Maybe you can tell be specifically what's going on."

"I finally acquired access to my files. A plethora of gibberish! A freethinker like me being labeled as bipolar disorder type one with a mixed bag of highly dysfunctional character logical traits, histrionic, enmeshed with narcissistic, borderline and sociopathic elements! What rubbish!!! How dare you describe me in such degrading terms!"

Fray stiffens more in his chair and responds with some

hesitation in his voice, "You have endured a lot of suffering in your life."

"Oh don't try to placate me, you-you half-wit! You are wrong to judge me by my many forays of self-discovery. Mundane commonplace sexual identity issues made me explore some tranny chat-rooms and a brief stint as a sassy courtesan. So what! I was not manic!"

"The incident in the truck must have been painful," Peter says.

"Speak not one more word about that black truck!" LaBoudy flashes with anger. "Cease your inquiry!"

Shaking his head, Fray remembers the many reports of LaBoudy being brought into the ER by the cops, screaming and yelling, dressed in black nylons, garter belt, six-inch fuck-me-heels, and a tangled, long red boa. Francis's usual M.O. had been to doll-up, walk the seedier streets in New Haven and wave at passing cars. When someone slowed up, Francis would quickly scamper away. Back then Francis loved the shock value of playing the part of a transvestite hooker. There were countless factious stories of him having sex with vets on leave that later died in Iraq or Afghanistan. Knowing the dead could not defend their reputations, he would gather the names from obituaries posted on the Internet. Francis would then attempt to tote his exploits in group therapy in order to soak up jaw-dropping reactions from his peers. Quickly, it was evident that group therapy was not appropriate, it being more a grab for the limelight rather than a mode to make healthy psychological changes. After being discharged from various treatment programs, his file wound-up on Dr. Fray's desk.

A fragile rapport had been established between Francis and Peter that allowed for some wildly intense therapy sessions. Peter discovered that Francis *never* had sex with anyone even in his most manic episodes. Francis's

15

defensiveness toward physical intimacy was that severe due to his abuse he suffered as a child. Auntie Barbara was supposed to have been Francis's guardian. There was the true grotesque tragedy of Francis at age 7 being forced to perform cunnilingus on his rotund 60-year-old Aunt.

Regretfully, despite all the counseling and therapy, Francis continued with his transvestite dress-up games for most of the summer until being replaced by a hyper-religious phase. The change was triggered by a particularly traumatic incident in July. All the roadside cock-teasing almost proved to be fatal. One night, a black Dodge RAM stopped and he was pulled in and beaten to a pulpy mess. Hours later back in the ER at Saint Roses, it was a pitiful sight. Francis's face was a swollen monster mask of blood and smeared lipstick and mascara.

"Alright Francis," Peter says, "We will defer the episode in the truck, but what about the church group?"

LaBoudy chuckles, "Oh that? What folly!"

"Folly?"

"The Pentecostal Church of Ultimate Salvation is to blame! I strolled in one day on a whim after getting bloody bored with the transvestite scene. I got back into men's attire. After a while I even began to accept handshakes and embraces after church services. It was all so lovely and syrupy! I heard sermons how the Lord heals all. Then there was talk of possession and demons! Soon I came to the conclusion that I never had bipolar disorder but was rather riddled with unclean spirits. Can you imagine that! Unclean spirits! Psychiatric medication was no longer an option. What I really needed was an exorcism! Hooray, old boy!"

Peter smirks.

LaBoudy reminisces with a fevered glint in his eye, "It was quite the dramatic spectacle during a faith healing service as I snarled and thrashed about on the carpet before the pulpit as the minister and others prayed aloud for my deliverance from the dark forces that spurred my fascination with uncircumcised penises and frilly panties! The congregation was relieved when I finally popped up, sweating, and out of breath but smiling and saying that I was okay and that the demons just vanished! Those worshippers that were fanatical believed the whole show and had shouted that the devil had lost and the Almighty had won! Others in the crowd who were a bit more intuitive clapped to be polite but did not holler halleluiah. I knew they had inwardly asked God to remove the sin of doubt from their hearts because the truth was I had given them a sense of uneasiness. Poor dears! I scared them."

Raising an eyebrow, Peter says, "The last time I saw you in this office you scared me. You had a strip of white cardboard from a box top wedged in the front of your shirt to resemble a preacher's collar. You stood-up on my desk and started reciting aloud scripture from Revelations. I was condemned to burn in hell for believing in pills rather than Jehovah. You were rambling and your speech was fast and pressured. And you still deny having bipolar?"

Laughing, LaBoudy replies, "I remember doctor, your saying to me, it's not the devil, Francis. It's the lack of Depakote! I loathe you for calling the ambulance and having me sent to that psych ward."

"How did you fare?"

"I cheeked my meds got discharged, only to rev up again."

"What happened next?

LaBoudy grins like the Grinch and answers, "It all went sour when I returned back to them on a Sunday in September. I walked in during the middle of a service, dressed only in white bed sheets and a pair of green flip-flops. The congregation at the Pentecostal Church of Ultimate Salvation all turned their heads and stared at me as I stood in the center of the aisle, rose up my arms and said aloud that God had been speaking to me during the wee hours of the morning! I made the minister stop his sermon! At first, the fanatical in the crowd had smiled with glee and sincerely wanted to hear from their brother who had tangled with evil spirits not so long ago. The others, again, looked apprehensive with tightening sphincters. I went on and proclaimed that I was God's son. The minister tried to explain in a frightened voice that everybody is a child of God and that while he appreciated my enthusiasm he wished that I would just relax and sit. I shouted back that he was a fucking imbecile and that I *really* was Jesus Christ incarnate and that all should bow down to me at this very moment! The congregation was aghast that day! Someone yelled out blasphemer! I shouted I'm the actual Second Coming!!!!! An elderly Puerto Rican gentleman walked out into the aisle and punched me in the neck. I retaliated by turning around and Tae Kwon Do snap-kicking the gent in the crotch so hard I'm sure I dislodged his old cancerous prostate. My gosh there was a lot screaming! Then someone else had the nerve to come out and grab me, the messiah, in a headlock! Can you imagine the disrespect! I bit! Scratched! Wrestled! It didn't take long to lose my bed-sheet robe and I became naked except for one green flip-flop. The police were called. It was an ugly scene as I was tasered, put on my belly and cuffed. Bare-assed and breathing heavy, I was left on the floor in front of the pulpit. Then back to the psych unit I went. Yes, what fucking folly indeed!"

Peter replies coolly, "A lot of chaos."

"No!" LaBoudy snaps, "It was not chaos! It was just misdirected greatness! Up until last week, I had been committed to a state hospital. Such a crime! While there I stayed mostly in bed. I was guarded and snippy. They diagnosed me with having severe depression after coming down from a full-blown manic episode with psychotic features. In reality I was quietly raging. I could not believe how quickly the church group had turned on me. I hate every one of them! And I now hate angels, saints, martyrs and all twelve apostles! You can even add old Saint Nick and the bloody Easter Bunny to my target-list! I would like to piss in all their open mouths!"

"Very dramatic, Francis. What is with the new accent? Is it British?" asks Peter in an irreverent tone, "It seems to come and go while you speak."

LaBoudy sneers and replies, "Well fine sir, when I was still back in that state lunatic ward, the staff pestered me to get out of my bed and to go to the community room to watch the telly. One evening Turner's Classic Movies broadcasted THE SILENCE OF THE LAMBS. The mental health workers were negligent in monitoring what the patients were viewing. I became mesmerized with the character, Hannibal Lector, played by Sir Anthony Hopkins. He's so smooth. So classy. So Sexy. It was then that I planned to reinvent myself again. If the Christians don't want me maybe, I should try being really evil. Why should I be good? Maybe sweet, gentle, Jesus-loving society needs a painful reminder that I exist. Maybe they deserve a really bad slap! With that realization, it was then that I brightened up and was released from that madhouse!"

Peter replies coldly, "I'm sure you were supposed to follow-up with the department of mental health for outpatient medication management and DBT. Did you blow off your appointment?"

"I don't need to answer to you!"

"You need help, Francis. You are not stable."

"Shut your trap, I am no longer court ordered for medication enforcement! I have my rights!" Feeling like a bank-robber that suddenly realizes that he has been bantering too long with the teller, LaBoudy quickly bolts up.

"Where are you going, Francis?" Peter asks with alarm in his voice. "You know deep down you need help! Think about why you really came here!"

"I got what I needed doctor! You are just not that observant!"

With a burst of crazed excitement, LaBoudy does an about-face and runs out of the office. "Ta-Ta!!!" LaBoudy shouts as he flees down the hallway.

Peter immediately buzzes the front receptionist to be on the lookout for the patient and to alert security. He then calls the medical director. "Hi, this is Dr. Pete. I just had LaBoudy come unannounced up to my office! He must have slipped past the receptionist. It's happened again. I know they're busy down there but who likes surprises this early in the morning. He just left!"

As the security guard comes up the main stairwell, LaBoudy had already absconded down the back way.

Peter hangs up the phone and stays in his office. It is against safety protocol to go running after manic patients. The police would have to handle it. With a sigh, Peter looks down at his desk to find his pen. He does not see it. It was a Mont Blanc inscribed with his name on it. It was old Christmas gift from his brother. The item has important sentimental value. He had been using it a short time ago before LaBoudy appeared. Peter searches his cluttered desk for another moment then in surprise and frustration says aloud, "Did LaBoudy just take off with my pen?"

FOUR

Monday, 10:22 a.m. The autumn air is crisp, the sky blue, and LaBoudy is ecstatic as he quickly scurries out of the rear of The Elm City Behavioral Health Center, prize in hand. A 1995, white Ford Tempo, with rusted side panels is waiting for him. In a rush, he yanks open the back door of the car and lays down across the seat.

"Drive! Drive!" LaBoudy screeches.

An elderly African-American security guard steps out into the parking lot, looking frustrated and winded. The Tempo pulls away and starts down the avenue.

"Magnificent! Absolutely magnificent!" laughs LaBoudy. He sits up and holds out Dr. Fray's Mont Blanc pen for examination. "Chauffeur, let's go on a long trip today." LaBoudy knows he cannot return home because a police car and an ambulance would surely be waiting.

"Where do you wanna go, Francis?" said the driver.

"I told you to no longer address me by name!" LaBoudy's tone suddenly turns nasty. "You are to address me as Sir! Now make haste to the highway!"

"Yes Sir."

The driver is Chester Dumont. The bowl haircut does not appear to match his age, nor does the red Winnie the Pooh sweatshirt given to him by his sister. He is 51, a year older than Francis, mildly obese, short, and squat, with thick bifocals, a graying little mustache and a hearing aid. There is also the label of borderline intellectual functioning. Chester's I.Q. is a tad too high to be diagnosed with mental retardation but is often described by others in the vernacular sense as "slow." He did however have certain skills that Francis did not possess, one being the ability to operate a car. LaBoudy has crippling surges of panic with the prospect of driving and has never obtained his license. Chester also has the fortitude to hold down part-time employment as a bagger at Super Stop & Shop. Francis never had a formal job in his life and is receiving 709.00 dollars a month from social security. Despite these facts, Francis often ridicules Chester calling him "Gump." They both live in the same state subsidized apartment building away from downtown New Haven. Chester does not like it when Francis gets mean but it is better than being lonely. Some months ago, he had to call Francis "Reverend," then "Jesus." Now it is "Sir." Chester does not understand. He liked it better when Francis was playing Halloween and dressing up like a woman. At least he could call Francis by his real name.

"See this pen, driver," said LaBoudy, "It belongs to Dr. Fray, that quack back there. I heard that a Mont Blanc costs a pretty penny. Parts of it are real gold. I took it!"

Chester glances back in the rear view mirror and asks, "How come, Fran- I mean Sir?"

"Because I should have some of the finer things in life. I always fancied this pen. I used to spy at it during those moronic therapy sessions. Plus, it's time for some retribution. How dare he imprison me in a loony-bin!"

The car started to pull up on the interstate. Chester felt nervous. He did not like the way Francis was grinning. It was spooky. Chester thought, *why is Francis speaking fancy, like some guy from England? Why does he call me driver? He knows my name. It's bad to steal. Why is Francis acting bad?*

They travel up on I-95.

"Many are going to feel my wrath. Oh, indeed they will be sorry." LaBoudy laughs aloud and leans back his head.

"The lambs will be crying!"

Chester's jitters get worst.

Up ahead there is an interstate Mobil station and a McDonalds.

"Driver, pull in there," Francis orders.

Chester suddenly brightens, "Oh good, I can go for an Egg McMuffin"

"Silence! No! We are not going to dine!"

Sulking, Chester pulls up front to Mickey-Dees.

"Driver, get out. Come around and open the door for me!"

"What?"

"You heard me! You are my bloody chauffeur!"

Chester gets out and opens the back door to the rusted Ford Tempo.

"Stand at attention and wait my return." LaBoudy abruptly marches forward toward the entrance of McDonalds. A stressed-out heavyset soccer mom pushing a stroller comes along on the walkway. The proper etiquette is to hold the door for her and her child. Instead, Francis quickly pulls the door closed behind him once he is in the foyer. He snickers when he hears her muffled voice on the outside, "Jerk!"

There are long lines in front of the McDonald's counter. Francis scans the room and looks at the many different faces. Young. Old. White. Hispanic. Black.

I hate you all so very much. So very much.

He then sees what he is seeking. The restrooms. He slips inside the men's lavatory, his eyes darting about. There is an empty stall at the end and he goes in and latches the door.

I must do this operation in a clandestine fashion. They cannot discover my treachery too early.

LaBoudy undoes his gray trousers and pulls down his boxers. Pointing about with his thin albino wiener, he begins to urinate on the walls but soon directs the stream downward into the bowl as he starts to get speckled with splash back.

"Damn it, I have wet marks on my attire!"

The peeing stops once his bladder is empty. He pauses for a moment and checks himself to see if he is ready for part two.

Yes, I feel it.

LaBoudy squats a bit with his white buttocks aiming to the side of the toilet. He begins to defecate. Long brown coils of feces come to drape partly on the seat while segments break off and land on the floor.

"A modern art sculpture!" Francis says with a suppressed giggle. "And kudos to that half box of Raisin-Bran."

He wipes himself then sticks the used toilet paper on the inside of the stall door. After bringing up his trousers he rummages through the pockets to find the Mont Blanc. The plan is to sign his first name on the wall of the stall but the pen will not write on the smooth metal surface.

"Foiled."

But still there are other ways to leave his mark. Leaning down he pads his crap with both hands and comes up with brown palms and fingertips. He then goes out of the stall with no intention to wash-up but rather to continue with his vandalism. Out in the main food area, he briskly walks up to the condiments counter and rubs his thumb on the silver button that dispenses the ketchup. He then quickly picks up a bunch of packets of tangy barbecue dipping sauce meant for the Chicken Nuggets, moves them around a bit in his hands then returns them to the little bin. Lines in front of the McDonald's counter continue to be long. The place is busy and no one takes notice of LaBoudy. There is only one empty booth left. He sits down for a moment and runs his palms across the table and on the seat.

This is one time in my life I wish I had E-Bola with a lot of blood in my stool!

Then his heart quickens as he sees a stack of plastic high chairs. Soccer mom and her toddler daughter are up in line getting a Breakfast Happy Meal. LaBoudy stands up and goes over and nonchalantly brushes his hands for a moment on the armrests of the first high chair in the stack.

Call me a jerk will you. I hope your little darling gets a nice case of lethal dysentery.

LaBoudy then decides to depart not wanting to press his luck and be identified. Small brown smears are left on both inner and outer door handles of the main entrance into the restaurant. As he comes down the walkway towards the waiting car, an obese family is coming forward on their way into McDonalds.

"Bon Appetite!" LaBoudy says to them with an impish smile.

Chester had done what he had been told and stood and waited by the car. He notices that Francis has that spooky smile again as he returns to the back seat. Chester closes the door for his friend. As they drive off, Chester wrinkles his nose and thinks he smells poop.

"Driver, do you know what I set in motion back there?" grins LaBoudy.

Chester is apprehensive to answer, "What?"

"Don't forget the "Sir"!"

"Yes, Francis; -I mean Sir."

"You see, I left a bit of a mess. Rhetorically I inquire, do you know what E-Coli is?"

Being quite perplexed Chester looks into the rearview mirror and just shrugs.

"It is a bacteria found in the gut. There is a lethal strain that produces toxins! It is rare but it does surface once in a while to cause some trouble for mankind. The fecal-oral route and improper hand washing are major factors! You know naughty children are always putting things in their mouths. Oh it could be quite dangerous if poor little Sally or rambunctious little Jimmy with his ADHD ingested that bad kind of E-Coli. Kidneys can shut down. Their blood becomes septic. Oh, very grim indeed. But of course, the authorities would first blame the meat packers. The hamburger did it! It was the bovine! But what about me! Could I carry that killer E-Coli in my bowel movement! One can only dream. One can only wait and see!"

"Huh?" Chester gasps.

Francis's speech is starting to become fast and pressured again. "Interestingly enough I also caught a fleeting glimpse of a young Negro teen with a mop-bucket working behind the counter during my little sortie into that bastion of fat and dimwitted Americana. He looked like one of those angry, troubled kind. You know, gangsta type. Surely that cruel white McDonald's manager will order him to go clean that --------- sculpture I left in the last stall in the men's room. A life changing critical choice is to be made. Does the Negro boy buckle to The Man and cleanup the human-filth for minimum wage and have heightened hatred for the world? Or does he snap? Walk off the job? Surely, it would be a violation of his parole. But he doesn't care! He's been incarcerated before. Maybe he will leave right away and go car-jack a frail granny at an intersection? Later score some crack-cocaine? Kill someone. Finally, years later, ending up shived-and-shanked in a prison shower. Oh, what a tragedy!" LaBoudy starts laughing loud. "You know I am so powerful I can take a shit and ruin lives!"

Chester is frightened. Tears begin to well up in his eyes. Then, he begins to openly sob as he drives.

"Chauffeur, what is your problem?!" LaBoudy flashes

with anger.

"You're talkin' about bad things, Francis! I'm scared! I don't want any trouble! I'm gonna drive home!"

LaBoudy has the urge to reach out and slap Chester in the back of the head for his insolence but chooses not to because he does not want to risk his sole access to a car. *Damn it! Damn it!* For a moment he wrings his soiled hands in frustration. LaBoudy then realizes that he needs to keep his plans secret in order not to frighten his chauffeur. Plus, he knows that Chester has a nosey sister that pops over once and awhile to check on her brother's affairs. Chester could blab. LaBoudy softens his tone. "Now, now, my simple servant, everything is going be okay. You need to drive on."

"It's bad to do bad things," says Chester, while sucking in snot and shaking a bit.

"Indeed, you are right my good man. I don't want to do bad things; I want to do great things. And every great figure has his trusted Igor. You should be happy, Chester. You'll be my assistant. We'll have fun!"

"I don't know, Francis. Those things you said seemed bad."

"No, no. It's all a game. I promise we'll start helping people instead."

"We will?"

"Yes, yes. We'll be good gents."

Chester calms a little as he continues on the highway with all the mid-morning traffic.

"In fact, if you do what I say and be a loyal Gunga Din, there may be a prize for you later in the day."

"Oh boy!" Chester suddenly gets excited. "What am I gonna get? What is it?"

LaBoudy smirks, "Well, if I have to use the restroom again; we'll need to find another McDonalds. I may buy you some of that cuisine that you desire so much."

"And a hot apple pie?"

"Your greed impresses me. But we will talk about rewards later. It is time to continue with some more of my plans."

"Yes, sir!" chuckles Chester.

"That's the spirit!" LaBoudy leans forward, patting Chester on the shoulder, leaving a few faint brown fingerprints. He then points. "I want you to pull in the left hand lane and slow down to forty miles an hour."

Chester instantly gets nervous again. "What?"

LaBoudy snaps. "Do you want to help people or not?"

Chester gives an apprehensive, "Yea?"

"Well, people are driving too fast. If you go over and slow down, people won't be in so much danger. 55 saves lives you know!"

"I thought the speed limit was 65."

"That's the maximum speed allowed by law. But if everybody slows way down below that, there won't be so many accidents. Don't you want to save babies and mommies?"

"Yes."

"Well, be a good American and do your duty."

Chester pulls the Ford Tempo into the left hand lane. He usually stayed in the right when driving. The left was always too fast for him. The speedometer drops down to 45 mph. A red Jeep Grand Cherokee comes barreling up from behind and instantly starts to tailgate.

"He's flashing his lights at me!" whines Chester.

"Tap your brakes hard!" orders LaBoudy.

"Okay, Sir!"

The Jeep almost smashes into the bumper of the Ford Tempo. There is a chain reaction of other vehicles having to break. Some car lengths behind, a Chevy mini-van plows into the back of a Toyota Prius. Shards of plastic taillight fly into the air. The Jeep swerves around to the right lane and as it passes, the driver blasts the horn and flips the bird.

"Hey, that guy's pretty mad!" says Chester.

"It's okay!" shouts LaBoudy with exhilaration. "You're teaching him to be a better driver and not to follow so close!"

Up ahead, there is highway construction. Jersey-barriers are set up. All traffic has to merge into a single lane.

"Oh, this will be wonderful!" claps LaBoudy. "Okay, chauffeur. I want you to slow down even more! We must respect the safety of those hard working souls of the Department of Transportation."

"What?"

"Just do what I say! We are coming into one lane. Single file. Bring down the speed and tap your brakes a lot."

"Okay."

With the accident between the mini-van and the Prius and the Ford Tempo crawling along at 25 miles per hour, it did not take long before I-95 heading back into New Haven is at a standstill.

"Someone is beeping their horn behind me! They seem upset," says Chester in an anxious tone.

"No, no, my little man." says LaBoudy with an unnerving grin. "They're not angry. They're beeping their horn to cheer you on. Everybody respects an extra careful driver."

"Really?"

"But of course. In fact, if you hit your breaks some more, you'll hear them cheer even louder."

Chester presses down on the brake pedal and a moment later there comes a longer sustained horn blast from a few car lengths back.

Chester giggles, "That was fun!"

"Yes! And you're also being a good citizen of Connecticut. I wouldn't be surprised, if you keep doing this each week, the governor will give you a special reward."

"Oh, boy! Oh, boy! What kind? What is it?"

"A big yellow ribbon, inscribed, CHESTER, THE SAFEST DRIVER IN THE NUTMEG STATE!"

"That's awesome!"

"Yes it is!"

LaBoudy turns his head for a moment and looks out the back window at the car behind them. It is a Honda. His eyes lock for a moment with the driver and it is not hard to read lips and to understand the use of the "F" word. LaBoudy quickly ducks down across the seat and goes into joyous hysterics.

I hope I'm making a Christian curse!

This was all a plan that began to be conjured -up during his last hospitalization. LaBoudy having fallen in love with the persona of the sassy serial killer Hannibal the Cannibal, he too wanted to toy with folks and hurt them. However, the major problem was that Francis's head would swoon with the site of blood and he would faint. Defecation was okay. In fact, he liked playing with kaka for some deep autonomy-versus-shame developmental reason but splattered gore was definitely out of the question. Francis knew that Hannibal was too debonair to ever be involved with coprophilia. There was a twinge of guilt concerning his inability to be a real hands-on murderer and Francis buried it but there was no way he would ever do things like chop, cut, and mutilate a human being. *Cannibalism? Yuck!* Francis's way to terrorize mankind would have to be more indirect. He would attack the society's infrastructure. Public bathrooms would be desecrated. Juicy boogers would be left on handrails. Bolts would be loosened on baby-changing stations to promote infant injury. There would be serial traffic jams. Francis believed every time he slowed down the highways there was potential for a wrecking ball to be sent into motion.

I'll make someone late for a job interview! He won't get the position because of the unacceptable tardiness. There will be subsequent marital discord. A threat of a divorce. Drinking! Finally, a murder suicide!

LaBoudy also had a plan to lurk on the roads near hospitals.

My driver and I will pull out in front of ambulances. We'll slow down; act stunned and won't pull over right away. We'll steal those precious moments needed to get someone to the operating room. Ah, too bad. Almost made it. A few seconds more may have saved grandpa's life. "HEE-HEE-HEE!" We'll kill hundreds this way!

Chester continues to drive on with his slow stop-and-go fashion. The rusted white Ford Tempo is the lead car in front of miles of stuck traffic. Behind the Honda is a black Dodge RAM. On the tailgate of the big truck are numerous bumper stickers. Some are faded and peeling while others are new. Besides the NRA decals, there are slogans such as GUN CONTROL MEANS SHOOTING WITH BOTH HANDS, and THE KENYAN WILL NEVER BE MY PRESIDENT BUT SARA PALIN WILL ALWAYS BE MY FIRST LADY, and WELCOME TO AMERICA, NOW SPEAK ENGLISH, and I'M A NEWTOWN-SANDY HOOK VICTIM BECAUSE THE GOVERNMENT HAS BANNED MY AR!

Inside the cab of the Dodge RAM, the driver is slamming his fist down hard on the dashboard while with his other hand he keeps blasting his horn. The man's ranting and swearing have now turned to primitive sounds of pure ---------rage.

Francis LaBoudy continues to recline across the back seat of the car, giggling, and picking brown bits out of his fingernails. Unknowingly, his grand scheme to set a wrecking ball into motion has begun.

FIVE

Monday, 11:56 a.m. It is almost lunchtime and Dr. Fray already assumed that his 11:00 am appointment is a no-show when he gets a call from the secretary that Paul Kosakowski is in the waiting room. The secretary reports that he appears, "up-set."

"You can send him to my office. Thank you." says Peter.

Before ascending the stairs, Kosakowski quickly charges into the visitor's bathroom to piss.

Peter removes the files from his desk, and arranges two chairs facing one another. A short while later, Kosakowski appears at the door, breathing heavy, red-faced and rambling, "I know I'm late. I was stuck in traffic. I almost busted my bladder. If you don't believe me, you can call the news station and check the road reports!"

"You look stressed," says Peter as he motions to the chair. "Come on in and take a load off. I-95 can be brutal."

Kosakowski plops down hard with an evident aura of irritability. He is 5'9, with a giant belly induced by Michelob, binge eating, and chronic stress. His beige polyester Hagars are stuffed tight. Dark sweat stains are under the armpits of his blue short-sleeve shirt. It was years ago when he had a brief stint in the Connecticut National Guard but he still keeps his hair buzzed short in military fashion. His eyeglasses look more like aviator shades. Kosakowski rubs the sore underside of his right hand as he talks, "You know I had to go so bad, so I swung into that McDonalds service center on the highway. And of course with my friggin luck, the men's bathroom is closed. They got some colored kid in there takin' his sweet goddamn time moppin' the place. I didn't want to be late. So I left and boom! I get stuck on the mother effin' road. I almost pissed my pants comin' here."

"Sounds extremely aggravating." says Peter with a validating tone.

"And not only that! There were some bastards in a white piece of junk deliberately drivin' really slow. Connecticut license plate, DPR-163. I couldn't exactly see their faces, but I could sense that they thought it was some kind of big friggin' joke. I bet they really were laughin'. Friggin' pricks!"

Peter nodded in a consoling manner but did not fully believe the client's interpretation of the actions of people in the white car. There was no other history of psychiatric treatment but the pathology was evident. Peter saw Kosakowski having the diagnosis of paranoid personality disorder. An individual with this type of illness often has irrational thoughts of persecution and believes that others are always intentionally trying to do harm. Peter knew it took time to build rapport with this type of client. He could easily sense that Paul did not trust him in the least. The approach would have to be one of gentle regard. There was also the conspicuous issue of decreased ability to control anger. Peter would tread lightly.

Kosakowski points his finger at the psychologist in a not so subtle threatening manner and sneers, "So, are you going to snitch to the court and say I was late and make my life more of a livin' hell?"

Peter gestures no with his head, and replies, "Don't worry, Paul. It's okay. I believe you made the best effort to get here. It is easy to see that you are under a lot of pressure."

This is the client's second therapy session. The court

mandated as terms of his probation that he attend treatment for anger management. Dr. Fray has to send a weekly letter to the judge regarding the client's compliance status. If the client missed his sessions, there would be a violation of probation. Kosakowski had no prior criminal history until the incident that occurred this past summer. His wife left him in August. During a meeting with the divorce lawyers he *lost it* and attempted to slap her. One of the attorneys sustained a dislocated shoulder and chipped tooth. The police were called, there were charges for assault and a restraining order was later implemented. The ordeal occurred a day before the client's 49th birthday. It was a monumental turn for the worst in Paul Kosakowski's life. There were no children involved but his ex-wife got custody of their Rhodesian Razor-Back, Brutus. She also got to stay in the raised-ranch in West Haven. Paul was now in a single room efficiency in the city that he feared and hated.

Peter leans forward a bit in his chair and asks, "So how was last week?"

Kosakowski loudly exhales and turns his gaze up to the corner of the office, seemingly to ignore the question. "I know you're not a real doctor, like a surgeon or a cardiologist but do you know somethin' about the body?"

Peter ignores the sarcasm and replies, "I know some. What's the question?"

"Do blacks and Ricans have bigger dongs than white guys? Is it really true?"

Peter shrugs in a nonchalant manner and says, "I'm not sure."

Kosakowski flashes his angry eyes toward the psychologist and laughs in a bitter tone, "Yea, a-course, you're a shrink! Why would you be lookin' at peckers unless you suck 'em on your day off."

"What is the purpose of the question?" says Peter

flatly.

Without warning, the client clenches his fist and whacks the armrest of his chair, then yells, "BECAUSE I FOUND OUT THIS WEEK MY WIFE IS DATIN' SOME SPIC FROM THE DOMINICAN REPUBLIC!!!"

Peter is startled and thinks the client may flip out and start breaking up the place, but Kosakowski quickly drops his head and appears to sob. Then there is a period of silence between the two. Kosakowski removes his eyeglasses and wipes his eyes with his big thumbs. Peter offers a box of tissues but the client swats them away. Kosakowski then puts his glasses back on and returns his gaze to the corner of the room.

There is another moment of silence.

Kosakowski begins to speak, still with hostility but now with some fatigue. "She has really done a number on me. Boy, oh boy, did she screw me over good. She even got me here with a friggin' headshrinker. I even saw it comin' but I still couldn't stop it."

"Saw what, Paul?"

"All the fuckin' signs! She wanted to work more hours. Always doin' overtime. And it ain't like I didn't keep a close watch. I waited outside in the parkin' lot when she left Dunkin Donuts, and made sure her ass was in my vehicle on the way home. You know the Arabs and the Taliban are always gettin' a bad rap about how they treat their women. But there is some ancient wisdom there. Keep 'em home or make them wear a veil if they go out in public makes perfect sense. If you let them wander, sooner or later they will be spreadin' their legs for some bigger cock."

"Paul, during our first session, you said that you were married for three years. Was there a time when you two were happy?"

Kosakowski exhales again with a gesture of reluctance

and annoyance but continues to self-disclose.

"It was alright in the beginning. Peggy was always shy. She was a fat girl. Trust me, the phone wasn't ringin' off the hook for dates before she met me. But, she did not look like someone who would give me problems. So I thought! The first year was okay but then she started whinin' and sayin' she was bored. She always wanted to go out to eat. I told her it is stupid to go out and pay for a meal that you can make way cheaper at home. Plus, you don't know if the friggin' cook just picked his ass and is now preparin' your food. I had to put my foot down many times."

"Was there ever a compromise?"

"Hey, we were okay in the beginning. We got Brutus when he was a pup. Trainin' a canine takes a lotta time. We stayed at home a lot. We would rent movies. I tried to teach her how to do re-loading but she wasn't interested."

"Reloading?"

"You know, makin' bullets. I had the whole set-up in my basement. I could produce all kinds of calibers and hot loads, 10mms, 45s, 9s."

Peter did not want the client to get derailed, like what occurred during the first session and perseverate about guns. He quickly redirects Kosakowski and says, "So what did you finally decide on doing together?"

"I don't know, on Sundays, we would go see my brother at the nursin' home. That big Polack never knew we were there. That car accident made him a retard. But listen, me and Peggy were happy until her friggin' sister started stickin' her nose into our lives!"

"How so?"

"How so! I'll tell you how so! You know how I feel about her from the first session! She's a friggin' dike for one. And like I said before, it's a cryin' shame but she is a state trooper! Can you believe that! A friggin' state trooper! Carries a gun, wears a badge and has a huge chip on her shoulder because she wasn't born with a humongous pair of swingin' balls! She never approved of me marrying her sister. She said I was too controllin'. All that Oprah bullshit! I couldn't believe it the day she came to my house, stuck her finger in my face, and said I needed to let Peggy get out more and have a job!"

"How did you respond?"

"I told her to get her finger out of my face because it smells like someone else's pussy!"

"How did she respond?"

"She accused me of being in a time-warp and that I don't think like a "modern person." I say I don't think like a modern day faggot. Listen, growin' up we had no parents. My big brother was like a gunny sergeant and I learned not to boo-hoo about things. I have always held a job despite years of asshole supervisors and bosses always watchin' me. All I asked for was some friggin' respect and loyalty. I wanted a woman that would be there for me when I got home. But like a jerk with no spine, I gave in. And Peggy gets a job doin' second shift at Dunkin Donuts. And the rest is history. Peggy is now out fuckin' some nigger-spic."

"How did you find out your ex-wife is dating someone else."

"I got my ways. One of the old neighbors keeps an eye on things. I got the intel that she was seen in this car with this wetback from work. Supposedly they've been going to church together. Some holy-roller place, the Pentecostal Church of the Ultimate somethin'-or-other."

"This all appears very upsetting. How do you think you will deal with the situation?"

Kosakowski again, points his finger at Peter in an intimidating manner and says, "Don't worry, Doc, don't start accusin' me of getting ready to do somethin' stupid. I'll stay away. My lesbo ex-sister-in-law said she would put a bullet in me if I got too close to her precious Peggy. But, I'm gonna bide my time. I know I'll have to pay out of my ass, but I'll get back my gun collection and my dog. I'm lookin' for a new lawyer."

"That sounds like the wise way to do it."

"If I was so wise, I wouldn't be here."

"It's a traumatic thing to go through a divorce. You need a place to vent. It's not a crime to get some support."

"Whatever."

"You mentioned in the first session, that your older brother raised you and was like a father figure."

"Yea, but I don't want to talk about this shit. He doesn't even know my name anymore. Goin' through that windshield scrambled his brain."

"It's sad."

Kosakowski looks down at the floor and starts to rub his hands together. He is fighting back tears again. He mumbles, "It is what it is."

There was another time of silence.

Then Peter asks, "Before Peggy, what were your other relationships like?"

Kosakowski brings up his head and looks back toward the corner of the room. "I was the bachelor type. I didn't need no naggin' housewife and cryin' brats in my life. But this don't mean I was queer or somethin'. It was fine enough for me to go once in a while to the Tokyo Health Spa to have some little cute nipper give me a happy-endin'. Plus, when Ronald got hurt, I had to take care of his sorry ass. Dealin' with those seizures wasn't pretty."

"It appears that you really tried to come through for your brother. Why did you finally decide to marry?"

"Ain't that the fuckin' million-dollar question! I curse my big mouth, meddlin' aunt for settin' me up with her friend's niece!"

"That's how you met Peggy."

"Yea."

"Was it the same year that your brother went into the nursing home?"

"Yea, it was."

"What's the connection?"

"ALRIGHT ENOUGH!" Kosakowski suddenly shouts. "Talkin' about this sad shit ain't helpin' me! If it weren't for the fuckin' judge makin' me come here, I wouldn't have to be thinkin' about this crap!"

Peter pauses for a moment then says gently, "Fair enough Paul, we'll change the subject. You are here for anger management. I know you refused group therapy classes and requested individual sessions. I want to help you with this issue."

"There is no fuckin' way I'm tellin' my personal business in front of a group of nut-jobs!"

"That's okay. That is why it is just you and I talking."

Kosakowski shoots a mean look, "Yea, and what will you blab to the judge?"

"The court doesn't need to know all the details of your life that we discuss here. Certain things are confidential. You have your rights of privacy."

"Still, what will you tell the judge?"

"The court will want to know if you finished the therapy sessions and that you have obtained some skills in how to control your anger."

"How' bout I slip you fifty bucks and you say I'm cured."

Peter briefly smiles back and says, "I won't be doing you any good if I did that. I know we really don't know each other. But I hope in time, you will find that I am really on your side. I see a man that is hurting and has a lot of stress and losses in his life. You have your brother's accident, the ending of a marriage, and the legal and financial problems. I know that you are a tough, hard-working man, but everybody has their breaking point."

Kosakowski laughs with scorn, "Her divorce lawyer got a taste of my breaking point. Fuckin' shark."

"Paul, can you define anger for me?"

"What?"

"Anger, can you try to tell me what it is?"

"I don't know. It's a feelin' or somethin'. It's being pissed-off. Like when being asked stupid questions."

Peter smiles and nods his head. "Anger is a natural emotion. It is hard-wired in our brains. When we perceive that something is not going our way or we are being violated somehow, it is normal to react and express anger. It is normal to be pissed-off."

"If it is normal to be pissed-off then why the fuck do I have to be here?"

"Good question. Anger is normal but how we express it is the concern. There has to be some control or else it will turn into rage."

"Rage?"

"Yes, rage is what gets us in trouble."

Kosakowski scowls and replies; "I can tell you are probably one of those liberal, Prius-driving', touchy-feely types; but, don't tell me you wouldn't want to crack a few heads if you lost your house, your dog, and now some dark-skinned-Jose'-fuck-face from the islands is doing' your wife up the corn-hole!"

For a moment, Peter felt a jolt of anxiety. He suddenly remembered his own divorce and all the seething, stuffed animosity. Peter answers, "Yes, I agree. I would likely feel hostility. But, I hope I would have the control not to do something that would make my life worse."

"Yea, well I guess I did make things fuckin' worse. I definitely screwed myself over. I never had an arrest record before."

"Well, I know you are not here by choice. But give

yourself some credit for talking about some painful stuff. Maybe together we can learn some things and make a bad situation better."

Kosakowski exhales loudly again and appears to soften a bit.

Peter asks, "Normally when you get angry, what is the first physical sign?"

"What?"

"How does your body react when you first start to get upset?"

"I break a friggin' sweat. When I start to get T'd-off I could be wearin' a bucket of Right Guard and it still won't matter."

"Okay, then what happens?"

"I feel hot. I could melt ice on my skin."

"What next?"

"I don't know! I see red. I get fuckin' mad! What's your point?" Kosakowski starts raising his voice.

Peter says calmly, "You're doing a good job describing how physiologically, anger can affect the body. One of the primary steps of anger management is being aware of the first signs as you start to rev-up. If you can catch yourself, then you can implement a strategy so you don't cross the line. Do you know what I mean by not crossing the line?"

Kosakowski casts his mean smile, "It means not going postal."

"Yes, not resorting to violence or even threatening someone. If you go down that road, what will happen?"

"Prison or cops takin' me out."

"That would be terrible. Think of anger management as self-preservation. Can you picture a stop sign in your head?"

"A what?"

"A stop sign."

"Yea."

Dr. Fray leans closer to the client and gestures with his hands, "When you start to experience the heat building as the anger grows you have to visualize the image of that stop-sign in your head. You have to yell to yourself, "STOP! I CAN'T CROSS THE LINE!""

"Yea, then what?"

"There can be many ways to handle a situation. And we will explore them through our time together. What I would like to try now with you are some breathing techniques."

"Sounds kind of fruity?"

Peter already expected that the client would be initially resistant to this type of coping skill; it appearing too new-age-y, but he had a plan to sell it. Peter replies, "Paul, special forces operators, martial artists and many other individuals in high stress situations learn breathing techniques to increase focus and maintain control."

Kosakowski smirks. "Yea?"

"Position your feet flat on the floor and sit up straighter in the chair. Relax your hands and close your eyes."

"I'll close my eyes but if I open 'em and see you removed your trousers, you're dead."

"I promise to remain dressed." Peter says with some humor.

The client shuffled his large frame uncomfortably in the chair and did what the psychologist asked.

"Take a deep breath through your nose and bring the air down to the bottom of your lungs. Hold. Now, slowly exhale out your mouth.

Kosakowski roughly snorts in then blows air out of his mouth that rustles some of the hair on the doctor's forehead.

Peter says, "Do it again. But this time do it slower and more gently. Relax. Breath."

Kosakowski continues and subtly appears to ease himself in the chair.

"Good, keep breathing. Concentrate on your breath. If your mind starts to wonder, try to focus back to just the air moving in and out. Good, keep going."

A few more minutes pass and Kosakowski opens his eyes. "Okay, I'm done" He says.

Peter asks, "How did it feel?"

"It's okay. I sort of know this already."

"How so, Paul?"

"Snipers. I read it in a sniper manual. Before they shoot someone they do that breathin' so they don't jerk the shot."

Peter internally cringes. After a pause, Peter reaches for a therapeutic connection and says, "Well, as I said earlier, individuals in combat have utilized breathing techniques, but how can you use them so that you obtain a sense of peace and control?"

Kosakowski leans forward and says in a superficial kind tone, "Doc, do you know what would really help me to blow off some steam and relax?"

Peter replies with hidden hesitation, "What, Paul?"

Past the lenses of his glasses, there could be seen an intense shimmer in the client's hateful eyes. Kosakowski says, "Get back my gun license. Tell the judge I'm okay so they can re-instate my pistol permit. Then I could go to the range. That's what gives me peace. I don't need to do this guru, hippie meditation bullshit! I want to go back to huntin' and skeet shootin'. I promise I ain't some asshole that would shoot up a school! I ain't like that! Do you fuckin' understand?"

A swell of uneasiness hit Peter again. It was something that the client had pressed for during the first therapy session. Kosakowski's gun license had been pulled. The police confiscated all his firearms after his arrest.

Combined, there were over 63 pistols, shotguns, and semi-automatic rifles along with boxes after boxes of ammo. With venom, Kosakowski cursed and blamed his sister-in-law for orchestrating the seizure of his weapons.

"So, what's your answer, Doc?" Kosakowski seethes. "Are you gonna help me get back my constitutional right to bear arms. Or are you gonna leave me unprotected in this fucked-up world? Home invasions, gang-bangers, al-Qaeda, an asshole government on the verge of collapse! How can I relax if I'm un-armed? Don't make me a sitting duck."

Dr. Fray stiffens in his chair.

"Are you gonna worm out of answerin' like last time, or give it to me straight?" Kosakowski leans his bulk forward and glares.

In the next second, there comes a series of muffled blasts from a horn. The sound comes from the outside and permeates the small room.

Kosakowski bolts up from his chair and bellows, "THAT'S MY FUCKIN' ALARM ON MY TRUCK!"

Unnerved, Peter rises up also and says, "Do you want me to call the police?"

"DON'T YOU DARE! I'll HANDLE IT! I'M GO'IN!"

In a hurried, furious mass, the client storms out. Rapid, thumping steps are heard going down the stairwell. Kosakowski busts through the doors of the reception area to the parking lot. The African American security guard is standing near-by. Kosakowski asks, "Did you see anythin'!"

The guard replies, "No."

With rage Kosakowski yells back as he passes the guard, "OF COURSE NOT SAMBO! BECAUSE THAT WOULD MEAN YOU ACTUALLY WORK FOR A LIVIN'!!!"

Kosakowski makes it to his truck that is parked on the

street. The driver's side window is smashed. He yanks open the door. The radio is still there but the floor mat has been turned over. Kosakowski whips his head around and scans the area. The alarm is still blaring. There is a large black woman and her grandchildren pushing a shopping cart on the sidewalk. Kosakowski's short sleeve shirt is now a darker hue, totally saturated with sweat. A blood vessel shows thick on his right, hot temple. "I KNOW YOU NIGGERS DID THIS!!!" He screams as his eyes flash to the individuals on the sidewalk then up to the boarded windows of the tenement house across the way. "I KNOW YOU DID THIS!!! YOUR LIVES DON'T MATTER TO ME!!! YOU HEAR ME?! YOUR LIVES DON'T MATTER!!! "

With his beefy forearm he roughly brushes the shards of glass off his truck seat and sets them in a glittering spray out on the asphalt. Jumping behind the wheel, he puts in the key, the alarm abruptly stops; he hits the gas. Smoke and burning rubber comes next as the large black Dodge RAM surges forward, tearing down the street, blowing through a stop sign in the distance.

Disappearing.

Dr. Fray replaces the phone receiver, pushes back in his chair, and rubs his forehead. He had notified the front desk of the occurrence. The manager of the treatment facility called and jokingly inquired about what kind of new therapy was being tried that was causing clients to run out the doors in a panic. *This is one awful morning!* Peter says to himself. He then wonders what he will write in the weekly update to the judge regarding the Kosakowski case. *The guy is nitroglycerin.*

Attempting to utilize his own breathing techniques, Peter closes his eyes and slowly inhales and exhales. It is time to decompress. He keeps up with the breathing but he soon finds it is not working. The recent session had stirred up some uncomfortable bits of his personal tragic relationship. Peter had been married for eight years. Brigitte, his ex-wife, often complained that she thought by marrying a psychologist there would be highly efficient communication and deep understanding in their blessed union. She also thought the lifestyle would be different. She was highly disappointed. When the private practice failed and the book thing never happened, so did the big dreams of financial success. They were never poor but they were never rich. In her frustration, she would often say that if he knew all this psychology-positive-motivational-bullshit why he couldn't help himself to succeed. In response, Peter knew that his own behavior was to clam-up and stuff the hurt. It was all more fertilizer for his deep insecurity. She left him for an investment banker in Greenwich.

Peter thinks, *Kosakowski is right; it is good to punch-out divorce lawyers.* He shakes his head, opens his eyes and laughs to himself without joy.

In the next moment, the phone on his desk rings again. The receptionist gives him the update that the police were called regarding the recent vehicle break-in. She also reports that the cops and EMS showed up at Francis LaBoudy's apartment but he was not there.

"Great." Peter says, rolling his eyes.

"Also, Dr. Fray, I was called by the Trinity Grove rehab center, to notify you that your client, Betty Farrell, eloped out of the program on Friday.

"Wonderful. Anymore bad news?"

"No, I don't think so? Sorry Dr. Fray."

Click.

Peter reaches out for the cup of coffee on the corner of his desk. There are only a few cold sips left at the bottom. Peter finds the taste a tad sickening. He tells himself,

Think of some good things. His mind brings up images of his new girlfriend. She is an art teacher at Yale. There are flashes of her nude, doing Yoga, with morning sunlight coming through his bedroom window.

"Accentuate the positive." Peter says aloud and he takes the last sip of bad coffee.

In the next week and a half, Dr. Fray's self-doubt would bloom into a bumper crop. Who would have expected that so many people would be massacred?

SIX

Monday Evening 9:18 and Betty Farrell has no idea that this will be her last night alive. Her expectations are to party-hardy and have a three-way. There are no premonitions of horror and death in the girl's racing mind. She loves the up side of her bi-polar disorder. Being only nineteen, she had been hospitalized in psych units over a dozen times. The doctors wanted her to take mood-stabilizers like lithium and Depakote but she would never really comply. She complained that the meds took away her "mojo." If she got too racy, she would often smoke weed, down some Captain Morgan's or try to score some Oxys. If neuro-chemically things got low, she would snort some lines to spark back up.

And then there was the sex.

Betty's career aspirations involved being a high-paid porn starlet specializing in double penetration but she was always willing to give it away to most anyone for free. By age 16, she already had two abortions. There were also the multiple cases of chlamydia, crabs, and genital warts. She had a baby girl last year that was immediately taken away by DCF and placed in the care of her aunt in Colorado. The child was born when Betty had a flare-up of herpes. When Betty was in various rehab programs, she always tried to hook-up with another client, either male or female and especially if the person had a criminal history. Dark and dangerous was a major turn-on. She would then use her sexual exploits to rattle others and bask in the Jerry-Springer-Show-like-attention. At one point, Betty got on a wigger- kick and attempted to mimic ghetto behaviors. Wearing a do-rag, black shades, and Baby Phat sweats she would often say to her Caucasian girlfriends, "You muthafuckers haven't lived until you rode a real, true gangsta' dick!"

Having WASP and Irish genes, Betty is white as snow. She had grown-up in the richy-rich, yuppie, countryside of Connecticut and had never talked to a person of color until being sent to rehab. Her wigger-kick abruptly ended when her boyfriend, Jamal, a.k.a. NO-LUV-4-U, bolted when she announced that she was having his "shorty." Betty was heart-broken, devastated and no longer attempted to speak in Ebonics.

In the past, there had been other rebellious, zing-your-parents, identity roles. There was the Goth-alternative-suicide-Wicca-period, with the black lipstick and black fingernails. Then there was the neo-hippie, Deadhead, vegan, smoke blunts on a daily basis phase.

Recently, Betty has been saying, "I don't know who I am. I just want to push it to the limit and have really cool, intense fucked-up experiences!" Her hair is now spiky-gelled and dyed platinum but there had been times when it was magenta, blue, green, in dreads, cornrows ...etc. Body modification was an additional addiction. Small chrome balls hang out of her nostrils from little chains attached to a bar in her nasal septum. Her left earlobe has a large blue disk extender. And of course, there is the eyebrow piercing, the tongue-stud, bi-lateral nipple rings, the dangly thing from the navel, and the tiny steel loop through the hood of her clitoris.

Ink work is also rampant. The name Courtney is tattooed on the right side of her neck in flowing script. "It's my daughter's name." She would say. "I want her to grow up and be relevant just like Courtney Love." Betty would also state to others that her major goal was to get back custody of her child and be a good mother but secretly she could not bear to touch the infant because she knew that Jamal's blood ran through its veins. She also despises how her body changed with the pregnancy. Before, she had been thin with perky breasts and a heart-shape butt. Now her ass is wide and her belly flabby. The tribal tattoos on her tits, inner thighs, and lower back are all misshapen due to the extra fifty pounds that she gained and still cannot lose. She often has to suppress and bury the painful truth that she is not mega porn star material.

Dr. Fray had started treating Betty in September but the private sessions had to be put on hold because she kept relapsing. Another inpatient rehab was the recommended therapeutic plan. Betty liked Dr. Fray and expressed that he was "nice." She agreed to go to the Trinity Grove Recovery Center in up-state Connecticut but with extremely weak motivation to stay clean. She often laughed and bragged, "There's not a rehab in this country that can hold me!" Betty was notorious for smuggling drugs into facilities or going AWOL. She considered it a big joke to try to B.S. the drug and alcohol counselors and later slip Dust to the other group members. Then there would be the other times when she would be caught going down on someone in a bathroom stall. Betty told Dr. Fray, "Hey, I'll go to your rehab. You meet the coolest losers there. Maybe this time I'll meet my husband to be. Want to high-five me?"

The duration of the program at Trinity Grove was 28 days but Betty only lasted a week and a half when she signed herself out last Friday. The major trigger for her leaving was that she did meet another "new cool guy." Troy was on probation and was mandated to complete rehab. He was older than her by two years. Betty being always the fan of the "bad boys" thought it was so hot when he told her he was going to bolt and take his chances with the law. Her heart then went aflutter when Troy screamed at one of the counselors to F-off when he was confronted about not paying attention in the treatment groups. Betty left with her new bad boy but he was more than just rebellious; he was a full-blown psychopath. The real McCoy.

It was now 9:22 p.m. The metallic gold Lexus 470 weaves along the black, woodsy, road. Betty is driving while Troy and Marco ride in the back. She is ecstatic with hyper-verbal, pressured speech and has not stopped yapping since picking the two up in New Haven. Rambling on, she manages to chain smoke and steer but sometimes crosses into the on-coming lane.

"There was no way I was going to stay in that fucking rehab while my bitch of a mother is in Aruba with her new boyfriend! I mean like, hello??!! What's wrong with this picture??! Mommy gets to party and I don't! Fuck that!"

Troy asks with a smirk, "Is this your mom's Lexus?"

"Yea, well my daddy bought it. My parents are divorced but my father still spoils her and pays for everything. She's gonna shit out her Prozac when she finds out I came home and took her wheels. Never mind that I'm also smoking inside her precious SUV. Fuck her! My dad's cool though. He's out in California with his new wife. She's a bitch too. I can tell you guys all about her. She's like really young. I mean she could be like my sister. And those boobs are definitely silicone. And the way she dresses! Let me just say..."

Marco mumbles with annoyance, "Does this chick ever shut the fuck up?"

With a mischievous snicker, Troy fumbles for a moment with something in the waistband of his jeans. He then gets loose a knife. There is a thumbhole on the side of the blade. With a flick of his hand comes a flash of 4 inches of ATS-55 high carbon steel. Shark-like teeth serrations run the full length of the cutting edge. It is a Spyderco tactical Folder. With ease it can slice right through denim or thick rope. It could even saw bone.

"Where did you get that?" said Marco.

Troy lightly touches the point of the knife then reflexively draws the tip of his index finger into his mouth to suck the droplet of blood. "Damn, this mother-fucker is sharp!"

Marco snaps, "I said where did you get it?"

"I got it today!" Troy instantly jabbers with excitement. "I was walking downtown around noon, next to that clinic where all the crazies go and saw this big ass Dodge truck parked on the street. There were these pro-gun bumper stickers plastered all over the back of the thing so I thought maybe the owner was a gun nut and had a piece stashed inside. So I *BAM!* – smash the motherfuckin' window. And boy-oh-boy that alarm was re-e-e-ally loud. I didn't have too much time to rummage around, but I flipped over a floor mat and found this little beauty!"

"Weren't you once a patient of that place where all the crazies go?" Marco sneers.

Troy ignores the question and waves the knife around as if it were his shiny new toy. He then runs his hand down on the back of the front passenger seat. "Hey, Betty is the upholstery real leather?"

Betty continues to babble about her father's new wife and misses the question. Troy asks again.

She replies, "What?"

"I said is this interior real leather?"

"I don't know," she says. "I guess. It's a fucking Lexus. Maybe it is. Anyway, I want to tell you more about that bitch that's sucking up my dad's money. She's a real...."

With just slight pressure, the blade pokes right

through the fine beige upholstery. Troy presses downward then turns the knife to the side, then up, cutting a lopsided triangle out of the back of the seat. He laughs and hoots, "Wow! This thing is like a fucking light-saber!" He flips the piece of leather to Marco and jokes, "Hey man, want to own a piece of a Lexus?"

Marco tosses the piece away on the floor and does not laugh.

Betty stops her monologue for a moment and calls from the front, "Hey, Troy what are you doing back there?"

"Nothing, baby." Troy says with a Cheshire cat grin. "You just keep driving! Okay."

She turns her head for a glance back and says, "Troy, I want you to do me hard tonight! Will ya?"

Troy laughs, "Don't worry baby, I bet a lot of people are gonna get fucked hard tonight!"

"ROCK-ON!" screams Betty with delight as she stomps down on the gas-pedal. "You are so hot! I love you!" The sound-system comes alive as she cranks up Cyprus-Hill's Insane In The Membrane.

"Do you really think, I'm a hotty, baby?" shouts Troy.

"You betcha! I really left that rehab so I could jump your bones!"

Troy howls.

Many girls find Troy handsome. He is 6 feet tall. Even though he does not workout, he has a natural long, lean, sinewy physique. His complexion is slightly amber which gives him a sun-tan-surfer-look. Highlights of blonde are in contrast to his dark wavy hair. Jeans, work-boots, and t-shirts are his usual attire. At first glance he appears to be an average 21-year-old drifter but once one looks into his frenzied, blue eyes and witnesses the malicious smile, the instability is blatant. There is a badly drawn, green blotchy tattoo of Taz, the Tasmanian devil cartoon character on his veiny forearm. The tatt says a lot. As a child, Troy was diagnosed with conduct disorder and attention-deficit-disorder with hyper-activity. The ADHD is still chronic. He always appears distractible, fidgety and has the need to be playing with something or breaking something. For him to stay focused for any length of time is a Herculean task. And then there are the other adult psychiatric pathologies. Childhood conduct disorder had morphed into full-blown dis-social personality disorder. Troy has the grave inability to feel remorse or guilt for his actions. He is driven to gratify himself without much thought how it would affect others. The young handsome man has as much empathy and compassion as a hammerhead shark or a tarantula.

Marco is also a sociopath, however, definite variants exist between the two. They met as teens in the Liberty Oak Juvenile Retention Program outside of New Haven. Marco is the older, wiser-one. He is now 24. A pointy black goatee gives him the sinister devil-look. His hair is jet-black, long, and stringy-straight. Pale white is his skin. Then there are the black jeans, black t-shirt, and long Columbine black Mafia trench coat. He wears a black baseball hat backwards with the insignia torn off. Little homemade crude tattoos of crosses and aces-of-spades done with a sewing needle and ink mar the back of his hands and some of his fingers. He is short, 5'5. Those that know him would be hard-pressed to ever recall a time when they saw him *lighten-up*. The only mark of color is the hidden bright blue image of the Hindu Goddess Kali tattooed on his chest. Marco's eyes are little dark stones full of hatred. Marco often called the kids that were into Goth, "assholes." Adolescent identity fantasies of being a vampire or a witch could never compare to the true-life scariness of his thoughts and potential to kill.

"Hey, you up-front!" Marco shouts, "Turn down the fucking music! I got a question!"

"What?"

"I said turn it off!"

The blaring music suddenly stops as Betty fiddles with the volume knob.

With a mean, pissed-off tone, Marco asks, "Are you positive that your little friends got the money with 'em!"

"Hell, yea!" says Betty. "Relax. They all got rich families."

"They better," threatens Marco. "If I come out here for fuckin' nothing, I'll shut-up your fat ass forever."

Betty shoots a look back toward Troy and says, "Hey baby, are you going to let your friend dis me like that?"

Troy ignores Betty's plea and instead stabs the front passenger headrest with the knife.

They all drive on.

Woodbury is approximately an hour drive away from the city of New Haven. It was once a little New England farming community that has now changed to an affluent hide-away for the wealthy. Many New Yorkers have their weekend country retreats down off various back roads. There are even some movie-star types with digs in the area. Rural pastures, horse fences, meadows and ponds are the prized scenery.

It is quintessential Connecticut.

In some parts, building is not allowed even for the rich and famous. There are protected land trusts. One of them is Mitchell's 42-acre nature preserve. There, the population of deer and wild turkeys flourish. Out on the preserve is one of the many old hay barns that is no longer in use. It is a large rotting, gray structure rising out of a long, lonely field of cow grass. The dark pine forests encircle the periphery. There is no good reason for humans to come here at night. Hunting is prohibited. It is a desolate place when the sun disappears. There are no houses around for miles and miles. It is all designated to be a quiet spot where wildlife can be at peace to breed or feed. Or stalk.

Tacked here and there on the decaying wood on the outside of the barn, are No Trespassing Signs. But at this moment there are intruders. Techno-trance music, sounding diluted and irritating comes from inside and disturbs the melancholy, sober, stillness of the evening. A silver BMW X5 SUV is parked out front. It is 9:36 p.m. Flickering white light flashes through the seams and cracks in the planks of the barn. It is an odd spectacle within the cavernous interior, as rays from a mirrored disco ball shoot up high above and sporadically illuminate the dark wooden rafters and gobs of hanging cobwebs. A battery-powered lantern gives additional light where two girls are huddled on a blanket. The October night air is chilly. They are cold. The younger one whines, "Are you sure they're coming? It's getting late. My parents said I have to bring back the car by 10:30."

Marsha, the older one, says, "Come-on, Zoë. Be good; don't ruin this."

Brendan is standing nearby shining his flashlight on the disco-ball that he strung-up on twine and let dangle from a lower crossbeam. He is grooving to the music pounding from the boom box while he periodically takes long swigs from a bottle of Bacardi. Yesterday was his 19th birthday but today is his party. He looks over at the two girls and slurs with a drunken smile, "L-L-Looks like you're freezing. Do you want to fire up another blunt to keep you warm?"

"It's fine, honey." replies Marsha with a nervous smile, as she clutches herself and shivers. She is wearing a Peruvian Alpaca sweater that she bought at a street fair but she is still not warm. "This is fun." She lies. "They should be here pretty soon."

Brendan gives a goofy grin and with uncoordinated

movements, puts down the flashlight and bottle of rum, then attempts to search the pockets of his bulky, oversized green army jacket to find his bag of weed and Zig-Zags.

Desperately, Marsha hopes that everything will go as planned and Brendan won't leave her.

I hope he doesn't get angry at me again. I just want him to be happy. Please God, make him love me!

They have been going out for a year and she is still smitten. She is enamored with the image of him being a musician. He is tall and lanky with thick hair, silver double loops in each ear and a handsome face. Brendan was expelled from the Gunnery, a prestigious prep school, for multiple offenses of blatantly selling Acid on campus and being a chronic no-show in class. When it happened he had explained to her that it was a good thing because he could concentrate more on song writing and getting a band together. Months go by and Marsha noticed that he hadn't been playing or practicing. Recently, she had gently inquired about how things were going and suddenly he became enraged and flew off the handle. He had screamed at her, calling her a fucking bitch, and told her that she was clueless about what it is like to be in a fucking creative rut!

Brendan's parents are in the midst of a divorce. His dad is an investment banker on Wall Street and had recently chosen to hide in the city and no longer come home. Mom, in a depressive funk, is overwhelmed. She now mostly stays with a butchy friend from Pilates class. The house has been empty except for Brendan staying in his room with the door locked and all the windows shut while having a cannabis clambake and popping pain-meds. Issues to High Times magazine lay unread and strewed about on his bedroom floor.

Since meeting Brendan, Marsha feels like he is her life raft and she is about to drown. Her parents are also in the process of divorce. Some time ago, she was *Miss Preppy*, involved in the yearbook committee, had 3.8 G.P.A., was senior captain of the Taft prep- school swim-team and had big plans to go to UCLA for pre-law. Everything was perfect until last year. In December, daddy came out of the closet and announced that he was tired of living a lie. Mom started hitting the Shiraz morning, noon, and night and got into a horrible car accident, shattering her pelvis and both legs, while driving drunk in her husband's Miata.

Marsha just turned 19 too and nothing is perfect anymore. Plans for college are dead. She now dreams of being her boyfriend's promotions manager and helping him book tour dates. The only problem is that Brendan has yet to create any of his own music.

But she has faith.

A week ago, Brendan told Marsha that he could get out of his artistic slump if he could go deep inside himself to find his well of creativity. He explained all the great musicians like Hendrix, Cobain, Nowell, Staley all experimented with different kinds of chemicals and even used heroin to be inspired. With tears in his eyes, he said that if she supported him with what he *really* wanted to do, he would make a reference to her in every song that he wrote. He hugged her hard. She cried and that night was the first time she swallowed and didn't spit it out.

He then made another request.

It was then Marsha found herself calling Betty.

As little girls growing up in picturesque Woodbury, Marsha was a friend of Betty Farrell. Their houses were close by. They grew apart in their early teens as Betty started to become more wild and strange. It was front news gossip in school about the drugs, the hospitalizations, getting pregnant from a "black guy," and being expelled from Taft. Not too long ago Marsha and her friends had often referred to her as a "skank" and a "ho." Now, Marsha seeks her help. She considered it a great stroke of luck that Betty had left rehab and snuck home. Promising crisp new hundred dollar bills drawn from her savings account, Marsha pleaded with Betty to hook her up with "a connection" as a special birthday present for her boyfriend. Betty's eyes had flashed at that moment. From various interactions with career criminals in rehab, Betty had acquired some diabolical, scammy behavior. She told Marsha that she would need "a lot of G-notes" to get her connected with a "legit dealer." Marsha said she would hit up Zoe for more money. With a sly grin, Betty had replied, "You go girl!" And the Monday night rendezvous at the barn was planned.

9:50 p.m. Headlight beams, piercing the dark, kept bouncing, showing up high then dipping down low, as the Lexus comes four-wheeling and tearing across the grassy field toward the barn. Segments of rusted barbed wire have come entangled in the front bumper of the SUV after it plowed through part of an old cow fence.

"They're here!" shouts Marsha as she hears the approaching vehicle over the droning of the boom box.

Zoë cringes. Her gray Taft Field-Hockey sweatshirt is also not warm enough for the nighttime temperature. Earlier, she got startled by the mice darting out from the shadows across the dusty floor. She hates mice! Zoe is 18 and also Marsha's cousin. Wearing her hair in pigtails and being almost anorexically thin, she appears prepubescent. Past psych testing showed she has traits of Asperger's' Autism. She is a brainiac in trigonometry and calculus but oddly related with people. Marsha always knew that her strange little cousin had an obsessive miserly knack for squirreling away money from years of monetary birthday gifts and Christmas cash from grandma and grandpa. Zoe agreed to give a loan to Marsha with the condition that they start "hanging together." Marsha never planned to bring Zoe along tonight, but she was the only one around with quick access to a vehicle. Brenden had totaled his Jeep months ago and Marsha's father trying a "tough-love approach" restricted Marsha's funds and refused to buy her a car until she decided to pursue college again.

9:53 p.m. Glare from high beams stream through some of the slits and gaps in the front side of the barn. Then the growing sound of the approaching engine abruptly stops. Marsha scampers over to the barn door and pushes it open on its corroded hinges. There is the clunking of vehicle doors opening and shutting. From outside comes an excited high pitch female voice. "HEY, HOME-GIRL READY TO FUCKING GET DOWN!!!"

Betty busts in, quickly squeezing Marsha, then forcefully kissing her on the mouth. Marsha was taken aback because Betty slipped her the tongue. "Remember coming here as little kids?" squeals Betty. "Isn't this place the bomb?"

"Yea," Marsha replies with a forced smile.

The next to enter is Troy. Cheerfully and loudly he says, "Wow! Look at this! Is this your own little private rave party!"

Staggering a bit, Brendan comes over and offers his bottle of Bacardi. "W-W-Welcome, dude." He slurs. "Want some?"

"Don't mind if I do!" Replies Troy gleefully as he takes the bottle of rum, tilts back his head and fills his mouth.

Zoë remains silent on the blanket, clutching herself.

Then Marco walks in. He is carrying a cheap piece of black, vinyl luggage that has been repaired various times with packaging tape. He quickly scans about with an expression of pissed-off-meanness.

"Nice to meet you, man" says Brendan as he offers his unsteady hand.

Marco ignores the gesture for a handshake, walks past Brendan as if he weren't there and turns to Troy and says, "What the fuck is this? Is this some kind of fucking joke?"

Troy just shrugs and smirks. The others shoot nervous looks at one another.

"What's wrong?" says Marsha with fear in her voice.

For a second, Marco suddenly softens as he makes eye contact with Marsha but then returns to his angry shtick. Looking away, he rants, "I was told there would be some serious buyers here and what do I get! A bunch of fucking hick youngsters! What a fuckin' waste of my time! I'm out of here!" He starts toward the door.

"Oh wow, this is like, a total let down!" says Brendan.

Marsha yelps. "Wait! Please! Don't go!"

It is hard for Troy not to laugh. He knows the ruse Marco is playing.

Marco turns around and points his finger at them and says, "Go back to smoking your little weed, stealing bottles from daddy's liquor cabinet and drinking Robo! What I got in this suitcase is only meant for rock-stars, and those willing to experience life to the fucking fullest!"

Frantically, Marsha pulls out wads of hundred dollar bills from the pockets of her cargo-pants and says, "Here! I got cash! Please don't leave!" Some of the bills fell from her trembling fingers and landed on the floor. "How much do you want? Please! Help us out here! This is supposed to be a birthday present."

"Birthday present? You should have hired a magician or rented a fuckin' pony!" Marco again looks into Marsha's eyes and feels something inside of him stir. He thinks, *This chick is beautiful!*

"Please." Marsha says with tears building.

Marco quickly stomps forward and snatches the wad

of money from her hand and stuffs it somewhere in his black trench coat without even looking at the amount.

"Okay, what do you want?" He says roughly. "And turn down that fuckin' music!"

Marsha gives Brendan an excited, anxious look.

Betty rushes over to quiet the boom box

There is a tense pause.

"I don't have all fuckin' night!" pressures Marco, "What will it be?"

Lowering and clearing his voice, Brendan tries to rally himself to appear all smooth and in control. "Hey, man. I'm a musician. And all the greats like Shannon Hoon from Blind Mellon, Sid Vicious, and a- uh, and a-uh, you know like Cobain, all used something to enhance their art. I really believe we should be free to explore our minds through chemistry and magic."

"What the fuck?" Troy snickers.

"I don't give a shit." barks Marco, "Just tell me what you want to move?"

"W-W-Well, I got booted out of school for dealing but I still got all of my contacts. All rich kids. Synthetics are popular, but I would like to sling something, with style. Something a great poet would O.D. on. Something classic! "

"Classic?" Marco questions.

"Yea, classic," smiles Brendan. "I know you're feeling me. Right?" He offers Marco a fist bump.

"No!" Marco ignores Brendan's hand gesture. "What the fuck are you talking about? You're a babbling drunk asshole!"

Brendan drops his goofy smile, "Oh man, don't be like that? I'm just a little tipsy, but I'm cool. Really. I'm straight. I'm good. Really."

"Then fucking tell me what you want?" Marco presses.

"Heroin."

"Why would I ever trust a fuck-up like you? Marco says with a squint. "You want to sling Heroin? You will get made in a fuckin' second by a meter-maid then be pissing yourself in front of detective while doin' a-tell-all."

"No, I'm not gonna do this forever. I just want to buy a one shot order of product, flip it, make a nice chunk of change, then leave for Cali to start my career. I don't want to even know your name. We won't see each other ever again. I promise."

"How much money do you have on you now?" Marco drills.

Brendan looks back at Marsha.

She stammers, "I- I- just gave him some. I'm not sure how much. There was at least seven hundred, I think."

"No longer count that," snaps Marco. "That scratch was just to get my attention and not to walk out on your ass. Now search your pockets again and show me what you got."

Marsha pulls out a folded white bank envelope stuffed with more bills and for a second time the currency is plucked from her hand. Pausing for a second, Marco does give a quick count before the envelope vanishes into his coat.

"Is there enough?" Marsha asks.

Again, Marco feels himself stir with a weird building hunger as he looks into Marsha's eyes for a third time. "You're really part of this?" He questions.

"It's just going to be once," replies Marsha with a sudden jolt of shame. "We just need enough money to last us one year. Our parents won't help us with moving to California. We want this to be just in and out."

What comes next is rare, Marco smiles. His lips curve upward into a nasty coyote-like grin. He says "In and out? I like that. In and out."

Marsha feels her skin crawl.

From the beginning it was Marco's and Troy's plan to sell the kids fake shit then bolt with their cash. There is no need to stick around. Betty was in on it from the start and was totally okay with her old playmate being beat for her money because she knew that in the past Marsha and her click of yuppie friends had talked behind her back. *You deserve to be burned, bitch!* Betty thought, *I know how you used to dis me!*

Suddenly Marco's boiling urge for Marsha makes him uncharacteristically divert from the plan. He thinks, *I'm gonna put her under and do her.* His impulsive decision would allow for a glimpse of hell on earth. With his mind rapidly calculating, Marco turns to Brendan and with an abrupt change of tone says jovially, "Hey man, if you are going to sell my product, I want you to sample it."

'Really?" Brendan is taken aback.

Troy and Betty both give surprised looks at Marco.

Marco ignores them both and continues with Brendan, "Of course, you should know what high quality shit you just bought. Every good salesman should know his product."

"Now?"

"Yea now. We're gonna celebrate a little bit. It's like shaking hands and cementing the deal."

Like a kid asking for permission for a new toy, Brendan turns to Marsha and says, "Hey, it's my birthday, right?"

"I don't know" Marsha says, "You want to do this now?"

Marco grins again at Marsha, "Hey, it's his birthday, Queen-Pin. You can't deny your man on his birthday."

Following Marco's lead, Betty shouts. "Yea girl lighten up! I'm freezing my ass off in this place; let's have some fun!"

Brendan reaches out and hugs Marsha. He kisses her

sloppily, "I love you! I really love you. Thanks for being so cool." His breath stinks of rum. Marsha shivers in his arms. "I love you too. I love you too." She says.

"Ah, really sweet," sneers Marco. "Okay Romeo. You ready?"

"Yea," replies Brendan with sudden nervous hesitation.

"I need to set this down somewhere," says Marco, motioning with the suitcase. He then looks over at Zoë sitting on the blanket. "What about her? We hooking up the kid too so she can play the clarinet better in band practice?"

Marsha suddenly panics. "Oh, God, I forgot" she exclaims. Her plan was to have Zoë go stay outside in the Bimmer when the others arrived but Marsha got distracted with all the excitement. Marsha leaves Brendan's side and rushes over and kneels down next to her little cousin. Sounding breathless Marsha says. "Okay- Zoë, I need you to be a grown-up girl about this. You can't tell anyone. And definitely not your mom and dad. We are pals, right?"

Zoe asks flatly. "Why did you give that guy all my birthday and Christmas money?"

Marsha quickly lies. "We're making a deal on band equipment."

"I want to go home, now." Zoe says robotically, "I don't like mice. I saw some earlier run across the floor."

"We'll go home soon."

"No. Now."

"Zoe, don't be a brat."

"I'm going to call my parents."

Grabbing her by the shoulders, Marsha shakes her cousin. "Don't you call anybody!"

"Ouch. You're hurting me." Zoë says, void of emotion.

Troy comes swaggering up and laughs "Hey you two, what's all the commotion? And you little sister, why do you want to leave? Don't you want to hang with the big kids?"

Zoë looks up at Troy with a constricted affect.

"You are a pretty girl. Do you know that?" Troy says smiling. "Do you like Hannah Montana? What kind of music are you into?" He reaches down to stroke her hair.

Marsha pulls her cousin away and states firmly, "Don't touch her! I'll handle it." She then brings her face close to Zoe's and starts talking fast but keeps her voice low. "Zoe, if you just let me finish this, I swear I'll take you to the mall and give you a three-hundred-dollar shopping spree. Plus, pay you what I owe you. How about that? Okay? Just go outside and wait in the Bimmer. I'll give you the key and you can start the engine if it gets too cold. I promise to come out and check on you. We will go home soon, I promise."

Zoë just shrugs and looks away. Marsha stands, takes her cousin's hand, and pulls her up. They start heading out.

"Aaw, come on, she doesn't have to go," says Betty, holding up the loose blunt that Brendan attempted to role earlier. "Maybe the little sweet-heart needs a puff. Do you want to party, honey?"

"She's not part of this!" snaps Marsha, "Come on Zoë just walk."

"What are you talking about, girlfriend?" replies Betty. "In certain cool, like-island cultures the mothers blow pot into their babies' mouths to have them fall asleep. I think it would be so-o-o cute to see a bunch of little Rastafarian rug-rats all high and happy. Ya, mon! Ya, mon!"

Marco and Troy both make eye contact. Even though no words are spoken, they both know that the situation has to be controlled.

Outside, a chilling wind starts to come across the open dark field, causing the dead brittle cow grass to rustle. Marsha leads Zoë out to the SUV. "Here just listen to your iPod. I'll turn the engine on so you can keep warm. I won't be long, I swear!" She gives an awkward hug to her little cousin. The wind grows stronger. Marsha shivers and clutches herself while turning around to hurry back. Peering out through the glass of the SUV's passenger seat window, Zoe's little face is stark white like a ghost child. She watches Marsha disappear back into the barn.

The others had already gathered around the suitcase that had been zipped opened and set on one of the blankets. The sweet stench of pot fills the musty air as Betty puffs smoke rings.

"Nobody fucking touch nothing but me," warns Marco.

Except for some ratty clothes, the suitcase was Marco's only real personal possession when he left juvenile hall seven years ago. From that time on, he has gathered in the suitcase a forever-changing inventory of pills, powders, and liquids. Triple wrapped in plastic bags and stuffed deep in the inner side pockets are bundles of shitty Mexican Black Tar along with very potent low-cut H from Colombia. In other compartments there are various vitamin bottles full of Ecstasy, Special K, Rophies, Oxy's, Percs, Xanax, Viagra.... There are also little dark vials of GHB and Poppers and sheets of Microdots and a few bundles of tealeaf joints laced with Dust. He also has a lot of K2, Spice, Ivory Wave, and Hurricane Charlie. At this time, he is out of real coke.

However, not everything in the suitcase is straight. There are dime bags of baking soda. It is some of the fake shit that he plans to pawn off this evening. Newbies are easily ripped-off. In the past, Troy would often carouse the college-bars and dance-clubs and find gaggles of drunk, gitty sorority girls. After a few Samuel Adams and shots of Petron, inhibitions would drop and it would be easy for them to misread Troy and consider him just wild, fun and harmless. Troy would usually lead them outside in the parking lot to meet Marco. Molly was a common request. If Troy gave the sign that they were virgins to it all, Marco would scoop the cash and reach into the part of the suitcase where he kept a Centrum-Silver bottle full of purple tablets inscribed with smiley faces. The girls would return to the club all excited thinking that they just scored something that was going to make them all groovy and touchy-feely, when in reality they just bought expensive caffeine-sugar pills.

Marco and Troy have been slinging and scamming on and off together for some years. Troy often comments on why Marco keeps on using the same ratty suitcase to display and sell his products. Superstition is the answer. Deep down, Marco knows it doesn't make sense but he used the suitcase during his first time dealing and things have been cool since. Narcs always seem to be oblivious. The suitcase is like a good-luck charm. A shield of protection. Marco also has a 25. caliber Tarsus automatic with an extra magazine stored in another side pocket as a second line of defense.

"What do you got in there for me?" says Betty as she raises her arms, snaps her fingers, and shakes her wide hips. Since having a kid, her belly had grown and accrued stretch marks but it did not stop her from wearing belly-shirts. The bubble-gum, goose-bump flesh hangs out over the top of her jeans. The navel piercing is kind of lost in the flab.

Marco, who is kneeling down, looks up at her and says, "I don't know if I have any Slimfast or TrimSpa in here. That's what you really need."

Betty drops her arms and pouts, "Hey, that's mean! I'm like a mother, you know. It's natural to gain a little weight." She looks over at Troy. "Troy, baby, make him be nice to me!"

With a smirk, Troy replies, "Marco, our girl here

deserves a Centrum smiley face."

"No!" says Betty. "I want some Mitsubishi. Got some? It's freezing in this fucking barn, I need to heat up!" Betty knows that tablets etched with the Mitsubishi symbol are real methylene-dioxymethyl-amphetamine.

Rummaging a bit through the suitcase, Marco uncaps some bottles and gathers some pills. "Here, take these." He says, holding out his hand.

"What are they?" she asks.

"Just take them!" commands Marco. "Beggars can't be choosers."

The pills are two Xanax and two tablets of Rohypnol. Marco does not want this chic any more spastic and chatty. E was totally out of the question. The combo he offers Betty is to put her down and shut her up.

"Should I take them, Troy? " Betty asks.

"Do as the man says." Troy replies and hands her the bottle of Bacardi.

Betty palms the pills into her mouth all at once, then washes them down with a gulp of rum. She cheers, "I'll be the first one flying tonight! Watch Out! YEE-HA! Hope this shit warms me up! It's getting drafty in here."

Anxious and tense, Marsha asks, "Should we hold up for a minute and talk about business. I mean, do we really have a deal? What are the terms?"

Marco again scans Marsha. He thinks, *She's like-perfect.*

The night wind from the outside comes whistling through the rafters and cracks in the barn wood.

"Terms?" Marco questions. "I got you baby-doll. No need to worry. I'm gonna hook you and your man up really good so you will be livin' large on Rodeo Drive." Reaching out he takes the rum bottle from Betty's hand. "Let's have a toast and a few appetizers." Marco pours out a few more tablets of Mexican Valium and looks back at Marsha.

"Take these." He says.

"No, I'm okay." Marsha says nervously. "I'm really here for my boyfriend. I thought I would just watch."

"Watch?" Marco balks. "You're part of this, Queen-Pin."

"I know." Marsha says shivering. She attempts a nervous smile and jokes, "I'm the designated driver." In her mind she thinks, *Oh my god, he's so creepy!!!*

In a sudden threatening tone, Marco snarls, "Open your mouth!"

Marsha is instantly filled with terror. Marco puts the pills out to her trembling lips like a priest offering communion. Brendan doesn't have the balls to intervene.

Marsha shirks back and says, "Please, no thank-you!"

In the next second, Betty snatches the pills from Marco's hand.

"What the fuck!" snaps Marco.

Betty puts the pills in her own mouth then forcefully kisses Marsha on the lips. Marsha struggles to get away but reflexively swallows then gags.

"Come on girl!!!" Betty takes back the Bacardi bottle and pushes it on Marsha. Marsha drinks, coughs and chokes on the rum.

"Are you okay, babe?" Brendan steps forward to hold and steady Marsha.

"W-w-what did I just swallow?" gasps Marsha.

Betty looks down at Marco, "Did I do good?"

Marco glares back at Betty and says, "Don't ever fucking jump in when not asked!"

"What was it?" quivers Marsha.

"Nothing! You need to relax girl." Marco says.

"That was funny!" Troy laughs.

Shaking and not knowing what to do, Brendan looks at Marsha and says, "You're okay? Right? It's all cool?"

"I said she's fine!" barks Marco. "Let Miss Queen-Pin

be for a moment! Get your ass over here lover-boy!"

Abruptly, Brendan abandons Marsha and goes over to Marco.

Marsha stands there dumb-founded.

Marco glares at Brendan and says, "Are you ready, son?"

Yea, I-I'm ready," says Brendan all jittery. "What do I do?"

"What do you do? Well, well." Marco mocks. "Why don't you start by getting that big old army jacket-off, roll up and let me see how good your veins are."

As Brendan starts to remove his coat with awkward motions, Marco goes into the suitcase, digging around a bit to retrieve the product and the *works*. Marco chooses the Columbian H. The heroin is cut with chalk but the purity level is very high. The plan is to snow the kid deep so there would be full, undisrupted access to Miss Preppy Queen-Pin.

"Okay, man, I got my jacket off!" puffs Brendan with excitement as if removing the jacket was some kind of athletic achievement. He kneels back down, shivering in his Life-is-Good t-shirt.

"Hold it, dude," says Marco. "We gotta cook this shit up." Marco brings up a bundle of capped syringes and jiggles them a bit in front of the others. "You see boys and girls when shooting smack you always use clean needles. Safety first."

Troy laughs.

Pulling out an old tarnished blackened, silver spoon, Marco sticks it into the baggy of dope. Panning and sifting a bit, he comes out with just about two Tic-Tacs worth of powder. The following ingredient consists of droplets of water from a little plastic squeeze bottle. Taking and uncapping one of the needles with his teeth, Marco then uses the point to stir together the liquid and drug that is on the spoon. "How about a little audience participation here," Marco says. "Anybody got a light?"

Betty and Troy look at one another then start fumbling for their lighters. Marco temporarily holds the needle sideways with his mouth like a pirate holding a knife between his clenched teeth. He takes the lighter that is placed in his free hand. Suddenly, the fire from the Zippo reflects in everyone's eyes. The flame licks the underside of the spoon as the mixture is heated.

Marsha feels nauseous. She can tell that Brendan is breathing heavy.

The flame is snuffed out and the lighter is dropped on the blanket. Marco takes the needle from his mouth and puts the tip back into the spoon to suck up the solution.

"Locked and loaded." says Marco with his awful smile as he holds up the now full syringe.

Marsha looks wide-eyed. Brendan gulps.

"Okay, Rock Star, get closer and give me your arm," orders Marco.

"Should I use my belt? I got one on," says Brendan.

Marco gives an examining squint then replies, "Nah, I see that big blue vein in the crook of your arm. It's totally cherry and waiting to get fucked by this spike."

Brendan's skin looks like a Geisha's in the glow of the electric lantern. Marco reaches out to position the kid's forearm.

"I don't see any tracks, son," says Marco. "You really are a newbie."

"Wait!" says Brendan, suddenly jerking away his arm. He looks at Marsha with glistening, scared, pink-stoned eyes. "Do it with me, Baby! We should experience this together!"

"What?" Marsha gasps.

"Come on, Baby! You and me. I love you." Tears start down Brendan's cheeks.

"You gotta be fuckin' buggin'!" Marco curses.

"Oh, that's romantic." claps Betty. "Come on girl. Do it for your man. You will totally be into it. It's awesome!"

"N-No." Marsha quivers.

Marco thinks to himself, *Maybe this is not a bad idea. A little H with those Rophies and I can do Miss Queen-Pin up the ass all night long and she won't even know it.*

"If you don't want to, Marsha, I'll shoot-up with your man." says Betty smiling but bitchy. "I think he's s-s-s-so cute! With those looks, he's gonna be a hard one to hold on to!"

The nausea keeps growing and Marsha starts to feel her head swoon. "N-No." She repeats with a bit of a slur.

"Yea, try it, sweetheart," says Marco with his coyote grin. He reaches out to pat Marsha's cheek but she flinches and pulls away. Marco's smile vanishes. He thinks, *don't worry, Bitch! Pretty soon you won't be able to flick a fly off yourself!*

"I'm the- the- designated d-d-driver." Marsha mumbles.

Troy laughs.

"OMG Marsha! You are such a weirdo!" Betty rants.

Marco snickers bitterly, "Well, let's get this primo shit into your boy before it cools down. You'll have time to decide later, Queen-pin." Marco firmly grabs Brendan's forearm and looks at him mean in the face. "Don't you dare jerk away again, Romeo. If you move too much, I'll miss the vein and get you in the muscle. You'll balloon-up like Jiffy-Pop and it will burn like a motherfucker. You understand?"

Brendan just nods and looks like a first-timer on a diving board.

Upward and slanting at a forty-five degree angle the needle pierces the vein and the plunger is pressed. It is a perfect hit. Hydrochloride salt takes off into the vessels on the way to the brain. A bit of scarlet is pulled back up into the syringe as it is removed.

"Wow." says Brendan with a sudden smile. Everybody stares at him. Then his smile drops and his face shows a grimace.

"Feel like you're gonna hurl?" asks Marco with disdain.

Brendan's cheeks begin to puff then deflate.

"Quick, Troy!" orders Marco. "Let's get him the fuck outside!"

Both guys take Brendan under the armpits and lift him off his knees.

"Oh no! Is he okay?" cries Marsha.

The two do not answer as they start dragging Brendan across the dusty, creaking floorboards to the doorway.

Marsha begins to get up to follow but she feels someone pressing her back down.

"You got to chill, girl!" says Betty with her hand still firmly clamped on Marsha's shoulder. "It's no big deal. Some puke the first time. He will be feeling like he's in heaven in a moment."

The opiate molecules had connected with the neurons that signal regurgitation. The three make it outside in the nick of time as a stream of Bacardi and an earlier meal of vegetarian chili and tofu hotdogs come spurting forth in an arc from Brendan's mouth. Inside the Bimmer, Zoë witnesses the vomit geyser.

A few moments pass.

Marco and Troy still have Brendan under the arms as they bring him back in. Marsha wants to get up and run to her boyfriend but she feels like her body is suddenly very heavy. No one is physically holding her down this time.

With brown vomit on his chin, Brendan is smiling goofy again, "I'm cool; I'm cool. I feel so warm. Oh-wow."

"Put him over there in the corner," barks Marco to

75

Troy. "He smells like shit."

"Why can't he be here n-n-next to be me?" whimpers Marsha with more of a pronounced slur in her voice.

"You don't want to disturb his high," says Troy. "Let him nod in peace. Plus, if you get too close and get a good whiff you may want to barf too."

Marco and Troy roughly plop Brendan down on his back in a darkened corner with the spider webs. The heroin has found receptor sites in the limbic area of the brain, triggering the release of dopamine and causing a wonderful sensation of warm, mellow euphoria. Other molecules of the drug hit different parts of the brain, converting into morphine in the neurons and blocking electrical impulses that would be interrupted as physical discomfort. No pain, just pleasure is the mode. It is physiological bliss. In the reward circuit of his mind it is Eureka! Brendan has true junky potential.

"I-feel strange." says Marsha, her eyelids heavy. She has continued to stay sitting on the blanket next to the suitcase. It has been about 18 minutes and the Rophies are starting to take effect.

"Want a puff?" Betty says, leaning down behind Marsha and putting the blunt to Marsha's lips. With her other hand she squeezes Marsha's left tit through the Peruvian sweater. Marsha does not inhale the pot nor remove the unwanted, groping hand from her breast. It is hard for Marsha to motor-plan. It is starting to get hard even to *think*.

"Get away from her!" snarls Marco as he walks forward. "Go find something else to do!"

"Oh, come on," says Betty with a pouty expression. "I thought you two fellas would like to see a little show here with me and missy prissy. You know I had my porn debut last year on a free amateur website. It was a group thing. Do you know what it was called?"

"Five dicks and a cow." Marco says with a sneer.

"Why are you such a mean asshole?!" snaps Betty.

"Move it!" barks Marco.

Betty steps away, flipping Marco the bird.

Marsha slowly topples sideways and comes to lay half on the blanket and half on the dirty floor.

Suddenly there sounds two horn blasts from outside. It is Zoë. Moments earlier, she tried to call and text her parents on her iphone but there was no service being so far out in the boondocks.

Marco flashes with anger and alarm. He yells at Troy, "Go outside and handle that!"

"You got something to make the little brat have a nice time-out?" asks Troy.

Hastily, Marco goes to the suitcase and searches around for a bit and comes up with more pills. "Go slip her these!" he orders.

Despite the commotion and recent piercing honks from the horn, Marsha stays down on the floor. She mumbles something incoherent. She doesn't even startle when Betty goes over to the boom box and suddenly cranks up the volume to the max and a track from DJ Icey comes blaring.

Troy walks outside to complete his mission.

Another dose of the Colombian H. is cooked-up but Marco does it in a bit of a rush. He wants to get to Marsha as soon as possible. *Damn, I can't wait to do this chick!* is the reoccurring, looping thought in his head. He even slips himself a Viagra before fixing up the needle.

"I'm ready!" Marco mutters to himself.

With syringe in hand, he comes up next to Marsha. She continues to lie sideways on the ground. Marco turns her so that she is now flat on her back. There is no protest as the sleeve of her sweater is pushed up. Her eyelids are at half-mast.

I hope she is not a puker," Marco thinks.

Taking some care, he injects the heroin into her left arm. The girl didn't even wince.

"Oh-yea, you took that nice, Queen-Pin!" Marco says panting. He discards the used needle by tossing it over his shoulder.

The whites of her eyes show through slits as they roll back in her head. Her pupils constrict. After removing his own coat, Marco wastes no time and pulls Marsha's sweater up, bunching it under her armpits. The bra is yanked down.

"Yes!" Marco says as he greedily dives down to suck on her nipples. He even bites and draws blood. There is a brief groggy moan induced by the painful stimuli but Marsha flutters on the brink of being comatose. Marco licks her face and tongues her mouth.

While Marco continues on, Betty is preparing to do her own thing. From an oversized spangled pocketbook that Betty has brought along, she takes out a jar of Vicks. Next, out of the pocketbook comes a white, plastic Harlequin mask. Scooping up gobs of vapor rub with her fingers, she smears the substance in the inside of the mask. She loves the menthol fumes. Leaving the still lit blunt on the floor, she finishes off the last couple of swallows of Bacardi. She flings the empty bottle. It does not shatter but rather hits the floorboards and rolls off somewhere out of the light. Even though it is cold, she takes off her shirt and unhooks her bra. Before putting on the mask, she runs some more Vicks across her upper lip.

"I am beautiful no matter what they say." she sings to herself.

The Rophies are starting to kick in but Betty still rises on up and dances to the techno, her naked pendulous, tattooed boobs swinging, her gut hanging, her wide hips swaying. After some moments she walks on over to Marco who has his black jeans unbuckled and is continuing to tongue and kiss the unresponsive Marsha. He has Marsha's cargo pants pushed down around her knees and is about to rip off her panties.

"Like it or not, I want some too." Betty says defiantly.

Marco looks up at her masked face and is startled, "Holy shit!"

Betty cocks one hip, snaps her fingers and replies, "Do you know who I am? I'm the phantom mistress of pleasure! It is so cold; my nips are so-o-o hard!"

"Get the fuck away!" curses Marco. He is surprised that the pills that he had given her had not yet done the trick

"Don't be so greedy!" says Betty. "Doesn't every rrr-real man want a mé·nage à trois?"

"Listen, you fat freak, loose the goddamn mask and disappear or I swear I'll shoot your ass!" Marco gives a threatening swipe in the air even though he is still prone.

"I hope you can't get it up, you faggot!" Betty screams back with hurt and anger.

In the next second, miraculously, Brendan comes stumbling out from the darkened corner. "Hey, w-w-what are you, d-d-doing with my girl?"

Marco bolts to his feet and scrambles to zip his jeans and re-buckle his belt. He thinks, *What the fuck is this, Dawn Of The Dead! They're not supposed to get back up!*

Even though, Brendan had been nodding with the heroin he was still sort of conscious. Through pinpoint pupils and heavy eyelids, he did catch glimpses of the drug dealer moving on top of his girlfriend. Having lowered inhibitions induced by the dope and booze, Brendan mustered some sort of impulsive courage that made him rise like Lazarus. "M-M-Marsha." He slurs with a space-cadet tone. "We g-g-got to go now."

Marsha does not respond,

Briskly and highly agitated, Marco walks over and gives a full force soccer kick to Brendan's groin. With an "Umpf!!!" Brendan immediately buckles and crumbles. A few moments later, Troy comes back into the barn and without hesitation joins in by slamming his steel toe work-boots into the side of Brendan's head, over and over. There is a one good shot square in the temple; a lot of the others miss and just strike Brendan in the shoulders and on the side of the neck.

Marco and Troy still keep kicking and kicking.

Finally, they stop.

Motionless and silent, Brendan lays balled up. Blood streams sideways, across his cheek and nose from his temporal skull fracture.

"Wow!" says Betty, her voice a bit muffled by the mask. "You stomped him good, Troy! That was cool, baby!" She shakes her boobs and approaches to give a hug.

Instantaneously, Marco intervenes and shoves Betty square in the chest. Betty lands hard on her rump but the force also sends the rest of her down and she whacks the back of her noggin on the floorboards.

"Christ, this heifer has tweaked my last fucking nerve!" booms Marco.

Betty stays down and rubs the back of her head. She cries softly under the mask and appeared suddenly exhausted. The blow appears to have knocked the mania right out of her. A wad of saliva hits her on the side of her bare stomach and then trickles down. Marco had spat a hawker at her. "There's a money shot for you, bitch!" Marco calls out. "Now lay there and go to sleep!"

She hears Troy laugh which makes her sob more.

Marco turns to Troy and complains, "All I want to do is screw that chick there on the blanket and split. This is a fuckin' clown show tonight!"

Looking over at Marsha, Troy sees that she is

motionless, on her back with her sweater pulled up and her pants pulled down. "Nice!" Troy says with a grin.

"Don't even think about it. There is no time for sloppy seconds," says Marco, sounding winded.

"It's okay. I'll finish my baby-sitting job I got going on outside."

"Bring her in here in case I need you to stomp on one of these fuckers again."

Troy looks down and sees speckles of Brendan's blood on his boots and on the cuff of his jeans and says with a smile, "You got it, captain." He leaves to go retrieve Zoë.

Turning and with hostile mumbling, Marco goes over to the boom box and gives another one of his goalie kicks. The music abruptly stops as the boom-box sails across the floor planks, its plastic housing cracking as it hits low on the wall. "I hate that kind of fucking music!" Marco growled.

Then there is a sudden odd silence in the barn except for Betty's soft muted, whimpering. It seems that the temperature drops even more.

Rubbing his hands, Marco begins walking back over to the drugged-out Marsha, saying as he goes, "I want to bang that pussy before my balls freeze off."

In the next second, Troy returns carrying Zoë hanging over his shoulder like a small game animal from a hunt. He announces proudly, "Looky, Looky, what I got here."

"Is she out good?" snaps Marco.

"Hell, ya. What were the pills?"

"Two Special K's and two Rophies."

"Damn, she's my little zombie baby now! When I went out the first time, I found some Mountain Dew on the front seat. She was all spazin' and trying to use the iphone. But I sweet-talked her and forced her to gulp some soda and take the happy medicine."

"Did she get through with any fucking calls?!" says

Marco with sudden alarm.

"It's cool. I checked. Ain't no service out here in the middle of East Bumble Fuck."

"Are you fucking sure?"

"We're straight! I-I promise.

Marco shakes his head with new apprehension and even more rumbling aggression. "We did our plundering, now is time for some fucking raping! But we still gotta high-tail it out of here soon."

"You got it boss-man, but we also should savor the moment," says Troy while placing Zoë down on the bare floor. "We scored some prime trim here."

The mixture of benzos and the anesthetic caused the girl to black out. Zoe is an unconscious rag-doll. The gray Taft Field-Hockey sweatshirt is roughly yanked off over her head by Troy. He then tears her bra away. "Wow!" says Troy, "This little one is definitely going to need implants in the future. Look how tiny her tits are!"

Marco doesn't pay attention. He is back down with Marsha. Briefly, he casts a suspicious look over at the still motionless Brendan then returns his attention back to his girl. Pausing for a moment, he looks down at Marsha's beautiful but comatose face and notices that she has an odd pasty complexion. He dismisses it saying to himself that it was just the effects of the lantern. Again, he kisses her while his hands knead and claw her breasts. Upon sticking his tongue in her mouth, he tastes something sour. "Ickk!" He exclaims as he brings up his head. "She's got puke in her cheeks!"

At that moment, Troy calls out from where he is with Zoë. Her sweatpants have been pulled down. "Take at look at this! I think I just popped her cherry when I was just diddling her. It's like a little fucking vice!" Troy holds up his bloody index finger, beaming ecstatically. "Can you imagine? A real fucking virgin! It is a special moment for the little darling; I'm her first!"

Marco ignores Troy and positions himself toward Marsha's waist and violently pulls down her panties. He mutters, "Finally!" When he flings away her underwear he feels that the garment is soaked. The panties make a wet smacking sound, landing in the darkness, out of the glow of the lantern. Marco lowers himself down on his belly, between her legs. A strong odor fills his nostrils. Wetness comes right through his black Motor Head t-shirt. He is lying in a large puddle of urine. Marco scrambled up to his knees. "Goddamn it! The chick pissed herself!"

Troy does not look over. He is fixated on his own prey. Standing up, over Zoe, he has his long, thin, uncircumcised cock out of his pants. It is flaccid like a white rubber worm. In frustration, he is jerking it, but it failing to get hard.

With disgust and sudden rage, Marco tears at his own belt, unbuttoning and unzipping his jeans. He feels cheated that his dream girl is being all too human and displaying bodily functions. It was not supposed to go this way. "Piss on me bitch! I'm going to drill you so hard that your cooch will be red for a year!" Leaning forward, his head rests on her chest as he works down below, pulling out his small penis from his frayed gray underwear. His dick is also soft and un-responsive. In frustration he keeps yanking it. "Fuck!" He growls. The Viagra is not working. Is it Betty's curse?

At that moment a startling realization occurs. Marsha's chest is showing no signs of rise and fall. There is no breath. Marco pulls up and looks back into her face. There is a blue hue. In a bit of a panic he slaps her hard on both cheeks. "Wake-up!" he yells.

Nothing.

He gives her a nasty titty-twist.

Nothing.

More slapping. He frantically checks for a pulse and puts his ear to her mouth and nose to detect breath.

Nothing.

Early in his passionate haste, Marco had accidentally cooked up over 500 mgs of heroin. Combined with the Rohypnol, vital electrical-chemical transmissions in Marsha's brain had been disrupted and suppressed. The autonomic impulses going to her diaphragm had ceased. She had stopped breathing approximately seven minutes ago. There was global neuronal death due to lack of oxygen to the brain.

Bounding to his feet, pulling up his jeans, and stuffing his limp member back in his shorts, Marco proclaims loudly and with fear, "Jesus! I almost fucked a corpse!"

"What?!" Troy exclaims. He is about to straddle Zoë.

"Stop whatever fuck you're doing and get over here!" yells Marco.

Zipping up as he goes, Troy hurries over and looks down. "Wow, she looks like she's toast! We need to get her in some ice! Try to wake her up!"

"We got no fucking ice, you moron! Where would we get fucking ice around here?" screams Marco. He hits Troy in the shoulder out of aggravation.

"How did she OD?" whines Troy while holding his upper arm.

"Who the fuck knows?! The chick is a fucking lightweight!"

"Do you think she is really dead?"

"Fuck ya!" answers Marco, while tugging the front of his urine soaked t-shirt away from his skin.

Troy reaches down and lifts Marsha up a bit by the shoulders, her head hanging back. He shakes her and yells, "Wake up bitch! Come-on!"

Nothing.

He also slaps and pinches her.

Nothing.

He tries again.

Nothing.

There is a *thunk!* as Troy let's go of the lifeless body, the corpse's head hitting the floorboards. He gasps, "Ah, we got to disappear, man! Let's just fly! The keys are still in the Lexus! YOU'RE RIGHT; SHE'S FUCKING DEAD!!!" Troy starts to turn to leave but Marco quickly reaches out and grabs him by the wrist and spins him around.

"Hold up, fuck-head! We can't leave it like this!"

"W-W-What do you mean!" Troy stutters.

"We got all these others fuckin' lying around here!"

"Fuck 'em! There all stoned out away!"

"They will wake up! They will remember who we are! Especially that fat whore over there!"

"Well, what the fuck are we gonna do? Hell with it! I'm going!!!"

With a quick body shot right under the solar plexus, Marco knocks the wind out of Troy and causes him to double over and make gagging sounds.

"You gotta cool your jets mother-fucker! Chill!" Marco reaches out and holds Troy by a tight fist-full of his two-tone hair. Troy is dry heaving and trying to find his breath. Letting go, Marco says with disgust, "Don't be a fucking skirt! We gotta think!"

Finally getting in some air, Troy rubs his chest and jabbers, "This is way too heavy man. I mean like, wow! We just need to split! It's like just bad luck with her OD'ing. It ain't our fault. We were just here to party a little. It was all good but- "

"Are you really that dumb and believe the shit you're shoveling!" hisses Marco. "This is not just feeling up some tipsy college girl. We got a dead teen-ager here! A rich, white one! Mommy and daddy, the police and the PTA are all going to be revved and screaming to string us by our nut sacks!"

"Oh man! Come on!"

"If you think you are going to tell your jive to the judge and walk, you are the world's biggest retard!"

"Yea, but- like this chick dying was kind of like your thing. I don't mean to bail on you but,"

Marco's eyes become more terrorizing. He takes a step forward, snarls, and pokes Troy hard under the Adam's apple causing Troy to *GAGGIK!* With venom, Marco spat, "You are a fucking accomplice, asshole! And, finger-fucking little miss pigtails ain't like just littering. Most times you drug a chick and rape her, she doesn't say shit because she doesn't fucking remember or she is too fucking embarrassed. With this fucking scene, your little virgin over there is gonna tattle-tail when she wakes up with her little sore snatch and cops start sweating her!"

"Oh, man this sucks!" Troy cried, rubbing his throat.

"It sure does! And like I said, you're a fuckin' accomplice."

"Dude, I still don't know! Christ! This is all too quick!"

"If you pussy-out on me, bitch, and try to bolt, I swear I'll shoot you in both eyes!"

Visibly trembling, Troy waves his hands as if surrendering. He knows that Marco has a gun. "Okay, Okay! I'm just bugging! I'm sorry!"

"I need you to be frosty! I ain't going to jail. You hearing me?"

"You're right! This is just a bad scene!" Troy feels like he is going to hyperventilate. He gasps, "What do we do?"

Marco rubs his temples for a moment. Due to the years of brutality in his young life, he did acquire survival traits that suddenly allows him to become in control. Marco says with abrupt bizarre, calmness, "We will put them all down."

There is a pause. Troy looks stunned. He wheezes,

"What?"

"You heard me."

"You're shitting me?"

Marco doesn't reply but just glares back with a horrifying intensity.

"You're fucking serious!"

Marco then asks coldly, "You want to be back in a fucking cell?"

Once before, Troy had done a yearlong stint. Having claustrophobia and the compulsion to be in constant motion, confinement was excruciating torture. At this moment, Troy has an instant revelation that Marco is right. Troy thinks, *If I get made, I'll be in prison for fucking ever.* Reaching into the back pocket of his jeans, Troy takes out the Spyderco. The tactical knife is shaking in his hand, "I got this, man. You can go slit their throats! I'll be outside getting' the Lexus warmed up!"

"Put the blade away, dude!" barks Marco. "And you're fuckin' staying with me in my line of sight. Like I really should trust your chicken-shit-ass! I gotta think."

"I'm with you man! You're right! I ain't spending my life in stir! I ain't gonna live in a cage forever! No fucking witnesses!"

"Great, I'm glad you just found your balls. There may be a plan."

"Really?"

"Yea."

"What?!"

"No more fucking questions. I got an idea."

Marco goes over to the suitcase and starts pulling stuff out. He begins cooking up syringes of heroin. Troy joins in to help but he is all thumbs. Clear plastic bags have been used as packaging material for the various drug bundles in the suitcase. Marco retrieves a bunch of the plastic bags. He also gets the role of duct tape that he keeps inside for periodic repairs to his beloved piece of luggage.

"Lets' off the rock star first." Marco says to Troy.

The two go over to Brendan who is still balled up on his side on the floor.

"Is he already dead?" asks Troy with a hard swallow.

Marco uses his foot to push Brendan over onto his back. The kid moans.

"Guess not." Troy nervously giggles, trying to hold down his fear.

There is wet and semi-dry gore on the side of Brendan's face as well as huge mutant-like swelling.

"This boy's face is ffffff-fucked-up!" Troy says in awe of his brutal work of head stomping with his steel-toed work-boots.

"Here, hold his arm out." Marco says as they both kneel down next to Brendan. Another dose of heroin is injected. Next, one of the plastic bags is placed over Brendan's head.

"What's the bag for?" asks Troy.

"We're going to make double sure that none of these fuckers ever talk!" Marco reaches out his hand. "Now give me that role of duct-tape."

Around and around, the tape is wrapped around Brendan's bagged head. Using his teeth, Marco breaks the role free.

"Looks like plastic mummy wrap." Troy laughs.

"Hold his hands to his side in case he starts to struggle," snaps Marco.

Troy does what he is told. The two wait. Brendan never stirs.

"I think that second shot of H. did him in," remarks Troy with astonishment.

"Okay, we'll still leave him taped up a bit to make sure he really bought the fucking farm," says Marco. He has the two other syringes held up behind each ear like how carpenters hold their pencils. "Let's do your fat girlfriend next."

"Girlfriend?" replies Troy. "She isn't my girlfriend! I got fucking standards!"

The two go over to Betty. The Rophies, benzos and the third of Bacardi are in full effect and she is passed out on her back, topless, and still wearing the Harlequin mask. Marco has feelings of vengeance as he sticks the needle in her arm and presses the plunger. "This will finally stop you from running your fucking month." He snarls.

The mask is pulled off her face. Heavy black mascara had run down the sides of her bloated cheeks from her earlier sobbing. Bright red lipstick was smeared across her chin. Her face is sticky like a glazed donut from all the Vick's vapor-rub.

"Fucking ugly looking!" Troy comments.

"Give me one of the bags." Marco says.

"With a mug like that, we should double bag her." Troy quips.

Having a long history of poly-dependence, Betty had acquired a bit of tolerance over the years. The hot injection of heroin did not kill her so quickly as it did Brendan. As the two bagged and taped her head, the sudden lack of oxygen caused some part of her primitive protective mechanism to respond. Loose and floppy, here arms came up.

"Shit! She's moving!" exclaims Troy.

"Hold her down!" says Marco.

It is still no great struggle. The two pin her arms and legs. Seen through the opaque bag and tape there are blotches and smears of the black mascara and red lipstick. There is also the glistening vapor rub. Facial features are hard to discern. Betty's head looks like decaying Chinese food wrapped in plastic.

She dies.

The two rise up after a little bit.

"Leave her bagged for now." says Marco. "Let's do number three."

Suddenly, no longer scared, Troy shows an excited smile. "Man, this is a rush! I am so amped! I'm still sort of shaking but it feels good! I can't believe that we are being this hard-core! We are stone-cold killers, man! Woo-weee look out! Ha-ha!"

"Tone it down!" snaps Marco. "Stay focused!"

They huddle around Zoë. The last needle is stuck into her little arm. Instantly, her little chest collapses.

"We won't have to bag and wrap this one," says Marco. "She's done."

"Alright! We're out! Mission accomplished!" Troy says clapping his hands.

"Hold-up, asshole!" Marco says with no patience. "Give me your knife!"

"What?"

"You heard me! Give it to me!"

Troy hands the Spyderco over to Marco.

"Now, go and put the clothes back on these chicks." Marco says.

"No way!" exclaims Troy. "You're fucking with me! They're dead!"

"No, shit. But we'll try to hide the molesting."

"I don't get it! Ain't murder worst?"

"Shut-up! Don't think. Just do as I say!"

Reluctantly, Troy bends down and starts to pull up Zoe's pant. Marco walks over to Brendan's corpse and begins to cut the tape and remove the plastic bag. He is careful not to nick the flesh and cause more injury to the body. The bloody tape and plastic are stuffed back in the suitcase. Betty's head is also uncovered in the same manner and wrappings gathered up. Marco finds one of the used syringes on the floor and sticks it back in her arm.

He wants it to appear that she injected the others then did herself last. *The cops will never buy it*, Marco thinks, *but it may throw them off for a bit. I just need time to run before they lift our fuckin' prints! Our fucking prints are everywhere! Christ!*

Troy becomes frustrated as he tries to re-snap Marsha's bra. He got the brasserie tangled and twisted with the sweater around the dead girl's shoulder. "Fuck! Fuck! Fuck! I don't know how to do this, man! And it's kind of giving me the creeps!"

Cursing, the two work together re-cladding the bodies. They both get nauseous when they have to deal with Betty.

Troy whines, "I can't wait to scrub my hands and get rid of that feeling of big dead tits!" He then looks up at Marco and confesses, "And by the way, I couldn't find that chick Marsha's panties."

"Let it be," says Marco. "Maybe they'll think that her and Brendan got busy before they all shot up and croaked."

"You mean like a suicide pact?"

"It's gonna be a fuckin' miracle if the police believe that shit."

Troy gets more excited, "Dude, we should write one of those e-mo suicide notes and leave it in Betty's hand!"

"What?"

"It can say something like, dear all you moms and dads! You didn't love us enough. So we all decided to end it. We are all having one last party. Best way to go. Signed Betty!

P.S. That kid that wants to be a rock star, I kicked in his face because he called me fat and wouldn't fuck me!" Troy starts with his crazy laugh. He asks Marco, "What do you think, man? Fuckin' brilliant right?"

"No. It's a really fuckin' stupid idea." says Marco.

"Why?" says Troy, sounding hurt.

"Forensics!" snaps Marco, "They'll know the handwriting don't match!"

Troy looks perplexed. "Oh?" he says.

"Enough!" barks Marco, "It's time"

"Time for what?"

"Time to split and run!"

Troy becomes hyper and bouncy again. "Dude, how much money did we score tonight? Let's take the Lexus and just make a fucking run to Mexico! What's that place where all the kids go for Spring Break? We can party on the beach! Get some of those chicks from Girls-Gone-Wild! Dude, it will be awesome!"

"Maybe you can get on an MTV special and say "Hi, Mom!" on camera!" Marco balks with annoyance. "Alright, enough fuckin' yappin'! Move it!"

Troy shrugs.

The suitcase is closed up. Grasping the handle of the luggage, Marco says to himself, *Okay, magic suitcase, protect me from all this bullshit.*

The two walk out and the barn door is shut. Outside, Troy looks over at the BMW SUV. "Can we take both rides? That would be sweet!"

"No!" says Marco. "It stays. We'll take the Lexus out of here and dump it in Waterbury."

"Why Waterbury?"

"The city is a shithole. Will leave the ride up in the hills where the Latin Kings are. In no time this ride will be stripped like there were piranhas."

"How are we getting' home?"

"They got a Metro-North in town. We'll have to hoof-it a bit to the station, then it's back to New Haven."

"Man, you're like fucking James Bond! Cleared our tracks, came up with an escape plan lickety-split and all! What made you suddenly so cool? Have you done this shit before or what?"

Marco does not answer but his thoughts begin racing like the Indie 500. A sense of panic comes back and starts building inside Marco even though he looks composed on the outside. He thinks, *Why did I lose my fuckin' brains over that Marsha chick? What the hell was wrong with me? Now, we're gonna be hunted!!!!*

The two get in the LX470.

Troy asks again, like a child wanting to know what he is going to get for Christmas. "How much money did we score?"

"Shut the fuck-up," says Marco coldly, while internally he is full of hot boiling fear, excitement, and rage.

The Lexus pulls away, high beams glaring and following the tire tracks in the field.

11:59 p.m. Back in the barn, the lantern is left on. The disco ball still hangs from the rafter. All four bodies are left displayed out on their backs. Zoë is in the middle of the floor. Marsha is to the side, still half on and half off the blanket. Betty is nearby on the bare dirty wood planks. Brendan is still in the darkened corner with the cobwebs.

Some time passes.

There is no more distant sound of a fleeing vehicle.

Silence.

Then comes, ever-so gentle pattering. One of the same mice that had scared Zoë earlier in the evening darts out from the shadows. Hunger is an urge that is known to override fear. The little rodent scampers over to the side of Zoe's head and starts gnawing the soft dead flesh of her earlobe. Its greedy, tiny mouth turns red.

Starting far away in the woods, the cold night wind returns. It rustles through the black pines and trees and moves out across the marred field. A high-pitched whistle sounds as the gust comes through the crack, slits and gaps in the ancient barn. The disco ball turns joylessly.

93

Some time ago, before Betty died, she abandoned a lit blunt on the floor. During all the commotion, it had fallen through a space in the floorboards and dropped down into the vermin's nest of wood shavings. The blunt had almost burned out, giving only the faintest scent of cannabis.

The wind carries through the interior of the barn. The little dying ember in the blunt suddenly flares up with new life like a tiny red warning button. It gets hotter. Some of the nesting starts to smolder. Then there is a flame. The wood of the barn is dry and brittle.

Ignition!

The mice scurry. Their itty-bitty hearts are pounding.

Thirty minutes later, it is a spectacular scene as bright orange blooms burst into the night sky, as the barn's roof explodes then caves in. The field is awash in a hellish glow.

SEVEN

Tuesday, 11:40 a.m. It proved to be the start of another clear nice autumn day but Mattie Gallagher could give two shits about the weather. He needs an eye-opener and there is no more booze in the house. It is time to go on a mission. Having slept in his shirt, he only needs to find his pants. The plaid golf trousers are found balled up at the foot of the bed. He gets into them and goes into the bathroom. While pissing in the toilet, he catches a glimpse of himself in the bathroom mirror.

"Glory be! You did yourself awful!" He exclaims while looking at his reflection.

There are black crusted stitches on his forehead from his Saturday night out on the town. Yesterday afternoon, he left Saint Rose's Hospital and like always, against medical advice. A new social worker in the ER had tried to push a 28-day rehab on him. He told her he would definitely go as long as the rehab facility agreed to let him out once a day for Happy Hour. The social worker didn't laugh. From the hospital, Mattie had gone directly to The Anchor Tavern to get ripped. He spent most of Monday evening in a drunken blitz.

Mattie mutters while he rubs his soar head, "Damn it, I don't remember when I came in last night. Wonder if the cold cruel world is still standin'?"

Below, from the downstairs living room, comes an elderly woman's voice, "Is that you I hear tinkling up there? So nice of you to rise. It's almost noon you know! You have some errands to do young man!"

"Oh, Christ!" Mattie curses.

The voice belongs to Mattie's cousin, Gretchen. She is 68 years old. They both live off her social security and her dead husband's pension. It is no secret that she too is a drop-down-drunk. She doesn't leave the house much anymore and she uses Mattie as a pair of legs to go fetch her milk, eggs, coffee, Irish Mist, Seagram's 7, Dewar's White Label and cartons of menthols.

"Are you alive up there? The cabinets been bare you know. You haven't been home for some days!"

"Yea, yea, I hear ya naggin'!" calls out Mattie as he takes a handful of Vitalis to smooth back his thin white hair. "Hold your water; I'll be down in a few!"

Slipping into his shoes, he then zips up a light blue windbreaker and hurries down the stairs, swearing as he goes.

Gretchen has her little withered body wrapped in a housecoat and fused into a Lazy-Boy. There is a nicotine haze about her as she chain smokes. Channel 8 news is on the television. Scenes of EMS workers and police walking through the ruins of a barn fire are being broadcasted. Gretchen turns down the volume with the remote when she sees Mattie. She exclaims, "Oh Holy Mary Mother of God, what happened to your head? Did the niggers do that to ya?"

Ignoring her question, Mattie makes a B-line for the three twenty dollar bills at the end of the cluttered coffee table. He snatches up the money and heads for the door. He starts feeling the shakes coming on. "I'll be back!" He says. Gretchen is still babbling about her order from the packy when he slams the door behind him and makes it out.

They live in one of the row houses on the New Haven, Fairhaven line. It is a poor area and they are the last old Irish to be living in a predominately black area. The only perk is that over the years there was an inundation of liquor stores. Mattie favors Fox's Spirit-Mart because it is close and the lady behind the counter is white and "not some dot-head." He walks fast down the street and sees his destination. With the ding of the little bell that signals that a customer has entered the store, his anxiety and irritability seems to ease.

"Well, look what the cat dragged in." Lucy says with good nature. Seeing the stitches on his head she then asks, "Gosh, what happened?"

Mattie quips, as he rushes pass her on his way to the vodka aisle, "I got hurt rescuin' all those orphans. Didn't ya hear?"

She laughs, "Boy, what a hero." Lucy is amazingly obese. The estimate is over 450 pounds. A large apron-wedge of fat hangs down between her thighs. Above her pronounced double chin appears to be a consistent jolly smile. Her graying hair is tied back tight in a bun. Bright colored moo-moos are her everyday apparel. Rarely did anyone see her come out from behind the counter. Seated on an extra-wide, metal machine shop stool is her full time perch.

With shaky hands, Mattie quickly twists off the cap to a pint of Bukoff, then starts to take in what appears to be life-sustaining swallows of the Russian potato juice.

"Whoa, hold up, mister!" scolds Lucy, "can't be drinkin' in here. It's not a saloon you know!"

Mattie takes two more gulps and then turns to her with a guilty smile. "Sorry, your majesty, I was just hurtin' a bit. But you may have conjured up a fine idea. You should put bar stools in each aisle. I would sit here all day long and never leave. I would have the freshest libations while ganderin' at your bountiful beauty."

Grinning and shaking her head, Lucy says, "Ahh, that's sweet. If you're Jonesin' that bad next time, I'll ring you out quicker than lightning and let you brown-bag-it outside."

"Good to know, you're kinder than Mother Theresa." replies Mattie.

"Did you ever think of slowing down?" Lucy asks with some hesitation.

Mattie responds with a mean glint in his eyes, "Now those are fightin' words, darling. It's like askin' a man in a whorehouse to contemplate celibacy. I was once court ordered to attend AA. During my first 12-step meetin' I raised my hand and asked to address the group. After given the floor I offered to sponsor a fieldtrip to the Anchor Pub and that I was buyin' the first round. I was briskly booed out of the meetin' but three fellow booze-hounds took me up on my offer. The four of us left and went out and got snookered that very evenin'. Raisin' our glasses for a toast, we all shouted, "Friends of Bill W. go screw your mother!"

"Oh, you are a rascal." Lucy laughs with resignation in her voice.

Turning away, Mattie then begins to shop, picking up three bottles of Dubra Vodka, and a Seagram's VO. With arms full, he comes up to the register and puts the stuff on the counter. "Give me also a cartoon of whatever smokes are the cheapest."

"Yes, sir. You also want your Quick-Picks? Lotto is up to 3.5 mil."

"Yea, and give me two Win-For-Life scratch-offs."

Lucy begins to work the lottery machine.

Suddenly, Mattie is hit with a thought that gives him a little excited spark. "And give me a pencil and one of those slips. I want another Lotto ticket but I want to choose my own numbers."

"You got the winning six for me?" chuckles Lucy.

"I got six for ya right here." Mattie jokes while

gesturing to his crotch.

"Whip it out, lover." purrs Lucy.

Mattie just smiles and starts to fill in the numbers on the slip.

"Those numbers mean something?"

"Oh, just what a little birdy told me."

"Really?"

"Well, a big birdy. A big, crazy birdy. Totally nuts and howlin' at the moon. He was calling out numbers faster than an auctioneer. They said that he cut off his own teet." Mattie hands her the completed Lotto slip. "I hope I remembered the numbers right. I confess I was a bit inebriated that other evenin' and those nurses in the emergency room were a bunch of heartless cunts. Not a compassionate bone in their bodies."

Lucy shakes her head with a sigh of empathy and runs the slip through the lottery machine. Before handing him the Lotto ticket she reads the numbers aloud, "Are these them? This what you want? 27, 28, 30, 31, 35, 37."

"Yea. Could be? Only the devil knows." says Mattie as he takes the ticket.

EIGHT

Tuesday, 1:05 p.m. at the Elm City Behavioral Health Center, Dr. Fray is back at his desk doing notes and waiting for his next appointment. It is hit or miss if the client will show. Her name is Rhonda Butkus.

A personality can be defined as a comprehensive menu of character traits. If a person is born with a neurological even temperament and experiences a nurturing, validating, loving childhood, he or she can be blessed with a healthy ego. That individual will have self-love, be able to learn, excel, see reality correctly, overcome losses, and make "good" choices in life. On the other hand, if a person is born with a neurological system that is hypersensitive to stress, coupled with an invalidating, traumatic childhood, he or she could seem as cursed.

Rhonda Butkus is one of the dammed. Her mother was an alcoholic who drank when pregnant. Booze infiltrated placenta, impairing development of the fetus's prefrontal cerebral cortex. As a child, Rhonda had difficulties with focus and concentration. There was hyperactivity and hissy fits that went way beyond what is expected during the Terrible Twos. Then the various stepfathers came along. The molestation started at age eleven. Little, spazy, Rhonda had just wanted comfort and attention but instead got a big hand over her mouth in the middle of the night and excruciating pain *down below*. Whenever the males left the scene, mother would accuse little Rhonda of being a "slut" and seducing "her man." More drinking, screaming, beatings and hell would follow.

The childhood nightmare left Rhonda as an adult with a severe case of Borderline Personality Disorder. Her emotions are raw like the skin of a burn victim. Having monumental abandonment issues, she seeks out anything with a pulse. There appears to be an on-going parade of hook-ups with addicts, criminals, and married men. When the guys take off, Rhonda will often self-destruct and scratch and burn her forearms and attempt to OD on sleeping pills. She literally has close to fifty inpatient psychiatric hospitalizations for self-harming behavior and suicide attempts.

1:09 p.m. The secretary calls from the floor below and moments later, Rhonda Butkus is standing at the door.

"Hey, Dr. Fray, I made it in." she says beaming.

"I see that, Rhonda." says Peter while gesturing for her to enter and sit down in his office.

Usually, she dresses in frumpy sweats, but today she is in a Slipknot concert T-shirt and tight black jeans that causes her to look like an aging groupie. Her curly red hair is no longer tied back but rather combed out big and wild. Fray observes that her lipstick is dark purple, almost black. Heavy charcoal eyeliner accents the crazy intensity in her gaze. Rhonda is pushing 50. Her age and complexion of crows-feet and worry-lines do not appear congruent with her new get-up.

"You look a bit different?" Peter says, while avoiding any condescending tone.

"Well, I have a new boyfriend. I needed to do a makeover. You know, try to be kind of hip. He has me listen to this new head-banger-hard-rock-stuff. I'm gettin' to like it. No more country for me."

"Hmm, interesting." Fray says, knowing that another disaster is likely brewing. He gently asks, "So what is the reason for the appointment today?"

Rhonda exhales and sighs, "Well, I think I finally found my soul-mate."

"Hmm?"

"Yea, I have been so happy. I don't need those P.T.S.D. support groups anymore, Dr. Pete. No more DBT. I hate those fucking groups. This man makes me whole. I'm so excited. His warmth has cured me of all my depression and hang-ups. Plus, he is so friggin, good-lookin'. I can get wet just thinkin' about his bod!" She then giggles. "I'm just in love. It's the best!" She shows Peter her bare forearms that are a latticework of old white bumpy scar tissue from years of self-mutilation. "See all these marks. I'm gonna cover them up. I don't feel like cuttin' no more. I'm gonna get these tattoos made with my lover's name entwined in mine with pictures of thorny roses. Is that cool or what, huh? Can't you see I'm truly happy, Dr. Pete?"

"I see you smiling, Rhonda." says Peter. "How long have you known this gentleman?"

She puts up her hand and there is sudden irritability in her voice, "Stop right there, Dr. Fray, I know what you're gonna try to get at! You think I'm runnin' into another fucked-up relationship but this one is way different. I know it! I feel it sooooo deep. I didn't come here for you to piss in my Cheerios. I already know what is good for me. Don't you dare make me cry!"

"Okay." Peter replies, in a gentle manner. "But what can I help you with?

"It's little Jesse! He's being a royal pain in the ass! He's all jealous and tryin' to break me and my man up!"

Jesse is Rhonda's 18-year-old son. Department of Child and Family Services had removed the boy from her care when he was age 7 for neglect and unfit parenting. He was shuffled from foster home to foster home until now. Being discharged from the system, he had nowhere to go, so he decided to live back with his mother. Peter knew it was a disastrous idea and had often thought, *No Jesse! No! Run away! Run away!*

"What do you think Jesse is feeling?" Fray asks.

"Who knows? He's a moody little teenage shit-head. I told him if he doesn't respect me, I won't allow him to get high in the house anymore. I'm still his mother. He has to live by my rules!"

Pete asks, "Do you think it is a wise idea to allow Jesse to use drugs?"

Rhonda again puts up her hand, "Listen, I'd rather him use at home then doin' it out in the streets."

"It is difficult to raise a teenager," says Peter. "You are right; they can be quite moody. But if you let your son do drugs at home, it doesn't mean that he won't use elsewhere."

"I don't care!" Rhonda flashes with agitation. "To be honest, I could give two-shits if he gets high! I just need him to stop cock-blockin' me with my new man!"

The doctor sighs inside. He pauses then asks, "How is he hurting your new relationship?"

Exhaling loudly, Rhonda rolls her eyes, and pats her thigh, "Well, for starters, last night he threw a fit because my man had to go on a job and he wasn't allowed to tag along. So immature!"

There is a pause. Fray frowns then asks, "What kind of work was it? How come Jesse wanted to go?"

"I don't know. Some kind of delivery job. Whatever. But Jesse wanted to chum around, but Troy needed his space."

"Troy is your new boyfriend's name?"

"Yea, ain't it sexy."

"It is interesting that you say that Jesse wants to break you two up, but also wants to hang around with Troy. What do you think is happening?"

"Well, Jesse and Troy were friends first. They met in rehab. Troy needed a place to stay so Jesse let him come over. That's how we met. I almost had an "O" the first time I laid eyes upon the man."

Peter knows he is poking a wasp's nest of dysfunction but still continues with his questioning. "So, has Troy been clean and sober since getting out of rehab."

"Oh yea." smiles Rhonda. "He ain't gonna use no more. He's full of charisma. He's got his act together. In fact, if Jesse would stop being such a brat, Troy would be an excellent father figure. Troy could be a great role model for my boy."

"I know that Jesse is 18. How old is Troy?"

Rhonda drops her smile and stiffens in the chair. "What does it matter?" She says defensively. "Age shouldn't mean anything! It's what's inside that counts, right? You're a shrink, you should know that!"

"It seems my question about age upsets you. How come?"

"Listen, Troy called me a MILF. Do you know what that means? A lot of younger guys like older women. Troy is 21 but he is really grown-up for his age. And plus, I'm not that old. I heard on one of those talk shows that being in your 50's is like the new 30's. So you can think like, you know, me and Troy are really kind of, almost, the same age. Understand? "

For a moment, Fray wants to smile due to her ludicrous comments, but then feels sad because he knows a crash is soon to follow. He still probes further, "Do you think, Jesse would ever accept another male who is just a few years older, as a father figure?"

Rhonda flares up and yells, "I don't give a fuck what Jesse thinks! What about my happiness? I finally found someone who is really special! I'm not going to be lonely!!!"

There is another pause. Peter says softly, "I see that you really suffer when you feel lonely. Life must be so hard for you."

Her anger quickly dissipates and tears well up in her eyes. With quivering lips she says, "Please, Dr. Fray, tell me that it's okay. Tell me I'm not a fuck-up. Tell me, that I should care about myself and really love this man."

"Rhonda, I agree you should care about yourself. That is a good thing. But what does your wise-mind tell you to do in a situation like this?"

Putting her hands over her eyes she weeps. Peter sits in silence, hoping that she will reflect for a moment and maybe have a hint of insight.

"Taz." She mumbles, with her hands still covering her face.

"What?" says Peter. "Sorry, Rhonda, I didn't hear what you said."

Dropping her hands, from her cheeks, she has an impish smile. Her black mascara has streaked her face. "Taz." She repeats with a slight giggle. The dark lipstick makes her grin a bit sinister.

"I don't understand, Rhonda." Peter replies. "What is Taz?"

With an unnerving glint in her eyes she answers, "He has the cutest tattoo of the Tasmanian Devil on his arm. I like to kiss it."

The doctor is suddenly hit with a memory of a past client. He quickly asks, "What is Troy's last name?"

Rhonda cocks her head and replies, "Its Bennett. Troy Bennett."

A brief chill runs up Peter's spine. A few years ago, he moonlighted doing forensic evaluations for one of the city's young offender's program. He recalls assessing a kid named Troy Bennett. There were numerous charges for burglary and larceny as well as an extensive drug history.

There was a rule/out diagnosis for emerging bipolar disorder but Peter saw something else that went way beyond typical manic impulsivity and garden-variety dissocial behavior. The teen gave off an unnerving vibe. Peter remembers thinking, *This one has the potential to do some really bad things.*

"Do you know Troy?" asks Rhonda with some excitement.

Peter would never break confidentiality and ignores the question. He puts a bit of sternness in his voice and asks again, "Rhonda, tell me how your wise-mind would guide you in a time like this?"

On cue, her lips begin to quiver again and there are more tears as she pleads, "Just tell me it's okay. You're the best psychologist in the world. You're the only one I can really trust. I tell you things that nobody else can get at. You're my savior."

Nodding his head no, Pete replies, "I need to hear from you. Tell me, what is the right thing to do?"

Her rage flames on. "YOU'RE AN ASSHOLE!!! DO YOU KNOW THAT!!! YOU FUCKIN' FAKE!!!" Rhonda bolts up, grabs her purse and starts heading for the door. Peter asks her to sit back down but his voice is a peep in a hurricane. She continues to curse and cry as she goes down the hallway. The ranting grows fainter as she departs.

Silence.

Peter exhales and hopes that he does not have a repeat of yesterday with all the emotional meltdowns. He surmises that a break-up is right around the corner followed by her racking up another hospitalization. Peter is unnerved and concerned about her connection with Troy Bennett. The doctor knows that Rhonda could be like a hemorrhaging swimmer among sharks. And there is her son. Again, Peter says to himself, *Run, Jesse Run!*

NINE

Tuesday, 5:30 p.m. in an upstairs bedroom of a haggard three family row house, off New Haven's Whalley Avenue, Marco lies on his back in a crumpled unmade bed, sweating and panting. His black jeans and dirty underwear are bunched down around his knees; his black t-shirt pulled up around his armpits. A pungent sharp stink of Marsha's dried urine is in clothes and on his skin. Moments earlier, flashbacks of her nipples and dead face played in his mind. Now, Marco feels stomach sick. The bright indigo tattoo of the Hindu Goddess Kali appears to glow in the center of his white clammy chest. Jizz pools in Marco's navel. Frantic masturbation was just a brief release from the pounding anxiety. The lucky suitcase was stowed safely under the bed. All day long, Marco had been flipping through local channels catching reports of the barn fire in Woodbury. He came up stairs after catching the Early NEWS 8 lead story. The media finally released the names and yearbook photos of the dead teenagers. Snippets of one of the hysterical, grieving moms flashed on the screen followed by an interview with classmates preparing to do a candlelight vigil. There were headlines such as "HORRIFIC TRAGEDY!" and "DEADLY INFERNO!"

Marco feels like he is going to burst. "Fuckin' almost prime time!" he says aloud. Audibly exhaling, he then wipes cum off his belly with a sheet. The old bed linen has images of baseball bats and catcher mitts. A few Yankee posters are still push-pinned to the closet doors. Marco's eyes dart about, his gaze going to the Little League trophy on the bureau and then to a fading team photo tacked on the wall under a crucifix. His late little cousin Joey is in the second row. The kid had been killed in a mini-bike accident years ago. Marco has his room. The lingering sorrow has still not been fumigated.

Gina, Marco's Aunt, had always allowed Marco into her home. Marco figured that she was looking for a replacement for her kid. She tries to be all nice and lovey-dovey but Marco will have none of that shit. He never allows her to hug him. It is way too late to learn nurturing and compassion. That boat had long sailed. Marco's biological parents were both addicts. His mom, Gina's sister, got HIV and OD'ed in a shooting gallery in Bridgeport and his father pissed off someone really bad while in prison and never woke up after a serious beat down. Since age 13, Marco has been running free, vicious and hollow.

He pulls up his shorts and black jeans, then covers his sticky belly with his dank black T-shirt. Running his fingers through his long, greasy black hair he stands up, and yells, "I can't stay in this fuckin' house anymore!!!!" He then spits a hawker at the crucifix on the wall.

Restless rapids are running through his mind. Marco knows going back to watch TV would only fuel his surging adrenaline. It would be easy to dip into his suitcase for some downers but he feels too paranoid to get stoned. *Can't get caught stuck-on-stupid! Got to stay sharp! A fucking SWAT team can come busting in at any time.*

Stomping out into the hall, Marco starts to pace and grill himself again. *Chill motherfucker! Chill!! You know you fucking lucked out pretty good! That fire probably destroyed all that forensic bullshit. Should have thought of burning down the fuckin' barn myself! Just got to keep low. Maybe I should split for Cali too. Go to think! Got to think ...*

There is a commemorative clock in the hallway of Pope John Paul. Marco sees the time and knows that it will be awhile before his Aunt returns home from the nursing facility where she works as a certified aid.

Can't believe that woman has a job where all day long she wipes old people's assholes. What a fuckin' loser!

Marco throws some jabs in the air to burn off some of the frustration. It is to no avail. The pacing and ruminating continues. He knows he needs to stay inside until it is at least dark. The plan is to meet up with Troy later on to divvy-up the money they scored. Marco is uneasy about his partner crashing at the home of some little-piss head that he had met in rehab.

Hope Troy that numb-nuts doesn't start bragging and telling shit to people. I know he's a fuckin' liability. Maybe I should shoot him in the back of the head tonight when he's not looking?

A few more minutes drag by on the Pope clock. Abruptly, there are flashes of Marsha's dead face again in Marco's brain. He can smell the urine. The stink seems to grow stronger, coming up from his goatee, into his nostrils.

Marco rants out loud, "I can't stop thinking about Queen-Pin!!! I'm starting to bug!!! She's like a fucking witch!"

Impulsively Marco rushes into his Aunt's room and tears off his black t-shirt, throwing it down like it was a diseased pelt. Marco then feels like smashing all the little Joey photos that align the walls but suddenly catches a glimpse of his tattoo in the mirror. The image of Kali appears to glow even bluer. Marco freezes in his tracks and does not follow through with his rampage. An odd momentary sense of focus occurs. Peering at his reflection, Marco examines his tattoo.

"You're a beautiful bad-ass work of art." Marco whispers to the image.

Years ago while Marco was locked up in a juvey detention center, somebody donated some books. One was a tattered text on world religions. Out of restless boredom, Marco had flipped through the pages and saw a classic artistic rendering of Kali. It was located in the chapter on Hinduism. Anything spiritual was mumbo-jumbo bullshit in Marco's mind. He never cared to read a single word about the deity's karmic mission but was rather just enthralled with the ferocious "cool" imagery. The Gene Simmons-like huge pointed red tongue. The three eyes. The blood. The severed body parts. Marco ripped out the page of the textbook, stowed it away in his suitcase and years later had the figure of Kali inked on his chest.

The goddesses' form is tattooed smack dab in the middle of his sternum. Her four arms curve out across Marco's scrawny pecs. She is standing on a supine Lord Shiva. Garlands of human skulls hang from her body. In one hand she holds a scimitar. In another hand is the decapitated head of the Hindu demon Raktabija.

Marco remembers how he bartered with the tattoo artist and traded a large amount of LSD and dimethyltryptemine for the job.

"Too bad that tattoo artist hung himself." mutters Marco, "The guy was awesome. Fuckin' rocking' intricate detail." Marco taps the image of the demon's severed head with his fingertip. Marco then thinks, *I have to admit, last night, I was good at killing people. Maybe I have found my hidden talent. I'm still too amped. But maybe I'll come to love it when I finally learn to be relaxed after doing some more murdering."* Again, he taps the image of the severed head on his chest.

Across the room on a small desk is Aunt Gina's old Gateway computer. Marco impulsively walks over and turns it on. An image of little Joey's face pops up as a screen saver. Marco spits at the screen and saliva runs down the front of the monitor. He then Googles one of his favorite websites, "GORE-PORN." Instantly, there comes up news stories on ISIS. There is an attached link to archives of uncensored combat footage from Iraq and Syria. Marco clicks.

There is a pause as one of the video-clips starts booting up to play.

"Com'on baby!" Marco asks aloud in anticipation.

Blaring Islamic music suddenly fills the small bedroom, briefly startling Marco. For some reason the computer's speakers had been cranked to high volume.

"Watching beheadings never gets old!"

On the small screen is a grainy image of a figure in a bright orange jump suit kneeling in front of a row of men clad in black.

"I love these fuckers," mutters Marco.

One man standing behind is jabbering in Arabic and holding a dagger. Then there is a terrifying war cry as the individual in the orange jump suit is pushed sideways to the ground. Some of the men in black start holding down his legs; his hands were already tied. Marco watches in amazement as he sees the one with the knife pounce down and begins cutting the captive's neck. Gurgling, whimpering, sucking sounds are heard and followed by the high whistle of air rushing from the victim's lungs and out through the huge gash in his throat. There is a brief pause in the video followed by the executioner working the stuck blade against cervical vertebra. There is another break in the video. The men in black are standing back in a row. The one in the middle holds up the severed head. Quick pause. The head has been placed on the chest of the decapitated corpse. Dark blood is pooling.

"Fucking cool as always!" Marco exclaims with awe.

He thinks, *I should join fucking ISIS but I don't believe in fucking Islam. There ain't no god. And I ain't blowing myself up for a fucking fairy tale. But got to love all the killing!*

There is again the shrieking war cry of revenge from the insurgents, "ALLAHU AKBAR!!!"

The Islamic music.

The screen goes dark.

"Gotta see it again." Marco says with his coyote smile.

Marco quickly replays the video.

He replays it again.

And again. "ALLAHU AKBAR!!!"

And again. "ALLAHU AKBAR!!!"

Every time, Marco studies the grim details. He tries to make out the expression on the victim's face both when alive then dead.

The guy looks scared shitless. Looks like he's drugged up a bit.

The execution clip is replayed again.

Marco's erection returns.

The blue color of the Kali tattoo turns black in the vibrant glow of the computer screen.

It is time to go back on a rampage.

TEN

Tuesday, 9:40 p.m. in a pigeon coup like efficiency on the border of West Haven, Paul Kosakowski is breathing heavy and sweating again. Army boots and skivvies are what he has on for the moment. His big beer-belly-stress-gut hangs way over the waistband of his underwear. There is a sharp whooshing sound as the blade of the katana cuts through the air. Paul grips with both hands a short Cold-Steel tanto. Giving a *"Ki!"* he swings and slashes again, ending with a dramatic, martial arts pose. Some of the empty Miller-Lite bottles rattle on the little, cluttered coffee table. In his mind, he pictures himself the avenger. Across the cramped room, in a mirror, there is the image of a fat guy in his underwear, playing with a short samurai sword.

"Those porch-monkeys would have turned white if I caught 'em near my vehicle with this baby in my hands!!!" Paul says aloud.

With no skill or grace he whirls about again, stabbing and thrusting. Breathing even harder, he finally sits down on his ripped, vinyl gold couch, the sword across his lap. Piled nearby and next to discarded empty pizza boxes and old greasy KFC buckets are stacks of magazines such as HANDGUNNER, SOLDIER of FORTUNE, GUNS & AMMO, TACTICAL KNIVES... Paul has already gone through all the latest issues. He is too restless and anxious to read now anyway. Molten anger is bubbling and sputtering inside with every moment-by-moment recollection of what happened to his truck.

Maybe it is time to bring out Mr. Whoop-Ass! A bitter grin briefly appears on Paul's sweat-beaded face. "The world is fuckin' with me. Fuckin' with my stuff. Friend, I need to hold ya now."

He never takes Mr. Whoop-Ass out during the day. The one window in the apartment has the blinds down to make sure not the slightest glimpse could be made from the outside. Kosakowski gets up and turns off the lights. Flickering, stark blue and white flashes come from the television that was left on mute, giving rise to constant morphing shadows in the darkened, dirty room.

"Come on Buddy let's see ya!"

As if praying to Mecca, Kosakowski gets down on the soiled carpet and begins to pull something out from under the coach.

"Come to Papa, baby."

It is a black fabric nylon case for a long gun. With the same titillation of undressing a lover, Paul slowly unzips the zipper that runs the full length of the object. Inside is his icon of power. Illegal to own in the state of Connecticut, it is a Bulgarian manufactured AK-47. The police had confiscated all of his other firearms including his four Bushmaster ARs that he had purchased legally. This assault rifle is new. Weeks ago, Kosakowski had done a manic three day road trip to Georgia. It was a private sale. The purchase of the AK was under the radar. Stashed about the apartment in a few gym bags there are also at least 40, East German 30-round magazines. Five old Soviet surplus ammo cans, stamped 7.62x39 are stacked in Paul's closet.

"There ya are, my friend!" Kosakowski exclaims as he rises, snapping up the weapon and quickly bracing the wooden rifle butt against his sweaty bare shoulder. He aims the barrel of the AK at various items in the room. The silent flickering TV. The mirror. The over-flowing trash basket in the corner.

"Pow. Pow. Pow." Kosakowski says with a smile. "They would shit green if they knew I had ya. I would definitely do some time in the big house."

Upon first acquiring the weapon, he had bought an adapter kit to modify the rifle to fire fully automatic. Another big illegal no-no.

"Wonder how I'd look with Aryan Brotherhood tattoos?" Kosakowski asks aloud as he pauses and squints at his reflection through the dimness, across the way in the mirror. At this moment, there is only a tattoo of the National Guard insignia on his chubby upper arm.

"Nah." Paul says with another joyless, mean laugh. "Nope, I won't let them take me alive. I ain't livin' behind bars for the rest of my life with all those mix-breeds. Me and Mr. Whoop-Ass will go down together fightin' like patriots. Fuck it." He kisses the cool black metal of the breech and tastes the bitter gun oil. In the next second, he angrily pulls back the slide, ejecting a live round that goes clinking and rolling off somewhere in the dark. Minutes tick by and Kosakowski does a bunch of dry firing and practicing dropping and slamming in magazines. He draws beads on the miniature icebox, the mound of soiled shirts and shorts in the other corner of the room, the mirror and the TV again. There are also fantasies playing his head of black youths running in fear from his Dodge Ram, screaming for mercy then being riddled with automatic weapon fire.

"Black lives never fuckin' matter!"

After a while, Kosakowski becomes physically tired again, and sits back down on the couch. The Katana and AK are crisscrossed on his lap. His body is spent but his mind still races. Playing with his sword and gun did little to channel the anxiety and pulsing internal rage.

"I can't calm down." Kosakowski moans. "I guess it's

gonna be another fuckin' night without shut-eye!" There is no more beer left to induce a drunken sleep. He quickly gives a glance over to the stack of gun magazines. There is one sure way to get some relief but the thought always makes him hate his own existence. The notion is so personally shameful, that whenever it surfaces into his consciousness, he feels like placing the barrel of Mr. Whoop-Ass under his chin, and blowing off the top of his cranium.

What kind of sick-o am I? Kosakowski asks in torment.

Hidden way down in the bottom of the pile of gun and knife magazines is another publication of a different subject and genre. The title is HOT 12 INCH. On the cover is a smiling, muscular, male Brazilian model in a thong. Inside, many of the glossy pages with photo spreads are rippled, and stuck together.

"Not again!" Kosakowski pleads, clenching his teeth. There is a stirring down below in his underwear. He is pitching a tent.

"FUCK!" Paul curses aloud. "I can't believe I'm doin' this!" He yanks out the gay porno mag from the bottom of the stack, causing the other gun and knife magazines to topple over and spill onto the rug.

Over on the coffee table amidst the beer bottles, empty Styrofoam cups and pizza scraps, there is an answering machine. A tiny blinking green light indicates that there are messages. They are the unanswered calls from Dr. Fray from both yesterday and today.

Kosakowski's voice is hot and pressured. "Come on! Come on!"

In the glow of the muted TV, Paul Kosakowski has put the gun and sword aside. His boxers are now down by his ankles as he frantically flips through the remaining good pages of HOT 12 INCH. Suddenly there are violent flashbacks in his mind of the shrimpy little transvestite with the red boa that he pulled into his truck and tried to blow.

It is now 10:00 p.m. On the television screen in front of Paul, silent images of the fatal Woodbury barn fire play on the news. Channel 30 then cuts away to broadcast the live Connecticut Lotto drawing. The fifty balls are released down into the clear plastic chamber, bouncing, colliding with each other like unstable molecules. The first one pops to the top. Then the next one. Followed by another. Then another... The announcer mouths the results but there is no sound from the set, there is just Paul's gasps and rapid smacking sounds of jerking-off.

The numbers flash on the screen. 27, 28, 30, 31, 35, 37.

ELEVEN

Wednesday 9:30 in the morning at the Elm City Behavioral Health Center, Dr. Fray is in a clinical team conference when he receives notice from the receptionist that Betty Farrell's father is in the lobby freaking out and insisting to be seen.

"I better handle this." Peter says in a troubled tone.

The others in the meeting nod knowingly and wish him good luck.

Mike Farrell is a big man, age 51, who once had the red complexion of a boozer, but now has a carrot-colored tan since living on the west coast. Dressed in a blue blazer, rose-pink shirt and white slacks, his clothes are wrinkled and gamey. A strong sour body funk overpowers his cologne. He has not bathed nor changed since flying in the other day from LAX.

"I'm so sorry." Peter says as he shakes the man's meaty hand and offers him a seat in his office.

"How could this happen?" Farrell asks in exasperation. Alcohol and dry-mouth-bacteria makes the man's breath stink.

Peter replies. "I don't know. This is such a shock. One of our staff members notified me late yesterday after catching a news report. This is horrible."

"It's a nightmare." Farrell says, running his big fingers through his frosted hair-weave. "My ex-wife cut her trip short in Aruba. She won't frigging talk to me. She's just numbing herself out on Ativan and some other shit!"

"How can I be of assistance, Mr. Farrell?"

"Well, looks like you are offering your help a little bit too late, don't you think? You were my daughter's shrink, goddamn it! I don't know why she wanted to come here to this cut-rate ghetto clinic. I always paid for top-notch rehabs. You know for the amount of money I shelled out on those fancy treatment centers I could have sent my little girl to fucking Harvard or Yale."

Peter didn't challenge the man's statement but felt a sudden jolt of counter-transference and disdain. Mike Farrell is a real-estate investor who after scoring some big financial hits left his spoiled wife and troubled daughter to go play in the sun. Betty described to Dr. Fray in one of her therapy sessions how her dad once blew back into town unannounced, signed her out of rehab, bought her new clothes, did some lines together, got drunk with her, and then took off again with no further contact for a full year.

"This is a terrible loss." Peter reiterates, "Your being her father, it must be so devastating." Peter found it hard to hold back his bitter sarcasm.

"No shit." Farrell snaps. "Listen, I didn't come here for your fake sympathy. We got something to solve here! I came here for some names."

"Names?"

"Yea, names! At least one other person was there that night. There were more than one set of tire tracks in that field. My ex-wife's Lexus, which I bought for her, is missing. It was supposedly spotted in Waterbury but who the fuck knows. But now it's gone. I got to find out who else was there at that barn!!!"

"What are the police saying?"

"They blew me off and told me to get some rest. Fuck that! I'm not sleeping till I get some answers! I can't even have a funeral yet for my little girl because they're still doing all those fucking morbid forensic tests on her body. She was burnt to a crisp! Oh God!!!!----" Farrell lets out a tortured sob.

Peter feels his own anguish.

Farrell catches himself, and wipes his eyes with the back of his big hand. In a choked, angry voice he continues, "There are already rumors. Total bullshit!"

"Rumors?"

"Yea, some classmates of the other dead girl are saying a bunch of nonsense. Saying that Betty had arranged some sort of drug-deal. They're trying to pin everything on my daughter because they know she had some problems. My baby wouldn't do something like that. Those other parents should have watched their kids better. All they're doing is looking for a frigging scapegoat."

"What do you think really happened, Mr. Farrell?"

"Someone else caused those kids to die! I know the cops mentioned something about trying to get prints off a half-melted soda bottle found in the BMW. I want to know from you, if Betty ever talked about anybody. Somebody that she was involved with that could have been sort of shady."

Peter raises an eyebrow and thinks to himself, *Which one?* He knows that Betty had been involved with a parade of dysfunctional souls. After clearing his throat, Peter gives a metered response. "As part of confidentiality in therapy, I have to watch what I say. But I'll tell you in all honesty, she didn't mention anyone recently."

"Are you sure?"

"Yes."

"Then what the fuck did she talk about?"

There is another pause. Peter replies, "A lot about you."

Farrell sucks in some air and fights back his tears as he speaks, "She was my little girl, my buddy. I used to call her my wild bucking mustang because she was so hard to control. Hell, I never believed in being one of those militant, crazy, strict parents. I told her to go to rehab and just learn to slow down a bit. Learn to party in moderation. In fact, a month ago, I told her if she finished rehab, I would take her to Catalina for a nice vacation to get away from her bitch of a mother. But then-" The tears burst forth and his voice gets stuck in his throat. Farrell buries his face in his hands.

Peter remembers Betty self-disclosing about her father's manic mood swings and cocaine binges. There were also the revolving younger and younger girlfriends, impromptu romps with stewardesses, and thousands and thousands spent on hookers. It was always easier to self-medicate when having a big bank account.

"You deserve to have answers to what happened to your daughter." Peter says softly. "But you don't have to do this alone. Would you consider grief counseling?"

Farrell ignores the offer and asks again, "Are you sure you don't remember any names?" For a second, his tone is almost pleading. "Anybody she was dating?"

"There is nobody she mentioned." Peter says somberly but in his mind he was trying to recall the roster of dangerous misfits that Betty used to brag about.

"Are you sure?"

"Yes." Peter replies.

"Then fuck you!" Farrell snarls as he uncovers his face and stands up. "I don't need a shrink! You're all a bunch of nuts! You did zero to help my daughter! I should sue you for all the bucks I spent for her therapy! I came here for some answers, and you got jack-shit! And if I find you're holding out because of that confidentiality bullshit, I'll make sure they pull your fucking license!"

Lowering his head and staying silent, Peter takes the man's hostile sorrow.

Before exiting the office door Farrell turns, points his finger at the psychologist and shouts, "I was a damn good father!!! Remember you're the one that fucked up!!!!"

Oddly, Peter is getting used to the sound of angry footsteps going away, down the hall.

TWELVE

Wednesday 4 o'clock in the late afternoon, Mattie Gallagher is in another pissed-off, cantankerous mood, having just lost a sizable chunk of change at OTB. He is still a bit lit from his liquid lunch and has just run out of smokes. Fox's Spirit-mart is close around the corner. The door jingles and rotund Lucy is in her permanent spot behind the register.

"Hello there, fella!" she says with welcoming glee.

"Oh, stop smiling." Mattie grumbles.

Lucy purses her thick lips in a pout. "Aww, my baby having a bad day?"

Mattie shakes his head in disgust. "The ponies I picked were so friggin' slow, I could've run faster, barefoot and with a bundle of bricks tied to my pecker."

The woman's deep bass laugh sets a quake through her expanse of tallow. "Now, that's slow!" She says with all grins and chins.

"Yea, you ain't kiddin'."

"But, maybe it was the jockey's fault. Can't always blame the horses ya know. Plus, I like animals."

"Aah, bullshit" Mattie flicks the air with his hand. "All of them need to get their tickets punched. They should deport all those midgets back to Venezuela or wherever the fuck they come from. And every one of those nags needs to be put down and packed into Alpo cans!"

"Honey, looks like ya lost a lot of money."

Mattie shakes his head again, and then leans forward, resting his elbows on the counter while rubbing his tired face with his palms. He asks, "What's the cheapest carton ya got?" He already knew the answer.

"I got Merit Lights for 62 bucks with a free lighter." Lucy replies.

"How about starting a tab for me?" Mattie mumbles. "You can see I'm a little short at this time."

Lucy stiffens slightly and instantly loses a little of her cheery tone. "Now you know I'll help you brown bag a quick nip but I don't offer credit in this store. Never have. Always cash up front. It's better that way."

With a mean squint, Mattie barks back. "My gosh, I never knew an ex-carnival fat lady that is also a money grubbin' Jew!"

Wavering an accusatory finger, Lucy says, "Hold on there fella, watch your mouth. This is not a place for charity. Ain't no soup kitchen here. Plus, people have to know how to limit themselves."

Mattie straightens up, anger popping. "Don't you preach to me woman! Don't you dare preach! The last I heard, gluttony is still a fuckin' sin in the Bible and from the looks of it, you must have bankrupted a few all-you-can-eat buffets in your day! And furthermore, I ain't no charity case. I've been comin' here a long time. I have been a good customer. Just yesterday I dropped forty dollars here. I thought elephants are supposed to have good memories!"

"Just leave!" Lucy shouts. "Go try your beggin' at the other packies. The Indians and Koreans will chase you out and shove a push-broom up your skinny ass!"

"Fuck you!"

"Get out!"

"I'm leavin'!"

"Good!"

Mattie pauses; he still desperately needs his nicotine. He takes a deep breath. In frustration, he digs into the front pockets of his trousers. He snarls, "You think I don't have money. I ain't no mooch! Give me a pack of Camels and you won't ever see me again!" From his pockets come handfuls of betting slips, coins and some crumbled singles. Mattie was sure he had at least enough for one pack of cigarettes.

"Fine!" Lucy says with a huff and reaches back to the display to get the smokes. She drops the pack down on the counter. "Anything else?" She says sternly.

"How about you being gone and the world a lot lighter." Mattie quips.

"That will be $8.75." Lucy orders, choosing to ignore his rude dig.

Anxiously and with trembling hands, Mattie un-crinkles the dollar bills and shifts through the small pile of papers for dimes, nickels, quarters and even pennies. All he comes up with is $3.82. "Shit!" He growls to himself.

Lucy smirks, "Looks like you're a little short. I guess it's a good day to quit smokin'."

Seething and red faced, Mattie replies, "You're an evil cow."

She looks down at his pile and sees the lottery ticket he purchased the other day. Sarcastically, Lucy gloats, "Maybe that will pay for the rest."

Suddenly an odd sense of panic, undefined premonition and almost euphoria comes over Mattie. He picks up the ticket and quickly hands it to her. "Check it!" He says.

Lucy takes the small, white and pale-pink ticket and feeds it into the lottery machine.

There is a pause.

Both are dead silent.

There are clicking sounds in the machine and then it did something that it never had done before. The small red matrix board begins to flash. There is buzzing and beeping. Beeping and buzzing! The matrix board spells out W-I-N-N-E-R!--T-O-P--P-R-I-Z-E!

The ticket pops back up from the enter/exit slot. Lucy instantly snaps it up. Her face is white, double chin quivering, her body a mound of tense gelatin.

"Hold it!!! Hold it right there, big Bertha!!!" Mattie's eyes are wide open and frenzied. With one hand he is reaching out while his other arm is cocked back ready to deliver a punch. "I'm okay with confessin' that I swatted a few broads in my day! I have no regrets in knockin' your God-damn teeth out and sendin' you to the moon if you dare hold onto that ticket for one more fuckin' second!"

Lucy is still stuck, trembling.

Mattie leans forward and plucks the ticket from her fingers.

The numbers read: 27-28-30-31-35-37.

THIRTEEN

Wednesday, 5:00 p.m., the autumn light is fading but the temperature is unseasonably warm. Vinny Gentile and his cousin Frank Miranda are sitting outside in the alfresco area of Dominica's Trattoria. It is New Haven's little Italy. Across the street, both locals and tourists are waiting in line to get into Sally's pizzeria. A bright white Cadillac Escalade comes slowly rolling up; the driver's large tanned muscular forearm is hanging out the window. It is local security for all the area businesses. No young urban blacks or Hispanics ever cross into this neighborhood.

"Heads up, Frankie." Vinny says, taking a sip of espresso then putting it down.

The huge SUV approaches. It is time to pose. Vinny leans back a bit in his chair, one hand on his Demitasse cup. Over the years he perfected the Bobby De Niro nonchalant, I'm-the-man smile. The driver gives a slight thumbs-up. Vinny reciprocates with a little nod. As soon as the vehicle passes, Vinny relaxes and is ecstatic. "Did you see that, Frankie! See that. See the respect I got. That was one of Mr. Penzetta's boys!"

In his usual patronizing manner, Frankie affirms, "Yea, I saw Vin. Nice."

Vinny leans a little farther back in his chair, his chest swelling as he speaks, "Yea, that's how it should be. The young ones should never lose respect for the old timers."

Frank gives another nod of appeasement. He never wanted to openly confront Vinny on the reality of the situation because he didn't have the courage. Plus, ever since growing up as kids, Frank was able to siphon some feelings of excitement and life through his cousin's grandiosity.

Both men each turned 50, but Vinny looks much younger. He has only a few wrinkles on his handsome olive skinned face. There is not a single gray hair in his well-groomed moustache and black pompadour. The barbell-set at home is used once in a while and he looks good in his wife-beater, even though he is sort of on the skinny side. It doesn't matter if it is either hot or cold; when Vinny is out in the city his trademark apparel is a black Italian leather sports jacket, open collar shirt and 18 Karat gold chains with a dangling horn of good luck to ward off the evil eye.

On the other hand, Frank is short and squat with a pasta belly. Male pattern baldness left him with a monk-do and some kind of mineral deficiency causes dark, sagging bags under his melancholy eyes. He never cares to buy clothes for himself but just waits for whatever his sister and 70-year-old aunt pick out for Christmas. The one piece of jewelry he has is a Saint Jude Medal from confirmation as a kid, but it is never on display because he isn't the kind to flaunt chest hair and Italian bling.

The young waitress from the Trattoria comes out to check on the two. "Can I get you guys anything else?" she asks with a smile and showing cleavage.

Flashing back a grin, Vinnie says, "Somebody as beautiful as you, I wish you were on the menu."

She giggles, "Oooh, you're sweet."

With a wink, Vinny says, "Give me another espresso with a little Galliano."

"Sure." She then looks at Frank. "You want the same thing?"

"Nah," Frank shakes his head. "Just another seltzer

water."

"Ya sure?"

"Yeah, it's my stomach again." Frank says with an apologetic tone.

"Do you want some TUMS?" she asks.

"It's okay, miss. I got some Brioschi."

Vinny scolds his cousin, "When you goin' ta see a doctor? You gotta get that looked at."

Frank mumbles, "I'm fine. I'm good."

The waitress turns away.

Taking out a pack of Marlboro's, Vinny strikes a match, lights up and breaths deep. Puffing out smoke and pointing his finger, he says, "You gotta learn ta take better care of your health, ya sad sack of shit. You know I love ya."

Ever since he was a teen, Frank was plagued with a delicate stomach. Of recent, the pain was getting worse. Popping antacids and chugging Pepto-Bismol wasn't helping. He is in secret torment, believing that he has cancer. But going to a doctor was out of the question after hearing about the latest medical trends involving colonoscopies. Frank always avoided his reflection in the mirror when he got out of the shower. The thick curly back hair, the man-boobs, fat belly and ischemic-nubbed penis resulted in a horrible body image and personal shame. There was no way he would expose his pathetic nakedness to the peering eyes of a bunch of doctors and nurses. And the notion of having a tube put up his bare ass appeared similar to some kind of Gestapo interrogation technique used to torture spies. Frank often pledged that he would rather die from rectal cancer than go through that trauma of getting his colon checked. With a sigh, he took another swig of seltzer and Brioschi.

Vinny leans forward a bit with a dirty smile. "Whatta think of the melons on that waitress? Oh mad one!"

"I don't know," grumbles Frank. "She's just a kid. Too young for me."

"Jesus, whattaya want, grandma in a thong? I gotta get ya some Viagra."

Frank looks down and broods. The subject of women was always a sore spot. Marriage or even dating never happened. At weddings, Frank was always the single guy that danced with the white haired aunts and heavy set Italian mamas. The old people commented that he should have been a priest. There was even a cruel rumor that he was queer but the accusation was false. Frank was not gay but rather suffered from a lack of desire. It was always easy for him to go with the premise that masturbation was a sin because ever since a young man he had been dead between the legs. He did not know why. It was just another mystery that yanked down his self-esteem.

Regarding Vinny, his sexual drive is always full throttle. He also never married but has a revolving stable of waitresses, female bartenders, and lonely housewives. It is not just his good looks and self-confidence but he has a shtick that a lot of women find irresistible. Vinny has no money, is always in debt and lives with their elderly Aunt Teresa, who makes his bed and does his laundry. When schmoozing with one of his dates, he sells the story that he has been sitting on a large sum of cash from a big score that occurred some years ago. He says that he is playing it really smart, lying low, and not spending any of the loot because he is still under surveillance from the feds. The romantic fantasy of being with a real-life bad-boy-mob-guy causes many women to easily drop their panties and have their legs up in the air. Vinny also gets a lot of presents, home-cooked meals, and even cash. False promises of pending fur-coats and trips to Florida make the ruse even sweeter.

In reality, Vinny was never connected with organized crime and never took part in any big heist. The only questionable behavior besides playing women is ripping off the state for Social Security Disability. After a stint with the Department of Transportation, he did a marvelous bit of acting portraying a person with an orthopedic work-related injury. The union rep was very supportive regarding the claim in exchange for a life-long kickback of $200 a month. Vinny is left with a guaranteed check of $1,600 clear, every four weeks, which in turn is usually gobbled up at the Indian Casinos in eastern Connecticut.

It is Frank who has the money. He and his sister own a catering business that does pretty well. Having no interest in vacations or fancy cars and not having any kids, Frank just squirrels away his cash. The only source of depletion is Vinny's frequent pleas for loans that he never pays back. Often Frank wonders if he stopped giving his cousin money, would the chumming around stop. It is a pathetic truth that he could be paying for friendship like a john pays for a fuck.

The waitress returns with the drinks. "Here you go fellas." She says with more smiles. Frank has a twenty-dollar bill on the table. Vinny reaches out and snatches the money, acting like it is his cash. He gives it to the girl "Here sweetheart this is from me to you. I see that you're workin' hard."

"Thanks!" She quickly takes the money.

Frank inwardly fumes.

Vinny knits his eyebrows a bit and lowers his voice, attempting a concerned and all-knowing tone. He asks the waitress, "So what's your goals? I sense that you got potential."

The girl laughs and replies, "Gee, I don't know."

Slowly leaning back again and doing the swelling of the chest, Vinny says, "I'm connected with some top level guys in this neighborhood. I could put a good word in for ya. Maybe ya wanna be hostess or lead bartender. One of these nights we should go out ta dinner and discuss your career."

"Wow. We'll see. Maybe. Thanks." The girl is still giggly but a little nervous.

Vinny gives a fatherly smile and nods. "Think about it, sweetheart. I always like ta help young people from around here ta get a good start in life."

As the waitress scampers away, Vinny gives his sneaky smile and leans forward again toward his cousin. His voice is now high and a tad hushed. "I guarantee ya, I take that broad out, get some vino into her, she'll be suckin' my sausage, no problem!"

Surprisingly, Frank finds himself responding with sarcasm. "Are ya gonna take her out to supper with my money too?"

For a moment, Vinny is taken aback. He responds with an offended tone, "Mother, Mary of God, you gettin' cheap on me! If you think I got short hands goin' for my wallet, we can stop hangin' together. Excuse me for sufferin' from a back injury. Maybe if the state of Connecticut would stop given all the friggin' money to all those welfare moulinyans, I would get a decent compensation check. My life ain't easy ya know being disabled, for Christ-sakes!"

Frank is startled. This was the sort of confrontation he feared. He quickly recants, "I was just jokin', Vince. No disrespect."

Vinny pouts for a moment but then returns to his jovial self. "So ya wanna bet me on how soon it will take for me ta be sliding my dick between that cutie's nice big tits?"

"Well, what about Gina?" Frank asks, "You finally met somebody nice. She lost her kid. She's kind of a fragile person. I don't think she can handle somebody cheatin' on her."

Rolling his eyes, Vinny says, "Oooh, why am I hangin' with an alter boy? Don't make me feel guilty! I don't like that. Gina's kinda slow. She buys everything I say. She'll never find out shit. I bet you double or nothin' on that one."

Again patronizing, Frank shakes his head and replies, "I know not to bet against you, Vince."

Taking a big swig of espresso and liqueur, Vinny then slaps the table with his hand and laughs, "That reminds me, we haven't gone ta the casinos this month. Whatta ya doin' tomorrow night, accept growin' more hair on your ass?"

Pensively, Frank looks down and takes another nervous sip of seltzer. He knows it is a bad idea because both of them always lose their shirts. Vinny also owes money to a lot of other people in town. Frank sometimes fears for his cousin's safety. At the crap tables, Vinny can get out of control, blowin' money like it is nothing. Vinny is an action gambler. Winning money really isn't the draw. It is rather the rush, the quickness of the game and the moment of attention when all eyes are on him right before he tosses the dice. Vinny is also a sucker for all the pretty cocktail waitresses with their plastic smiles that push cheap free booze.

Being at gambling tables was never Frank's thing. He found it too intimidating. Slots were his addiction. Finding an empty row, he could spend hours throwing in quarters, robotically pulling down the lever, watching his coins disappear. He is an escape gambler. Again, winning money is not the source of the compulsion but rather emotional distraction. Frank was comfortable among the zombie horde of widowed senior citizens, with unresolved grief issues, and depressive symptoms. They would all be in a trance, fixated on the little spinning icons of cherries, diamonds, and lightning bolts. It was good not to think about life for a while.

"Come on, Frankie!" Vinny prods again. "Let's go tomorrow night. I'll get ya one of those things. Ya know, what old people wear to pee in."

"A catheter bag?"

"Yea one of those, so you don't have ta get up and go the bathroom. Just in case you're on the slot machine that's about to spill its jackpot. You don't wanna leave to go take a piss and some old bitch sneaks over, drops in her quarter, and bingo! Steals your big win after you been feedin' that machine for hours."

Frank smirks, "That's okay, Vince. I think I'll take my chances on that one."

Vinny claps his hands then stretches back his arms. He is a bit revved up on all the espresso. "We're goin', buddy. I'm juiced. Somethin' excitin' is about ta happen. It's in the air, do ya feel it?"

While taking another sip of seltzer, Frank catches in the corner of his eye, a cab pulling up to the curb.

FOURTEEN

Wednesday, 5:22 p.m., Mattie Gallagher stumbles a bit as he gets out of the cab. Earlier, having no money to celebrate his amazing win, he frantically hurried home and stole the last two hundred dollars from his cousin's purse as she lay slumped and blitzed in a recliner from her afternoon binging on Seagram's VO. The lottery claims office is closed and Mattie plans to be there at the crack of dawn tomorrow to claim his prize. Tonight, however, he wants to tell the world that he is no longer a loser and rub his success into the faces of all those who had crapped on him.

Dominica's Trattoria is up ahead. Mattie takes another gulp of Smirnoff Red, from the brown paper bag, as he staggers up the sidewalk. He bought the pint on the drive over and it is now almost empty. The vodka was just a liquid appetizer in lieu of the serious partying planned for later in the evening. There are two men sitting in the outside café area. There is a surge of even more excitement as Mattie recognizes their faces. "W-W-Well, well, what do I see!" He proclaims loudly with a slur. "Two I-talians, just a few steps up from the niggers! H-Hello ya slimy fucks!"

Instantly flashing with anger, Vinny knows the voice as he turns around to look. Frank just rolls his eyes and almost smiles. Mattie comes up next to their table but is still on the sidewalk.

"Jesus, Mary, and Joseph!" Vinny fumes. "Why would a worthless, Mick, piece-of- shit-drunk, like yourself ever have the balls ta step into this neighborhood? You can't tell me you're that cocked or stupid?"

"Pipe down, ya little skinny guinea!" Mattie replies. "Or I'll give ya another beatin'!"

Vinny clenches his fist and gives a gesture that he is going to rise up but Frank reaches out and grabs his cousin's elbow. Frank says, "Let it go Vince, He's harmless. It ain't worth it."

The three men grew up together as kids. Somewhere around in their teens, Mattie gave Vinny a bloody nose in a scuffle over a stolen bicycle. They have been rivals ever since.

"That's right, Frankie, keep ya boy on a leash!" Mattie laughs. "By the way, I heard that last wedding ya catered gave the bride a case of the Hershey squirts! Her white dress got ruined."

Showing more bravado, Vinny snarls, "Don't make me get out of this chair ya wrinkly-friggin' bastard! I won't know where ta put the body! Youse better keep movin'!" In reality, Vinny has no intention of getting into a physical altercation, even with an old alcoholic nemesis. He has a fear of fistfights and is squeamish of blood. To compensate for his aversion to brawling, Vinny mastered the art of threatening with a loud mouth bark but with no bite.

"Don't get your panties in a knot!" Mattie snaps back. "Ya think I came down here to see you two degenerates! I'm goin' up the street to Capri's to have a nice meal."

"They won't let you in!" Vinny sneers. "You can't afford it!"

"The hell I can't!" Mattie hollers.

"Who ya been blowin'?" Vinny says back.

"The question is, who will now be blowin' me!" Mattie says as he reaches down with nervous fingers into the front pocket of his golf pants. He pulls out the little square white and pale-pink ticket. "FEAST YA EYES ON THIS, FELLAS!!!" With a quivering hand, he dangles out the evidence of a fortune. "You wops are lookin' at three and a half million dollars!"

Both Vinny and Frank are stunned and rendered speechless.

With sweet revenge in his voice, Mattie gloats, "After I cash this in tomorrow, I can go to Capri's every night if I want. I can order the best guinea wine; have a nice big, fat steak pizzaiola. Maybe bend over one of those big titted I-talian waitresses and fuck her right in the ass in the main dining room and after, wipe my pecker on the tablecloth! Whatcha think of that, ya bunch of mutts?!" Mattie starts to laugh again, loud and mean. He then starts to cough, his balance wavering, and he almost falls down.

This time, Vinny does stand up. He reaches out and tries to snatch the ticket from Mattie's hand. But the old Irishman pulls back and quickly but clumsily stuffs the ticket back into his pants pocket. A vein on Vinny's temple is bulging, and he is quaking and appears to have tears in his eyes. "You can't have that!" He says with a gasp. "It ain't right! You can't have that money!"

"The hell, I can't!" Mattie spat. "I'm gonna live it up every day! And I'm given' a big middle finger to all youse greasy fucks every time I see ya!"

"Get the fuck out of here!" Vinny abruptly screams; his voice sounding oddly high and shrill.

Some of the customers waiting in line across the street turn and look. The waitress comes back out from the restaurant. Frank is shocked. He never saw Vinny this worked-up. He reaches out and tugs at his cousin's jacket, "Come-on, Vince! Let it go! Just sit down."

With his eyes watery but blazing and pointing with his finger, Vinny yells, "Get out of my sight, you Irish cock-sucker! LEAVE!!!"

Despite decrease inhibitions and poor judgment caused by inebriation, Mattie was wise enough to back off.

He is suddenly spooked by the furious intensity in Vinny's face. Taking some steps into the street, away from the two at the table, Mattie then yells, "Fuck it! I changed my mind! I'm gonna go down to the shoreline to the Captain's Catch to have a nice fried clam dinner! Don't wanna be around you types anyway. Plus, I fart up a storm every time I have guinea food!"

The cab was still on the street hoping to find another fare. Mattie waves it over. Grumbling and swearing, he staggers and gets into the back of the vehicle. He flips the bird as he takes off.

Vinny plops back down into his chair, looking beaten and exhausted. The waitress looks but stays away. Dropping his face into his hands, Vinny moans, "Ain't no friggin' justice in the world. God, I'm the one who deserves that money."

Frank pats his cousin on the shoulder and tries to be consoling, "Ah, what do they say? Every dog has its day. Forget about it. That bastard will take that money and finally drink himself to death. Don't let it get to ya."

Surging up, Vinny bangs the table with his hand making the glass and cups chatter, "You know he will be back around and go rubbin' it in our faces! He got the best of me once! Sucker punched me, the fuck! This is not right, you know it!"

Again, Frank tries to be soothing. "Vince, you were just a kid when that fight happened. And he was a lot older. It wasn't a fair thing, anyway. You did your best. How bout you come over tonight and we'll watch a game and relax. Forget about all this. I'll warm up some manicotti and I got some lamb chops. Very nice. We'll even talk more about goin' to the casino, if that makes ya happy."

"Casino!" Vinny becomes more irate. "What the fuck youse talkin' about! Every time I lose a dime, I'll be thinkin' about that Irish fuck winnin'! I'll go crazy! I know it!"

"Vince, there is nothing we can do about it." Frank shrugs. "It is what it is."

Bolting up again for a second time, Vinny is a live wire. "Fuck that! I ain't lettin' it be! I'm the one who always dreamed of hittin' big! I prayed for it all the time. God owes it to me; not that worthless mother-fucker!"

"Come-on, Vince." Frank looks startled. "Lower your voice, you're makin' a scene. The waitress, she may get the manager. We may get asked to leave!"

Vinny becomes even louder. "I don't care who hears! I ain't takin' this sittin' down! I got an idea!"

"What?"

"Get off your ass and come with me!"

"Where?"

"We're gonna go see Mr. Penzetta! He'll know what ta do! The office is around the corner"

"When?"

"Now!"

"No!"

"Yes!"

FIFTEEN

Wednesday, 5:50 p.m., the white Cadillac Escalade is in front of the office of Wooster Street Contractor's Project Inc. There is also a silver convertible Chrysler Sebring and a long black Mercedes S class parked in the lot. Inside, Sal Penzetta is meeting with a cohort. Penzetta is the real thing, connected with the Sabino organized crime family in Queens. Responsibilities involve the control of New Haven construction permits and the laundering of money through local restaurants.

Frank's guts are on fire. He couldn't believe that Vinny suddenly has the *cohunes* to want to walk into the tiger's lair. Over the years, Frank saw how his cousin could lay it on thick, playing his Pacino-De Niro charade in front of his harem of dumb waitresses. However, whenever one of the real connected guys would come around, Vinny would scamper away never wanting to get too close to the flame. A long time ago, Vinny was once approached to help unload stolen cases of Pellegrino. A panic attack ensued and Frank found his cousin in the ER faking appendicitis. Over the years, Vinny changed the story and told everybody that he had been asked to do a hit. Vinny was fun loving, irresponsible and a cheat but no killer. Throughout his whole life, Vinny never once even held a gun.

Trying to keep up with the fast steps of his cousin, Frank worries aloud, "I don't like this, Vince! It's a bad idea. What's gotten into you? These guys don't play around. You know that!"

"Shut-up, Frankie! It's pride! I don't want that bastard to have that money! I know Penzetta won't tolerate that Mick comin' around here and disrespecting our people!"

"Ah, sweet Jesus! Are you for real?"

"Fuckin' A!"

The two make it to the front door of the office. Frank is out of breath. Before Vinny can knock, the door swings open. Standing there is the driver from the Escalade and his ability to intimidate is a breeze, being six-two, with a shaven head, skeleton tattoos and jacked with roid enhanced bulging bi's, tri's, and pecs. The guy is in his early twenties and had been recruited from the neighborhood not just because of his physique but also because of his reputation of being a true badass. He is into mixed martial arts, Muay-Thai kickboxing and Brazilian Jiu-jitsu. A claim to fame is having won some preliminary MMA fights at the area Indian Casinos. His self-proclaimed nickname is Beef.

"Yea?" The muscleman asks with a hostile tone.

Stammering a bit, Vinny replies, "Auh, how ya doin'. I saw ya pass by a little earlier. Ah, thanks for give'n some acknowledgement. Appreciate it."

"I don't remember."

"Really?" Vinny suddenly sounds hurt.

"Really."

"I'm Vinny Gentile, an old timer from the neighborhood."

"Never heard of ya." Beef huffs.

"Are you sure?" Vinny presses.

"I said I don't know ya! That it?" Beef's voice has mounting irritability.

"No, auh, we're just wonderin' if we could see Mr. Penzetta for a moment."

"You got an appointment."

"No, sorry but-"

Beef starts closing the door.

"Wait!" Vinny blurts out in desperation. "I swear it's important; on my mother's grave!"

There is a pause. The door is three-quarters closed. A sound of a low grating voice comes from inside the office but the words are not discernible. In the next moment, the door opens wide and Beef waves the two in. Frank is pale and clammy and feels like at any moment he is going to have a hot streaming burst of diarrhea. Vinny is shaky and ecstatic.

The office is small with just a few metal folding chairs and a large cluttered desk. It is dark except for a lamp in the corner. The blinds are drawn down shut. Cigarette smoke hangs in the air and poisons the oxygen. Through the haze there could be seen a Saint Theresa's church calendar tacked up on one of the unfinished walls along with commemorative plaques and community service awards from the police athletic league and the New Haven Jaycees.

Behind the desk, sits Sal Penzetta in a blue Nike jogging suit. He is fat with a bull neck and clubby hands. It is easy to identify that he is wearing a toupee. The rug is a cheap one; the black wig hairs have an un-natural, artificial look. A Rolex hangs on his thick left wrist; it is real. The gold luster on the watch is dulled due to the nicotine residue. Near the corner of the desk there is an ashtray overflowing with cigarette butts. Sucking on a fresh Winston, then exhaling a small cloud, Penzetta hacks then grumbles, "Hey, can't you see that's full. Empty that."

"Oh, sorry. Sure Mr. Penzetta." Beef quickly comes forward to take care of the ashtray.

Vinny and Frank just stand there at attention, eyes stinging. Nobody offers them a seat.

Looking up with a stone-cold stare, Penzetta asks, "So?"

Vinny's talks fast but it is easy to tell that he has cotton-mouth, "Gee, Mr. Penzetta, we have all the respect for you and what youse do for the neighbor. I'm, auh, Vincent Gentile and this is my cousin Frank Miranda. It's-it's really an honor ta talk ta ya. I see ya around town once and a while. And, I, I always give a wave. Maybe sometimes youse don't see it. But anyway, I just always think the best about ya. And-and, so does the rest of everybody I know."

"I'm late for supper. What's this about?"

"Right, gee, I'm so sorry, Mr. Penzetta! I know you're a busy man! But I just found somethin' out that may affect this fine neighborhood."

"Yea?"

"Well, there is this guy we know. A real low-class cavone. He's not even Italian. He's a Mick. A scumbag drunk. And oh my god, he just came into a bunch of money! And he says he's gonna come back around here like some big spender, orderin' big meals and makin' us all look bad. It's just not right! So disrespectful!" Vinny is now shaking both with nerves and worked-up anger.

Cocking an eyebrow, and breathing out more smoke, Penzetta replies, "I don't understand what you want me to do about it?"

"You know." Vinny says with a quick plastic grin.

"No, I don't." Penzetta says with some irritation.

"You know." Vinny winks.

Annoyance turned to a brief flash of scary rage as Penzetta snarls, "Listen up, I don't know what you're implying!"

Vinny is visibly trembling. "I-I just thought he shouldn't be allowed in the restaurants. He talks bad about Italians! Our people! He's got no manners. I just thought you may wanna know!"

"Do I look like a fuckin' maître d? This doesn't concern

me; this is chicken-shit." Penzetta scolds. "You have embarrassed yourself by comin' here."

Beef the muscle man takes an opposing step forward.

Gas bubbles swell even larger in Frank's colon as he prays that his cousin will not utter another stupid word and that they will be allowed to leave in the next second.

Vinny's voice cracks almost sounding like he is about to cry. "B-But Mr. Penzetta, the dirty bastard just won three and a half million dollars! And that's not how it should be!"

At that moment there is a sound of a flushing toilet. From a small side bathroom, a door opens. Out steps a man in his late fifties. A bit of a gut hangs over his belt but he is stocky and still solid. His cheap gray sport's jacket has an imprint of a compact Glock Model 30. Even with all the smoke, the stink of Brute aftershave is evident. The man still has the paper towel used to dry his hands, balled up and going from palm to palm.

Vinny looks over and swallows hard. *Oh, no!*

It is Don Blaisdale, ex-detective from Bridgeport PD's burglary-theft division. Recently, he had jumped ship from the force when he got early word that the mayor was going down big time for accepting over sixty grand in thank-you money and a free condo in Stamford. Over the years, Blaisdale got his share but was crafty enough to sneak-out under the wire. Coming now to hang with Penzetta was comfortable and matched his level of morality.

"What's this jerk-off doing here?" asks Blaisdale with a tone of angry surprise. He tosses the wad of wet paper towel and it bounces off the shoulder of Vinny's leather jacket. Frank feels faint. Vinny shoots a look that is a mixture of dread but also boiling frustration. Meekly he replies, "Hey, that ain't nice."

"What are you gonna do about it, lover-boy." Blaisdale barks.

At that moment, Vinny is struck with the realization that he has made a big-ass blunder. He would have never entered the office if he ever dreamed that Blaisdale was back in town and was now chummy with the boss.

"You know this guy?" Penzetta asks Blaisdale.

Baulking, Blaisdale sounded-off, "Yea, I ran into this sleaze-ball once. Look up the definition of the world's most pathetic wanna-be and you'll find a picture of this greasy asshole."

The bad blood started approximately a year and a half ago, when Blaisdale, off-duty, came trolling around some area joints and kept stalking a particular female bartender. He became infatuated. The girl rejected him kind of hard. One evening, she had leaned over the counter and swapped spit with Vinny as the spurred detective sat nearby on a barstool, brooding and downing bourbon and sodas. All his life, Blaisdale had a hard time making it with women. Hookers were his usual outlet. He was physically un-handsome, having a broad blockish forehead offset with a slit for a smile and a mashed nose. The most unsettling feature was his optic bulging caused by a fucked up thyroid. That night at the bar, he overheard the two lovebirds making fun of his face and saying some comment about him having Ping-Pong balls for eyes. On his way out of the joint, Blaisdale went and shouldered Vinny. Vinny chose to respond with a bunch of flashy, dramatic statements such as "How dare youse do that! Do youse know who I am?!!!" And "I'm gonna have youse wacked!" Blaisdale countered by pulling out his wallet and flashing his badge and snapping it on the bridge of Vinny's nose. The cop then called the female bartender a "cunt" and gave the Italian Stallion a bitch slap across the face before storming out and vowing to "fuck 'em up" if they ever crossed paths again in the future. It was an ugly scene and Vinny almost had another bout of psychosomatic appendicitis.

At the present moment, the smoky office now seems hotter. Frank's anus is straining like a New Orleans's levee about to let loose. A big hand taps Vinny's shoulder.

"Time to go," orders Beef.

"Yea, throw 'em the fuck out," gloats Blaisdale. "Before he starts cryin'.'

"Hold on a second." snaps Penzetta. The boss man has a sudden expression of heightened interest. "Say again, what kind of money this guy has?"

"Three and a half million!" Vinny whimpers.

"How did he get it?" Penzetta asks.

Vinny gestures with jittery hands. "The friggin' lottery! Can youse believe that!"

"How do you know the guy is not yankin' your chain?" Penzetta questioned.

"I swear to God, I saw it with my own two eyes!" Vinny points toward Frank. "Ask my cousin! He saw it too!"

For a horrible minute, Frank comes under Penzetta's brutal gaze. The boss asks, "So is it true?"

Nodding, Frank stutters, "The-the-the guy had something' he was showin' off." Uncontrollably, Frank then leaks some silent but putrid gas. A stink resembling old liverwurst and rotting broccoli wafts and mixes with the smoky air. Inside Frank screams to himself, *Please don't ask me nothing more!*

Penzetta then sort of sneers, "Ah, sounds like bullshit. How come the guy still has the ticket? How come he hasn't cashed it in yet?"

Vinny blurts, "He just won! He just found out! The bastard says he's gonna go ta the lottery office tomorrow ta claim his prize!"

There is an abrupt new level of energy in the small room. Penzetta and Blaisdale both make eye contact, both feeling like hyenas with news of a fresh kill in the area.

"Sit down, boys." Penzetta says with some mock kindness that seems twice as unnerving.

With wide eyes, Frank looks at his cousin, conveying the sediment. *NO! LET'S GET OUT OF HERE!*

"Come on, sit!" orders Penzetta.

There is the scrape of the metal folding chairs as Beef pushes the furniture forward. Obediently, the two men sit while Blaisdale and the muscleman continue to stand.

Leaning forward a bit across the desk Penzetta threatens, "For your sakes, I hope this is not some fairy-tale. Again, are you sure what you are tellin' me is on the level?"

Frantically nodding his head *yes*, Vinny confirms, "That Irish bastard seemed really confident and ballsy!"

Penzetta gives another darting look over a Blaisdale, sucks in some more smoke, exhales and coyly says, "I still don't know how this matter concerns me. The only thing I can offer is if the gentleman wants to meet with me to discuss investment options."

"What?" Vinny says sounding flabbergasted. "Youse wanna help him?"

In an untypical manner, Penzetta smirks and replies, "Your bad blood with this guy has nothing to do with me. Like I said, I'm a contractor, a businessman. Suddenly havin' a lot of money can be overwhelming for some people. They don't know how to handle it. They can act rash. The money goes to their heads. Again, I can offer my services and help the gentleman manage his funds."

With a hurt look on his face, Vinny again whines, "I don't get it."

"You don't have to!" Penzetta snaps, hostility returning in his voice. "This is what you are going to do; you are going to work with Mr. Blaisdale so this guy can be contacted."

Frank's fear bumps up even higher. It is hard to

believe what is happening. Less than hour ago he and his cousin were just hanging out and shooting the breeze and suddenly now they are in something like quicksand. He fears for both of their lives but oddly also for Mattie Gallagher. Frank viewed Mattie has an irritating clown but did not hate the guy. *This is wrong! This ain't right!* Frank wails inside.

Perplexed and frightened, Vinny takes a quick glance over at the ex-cop and is jolted by Blaisdale's hungry, awful bug-eyed stare.

"I want this contact to be made tonight," says Penzetta. "I think it's best that we talk to this gentleman before he makes it to that lottery office tomorrow."

"I agree." Blaisdale says with an evident fervor in his voice.

Penzetta could easily see that Vinny is soft like pudding. And the cousin smells like he literally shit his pants. Fear and intimidation are great motivators but Penzetta knows that if he scares a man too much, the man cracks and nothing gets accomplished. At that moment, he decides on giving some false hope to push things along. "Listen up, both of youse." Penzetta softens again his tone. "If that gentleman decides to take his good-fortune and invest with us, down the line there will be some compensation for your effort. You understand?"

Some light bulbs go off for Vinny. He then understands what Penzetta is implying by the word "invest." Miraculously things are suddenly brighter in Vinny's mind. Trying to be honest with himself, his original intentions for coming to talk to Penzetta where not fully thought through. It was an impulsive act. Vinny had been caught-up in the moment and was swept up by jealousy and revenge. He just wanted Mattie's good luck to be ruined. In a shortsighted way, he initially would have been satisfied in having the Irishman jacked up by bouncers and thrown out of a restaurant, followed by the lottery ticket being torn up in front of Mattie's face. Now, the reality set in that there is a much greater matter at hand. There is three and a half million dollars up for grabs.

Like a little boy asking about Christmas, Vinny peeps, "Compensation? Really?"

Penzetta smiles like a crocodile, "That's right, tough guy. Youse better get goin'. Time's tickin'."

Vinny pops out of his chair, smiling and all jumpy, "Oh, God. Thanks Mr. Penzetta. I'll get right on it!" He reaches out to shake the boss's hand but Penzetta doesn't offer up.

"We'll shake later." Penzetta says. "After we talk to your lucky-ass Irishman."

"You got it, Mr. Penzetta!" Vinny turns and gives another anxious look over at Blaisdale.

Getting up on wobbly legs, Frank puts his head down and is so grateful to leave, however, before he can take two steps, Penzetta calls out. "Hey, you!"

Frank is visibly startled. He slowly turns toward the boss.

"Don't ever disrespect me and pass gas in my presence." says Penzetta. "Ever do it again, and I'll have your ass stitched up! Didn't anybody teach you manners?"

With a gulp, Frank gives a barely audible, "Sorry." He then quickly continues toward the door.

Penzetta gestures with his head to Blaisdale to follow the two out. Beef stays behind.

The door of the office slams shut. Once outside, Vinny quickly turns toward Blaisdale and says with an anxious smile, "I guess we gotta bury the hatchet, cause we're on the same team."

In the next split-second, the ex-cop grabs Vinny by the throat with one hand and pushes him hard against the outside brick wall of the office. Frank is stunned and just watches mouth agape. Vinny gurgles, wheezes and tries to pry-free from Blaisdale's claw-like grip that is tweaking his Adam's apple.

"Who the fuck do you think you are, ya piece of shit!" Blaisdale snarls. "I always hated pretty boys like you!" The ex-cop presses even deeper into Vinny's windpipe while reaching down low with his other hand to put a vice squeeze on Vinny's crotch. Frank watches in terror, as his cousin tries to turn at the waist and bring up one of his thighs to block his balls from being crushed.

Finally Frank yells, "Come on, knock it off!"

Blaisdale suddenly lets go, and Vinny buckles over gasping and coughing.

"Oh, Jesus!" exclaims Frank.

Smiling with sick glory, Blaisdale laughs, "Come on, aren't ya gonna fight back?"

Vinny remains hunched over.

"I said, come on!" The ex-cop snarls. "Show me what you got!"

Still Vinny does nothing but cowers.

"Boy, I wish that whore bartender was here to see this!" Blaisdale mocks. "Seems to me you both got pussies."

Slowly, Vinny straightens up, spittle hanging off his chin, tears glistening. He rubs his sore throat and winces from radiating pain from his nuts. Blaisdale, again, pushes him against the wall and gives him a stinging slap to the left side of the face. "Listen up, faggot! What's the name of the guy who's got the lottery ticket? Tell me right now or I'll start takin' apart your skull!"

Before Vinny could utter a syllable, Frank blurts out, "Gallagher! Mattie Gallagher! That's his name! Let my cousin go! Please!"

With his protruding blue icy eyes, Blaisdale flashes over a vicious glance, "That right, you stinky-fuck? You better not be lying! I don't mind killin' two for the price of one!"

"I swear to God!" Frank cries. "Please just let Vince go! Please!"

Blaisdale glares back at Vinny, still pressing him against the bricks. "Is that right? The name's Mattie Gallagher? Tell me yes or no!"

Sounding defeated and broken, Vinny replies weakly, "Yea, that's him."

"Okay, good!" smiles Blaisdale. "Now, where's the guy. Where's he at?"

Vinny looks back at the ex-cop with a pleading expression, "I'll tell ya, but what about my compensation? Mr. Penzetta said I will get some reward for makin' this thing happen."

Blaisdale responds immediately with a nasty quick uppercut right under Vinny's sternum. Vinny instantly folds and loses his ability to breath.

"Oh, come on! No!" screams Frank.

"Compensation?" yells Blaisdale.

Gulping like a fish on land, Vinny went to his knees.

"Listen up grease-ball!" rants Blaisdale. "I'll tell you what kind of compensation you're gonna get! You're gonna tell me where this guy is with the lottery ticket, and then you can walk away with your life! That's it! Nothing else! Not even a fuckin' dime! You can go cry to that slut at the bar and tell her how you got burned for makin' fun of the man with the eyes like Kermit The Frog!"

The shock to Vinny's diaphragm lessened a bit. Trembling, Frank helps his cousin up.

"Okay, you two guinea queers!" seethes Blaisdale. "Tell me where this Mattie Gallagher is right now!"

Frank goes to talk but Vinny, even though winded, answers the question, "M-Mattie said-" Cough. "He- he was headed-" Cough. "Back downtown to celebrate tonight."

"Where?" snaps Blaisdale.

Taking another painful breath, Vinny says, "He- he told us that he was gonna stop off first at one of those –" Cough. "Those-those Chinese all-ya-can-eat spots before he started some heavy drinkin'."

Frank thought, *WHAT? He could not believe that his cousin was actually giving the wrong information to this madman.*

"There are a million Chink restaurants in this city!" growls Blaisdale. "Which one?"

"I know which one." Vinny lies. "The- The China Happy Buffet, the one off Whalley Ave, on the edge of the-the nigger section." Cough. "It's -its right on Fifth Street."

Squinting with suspicion, Blaisdale asks, "Why the fuck would a guy go eat there when he knows he gonna be a millionaire?"

"Who knows?" Vinny says with a sideways glance, still holding his mid-section. "Like I- I said before, the guy's got no class. But that's the best bet if you want ta find him at this moment."

"You better not be fuckin' with me! I better find this guy! What's his home address?"

Vinny quickly lies again, "I heard he lives with his uncle on Orange Street."

"What's the fuckin' house number?"

"Ah- 21."

"How do you know that?"

"I grew up in that neighborhood."

"Are you sure you're not fuckin' lying to me?!"

Vinny nods no and Frank just stands there like a deer stuck in high beams. The ex-cop stares at the two for a moment with his unblinking, drilling eyes, his greedy mind racing. Inwardly, he knows he is getting his chain jerked. Blaisdale could always sense when a man is untruthful but the excitement of scoring all that money makes him deaf and blind to his own gut instinct. He also rationalizes that if worse comes to worst all he really needs is a name because he still has contacts on the police force that would run computer searches that would give anything from addresses, next-of-kin, social security numbers to dick lengths. Impulsively and a bit crazed, Blaisdale then says, "I'm leavin'! But if I can't find Gallagher, I'm gonna come back to hunt ya! And if this is all a bunch of bullshit, you two won't be livin for very long!"

At that moment, Frank wants to cry for mercy, and say it was all a big mistake, but he keeps silent. Blaisdale turns to leave and gives a coup-de-gras to Vinny by cuffing him in the back of his head and saying, "Remember, you ain't nothing! This is my town now and I'm here to stay. And if you wind up still breathin', I'm gonna spread the word in this neighborhood that you are a ball-less, weak-ass punk. Be prepared to be a walking joke on these streets."

Vinny just hangs his head and does not say anything back as the ex-cop storms away with hard-pounding, rapid strides. There is the burning of rubber as Blaisdale tears out of the parking lot in the silver convertible Chrysler Sebring and disappears down the street. In the next second, Vinny and Frank quickly rush away from the front of Penzetta's office. Down a back alley they go as Vinny holds the sore spot under his breastbone, while his cousin quacks loud farts with each hurried step. They finally stop, both out of breath, near a large green trash dumpster.

"We're goners!" gasps Frank.

"I hate that bugged-eyed fuck! " cries Vinny.

"Mattie said he was goin' down to the shore-line. When that maniac finds out we sent him on a wild goose-chase, he'll come back to get us! What are we gonna do?"

"I don't know! I gotta think! This didn't go right!"

"Didn't go right? Our lives are over! Look what you did?"

Turning skyward, Vinny makes his hands in the prayer position and wails, "Oh, mother, Mary of God! What the fuck?!!!!"

Rubbing his balding head, Frank says, "You gotta go back to Penzetta and tell him you're sorry and that it was a big misunderstanding!"

"I can't go back in there after all that!

"What then?!" shouts Frank. "We're doomed! And poor, Mattie too!"

Despite his pounding fear, Vinny was still equally juiced with anger fueled by humiliation. "What the hell are yous talkin' about?! Why the fuck do yous have pity for that Irish cock-sucker?!"

"Vince, you know this isn't right! Mattie is in danger! Who knows what that creep will do to him to get hold of that ticket!"

Sucking in some air, Vinny waves his finger in his cousin's face, "Look, don't try to give me any fuckin' guilt. Youse know Mattie would take that money and be dead within a month after all that partyin'. His liver will explode! Getting' that money out of his hands will probably save his life!"

In disgust, Frank shakes his head, "Ah, ain't buyin' it! This is wrong and you know it! It's like a sin or something!"

"What the fuck are yous sayin'?" Vinny yells back. "Go ahead and fuckin' judge me! I don't give a fuck! Why don't yous jump ship! Get out of here, youse fuckin' fink bastard!"

"I ain't gonna leave ya! But you gotta go back and plead to Penzetta. Tell him we just want to walk away from the whole thing!"

"No! I can't do it!"

"Then what? What are ya gonna say when that cop comes back around? Are ya gonna give up Mattie to him?"

"I don't know! Fuck! I gotta think!" Vinny keeps rubbing the sore spot where he got punched and paces around in a circle.

Frank assumes that at any moment his cousin will double over and say it is the return of his appendicitis and try to escape to the sanctuary of a hospital. Surprising, Vinny instead snaps his fingers and exclaims, "I just thought of a plan!"

"What?"

"I got it!"

"What is it?"

"We got to get to Mattie first before Blaisdale!"

"Okay!" Frank says. "We can warn him and tell him to skip town as soon as possible!"

"No! He won't believe us! He'll tell us to suck his ass!"

"What then?"

"We gotta get hold of the ticket ourselves!"

"What for?"

"Once I get hold of the ticket, I'll bring it right back to Penzetta and present it to him! That will make the boss friggin' happy! Then I'll ask in return to get that cop off my friggin' back. Penzetta's got to show some loyalty ta a fellow Italian. Blaisdale ain't Italian! Fuckin' blue-eyed Nazi bastard!"

Frank again shakes his head and pleads, "Jesus, I don't know! We shouldn't get deeper in this mess and make matters worse!"

"Matters worse! This is a way out! Plus, then I will get my compensation! Deliverin' Penzetta three and a half million dollars got to make anybody grateful!"

"But how are you gonna get the ticket!?" yells Frank.

Vinny pauses; his frantic, scared brain was zooming. He then says, "We got to lift it off Gallagher."

"Steal it from him! How? You can't do that! You ain't no pickpocket! You can't sneak-up on him!"

"I know! I know! Not me!" Vinny says.

Frank's anxiety suddenly peaks even higher. "I hope you're not askin' me to do it! I don't got the nerve, Vince! I'm sorry! Please!"

"No! Fuck, no! Not us!" Vinny jabbers. "We'll keep our hands clean as much as possible! I know somebody who may do it!"

"Who?!"

"Gina's got a nephew? He's stayin' with her. A real low-life. The kid spent most of his life in reform school, a history of jackin' cars. I met him once. A scary little fuck. Always dresses in black. A fuckin' weirdo. Gina says she knows he's up to no good, probably dealin' drugs but she don't got the heart to boot him out because she promised her deceased sister to look after him."

"God, I don't know, Vince!" Frank gasps while rubbing his forehead. "This is gettin' worse We're dealin' with all bad people, here!"

"Listen, all the kid has ta do is get close and reach into Mattie's pocket and get the fuckin' ticket. Mattie's probably so friggin drunk by now, he won't even remember that he won the friggin' lottery! Then the kid will give me the ticket and I'll bring it back to Penzetta! Done deal!"

"Yea, what happens if Mattie comes around and remembers that he has been ripped off? What then? You know he's gonna flip out! He may go to the police!"

Vinny spat, "You think the police will believe anything that piece-of-shit drunk says! Plus, Penzetta will handle Mattie for sure."

"I don't know, Vince. I don't think you can pull this off."

"Why not?" asks Vinny.

Frank looks down at the ground then sighs with despair, "This isn't you, Vince. This is too serious. Maybe you should skip town."

"What?"

"This is too real. These players are all too tough." Frank keeps looking at the ground.

"What are sayin', Frankie? Youse think I'm soft? Just a big-mouth!?"

There is an uncomfortable pause.

Frank glances back up and notices that Vinny's eyes are welling again.

"Fuck!" Vinny curses as a tear rolls down his cheek and he rubs it off like it is an embarrassing bit of snot. "Don't look down at me, Frankie! I bet you're thinkin' I'm fallin' apart here! Cryin' like a fuckin' skirt! I bet you think I'm yellow because I let Blaisdale rough me up! But I'll get him back! Just youse wait! All my life, I've been lettin' things slide. But today, was a very fuckin' bad day! It seems like everybody from my past has come up and rubbed my face in shit! I ain't lettin' no Irish-fuck-head have money that I should be havin'! And I ain't gonna let some bugged-eyed asshole disrespect me and grab my balls and ruin my reputation in my neighborhood! I'm gonna fight back! I'm gettin' my compensation! Yous wait and see!"

At that moment, Frank was still full of dread but also surprised with his cousin's newfound courage. He wonders if it was caused by total desperation, rage over losing-face, greed for money or a combination of all three.

"I gotta go find, Gina's nephew." Vinny says. "I think the kid's name is Marco."

Frank just nods.

A stray alley cat suddenly leaps out from behind the nearby green dumpster. Both men jump and are startled.

SIXTEEN

Wednesday, 11:05 p.m., the main dining room at the Captain's Catch restaurant is closed, desolate and dark but the little Tiki bar with the lobster traps and fake fish on the walls is still open. The place is a bit of a dive. It is in walking distance to multiple senior housing complexes, making it a convenient haven for old alcoholics. 68-year-old Wilma Shea keeps an un-lit Virginia Slim between her bright-red smudged lips, removing it only to sip and down her nightly procession of Black Russians. She is babbling to 72-year Carl Mazuroski who really isn't listening due to age related deafness and having just finished off his sixth Crown Royal. Ralph the bartender is bored and morose. It is a slow night. A few moments ago, he thought he had another patron, when a *guido* in a leather sports jacket popped in, but the guy abruptly turned around and left. ESPN highlights play on the TV hanging up in the corner. Ralph can't bear to watch having just lost a week's salary to his bookie for picking the Steelers. He takes his tip jar, rattles it a bit and spies a pitiful $8.75.

"I'm fucked." He mutters to himself. With a visible sigh, he then looks to his left. There is old drunk totally passed out with his head on the bar. Ralph was going to give him a little more time to sober-up before booting him out. The codger had been a pain-in-the-ass for the entire evening, jabbering about coming back and buying the restaurant and licking all the waitress's private parts.

Ralph again mutters to himself, "I really hate my fuckin' life."

Suddenly, he sees a tall blonde kid come into the lounge, all jittery, with wild blue eyes darting about, searching the room.

"Help you with something?" Ralph asks with a subtle inquisitive tone.

"Uh?" Troy responds, sounding dumbstruck. He pauses and then his gaze becomes locked in on the old drunk passed-out on the bar. Abruptly, Troy walks up to the intoxicated geezer and begins taking him under the arm.

"You know this old dude?" Ralph asks.

Troy stammers, "Y-yea, I'm his ride."

Wilma Shea turns around and calls out with a happy inebriated lilt in her voice, "Are you his grandson? You are so handsome. It's nice that you're lookin' out for your poor old grandpa."

Flashing a nervous smile, Troy replies, "Yea, that's it." He then boosts the old man backward, grabbing him under the armpits. "Come on grandpa, time to go."

Mattie Gallagher is woken-up by all the jostling and being forced upright off the barstool and on to wobbling legs. He looks into the face of the young blonde fella that is holding him steady. Mattie asks with slurred speech, "Arrre you the cab driver?"

Troy responds, "Yes sir. I'm here to take you home."

"Okay, my g-good man, show me to-to my ch-ch-chariot."

The two begin to leave the bar, with Troy hugging Mattie around the waist and supporting him under one shoulder.

Wilma Shea waves and says, "Have a good night, you two cutie-pies!"

Muttering more profanity, Ralph shrugs and scoops up the three quarters left behind.

Through the small lobby the two go. Finally, they

make it outside. The night autumn air is chilly. Troy gasps. There in the parking lot is a West Haven patrol car with its stark bright headlights on, illuminating the front entrance to the Captain's Catch. Sitting in his vehicle with the window down, the cop chats with a waitress that is leaning against her Honda Civic.

"Shit!" Troy exclaims.

Being out in the cold appears to suddenly pep up Mattie. He asks, "Where's your cab, son? We can't be dancin' together all night."

Squinting against the glare of the headlights, Troy frantically scans about the parking lot. Marco is nowhere to be seen. The plan was to get the old man out of the bar, bring him to the side of the building; both would do a lightning quick, coma-causing beat-down. Next, rifle his pockets and get the lottery ticket. Then they were supposed to jump into a waiting car driven by some greaser named Vinny. Having a cop show up out of the blue was definitely fucking up the works.

"I g-g-gotta piss." slurs Mattie.

Troy's mind is speeding. "O-Okay, we'll go to the back of the building!"

The two start up again, one holding up the other. Troy keeps his face turned away from the squad car's glare. There is an additional lot behind the restaurant. Off to the left is a late model Chevy Impala parked but with its engine running.

There they are! Troy shouts to himself internally.

"I need to take a leak now!" Mattie complains as he starts to clumsily search for his zipper.

"Okay, okay!" snaps Troy as he nervously looks over at the car, waiting for some kind of signal of what to do next.

"Oh boy, too late." says Mattie with a drunken giggle. A dark urine stain quickly grows on the front of his golf-pant and down his right inner thigh.

Abruptly the back door of the Impala opens and Marco comes out and starts forward with rapid steps. There is a pitch-black corner under the eaves of the building, away from the pale glow of the parking lot lights. Marco plans for him and Troy to quickly drag the old man into the dark spot to finish the job and leave lickety-split before that cop in the front decides to stop flirting and do a drive-around.

With an anxious voice, Troy calls out as Marco approaches, "Are we still doing this?!"

"Yea, but shut up about it!" Marco growls as he comes up upon the two.

Mattie knits his brow and slurs, "Who-Who-Whos-s's this long-haired Bela Lugosi?"

Suddenly, at that moment, the back door of the restaurant opens and two Ecuadorian dishwashers start to haul out a huge slop barrel from the kitchen. Marco and Troy both freeze. The workers briefly look over then turn away, putting down the barrel in order to take a break and light up some cigarettes. Troy looks at Marco with heightened frustration, relaying the sediment, *What the fuck do we do now?*

Marco seethes, he had gotten amped to pounce and do some violence but now there is a delay. A tense pause ensues. Then he says lowly, "We got to move this."

Mattie is confused and irritable, "Hey, where the fuck's my cab. My piss is freezing on me!"

In the front seat of the Chevy Impala, Vinny is in a state of jittery fear. He almost fainted when that cop showed up. Every nerve in his body told him to put his foot on the gas pedal and tear outta here. *Jesus, I am a friggin' coward! Why didn't I skip town?! What the fuck made me so crazy? What was I thinkin'?!* For some hours the three had been searching local dives around the West Haven waterfront for Mattie. Vinny didn't plan on Marco having a partner, this kid named Troy. Vinny berates himself and prays, *Why did I ever choose these two creeps! Mary-mother of God, get me out of this!* Then in the glare of his own car's headlights, he sees them hustling Mattie forward toward his vehicle.

"No! No!" Vinny cries. "What the fuck are they doin'! They can't bring him here!" Vinny then bites down on the knuckle of his own hand.

Outside, Mattie is starting to resist. "Hey, I don't see no cab here! Who are you guys anyway?!"

"Come on! Just keep going!" Troy urges while still holding and pulling Mattie onward.

Marco steps ahead and opens the back door of the Impala. From inside, Vinny yells out, "Hey, this ain't the plan! I can't have him see me!"

"Shut up!" barks Marco. He then snarls with a fast but hushed voice. "We can't do this thing here! We got wet-backs watching in the parking lot!"

Vinny clamps his hands over his face.

Both Mattie and Troy are now up next to the Impala.

"I ain't getting in the back of that car!" hollers Mattie.

Impulsively Troy says, "Well, then sit in the front!" He yanks open the passenger door with one hand, then spins and presses Mattie forward, pushing him awkwardly and roughly into the front seat. One of Mattie's legs is sticking out. Troy quickly reaches down and takes hold of the old man's urine soaked leg, lifts it up, and crams it into the car. With a loud slam, he shuts the passenger side door. Marco spontaneously, jumps into the back seat then leans forward to take hold of Mattie by the back of the collar. In the next second, Troy squeezes into the rear seat next to Marco. The back passenger door is pulled closed with another loud bang.

"Hey, what is this?!" Mattie yells with fear and anger.

Marco calls out to Vinny, "Let's go right now! But

don't burn rubber! Keep it cool!"

For a moment, Vinny seems to forget how to shift the car into drive. He then finally puts the Chevy in gear and grasps the steering wheel with a white boned grip. The two Ecuadorian dishwashers watch with mild interest as the black Chevy Impala slowly pulls out of the parking lot. They hear distant, muffled shouts coming from within the car. There was also a brief glimpse of someone's fist banging on the inside front passenger window. Once the car hits the street, it suddenly picks up speed and peels-off into the night. The dishwashers shrug and throw down their cigarette butts. As they resume picking up the huge slop bucket and start toward the dumpster in the corner of the parking lot, the West Haven squad car pulls around the building in a lazy roll-by.

11:31 p.m. Already some miles away, the Impala zips along, following the long road next to the shoreline with its rows and rows of condominiums. Inside the car there is chaos.

"Where do youse want me ta go?" shouts Vinny.

Marco yells back, "Just get out of this area! We got to go where it's fucking quiet!"

Even though old and drunk, Mattie fights spastically, wiggling and turning about in the front seat. At one point, he almost gets hold of the door handle but Troy leaning over from the backseat, blocks his escape by wrenching back his arm and pulling back his head. Marco also comes forward and punches Mattie behind the ear. The blow does not knock the old man out but just makes him holler louder. Mattie turns and tries to bite Troy's hand.

"Fuck!" curses Troy.

"Oh, God!" exclaims Vinny.

It is at this moment that Mattie finally realizes who is driving the car. Initially there had been no time to recognize faces as he fought for his life. But the voice finally sparked recognition. For a second Mattie stops struggling with his backseat captors and looks over at Vinny with fury and dismay.

"IT'S YOU!!!" screams Mattie. "I CAN'T BELIEVE IT'S YOU, YOU FUCKIN' RAT!!!"

Vinny cowers, clutches his teeth and drives even faster.

"I'LL KILL YOU!!! YOU ROTTIN' BASTARD FUCK!!!" Mattie squirms and lunges across the seat in an attempt to claw Vinny's eyes and barely misses taking hold of the steering wheel. The car swerves and almost sideswipes a telephone pole. Marco and Troy yank, slap and pull the old man back.

"I KNOW WHAT YOU WANT! YOU AIN'T GONNA GET IT!" rages Mattie. "I'll SWALLOW IT FIRST BEFORE YOU GET ONE FUCKIN' CENT!!!" The old man with his left arm uncontrolled at the elbow, is able to dig into his front pocket where he has the ticket in his tattered wallet. His trembling fingers have no fine-motor dexterity but when his hand is pulled away, the tip of his index hooks the wallet. With peculiar physics, the wallet flips out of his pocket and over onto Vinny's thigh.

"JESUS!" Vinny yelps as his peripheral vision instantly identifies the object. Despite his pounding fright and adrenaline, Vinny is able to slap down on the wallet like he was smashing a giant bug on his upper leg.

"NO!" wails Mattie as he comes back at Vinny.

Troy takes hold of the side lapel of Mattie's jacket. The material begins to rip as the old man fights against his restraint.

"Enough of this shit!" snarls Marco. "Gonna knock this old fool out!" Quickly and viciously, Marco starts pounding harder on Mattie. But the Irishman isn't going down. He takes the blows to the top of his head, shoulders and to the side of his neck. Thrashing about, Mattie again attempts to bite Troy, this time clamping down on part of his thumb.

"Fuck! Ouch!" Troy winces. He pulls back his hand.

"YOU THIEVES AIN'T GETTING' MY MONEY!" screeches Mattie.

Marco attempts to reach over to choke Mattie but Troy also comes forward again, this time with his knife! The Spyderco has been flicked open. Troy is boiling. He yells, "THINK YOU'RE GONNA BITE ME, YOU WHITE-HAIRED-MOTHER-FUCK!!!"

Troy brings the knife around and presses it against Mattie's throat. Instinctively, Mattie tucks his chin. High carbon, razor shark-teeth serrations pierce under the old man's lower lip and the sudden pain caused him to open wide and cry out. The blade inadvertently cuts diagonally upward then saws vigorously through the cartilage of his nasal septum. A piece of Mattie's nose flies off.

"AAAOWWW!!!"

With a twist of the wrist, the knife comes horizontally across Mattie's mouth. Biting down on the shiny cold steel causes Mattie's incisor to instantly chip. With force, Troy yanks back the knife to free it and by doing so slices open the old man's cheek right to the mandible joint and laterally filleting his tongue. The pointy tip of the Spyderco breaks off and is now imbedded somewhere in the old man's gums.

"AAAGGGKK-CCCK!!!"

At this moment, Troy and the others are unaware of the severity of Mattie's wounds. But then bright gouts of blood come pouring out. Reflexively, Mattie brings his hands to his face, feeling the slimy flaps of his bisected cheek. He sucks in, causing blood to go down his windpipe. Next come spasms and regurgitation.

Vinny cared for his Chevy like it was a Cadillac. It was the one possession he truly owned. With pride, he always kept the car Armor-All'd and spotless even during the snowy months. Obsessively, he consistently was shaking out the floor mats, wiping down the console, vacuuming the rugs, and spritzing the interior with Winter-Green-air-freshener.

Tonight, the pristine Chevy Impala is to be defiled. In a torrent of blood, partially digested whole-belly fried clams, French-fries, tartar sauce, stomach-acid and large amounts of vodka and scotch-whiskey, the passenger side inner windshield and dashboard is splattered.

"WHAT THE HELL?!!!" screams Vinny, the side of his face speckled with bits of fried batter and ick. Instantly the cabin of the car is filled with the stinging odor of gastric juices. Barf from Vinny's own stomach almost comes out to be added to the stew. Vinny thinks, *Oh God, I think I'm gonna pass out!*

Mattie goes into a frenzy as he chokes and gags, his small body contorting and twisting in the front seat. His knees bang against the glove box. Then his body falls sideways into Vinny. Mattie's thin spindly legs begin to kick at the passenger side window and door.

"HOLD HIM! HOLD HIM DOWN!" hollers Marco as he and Troy continue to lean over from the backseat, grasping and trying to restrain Mattie as the car swerves about the road.

"Where's the ticket?!" shouts Marco. "Make sure it don't get soaked with blood!"

Vinny doesn't answer but just grits his teeth as his head swoons and he tries to keep the car on the road. There are more wet, wheezing sounds, and a terrible sputtering of anguish. Blood from Mattie's nasal and oral lacerations keep spilling down his trachea, causing him to aspirate. Mattie has one hand free again and with jittering fingers, he makes a futile attempt to pinch-close his sliced tongue and cheek. The gore keeps flowing driven by

Mattie's pounding heart. For a brief moment, the front interior of the car is illuminated with stark light when passing a street lamp. In that fraction of time, Vinny looks over and makes direct eye contact with Mattie.

Oh, Jesus Christ! Vinny cries to himself. *Look at all that blood! I wanna faint!*

The old man lost his rage and ability to fight and now has a look of total helplessness and dread. Mattie could no longer talk but his terrified eyes show defeat and are pleading to Vinny for mercy.

What did I do? Vinny wails internally. *This is a sin!* The image of someone being that helpless and mangled is too much to bear. Vinny is abruptly flooded with a giant wave of regret that sparks a smidgen of inner fortitude. There is also the fear and big-ass realization of being part of a potential murder. Vinny cries aloud, "I'm sorry Mattie! Hang on buddy!" Up ahead on the right is the exit for interstate 95 North. The tires of the Impala squeal as the vehicle makes a hard quick turn and flies up the ramp,

"Where the fuck are you going!" Marco yells.

Vinny shouts back "Don't hurt him no more!"

"I said, where the fuck are you goin', asshole?!!!"

"He could be dyin'!" Vinny screams, "We gotta get him ta the hospital!"

"Are you fuckin' nuts?!" Marco has the urge to come forward and rip Vinny apart but the car is traveling way too fast.

"This is bullshit!!!" Troy shouts.

"We'll just dump him a few blocks away from ER!" Vinny says. "Then we'll take off!"

"Where's the fuckin' ticket?!" Marco yells.

"I got it!" Vinny cries with shame in his voice.

The two in the backseat, shoot looks at one another. Troy brings up the knife but Marco slaps his partner's forearm down and hisses, "Not now! Not while he's fuckin' driving! We'll crash!"

The traffic is very light this time of night as the Impala speeds down I-95 north. In the distance there is the H sign marking the exit for hospital.

"We're almost there, Mattie!" cries Vinny. "Saint Roses will take care of ya!"

"This old dude can ID us!" snarls Troy.

"Penzetta will handle it!" Vinny yells back.

There is a gurgling and high pitch whimpering as Mattie's eyes roll back in his head, showing flickering whites.

"Who the fuck is Penzetta?" Marco asks.

Vinny doesn't answer but presses down harder on the accelerator and is now reaching over 90 miles per hour. The exit is quickly approaching. Also up ahead there is a lone white vehicle putzing along in the side lane. It appears to be traveling oddly slow.

"I said, who the fuck is Penzetta?!" Marco barks. "And you better bring it down to 65 because we're gonna get attention from a fuckin' statey!"

The Impala keeps speeding along. The exit to the hospital is close. Vinny starts to decelerate but unexpectantly that slow moving vehicle seems to suddenly and purposely pull into his lane.

"WOOA!!!" screams Vinny. The two in the back also freak. By luck the Impala swerves and catches only a bit of the bumper of the intruding vehicle. The old white Ford Tempo goes for a spin and hits one of the yellow barrier barrels full of sand. Doing a couple of 360's, Vinny and the others, whirl down the highway, missing the exit but miraculously not crashing. The Chevy stalls sideways in the middle of the highway but at that moment there are no other involved vehicles. Marco and Troy were tossed around a bit in the back of the car but are uninjured. Mattie is not that fortunate and had smacked his head on

173

the side window and acquired another gusher. Like a crumpled, soiled ragdoll, Mattie is stuck down in the well of the front seat, motionless.

Marco is the first to shake off the feeling of being spun around and dazed. He shouts to Vinny, "Come on, let's get out of here! Drive! Fuckin' drive before the cops come!"

Suddenly there are high beams of two tracker trailers approaching in the distance. Vinny swallows back his own puke, shakes his head to get refocused then re-starts the engine. The Impala begins heading north with part of its left front scraped, dented and showing signs of white paint from the Ford Tempo.

"Mattie ain't movin'!" says Vinny. "I think he's out! We gotta turn around and get 'em ta see a doctor!"

"WHO THE FUCK CARES!" says Troy.

"FUCK THAT! NO DOCTOR" yells Marco. "YOU JUST KEEP DRIVING!!!"

"WHERE?!" Vinny cries.

"SOME FUCKIN PLACE QUIET!!!" Marco shouts.

Behind them, way in the distance there are the flashing blue, red and white lights of the highway patrol.

Inside the stalled, wrecked white Ford Tempo, Chester is sobbing like a little girl but is physically unscathed. From the back seat, there is the crunching and clinking of shattered auto glass, as LaBoudy shifts around a bit then sits up. He has a bruised elbow but is also okay. He moans. But then giggles. Little shards of glass sparkle in LaBoudy's hair and on his face like glitter.

SEVENTEEN

Thursday 12:50 am, throughout the small raised ranch it is dark except for the sad glow that shines out from under the door of the upstairs bathroom. Frank is sitting on the toilet, brown trousers bunched up around his ankles, his elbows pressing into his fishy-white hairy thighs, while his hands are in the prayer position, his head bowed. There are beads of sweat on his pudgy neck. Upon coming home, he had raced upstairs to the crapper in an attempt to relieve that horrible pressure in his bowels but there was no relief. All that came out was more gas and some hot liquid stool. The nagging, burning pain and sensation of being constipated does not go away. He continues to sit there and sit there, trembling and rocking at times. It is like he has an evil spirit in his colon that just won't leave. Frank knows that the insanity he just experienced was sure to make his innards turn to lava.

I can't believe what is happening!

But the guilt of not being with Vinny is worse than the physical agony. The Saint Jude medal is pressed between Frank's palms and he has recited a mixture of Novenas, Hail Mary's and the Lord's Prayer. But there is no feeling of comfort from above.

This is so bad! Why! Why?

Frank's sister had gone with her girlfriends to Atlantic City. She would not be back until tomorrow. The dead stillness of the empty home seemed to amplify the feeling of pending doom. Conflicted and perseverating thoughts were growing and circulating in Frank's mind. He kept wondering why Vinny didn't force him to come along to help find Mattie. Over the years for any small thing, his cousin would run to him to get him out of a jam. It didn't make sense that at this ultimate dire time that Vinny would go and try to handle this calamity solo. A paranoid notion then popped into Frank's head.

I wonder if he's planning to get the ticket, cash it in on his own and jump ship. Can the idea of getting all that money make him grow those kind of balls? What about me? Would he leave me here alone, hanging in the breeze, with Penzetta and that psycho cop? Could he be that selfish? Vinny, how can you do this to me?

The pain in Frank's bowels surge up a few notches causing him to cramp over and moan aloud. Suddenly there is the sound of a car pulling into the driveway.

"Vinny?!" Frank cries in exhilaration. He then has a jolt of guilt for doubting his cousin. Forgetting to wipe or flush, Frank rises and yanks up his bacon-stripped-underwear and polyester brown pants. There is now no time for his gastro-intestinal problems. As fast as his short legs will go, he scampers down the stairs and exits out the front door. The Impala is parked but the engine is boiling and idling fast. Frank squints in the glare of the headlights, his hand coming up to shield his eyes.

There is a pause.

The driver side door of the Chevy then opens, and Vinny comes forward on wobbly, zombie legs. When Frank sees his cousin's face he instantly becomes frightened. There is that horrible traumatized look, like something seen on the face of a prisoner in a World War II death camp.

"What happened?" Frank asks with a quivering lower lip.

Opening his mouth, Vinny goes to speak but instead instantly bends forward and heaves. There is a sick wet loud splattering of fluid on the asphalt.

"Jesus!" cries Frank.

Rising and wiping his mouth, Vinny takes some steps forward and would have collapsed but Frank catches him and props him upright.

"Oh, my God!" says Frank. "Are you okay? Oh, Christ what happened?"

Sobbing, Vinny says, "I-I-I tried ta save him!"

"What? What do you mean?" says Frank. "Where's Mattie? What the hell happened?"

Vinny doesn't answer but instead reaches down and searches for his cousin's hand. With a breathy rasp, he whisperers into Frank's ear, "Hold on ta this!"

HOLY SHIT! Frank says to himself as he feels the small piece of paper being pressed into his palm. At that moment, the back doors of the Impala open and Marco and Troy emerge, their faces obscured to Frank because they stand behind the glare of the car's headlights.

"What are we doing here?" Marco calls out, his voice angry and menacing.

Sounding scared but also irritable, Vinny shouts back, "I told youse two; we're stopping to get directions ta where we gotta go!"

"Let's all move in the house. I need to piss," says Marco ominously.

"No way!" Vinny snaps. "We're leavin' in a moment!"

Troy calls over to Marco with an anxious hunger. "Hey, it's pretty quiet right here! How about now?"

Quickly scanning the street, Marco sees that all the houses are dark and silent. It is a clean peaceful neighborhood, mostly populated by elderly Italians.

"Maybe?" Marco hisses back at Troy. "Hold it! Let me think."

Suddenly the porch light goes on across the street. 78 year old, Miss Ferraro who really never sleeps at night is startled by the outside voices and is now peeking out her screen door.

"Shit!" Troy curses. "Looks like an old lady over there is watching!"

"Change of plans again." Marco says to Troy. "It ain't happenin' here!"

Vinny abruptly turns and starts back to the Impala, his gait still unsteady. "Get back in the car! We're goin'."

Still squinting, Frank catches sight through the dirtied windshield, of just the top of Mattie's head. The old man is slumped way down in the front passenger seat. There is an instant swell of terror, but then Frank's mind seems to shut off and deny what he is seeing. Frank cries out to his cousin with almost prepubescent voice, "W-w-what do you want me to do?"

"Just stay here!" Vinny replies choking-up. "I'll see youse in a couple hours!" He gets back behind the wheel. The other two, like phantoms, don't say anything more and slip into the rear of the running vehicle. Miss Ferraro continues to spy from across the street. Frank knows he should not let his cousin depart but his own yellow-streak keeps him frozen. He catches the last parting glimpse of Vinny's haggard tear-streaked face.

EIGHTEEN

Thursday 1:22 am, slow and conspicuous, the Impala drives on into the night. The fear of now being pulled over by the police keeps flashing in Vinny's troubled mind. He compulsively checks the speedometer. *I know Penzettta would have me whacked in prison, if I ever got caught. Probably give the job ta a bunch of Mexicans that would gang rape me in the shower then shiv me fifty times like a fuckin' pincushion! Mother Mary, how can I survive this? God, I know I'm goin' to hell for killin' Mattie! Jesus, I didn't mean it!*

From the back seat, Troy questions, "I thought when we stopped we were supposed to pick up some blankets to wrap up this dead geezer? You also said we were to get some shovels? What's the fucking deal? "

Vinny gives a nervous look in the rear-view mirror, and then replies, "I changed my mind. Can't have any fibers in the car from the blankets? Can't be too careful when it comes ta forensics. Plus we're goin' ta the lake. We won't be doin' no diggin'?"

"Are we going to keep joy-riding around all night with a fucking corpse uncovered in the front seat?" Troy replies. "Maybe we should lean the body over toward you. Rest its head in your lap. Like you're a faggot getting a blow-job while you're driving."

"Fuck yous." Vinny says with a gasp. "Have some fuckin' respect!"

"Inquisitively, Troy asks, "Respect? You say you're some Mafia dude, right? I thought Mafia dudes are supposed to be all cold and cool and don't puke like a little baby-ass when they see the sight of blood."

Marco cuts in and barks, "Keep the body upright and uncovered. It will look weird if you have just one guy driving in front and two guys sitting in back." He looks at Troy and orders "Put the seat belt on the body so it stays put."

"What?" Troy replies with a nervous laugh. "I don't want to fiddle around with no more dead people! Can't we just stop and cram the mother-fucker in the trunk?"

"No!" Marco snaps, "With our fucking luck someone will roll up on us. Just fucking do what I say!"

Grumbling and swearing, Troy brings himself forward, hanging over halfway into the front seat to reach, tug and maneuver the body into a better seated position. Vinny catches a bit of Troy's elbow as the kid jostles about. Troy's hands become slicker with blood. It is a bitch to find the seatbelt and get it hooked around the flaccid corpse as the car sways on the turns. Mattie's pale blue windbreaker is slippery and sticky with gore. Vinny cannot endure looking over at the ghastly sight because he will surely barf again. Finally there is the sound of a metallic click as the seat belt is secured.

"Good, finally!" says Troy as he plops back down into the rear seat. He then reaches out and pats the back of Mattie's slumped head. Laughing, Troy says, "Now he looks like he's just sleeping after a wicked ketchup fight."

Vinny, again cringes, squeezes the steering wheel and checks the speedometer.

Suddenly, Marco says with heightened nasty tone, "Show me the ticket again."

There is a tense pause in the Impala.

"I-I already showed it ta yea." Vinny replies, his voice cracking. Earlier, when getting back into the car at Frank's house, Marco had instantly demanded to see the Lotto ticket. An ingrained ability to scam and lie came into bear, and Vinny flashed a piece of cocktail napkin that he had in his top shirt pocket.

Marco growls, "I want to see it again."

"Why?" Vinny replies, trying to put some force into his voice. "Don't worry you're gonna get paid."

"I said, I just want to see it!" Marco snaps.

"Yea!" Troy says with manic excitement, "Pass it back here! I want to take a look and see what it is like to hold a million dollars!"

Vinny knew he had to try harder with the Mafia shtick in order to keep these two at bay. "Listen, this ticket don't concern you." Vinny taps the empty breast pocket of his leather jacket. "It stays right here with me! This is property of Mr. Penzetta. There is gonna be no more show and tell, *capisce?*"

"Well, thing's have fuckin' changed." Marco snarls. "There will be an extra charge for taking care of this body."

Troy sings, "Yea, boyzzzzzes! Mo-money! Mo-money!"

"Sure." Vinny lies, "When I tell Mr. Penzetta that youse guys were professional, you'll get your compensation. Maybe youse two will do some more jobs."

"Wow!" Troy laughs, "We'll get gigs as hit men! That would be rockin'!"

"Tell me more about this Penzetta guy?" Marco says with a squint.

There is another pause. Vinny again tries to sound mysterious and authoritative, "It's best youse don't ask no more questions about Mr. Penzetta."

Marco then inquires, "Who was that other guy back at the house? He seemed more scared than a bitch."

Quickly, Vinny snaps, "Forget about him! He ain't got nothin ta do with this! And I said ease up on the questions."

Troy laughs, "Hey, but can I ask about Marco's Aunt

Gina. She's got a nice rack. You been dating her, right? Does she fuck good? Does she suck cock?"

Sparking with anger, Vinny replies, "You'll do better, kid, if youse show some class."

"Uh, sorry, dude!" Troy again keeps laughing but does sound oddly a bit embarrassed. He reaches out with a bloody hand and pats Vinny on the shoulder, "I'm just joking with you man!"

Vinny is startled and flinches as he feels Troy's unexpected touch coming from the backseat.

In a cold voice, Marco asks, "Where are we going again?"

"To the Housatonic River in Monroe," Vinny answers.

"Is it quiet there?" Marco asks.

"Yea," Vinny says. "It's the friggin' boondocks out in the woods. There's this boat launch. There ain't nobody around, especially this time of night."

"Good," Marco says with a weird calm but with wrath in his eyes. At this moment, Marco is struck with how unexpectedly this whole scene came to be. It was earlier this evening when Vinny showed up out of the blue at his Aunt's house all wired and telling this big story about needing some outside muscle for a special job for the mob. The guy had all the lingo but Marco could tell that the dude was a flaky, lightweight. It was like a fly asking a spider for help.

You're my fuckin' meal ticket! Marco thinks to himself, as he gives a predatory stare to the back of Vinny's head. *A free fuckin' holiday turkey!*

"Can we crack a window in this car?" Troy whines. "I think our dead dude's sphincter just said hello."

NINETEEN

Thursday 1:56 am, the Impala took a slow right turn off the main route and started rolling and bumping on an unpaved back road. They are now miles away from the city of New Haven and out in the burbs and the lake area of Monroe, Connecticut. The high beams cut through the blackness, briefly illuminating spans of aligning dark dense pines. Ruts and stones torture the car's old shocks, causing the occupants in the vehicle to be jostled. Mattie's lifeless head keeps bouncing up then coming back down, hanging slack and limp.

"Hey, man!" Troy calls out from the back seat. "Are we going 4-wheelin'? You ain't getting' our asses lost, are you? I hope the fuck that dude told you the right way to go."

For the millionth time, Vinny gives another death grip to the steering wheel. He does not answer Troy's question. Vinny knows exactly where he is going having been to this area every season to go fishing. It wasn't hard for Vinny to sense that the two may be crazy enough to do a double – cross and try to rob him of the big enchilada. Vinny thinks, *Won't they be fuckin' surprised when they find out I don't got the ticket no more! Fuckin' hoods!*

The dirt road is becoming narrower and steeper as it descends toward the water's edge. Thick spruce branches start to scrape the sides of the car causing Vinny to wince. Visibility suffers as a cool mist begins to materialize, choking and obscuring what lies ahead. The high beams had to be cut off because there was the rebound of a blinding eerie glare.

"It's getting fucking foggy," Troy bitches from the backseat with a bit of trepidation in his voice.

The tires suddenly start to roll on a smoother patch. It is the concrete of the boat ramp. Vinny quickly hits the brakes and stops. If the car went any farther they would have gone into the water.

"We here?" asks Troy with excitement.

"Yea," Vinny replies, exhaling with fear.

There is another one of those intense pauses. Then Marco goes for the door handle. The dome-light in the Impala pops on and Vinny makes the mistake of glancing over at the corpse. Mattie's dead blue eyes are still open; his face is swollen and coagulated with a maroon crust. All the facial lacerations are nasty but not the primary cause of death. It was rather Mattie's old booze labored heart that went into defibrillation during all that pain, choking, rage and terror.

"Jesus!" Vinny curses and quickly scrambles out of the vehicle, sucking in the damp night air, desperately fighting back the urge to wretch. The other two exit the car and also breathe deep, clearing their lungs. Marco spits out a hawker as if to remove a bad taste in his mouth. The inside of the Chevy, even with the windows open, holds that putrid sweet and sour stench of bodily fluids.

"It's fucking cold out here," says Troy with a jittery laugh.

The mist from the pitch-black lake slowly swirls about. There is an unnerving quietness that makes one's words have a slight echo.

"So," Marco says calmly. "You want us to roll the body into the water?"

"Yea," Vinny says with a gulp and looking more green than ever.

"Are we going to tie some rocks to his feet and sink the fucker?" Troy asks.

With hesitation, Vinny replies, "Yea, okay."

Troy complains, "But we got no goddamn rope! And I ain't going into the fucking woods to look for vines. I ain't no fuckin' Boy Scout! It's too fucking dark out here!"

"Screw it," Marco says. "Don't worry about that. I heard the body gets all bloated and somehow always gets loose and comes popping up. We'll just drop the motherfucker in the drink and be on our way. That good?" There is a frightening mocking tone in Marco's voice as he glares at Vinny through the murkiness.

"Yea, okay," Troy calls out tauntingly to Vinny. "I bet this lake is full of bottom-feeders, like eels. They'll eat out this dead dude's asshole and brains. Probably won't be nothing left by spring!"

Oh, mother of God! Vinny whimpers internally. He takes some uneasy steps away from the two.

"Let's get our boy swimming!" Troy says with another anxious laugh and returns back to the car. Marco follows over to the front passenger side. There are some muffled sounds of bickering as the two jostle with the body and pull it out of the Impala. They then start dragging the corpse toward the water's edge.

Vinny turns away and comes to face a large towering pine. In the darkness, Vinny reaches out with a trembling hand to feel the cool, wet, umber bark. The touch of the tree gives rise to a brief moment of comfort. Vinny inhales deeply and smells the scent of the night woods. He remembers those happy times coming out here to fish with Frank. *Dear God, I wish I had a friggin' time machine!*

Marco and Troy stop for a moment, leaving the body on the ground. Troy bends down and pilfers Mattie's pockets. "Fuck, only two dollars!" He curses.

Vinny quivers as he hears the two mumbling and resuming dragging the corpse down the slope. Like ghouls, they are obscured in the fog. Then there is the sound of some splashing as Mattie's body is rolled and kicked off into the mucky, reed-clogged abyss.

Oh, Christ, have mercy on his soul! Vinny cries to himself. *Oh, Mattie!* Vinny now reaches out with both hands to steady himself against the tree. He prays some more and keeps trying to assure himself with the plan. After the body is dumped, the next step is to drive back to New Haven. Marco and Troy are to take the car and burn it while he goes right away to Penzetta to present the ticket.

Maybe it will all work out? Imagine that! Vinny says to himself

The most damning sin was that despite all his regret and fear, Vinny still had the contradicting, greedy, selfish thought of getting his compensation.

God, I know I shouldn't think this way! But boy, a little taste of that money for all this trouble I'm goin' through would be really nice! Oh, shit, I know that ain't right! I should be happy just ta get out of this with my life! Pray I don't get sent to friggin' prison! But if I make it through this, holy mackerel, I'll be just like a real wise guy; whackin' some pigeon for a big score! I'll be the real deal for once in my fuckin' life!

Out from the mist, Marco comes up the slope from the water's edge with sneaky but hurried, steps, wet pebbles, softly crunching under the soles of his sneakers. He did not have his lucky suitcase with him but he did bring along one of the usual stowed items. Rising up the Taurus .25 caliber automatic, he pulls the trigger. A sudden, high-pitched pop is amplified across the dark lake. An itty bitty brass shell casing glows for a split second due to the muzzle flash as it tumbles through the air then falls out of sight. This is the first time Marco ever attempted to shoot someone. In the past, he once waved the gun at some teen-age jocks that didn't want to pay for their weed, but that was the extent of his firearm resume. In fact, he only practiced once with the stolen piece. When first getting it, he had taken some reckless pings at a stray cat in a parking lot in Hartford.

"Jesus!" Vinny flinches as the little bullet nicks some bark off the tree, about three feet above his head. A second misaimed shot rustles a branch over to his left. The third round zips somewhere harmlessly off into the night.

"What the fuck?!" Marco curses in frustration, as he expected his victim to have already dropped. He had been shooting at a distance of approximately 10 paces. But now Marco decides to rush forward and try it again at a closer range. With more luck than accuracy, the fourth bullet, strikes Vinny in the upper back as he goes to turn and cower. The round quickly loses its energy as it penetrates Vinny's leather jacket. It did pierce the skin and muscle but is stopped by the hard bone of the right scapula.

"AAAAOOOWW!!!" Vinny screams, feeling like he got hammer-fisted in the shoulder blade. With more psychological shock then actual physical trauma, he crumbles to the ground and shrieks, "OH GOD, I HAVE BEEN SHOT!!!" Curling up in a sideways fetal position, he has his left arm crossing his body, reaching over to hold the area of injury.

Marco is like a novice primitive hunter, who comes up upon a wounded gazelle that sprained a back leg. It is easy for him to get up close and personal, leaning forward and pointing the gun just a few feet away from Vinny's head. The Taurus shakes in Marco's hand. Adrenaline is pounding. In his frenzy, Marco feels self-actualized. It is a fantasy come true to have the thrill of actually shooting a human being. From Gangsta Rap, to memoirs of combat soldiers, to diaries of serial killers, all hailed the exhilaration of imposing one's will on another with a pull of a trigger.

"TIME TO DIE, MOTHERFUCKER!!!" Marco seethes with delight. He fires.

POP!

Vinny's body seemed to ball-up even tighter. The bullet only grazed some of Vinny's black Italian pompadour and kicked up a little bit of wet earth.

"No! Pleassse!!!" Vinny cries in such a high-pitched tone, that it sounds impossible to be his own but rather cast from some hidden ventriloquist. He now has his left hand clamped on the side of his face in a futile attempt for protection.

"Did I fucking miss again?!" Marco curses in sudden bewilderment. He thinks to himself, *Am I that bad of a shot or am I shooting fucking blanks?*

Almost mercifully, Vinny's mind begins to slip. The internal terror causes the sensation of an immense orchestra playing a score backward at a deafening volume. There are also wacky, dreamy flashes of relative's faces and one coherent memory of Vinny at age seven stealing a whole dish of Italian pastries at a wedding. Next there is an odd feeling of floating. To dissociate is like an appetizer before the main course of death is served. This time Marco sticks the tiny muzzle of the automatic against the back of Vinny's shielding hand.

POP!!!

The sixth bullet zips through Vinny's palm and enters near the side of his nose. It then changes direction and drills upward and comes to rattle around a bit in one of his sinus cavities. Because there was gun barrel to skin contact, the hot gasses from the ignited gunpowder had filtrated the back of Vinny's hand then exploded out, leaving a little blackened ragged star as an entry wound.

POP!!!!

It is the thinner bone in the temple that allows for the seventh round to travel into the cranium. The small copper jacketed slug slices through the fatty brain tissue then strikes the inner opposite wall of the skull. Next, it ricochets downward where there is respiratory circuitry and other vital do-hickies.

POP!!!!!

The eighth shot hits higher up on the frontal part of the skull. A divot is left as the bullet fragments. There is no penetration. However, it does not matter because it was the seventh bullet that bought the deed to the farm.

"Fuck!" Marco curses as the slide to the Taurus locks back signaling that the magazine is empty. There is a burnt whiff in the air. Even though it is a small caliber pistol, Marco's ears are ringing from all the gunfire.

"DUDE, IS HE DEAD?" calls out Troy as he bounds up the slope.

"I DON'T KNOW!" Marco replies. Nervously, he gives a quick kick to Vinny's rump then instantly steps back as if he just prodded a dangerous snake. The body doesn't stir. A part of Vinny's brain stem has been nicked and flooded with blood. Neural electrical activity has ceased along with breathing.

"Shoot him again!" Troy says, "Make fucking sure he's toast!"

"Yea, okay!" Marco's hand is shaking as he searches in his jean pocket for the extra .25's he brought along. Being so juiced and excited, fine motor dexterity has gone out the window. A few of the little slugs fall from his grasp as he tries to find the magazine release. He only manages to reload four rounds.

"Come on, man!" Troy says all jittery.

"Ah, fuck it!" Marco snaps with impatience, as he racks the slide. He leans down again to press the pistol point-blank to the side of Vinny's head.

"Cool!" Troy laughs. "Cap that mutherfucker again!"

"Wooh, hold up!" Marco says, suddenly aiming the

gun away. Even though it is dark, he sees glistening wetness.

"What' up?" yells Troy.

"I see the blood now. This fucker is bleeding a lot!" Marco says.

"So?" Troy asks.

"The Lotto ticket, dumb-ass!" Marco barks. "You think they'll accept a ticket soaked with fucking blood!"

"Shit!" Troy swears.

"Go search his jacket!" Marco orders. "Get that ticket before it gets ruined."

"Okay, but keep that gun ready just in case this fucker is playing possum and tries popping up like Jason from Friday The Thirteenth!"

"Come on! Fucking move it!" Marco says.

Troy bends down and with some caution rustles Vinny's shoulder. The body does not stir. Next, Vinny's corpse is turned over onto its back. Through the dimness, they could make out the contrast of dark streaks flowing out from the corpse's nose and mouth against pale white skin.

"Yea, he looks dead!" Troy says with a tone of wonderment.

"Go in the top pocket of his jacket!" Marco commands with bounding pressure in his voice.

With clumsy hands, Troy feels around in Vinny's front jacket pocket and pulls out a wad of cocktail napkins. Marco quickly snatches the wad from his partner's grasp. He knows the texture of the paper of a lottery ticket.

"This is not it!" Marco snarls. "Look again!"

Troy whines, "I am! I don't fucking see it! It's fucking dark you know!"

"Feel everywhere! Maybe he stuffed it down his pants!"

Troy pauses for a moment and says to Marco, "Dude,

this will be the fucking second time tonight I'll be fiddlin' with some dead guy! This is getting kind of weird!"

"We're talking millions of dollars here! Strip the motherfucker and get the ticket!"

Cursing some more, Troy starts fingering Vinny's front pant pockets. With his patience gone, Marco sticks the Taurus .25 auto in his waistband and kneels down and joins in with the search. They start to pull down the corpse's trousers.

"I don't wanna see no dead guy's pecker!" Troy bitches.

"Shut-up! Keep looking!" Marco yells as he yanks down the urine soaked boxer shorts and checks for the scrap of paper around the inner thighs and under dead Vinny's slippery wet ball sack.

"It ain't here!" Marco gulps, this time swallowing back his own bile.

They then roll the body on its stomach.

"Oh dude!" Troy gags, "He's prairie-dogging; I'm going to hurl!"

Marco stands up.

"Maybe he stuck it in one of his shoes?" Troy says.

Not answering Troy, Marco needed to vent his own revulsion and pulls out his gun and starts shooting again.

"WHAT THE FUCK!" Troy screams. He is still in a crouched position next to the body when one of the hot little shell casings bounces off his nose.

The left white clammy ass cheek of Vinny's corpse quivered as it received a peppering.

"Man, I think you made me deaf!" Troy complains. "You shot too close to my ear."

Seething, Marco just stands there still pointing the empty Taurus. He then mutters, "I need to wash my fuckin' hands."

Suddenly from across the lake on the opposite shore, a spotlight turns on and cuts across the fog.

The two freeze as they are bathed in a stark glare.

Twenty

Thursday 10:48 am. The morning sun is flooding through the bay window and casting a yellow glow in the living room. Frank has his back to the light, as he lies balled up on the couch. He has a pillow covering his head. The plastic slipcovers are moist and slippery because of all his sweating. Hours and hours of catastrophizing have left him numb and drained but an internal current of fear still fuels a torturous insomnia. His intestinal distress has now morphed into a single pulsating red-hot beacon.

If this don't stop, I don't mind dying. Frank says to himself. *I really mean it.*

Suddenly, shrill and loud the phone rings in the kitchen, breaking the stifling silence. Frank is jolted but he does not rise up. It would make sense to launch off the couch to catch the call but he is frozen.

What if it's news I can't face!

There are more piercing rings then the answering machine is activated.

"Hi there! You have reached Frank and Mary's fine catering; please leave your message after..."

Dear God, let it be Vinny!" Frank prays.

There is a mixture of letdown and relief as the voice of a jittery bride-to-be comes on and leaves an inquiry about the price break between jumbo shrimp cocktail for 30 guests versus scallops wrapped in bacon.

Frank then curses himself for not lending his cousin his mobile phone. In the past, Vinny would run through his minutes then not pay his bill. His services were always

193

being dropped. When a broad would ask for his cell number, Vinny would make the excuse that he needed to be mums for awhile because the FEDs were listenin' in. Sometimes the charades were all so amusing.

"Where are you, Vinny?" Frank whispers to himself. "Come on. Come home."

Outside on the residential street there is the occasional sound of a passing vehicle. Everytime, Frank would tighten up hoping the Impala would pull into the driveway. More minutes lapse, which drag into another agonizing hour. There is the reoccurring realization in Frank's mind that in the front pocket of his trousers is a tiny square piece of paper worth over 3 and a half million dollars. It seems so unbelievable. The slogan for the state lottery is to PLAY A DREAM. In his heart of hearts, Frank wants this dream to end and would gladly rip up the ticket, go back in time and erase all this horror.

12:01 p.m. Exhaustion is finally winning over Frank's vigilance and foreboding. He starts to fade. His eyes flutter then he falls asleep. In that brief moment while he slumbers, he does not hear the sound of the giant metallic pearl white Cadillac Escalade stopping out front.

12:04 p.m. The sliding glass door in the back of the house explodes. The two are like nightmarish juggernauts, storming in, going through the kitchen, searching, and coming into the front living room. Frank eyes pop open in a panic but he then does the ostrich technique, shutting his eyes and clamping the pillow tighter around his head.

"THERE'S THE LITTLE FUCKER!" Blaisdale roars.

Beef lunges forward past the ex-cop and scoops up Frank off the couch like he is just a laundry bag full of shitty diapers. In the next second Frank is sailing in the air, coming to crash against a hutch filled with his sister's collection of Precious Moments figurines. Blaisdale goes over and quickly pulls down the shades as Frank withers on the carpet midst the shards and broken bits of knickknacks.

"How ya doin' asshole?" Blaisdale snarls.

Frank cannot speak. Oxygen is not getting in. It is like being in a sudden car crash and everything is a topsy-turvy blur. Finally Frank's diaphragm relaxes and he gasps. Beef comes over and drops a knee on Frank's belly causing Frank to blast out an extraordinarily loud wet fart.

"What a fuckin' pig!" yells Blaisdale.

It is hard again for Frank to breathe; he is about to pass out. Beef eases up and removes his knee. Coughing and sucking in air like a dying pollywog, Frank's eyes roll into the back of his head. Blaisdale walks over, leans down and starts slapping Frank on the cheek. He barks, "Okay, come on! Don't check out on me now, ya smelly fuck, we gotta talk!"

Slowly, Frank refocuses and stares up at the red angry face of Blaisdale. The ex-cop's bulging eyes look even more pronounced and grotesque. Then the corners of Blaisdale's mouth curve up into the most vindictive smile as he says, "I got some good news for ya! You know that fuckin' spineless pretty-boy *paisano* of yours? Guess what! He's no longer in this world'! Whattaya think of that?"

Like being hit with a concrete slab, Frank is crushed with a wave of despair. He lets out a choking sob. Blaisdale cuts a wider grin and Frank is then instantly sparked with an unexpected rage that he never knew existed in his psychology. Making his hands into claws and flaying upward at the ex-cop's gloating face, Frank shouts, "Stop smilin' you fuckin' murderer!"

Blaisdale catches Frank's wrists and Beef instantly gives a quick boot-kick into the side of Frank's ribs.

"Oh, scratching like a little fuckin' girl are ya!"

Blaisdale says with some surprise. He does drop his smile.

Frank cries aloud in pain but with more fury.

Pressing down and pinning Frank's arms across his chest, Blaisdale says, "Listen up! I didn't kill your fuckin' cousin. Maybe if you two gave me the right information and did what you were told, your boy wouldn't be headed for some fuckin' autopsy table!"

Another sob went shuttering through Frank.

"But I knew you fucks were lying to me!" Blaisdale hisses through clenched teeth. "Gallagher don't got no uncle. But I did find that Irishman's aunt last night. That drunken old bitch got uppity with me and I slapped the fuckin' dentures right out of her mouth. But it don't matter, it looks like Gallagher ain't ever comin' home either. Now, tell me what happened to the fuckin' ticket!"

It is hard for Frank to get his mind around what was being said but he did know that he would not allow the ticket to be handed over to this fiend. He expected to die and had nothing to lose. The notion of pending death was oddly liberating and sparked a vengeful defiance.

"I said, now where's the fuckin' ticket?!!!" Blaisdale shouts.

Frank only manages to shake his head no.

"No, what?!" Blaisdale growls.

Frank does not answer.

"Okay!" Blaisdale seethes as he releases Frank's arms and stands up. He then draws his compact Glock Model 30 from a hip holster that has been hidden by his wrinkled sports jacket. He points the gun down at Frank's face. "See this!" Blaisdale threatens, "You're gonna fuckin' wish for a bullet if you don't tell me who's got the mother-fuckin' ticket!!!"

Frank cringes but still says nothing.

Blaisdale glances over at Beef and says, "Give this fuckin' little prick a taste of your talents. And I hope he doesn't shit himself cause he stinks fuckin' bad enough!"

Coming forward again, Beef leans down over his victim. Jostled about, Frank is positioned so that he is now lying on his side. The muscleman takes hold of one of Frank's arms and bends it at the elbow, trapping it. Next, Frank's wrist is placed in a gooseneck jiu-jitsu hold. There is instant sharp agony as Frank's tendons and radial nerve are over-stretched. Frank screams and tries to squirm away but is pinned between his assailant's legs. Beef then eases up on the hold and Frank could not help but whimper in relief.

With his smile back on his face, Blaisdale chuckles. "Boy, that sure must smart like heck!" He again gestures to Beef and says. "Do it some more."

The prolonged excruciating tearing sensation in Frank's wrist makes him cry out even louder, wiggle and spaz.

"Wow!" Blaisdale mocks. "I hope that's not the hand you wipe your ass with because you're gonna have to start using the other from now on."

Finally, Beef releases the pressure and Frank cries, tears streaming down his cheeks.

"Do I have your attention, now?" Blaisdale sneers. "We gotta talk, right? It's fess-up time. Or are you gonna be still fuckin' stupid?"

Holding his throbbing wrist Frank gasps, "P-p-please, just k-k-kill me."

"No!" snaps Blaisdale. "That's not how it works! You're gonna unburden yourself with the fuckin' God's honest truth and tell me where that ticket is! Do you know why? Do you?"

Frank doesn't answer but just stares in horror as if looking into the face of the devil.

"I'll tell you why!" Blaisdale rants. "Because you don't want me to get more fuckin' upset. I have been up all night searchin' places and findin' out where everybody fuckin' lives. I haven't got one second of shut-eye and not one drop of coffee. And if I don't get my caffeine I get cranky and impatient. And you'll suffer way fuckin' more than Vinny! Do you wanna know what happened to your faggot cousin? It's really bad. Do ya wanna hear? Do ya?"

At that moment, Frank wishes he were deaf. He shakes his head no.

"Too bad!" shouts Blaisdale. "You're gonna hear it anyway! Less than an hour ago, I rolled up on that house where your aunt lives. There were squad cars out front and they were doin' a preliminary notification. I walked over to one of the detective buddies I know and asked what the fuck happened. He tells me that two stiffs were found out by the Housatonic along with a cashless wallet belonging to a one Vinny Gentile. I pressed him a bit and he gave me some details that weren't so pretty. It seems that your cousin was found all shot up and with his pants pulled down. That's an embarrassing way to go. Why do you think his pants were pulled down?"

Frank feels that rage building inside of him again. He hears that sick delight peaking in Blaisdale's voice.

"You know what I think?" Blaisdale suddenly grins again, "They tortured him. Probably shot him in the balls and put a round up his rectum. Boy, there's a bad way to go. And what an epithet! Here lies Vinny the coward with his nuts blown off and butt-fucked with a bullet. Too bad that couldn't be chiseled into his fuckin' headstone. But it's okay, cause I'll make it my fuckin' pledge to tell everybody in your guinea-wop neighborhood this juicy information so they have somethin' interestin' to talk about and remember your cousin by."

Forgetting his hurt hand for a moment and still lying on his side, Frank goes for an awkward swipe at the ex-cop's leg. Instantly, Blaisdale does a side step while Beef gives another boot-kick.

"AAAAAHA!!!" Frank screams.

"Wow, aren't you all tough flippin' out down there on the carpet!" Blaisdale says with greater surprise. "But listen up shithead! I'm only tellin' you this story, so you can choose to be smart and give up where the ticket is or get tortured like your cousin but – worse! And I mean fuckin' worse!"

There is an odd pause of silence and the ex-cop sees that fear has left his victim's face and is now replaced by a determined intensity.

Abruptly Frank blurts out, "Gina's nephew got it!"

Blaisdale seems briefly taken aback. "Who?" He asks.

"It's a kid named Marco and his friend!" Frank exclaims. "They got the ticket!" His sudden lie was not meant to avoid torture but rather to seek payback. It was an odd moment of bravery. Frank no longer cared for his own wellbeing but rather was electrified with the notion of unleashing this psychopath on the punks that took his beloved cousin's life. He shouts up into Blaisdale's face, "GO KILL THEM!!!"

Excited, the ex-cop grills Frank on such things as the whereabouts of Gina's apartment, and physical descriptions. Frank quickly rambles on and gives as much info as he could muster including Vinny's impromptu plan to get the ticket and how his cousin must have got double crossed by the two hoods.

Blaisdale mocks, "See what fuckin' happens when wannabes try to play for real. They're so fuckin' cherry that they just can't help but be screwed. It seems to me that not only was your cousin a fuckin' coward he was also a certified fuckin' retard! What was he thinkin' goin' alone with those two guys? I bet you're glad you didn't tag along?" The ex-cop gives an inquisitive squint as he continues to peer down at Frank.

Frank just glares back while feeling another stab of shame and wishing that the ex-cop would also somehow die cruelly.

"I got somebody right now stakin' out the parkin' lot of the lottery claim's center in Newington!" Blaisdale boasts. "I hope those two you're talkin' about are dumb enough to show up and try to claim that big fuckin' juicy pay out!"

Slightly nodding in agreement, Frank seems calmer but internally his blood is pounding through his system like a torrent.

The ex-cop gives another suspicious squint and says, "But, should I buy this story you're tellin' me? You know you two tried to burn me once already."

Frank takes a shallow breath and says with anger in his gasping voice, "I never wanted to be a part of this whole thing! I really didn't."

Waving a scolding finger, Blaisdale says, "Yea, but you were there! You were fuckin' there. You never said a peep when your pretty-boy cousin was tryin' to jerk my chain. You never said a word. That makes you guilty. How does it feel to be a piss-ass' little weasel?"

Casting his eyes away, Frank suddenly feels sapped, knowing the ex-cop is right. He was guilty of being yellow, guilty of a not wrestling his cousin to the ground and stopping him from his madness. But instead he enabled Vinny like he always did.

"So, how much was supposed to be your take?" Blaisdale asks with a dirty snicker.

"I never cared about the money," Frank mumbles.

"Yea, right," Blaisdale spat with disgust. He then looks over at Beef and says, "Well, it's time to go hunting again. I guess we better make this quick."

Frank's vengeful courage is now replaced with a mixture of fear but also sudden peace as he assumes he is now going to be offed. *How are they gonna kill me? Please*

God, let it be quick. At least it's over. That's good. My sad life is finally over. Yes. Yes.

Blaisdale has that morbid passion in his voice again as he goes searching in his sport's jacket. He starts building himself up for another rant, "You know, you two fucker's got me in hot water with Penzetta. He was all steamed because I didn't partner-up with Vinny to go find that Irishman. But there was no way in hell, I was gonna be civil to that pansy-ass-cock-suckin' cousin of yours. No fuckin' way! But I'll make things right. I always get my man. I'm a fuckin' gggggggreat detective you know! I just wasn't suited for the American criminal justice system. It's too soft here in the states. Too much of that human rights bullshit. Give me a badge in San Salvador or even fuckin' Russia. Then I'll show ya how to have fun!"

Still lying there on the carpet, Frank cringes and waits for the end. Blaisdale re-holsters his Glock and then finds the silver cigarette lighter in his inside jacket pocket. Blaisdale gives the nod to Beef. The muscleman pounces again, coming forward then squatting down and hauling Frank up into a sitting position.

"Oh, Jesus! AAAAAGGG!!!" Frank gasps as he is trapped in a Full-Nelson hold. It is now hard to speak or take in air. Beef has him pinned from behind and Frank can feel large steel-grip hands pressing down and causing almost all seven cervical vertebrae to be on overload. *He's gonna break my neck!"*

"Ease up a bit," Blaisdale chuckles as he kneels down in front of Frank. "Don't make him into no Christopher Reeves. We can't have our little weasel here, all paralyzed and unable to feel his just rewards. Man, that's one thing I wouldn't wish on my worst enemy is a fuckin' spinal cord injury. The idea of it just gives me the creeps. When I was a rookie, I remember this cop that took a .22 high up between the shoulder blades and wound-up for life in a fuckin' wheelchair. He was pretty much dead from the torso down. Couldn't feel a thing. I heard that everyday some nurse had to go in and finger the shit out of his kiester because he could no longer tell when it was time to take a crap. God-damn, that's a sad way to exist."

Panicking, Frank does not really comprehend what his tormentor is saying. He just prays for the final curtain. *BLESSED MARY MOTHER OF GOD WHERE ARE YOU? PLEASE LET IT JUST END!!!* For a brief moment Frank thinks of his sister, then his own mother.

There is a clicking sound as the lighter in Blaisdale's hand produces a small unstable blue flame. The ex-cop pants with an almost sexual urgency, "Don't worry, you ain't gonna die today. I just want ya to feel something so you'll never forget to tell the fuckin' truth."

Abruptly, Frank is pulled up to a standing position while the ex-cop still sort of kneels before him. The lighter is held so that the flame licks up near the zipper of Frank's brown polyester trousers.

"AAAAAAAHHHHH!!!!...." Frank's scream is partially blocked in his throat because of the Full Nelson. He wiggles and buckles and tries to cross his legs to protect his crotch from the searing heat. Blaisdale takes hold of Frank's belt and attempts to hold him steady as he brings the lighter around to burn about the buttocks.

"AAAAAAGERRRRR!!!!"

"Better not fuckin' cut one!" Blaisdale howls and laughs, "The flame may go right up your asshole and your colon will catch on fire!"

"AAAAAHHHHHH!!!!"

The ex-cop stands up then curses as the Zippo temporarily loses its flame. Blaisdale barks at Beef. "Lift this fucker's head back for one second. I want him to feel the burn someplace different!"

The downward pressure on Frank's neck is released

but then replaced with a jarring backward yank. Blaisdale is ecstatic with the kinky evil joy of torturing another human being but in his excitement he has a decline in his fine-motor dexterity. He swears again in frustration as he clumsily thumbs the silver square lighter. Finally there is ignition.

"Yes!" Blaisdale says with almost a cheer.

The fluttering blue and yellow flame comes into contact with Frank's Adam's apple.

"AAAAAAAAAAAAHHHHH!!!" Frank is now able to scream aloud because his neck is no longer crammed forward. He thrashes, kicks out and sort of jogs in place while trying to tuck his chin. It feels like he is being cut from ear to ear. The sensitive skin of his throat instantly blisters with second and third degree burns. Mercifully, the lighter goes out again.

"Ah, fuck!" Blaisdale yells. He then tells Beef to let him go, knowing that the victim is screaming too loud and could alert neighbors. Frank instantly collapses to his knees and is wailing and crying. His trembling fingers quiver before his throat but he dares not touch the roasted flesh. It is hard to breathe again. Everything is swelling. But besides the growing tightening of his esophagus, a surge of minestrone-like vomit comes shooting out, followed by a flash of even greater pain.

"Ah, shit!" says Blaisdale. "He got puke on my shoe!"

As if touched by an intervening angel, Frank passes out and falls sideways. There is a moment of blessed relief from all the hurt and terror. Unfortunately, it is short lived as Frank regains consciousness, gagging, spurting out barf, sucking in and searching for air.

The two demons are still there. Blaisdale looks down at his victim on the carpet and says, "Try not to choke to death, you fuck. I still want you alive. We're gonna go look for those two cowboys. You better pray to God, they got the ticket because if they don't, I'm coming back with a whole container of lighter fluid and a long screwdriver. If you are holdin' out on me again, this will seem like a friggin' massage compared to what will happen to you next."

Frank does not respond; he lays there shaking, on the verge of going into shock. There are some brief snapping sounds as the broken bits of Frank's sister's Precious Moments figures are crunched by one of the two's heavy departing steps. The ex-cop and the muscleman leave the same way they came in, out the backdoor. Large but quiet, the Escalade pulls down the street and disappears. Old Miss Ferraro watches from across the way, questioning herself if she actually heard screams.

12:52 p.m. The happy yellow sunlight is peeking through gaps in the shade and Frank continues to be on the floor but is not just trembling but rather writhing in heightened agony. The pain from his blistered throat seems to intensify with every passing second and it competes with the burns on his groin and buttocks. His wrist also throbs like a muther. With all the excruciating stimuli he is about to pass out for a second time but then the phone rings.

Then it rings again.

And again.

The answering machine is activated.

"Hi there! You have reached Frank and Mary's fine catering. Please leave a message after the tone...."

Aunt Theresa's voice comes on. She is hysterical, wailing and screaming in Italian. It is a horrid operatic sound, full of sorrow, wrath, and almost insanity. At that moment, Frank struggles upright and lets out a bellow of his own misery.

I can't take this! I really can't take this no more! is the flashing message in his brain. On unsteady legs, he does a hurried limp out of the living room. He needs to get away from his Aunt's banshee-like cries. Stumbling, he grabs the set of car keys off the kitchen counter as he heads for his car. The garage doors are closed shut and the space is dim and occupied with two vehicles. One is a white Dodge Mini-Van with the logo and number of the catering business air-brushed on the side panels. The other is a 1984 maroon Lincoln Continental. What Frank planned to do next, had already played out in his head numerous times in the past.

Today, I'm gonna do it for real! God, forgive me! Please, just forgive me!

His left wrist and hand had ballooned up leaving him only the use of his right. Desperately, he pulls down the coiled green garden hose from the wall. Having OCD traits, the tools and various hardware items in the garage were organized on shelves, hooks and boxes and it was easy to find the gray packing tape despite his frenzy. Frank drags a length of the unwinding garden hose to the back of the Lincoln. He grimaces in pain as he kneels and rams a section of the green tubing up the exhaust pipe. The next part is difficult. Using his teeth, he frees a strip of the packing tape. This time he cries out in agony because tightening his jaw and moving his neck causes the horrible burn on his throat to flare-up. Then the tape folds in on itself and gets tangled.

"AAAAARRRERRR!!!" Frank wails.

He tries again with his mouth and gets the roll working. Lowering himself to the cold cement floor, he starts wrapping the tape around the junction between the tail pipe and garden hose. It is a clumsy job having use of only one hand but an adequate seal is made. Struggling and gasping, he stands back up and opens up the driver's side. Next, the key is put in the ignition, allowing Frank to partially lower one of the back power windows. The other end of the garden hose is then stuck snuggly through the opening.

I hope this works! Frank prays.

As he goes to sit behind the steering wheel, he yelps in pain because of the burns on his ass cheeks. Quickly he pulls the driver's door closed and leans on his right hip to ease the pressure off his cooked skin. Stabbing at the control buttons he makes sure all windows are completely up except for one behind that has the hose snaking in like a green rubber viper.

Here we go! Frank says to himself. He proceeds to start up the Lincoln. The big engine sputters and stalls but there is electrical juice. With a metallic hiss and a click, the tape deck finishes its automatic rewind. In the next second Dean Martin comes blaring through the sound system. "You're Nobody Until Somebody Loves You" is the song. Frank jumps and is startled, bumping his right wrist on the steering wheel. As fast as he can, he reaches over and shuts off the music.

"AAAh, fff-ff-fuck!" Frank garbles in anguish.

Once again he tries to start the car. The V-8 goes into convulsions but still does not turn over. Finally on the fourth attempt the engine starts to run. Instantly, exhaust comes spewing out from the garden hose in the back seat.

Panic messages flash in Frank's mind, *OH GOD! OH GOD! I'M REALLY DOIN' IT!!!*

In this moment of immense terror, an odd recollection then pops up in his head. There is the memory of how his sister would no longer ride in the Lincoln after finding balled-up pantyhose and a used Trojan on the back floor mat. Vinny used to love to borrow the Town Car for first dates.

"I'm comin' to join ya, Vinny," Frank cries.

Carbon monoxide begins to fill the interior of the

vehicle. Frank coughs and moans. Suddenly he feels like he is going to throw-up again.

OH. CHRIST, I DON"T FEEL GOOD!!!

The temperature inside the Lincoln rapidly rises. CO starts to combine with Frank's hemoglobin.

I'M GETTING DIZZY! OH. JESUS, IT'S HOT IN HERE!!! OWW! I HURT!!!

Frank is on the verge of fleeing out of the car but another part of him keeps him put and yearning for sweet peaceful death.

MOTHER OF GOD, WHEN AM I GONNA PAST OUT? PLEASE!!!

Toxic white vapors are now obscuring the view through the Lincoln's windows as the end of the garden hose belches and putt-putts. Frank is wheezing and sweating and his skin is flushed pink. A rapidly growing intense headache makes him swoon and start to lose it. Some weak internal survival mechanism prompts him to reach across for the door handle but his coordination is now too impaired. Finally he slips into unconsciousness.

A few seconds pass and without warning one of the garage doors begins to lift up. Old Miss nosey Ferraro strains with all her might as she pulls up on the outside handle. Poisonous gas comes bellowing out like the furies from Pandora's Box.

Twenty-One

Thursday, 6:07 p.m. On the New Haven, Hamden border there is the neighborhood eyesore. It is a tiny gray-paint-peeling cape with a corroded Pontiac Grand Prix on cinder blocks decomposing in the front yard next to a rusted swing-set. In the upstairs bedroom of the house, 18-year-old Jesse Butkus is practicing his coping skills. Vintage Pink Floyd drones in his headphones, as he lies on his bed amidst dirty laundry and twisted blankets. Tattered posters of Bob Marley and old 80's hair bands adorn the walls. The sweet stench of cannabis hangs in the air. He had finished what was left in the bong, and now just nurses a joint. There is some bad shit going down; he could sense it. Unexpectedly Troy had come ducking in today around 3 o'clock in the afternoon with some mean dude that dressed in black that gave Jesse the creeps.

Man, I wish they both say see'ya and split forever.

Last night, when that spotlight came shining across the lake after Vinny was shot, Marco and Troy were sure that the game was up, but they managed to toss the gun into the water, jump into the Impala and flee. They had dumped the car in Bridgeport before making it back to New Haven on a late night Metro North train. Both had congealed blood on their clothes like Halloween monsters.

It's my f-upped luck that they wanna crash here. Jesse thinks. *This totally blows!*

Jesse was also super grossed out and miffed at his mom. A little while ago, when he went downstairs to nuke a ham and cheddar Hot Pocket, he saw Troy banging her doggy-style in the living room. Rhonda's large white fat ass had jiggled with each rapid thrust. The two didn't even stop fucking when Jesse walked pass. To make matters worse, that guy Marco was just sitting nearby on the couch woofin' down peanut butter and jelly sandwiches, with dried blood under his fingernails.

So wrong!

At the present moment, there comes a quick knock at his door and Rhonda barges into his bedroom and says, "Jesus! Whatta havin' your own private clambake in here?" She waves a hand through the smoky haze.

Irritated, Jesse turns his head away and does not want to make eye contact with his mother. Intrusively, she walks up alongside his bed, leans forward and pulls his head- phones away from his ears.

"Hey, listen-up," Rhonda says. "I'm steppin' out for a bit. My sponsor called and she's being a real ball-buster and draggin' me to a meeting tonight. Plus, Troy told me to go take a hike for a while. Him and his friend got some serious business to talk about. They're out back hangin' at the picnic table. Promise me you won't be a little bitch and go bother 'em. Okay?"

Even though he is stoned, Jesse's disdain and hurt still shows in his slitty pink eyes. Rhonda reaches down and plucks the joint from her son's fingers. She takes a quick hit then gives it back to him. "One for the road," she quips. "I need something to get me through a whole fuckin' hour of havin' to listen to that 12 Step, Higher Power bullshit." She does an about-face and says, "Bye!" in a pissy tone as she departs.

Jesse clamps on his headphones. He suddenly feels like crying but fights back the urge and sucks deep on the dwindling tiny nub of weed.

This sucks! Suck! Sucks! Sucks! He mutters.

All through Jesse's young life there had been a lack of

care and respect. During his last foster care placement before returning to live with his mother, he was nicknamed Garth and continuously razed because of his resemblance to the Wayne's World character from the 90's. Many times he thought of getting rid of his shaggy blonde hair and doing something cool like shaving his head but he didn't have the balls. He is tiny and emaciated. Secretly, he yearns to be jacked and be a badass and be popular with the "hoes." But his only motivation has been to scurry around like a mouse and build up his weed stash, escape back to his room, listen to vintage rock, smoke and once in a while play Grand Theft Auto. He had hoped that Troy would have been someone awesome to hang with but it was a bust. Jesse came to the realization that Troy was just stone cold and grimy. Earlier, Jesse had eavesdropped on the stairwell and heard Troy talking to Marco about his mom, saying that he "only fucked the pig to get free rent like a nigger." Internally Jesse felt festering anger and guilt for bringing this guy home to take advantage of his mother even though he knew she was always porkin' bad dudes.

Troy promised we'd be buds and do some wild shit together as soon as we jetted from that cheesy rehab. Now he just blows me off! I can't believe I got played so he could get a crib! I am so dumb! I am a fuckin' Garth!

The Pink Floyd CD finishes and there is a silent vacuum in his headphones.

Bummer.

Jesse feels too stuck-on-stupid to reach over and hit replay. Some time passes. Then there comes a knocking down below on the front door. At first Jesse is unaware of the noise because his hearing is obstructed but then the knocking turns into frantic pounding. A vibration comes up through the floorboards and into the bedroom. Slowly, Jesse pulls off his headphones.

"What the hell?" He says to himself. "Why's King Kong banging at the gate?"

The battering continues. Jesse's first reaction is to just chill and hope the sound would stop. Then there is an outside muffled but enraged voice calling to the answer the door.

Sound's like whoever it is, is really fuckin' buggin'!

A jolt of fear prods Jesse out of his cannabis-induced lethargy. He thinks about going to hide in his overflowing, cluttered closet but then he feels too scared not to obey the angry stranger's demand to open the "F-in' door."

I hope this dude doesn't kick my ass!

Trembling, Jesse gets out of bed and starts putting on his jeans. He had been laying in his underwear and a Led Zeppelin t-shirt. With one foot bare and other clad with a holey white sock, he patters down the stairs with some haste despite all the Mary Jane in his system.

Who the fuck is this?

There is a small crack growing in the old plaster near one the hinges as the door shakes with each blow. Jesse is now in the hallway feeling a mixture of fright and vertigo. With a quivering hand he reaches out for the doorknob but in the next second the door gives way. There is the cracking of wood as some of the molding and part of the doorframe splinters and goes flying.

"WOW!!!" Jesse says.

Michael Farrell comes busting in. He is a man on a mission. Some hours ago, reporters had caught up with him and he vowed publicly on camera that he would personally track down whoever killed his beloved Betty.

"Which one are you?" He yells as he takes his large hand and grabs Jesse by the throat, slamming the kid against the wall and jamming the barrel of a small black revolver against Jesse's forehead. Still wearing the same clothes that he had on since his flight from California,

Farrell's 800-dollar sports jacket is a wrinkled rag and his hand-made tailored pink shirt reeks.

"Hey man, what the fuck!!!!?" Jesse screams.

The gun is a starter's pistol loaded with blanks that Farrell used once at a swim meet. Farrell recently retrieved it from his ex-wife's house. He wished for a real firearm but this was the best he could scrounge up. It is ironic that he is utilizing the starter pistol because it is a keepsake; a memento for that one brief attempt when he tried to coach junior-high athletics and get his daughter involved in something wholesome. The good dad and good daughter thing never worked. They both showed up to swim practice high. Plus there were allegations, that Farrell was stealing peeks at Betty's teammates when they were in the locker-room. Jesse knows nothing about guns and at the present moment truly believes he is on the verge of getting a real bullet in his brain. He tinkles.

"I said which one are you?" Farrell bellows as he digs the barrel harder between the kid's eyes. "Tell me or I'm gonna fuckin' shoot!"

Whimpering, Jesse says his name.

Farrell shouts, "So were you one of the punks that left that drug rehab with my Betty!"

At the moment, Jesse's mind races but then he remembers that crazy chick that was all over Troy and how she mooned one of the counselors when they were bustin' out of the main entrance to the rehab facility.

"Fucking answer me god damn it!" Farrell snarls as he shakes the kid and jabs him hard in the sternum with the starter's pistol.

"Ouch! " Jesse cries. "Okay! Okay! Dude ease up! I saw her. Okay! We just all bolted together! That's all! I swear! It was their idea to leave! I just tagged along!"

Farrell shouts back, "Yea, but were you there when she died in that barn? Were you there, you fucking little creep?"

Whether it is national or local news, Jesse did not have the slightest interest. He could give two shits about CNN, Action News 8, or the New Haven Register. With total sincerity, he is completely clueless about the demise of that wild fat girl with the annoying motor mouth. Flashing a stunned look, Jesse responds with a "W-what?"

Instantly, Farrell becomes more infuriated. "Don't play fuckin' innocent with me! What happened! I know you know! Who ended my baby daughter's life?" With an impulsive reflex, he bangs Jesse on top of the head with the starter's pistol. The kid wails louder and sags to his knees, jabbering, "Please don't kill me! Please don't kill me...."

"Where's your fuckin' buddy, Bennett?" Farrell yells, his face crimson and still holding the kid somewhat upright by a fistful of t-shirt. "Troy Bennett! I heard he was the fuckin' snake that got my daughter to leave that rehab! Where the fuck is he?"

Visibly trembling with terror, Jesse replies, "He's out-outside. In the back!"

"He's here?" Farrell barks. "He's here right now?"

Jesse shook his head yes like a celebrity wobble figurine.

"Where out back?"

"By-by the-the sh-shed," Jesse stutters. He's out smokin' on the picnic table."

"Two birds with one fuckin' stone!" Farrell exclaims. He then let go and Jesse sank completely to the floor. On the verge of giving some punitive stomps to the kid's ribs and face, Farrell holds back. At that moment, Jesse appeared so puny and pathetic, cowering, balled-up in the fetal position.

Exasperated, Farrell asks, "How old are you? Fucking 12? 14?"

Jesse peeps, "I'm 18."

"Yea, right!" Farrell snaps. "Dream-on you little fucking snot. Anyway, you stay put! Don't you dare fucking move! I'm going to check out back! You better not be fucking lying!"

Curling up tighter on the floor, Jesse doesn't say another word. In an enraged bluster, Farrell goes out the front door and starts around to the back of the house. The autumn night air is crisp and cold. Frost-coated dead leaves crunch under foot. It is pitch black except for the scattered glow from nearby homes.

"Need a fucking flashlight!" Farrell mutters to himself. "But nobody is gonna hide from me!"

Early in the afternoon, Farrell snuck on the grounds of the Trinity Grove Rehabilitation Center. He knew that the administration had their strict confidentiality rules and would not give out any information about the other clients' involvement with his daughter. To circumvent the problem, he walked next to the fence near the outdoor smoking section and started tossing wads of twenty-dollar bills over the chain-link. One of the support staff monitors came out to meet Farrell. Flashing another five hundred dollars it was an easy pay-off to get some names and an address. Farrell's next step in his plan was to hunt down the last people that saw his daughter alive and "beat the fuck out of them until he got answers."

"I'll get 'em!" Farrell huffs to himself. In the next second, he bangs his foot and almost trips on a rusted lawnmower that had been left in the back yard.

"Fuck!" he curses.

Suddenly to his left there comes the sound of jostling and creaking. In the dim, there appears to be a figure trying to clamor over some sort of wall. It is Marco.

"Freeze!" Farrell hollers. "Or I'll shoot!"

Troy had already sprinted across the small yard,

completed a quick scramble and made onto the other neighbor's property. Unfortunately for Marco, the right cuff of his black jeans is hung up on one of the pointy tips of the weathered picket fence. "Fuck! Fuck! Fuck!" Marco swears, as he struggles to free his leg and hoist himself over the barrier.

"I said don't move!" Farrell shouts, as he rushes forward with his cap gun.

Even in the darkness, Marco can see that the man is holding some type of weapon. He surmises that it is either a detective or some mob guy looking to revenge Vinny's murder. There is then the sound of ripping material as the jean cuff tears free, causing Marco to fall backwards. With a thud, he lands hard on his butt on the cold damp earth. At that moment Marco is helpless.

"Are you Bennett?" Farrell pants with adrenaline as he towers overhead and points downward with the starters pistol.

Marco's sudden fear instantly triggers a protective surge of rage and he doesn't answer but just growls back like a wolverine caught in a trap.

"Did you hurt my daughter?" Farrell boils.

There comes the thumping of fast strides and more crunching of brown leaves as Troy bounds back into the yard. Charging through the blackness, he begins to hold the Spyderco high in the air in an ice pick grasp. The reason for his return was not out of loyalty but rather to feed his newly found adrenaline-pumping addiction to killing.

"Hey!" Farrell says with alarm. He begins to turn and point the starters pistol at the approaching figure but it is too late to cause any type of halt. There is a glint of steel in the nighttime, ambient illumination. The fully serrated blade comes arching and gouging down through Farrell's sport's jacket, catching him in the shoulder, piercing into the meat of his right deltoid and exiting with a 6-inch ragged laceration out through the back of his arm. Troy almost inadvertently stabs himself in his own thigh as he finishes powering through with the knife. Reflexively, Farrell pulls the trigger to the starter's pistol before dropping it. There is a high-pitched pop that makes Marco flinch as he still sits on the ground. Being juiced with a savage burst of adrenaline, Troy didn't even realize that the gun went off, but rather continues to carve at his victim with the Spyderco.

"GONNA KILL YA!!! DIE FUCKER!!! DIE!!!" Troy screams. Unknowingly, he keeps nicking his own free hand as he attacks with wild slashes and jabs.

With his right arm going numb, Farrell gets diagonally cut across the left palm, sliced twice shallow across the belly, gashed in the chin, and punctured hard and deep in the upper right chest. Like his attacker, he too is full of primitive survival energy, which causes him not to feel the real pain of his wounds.

"Shit!" Troy curses as he unexpectedly loses hold of his knife. In the past second when he had plunged the Spyderco into the man's plural cavity, the blade was briefly obstructed as it glanced off a rib, causing Troy's hand to slip down the handle and catch part of his index finger on the shark-tooth-like serrations. Slick with his own blood as well as his victims, his weapon slipped from his grasp. This gave Farrell the opportunity to fight for his life. Mike is a big man and had played some high school football, so instinctively, he charges forward, head down like a bull wounded by a matador. Troy is tall and lanky and is easily tackled. For a fleeting moment, Farrell has the advantage of being on top in the mounted position. With fury and terror he clamps down on Troy's throat with his left hand and starts to squeeze with all his might. On all fours nearby, Marco is frantically searching the grass for the dropped starters pistol, thinking that it is a real firearm. "Where the fuck is it?" Marco curses.

There on his back, Troy squirms and desperately tries to pry off the tremendous grip that is on the verge of collapsing his trachea. Suddenly the pressure ceases. Farrell rolls sideways and comes to be supine, next to Troy. Even a father's vengeance is no match for rapid blood loss and a collapsing lung.

My God, what's happening to me? Farrell says to himself in a horrified panic. He appears to be frozen with paralyzing fatigue as he desperately wheezes. *It's hard to breathe!!!*

"Found it!" Marco says as he comes up with the starters pistol. Without hesitation, he starts firing at the big man on the ground. There are four quick blank shots then the clicking of spent chambers. Troy gets to his feet but is coughing and holding his bruised throat. He wretches then stammers, "D-d-d ya kill 'em?"

"I think so!" Marco says.

"F-F-F- fucck you!" Farrell blurts out with a spurt of red saliva.

"Shit! He's still alive!" gasps Troy.

"Fuck!" Marco curses. With more emotion then rational thought, he points the gun again and keeps pulling the trigger hoping there would be one leftover live round. After a series of more empty clicks, Marco tosses the gun away in frustration.

"Who's this guy?" Troy asks aloud.

"I don't know! " Marco barks back. "Maybe a cop!?"

From the ground, Farrell proclaims with a wet gurgle, "I'm Betty's – fa-father!"

"Who?" Marco snarls.

"Holy shit!" Troy squawks with surprise, "He said he's the dad of that fat chick we bagged!"

At this moment, Marco becomes more enflamed. He

remembered how that girl had disgusted him and how glad he was to wrap her head in plastic. What made matters worse was that it had to be her father to make him feel a jolt of fear those moments ago when he was caught up there on that fence. *That cunt may have tried to get some more revenge from the grave, but now dear old dad is gonna pay for making me look like some joker!*

"What are we gonna do with him!" Troy jabbers. "He's talking but he ain't moving. He's hurt! I think I stabbed him pretty good. Do you think you shot him some?"

"Who the fuck knows!" Marco says seething with rage. "But let's drag this sucker into the shed!"

A chilly, autumn wind comes blowing across the dark yard creating a miniature twister of dried brown leaves. In the distant, a few houses down, a fat old Rottweiler that was left outside, is barking and straining against its chain, excited by the sounds of the fight. The people in the neighborhood are used to domestics and drug raids. Having their own sins, nobody in the vicinity feels inclined to alert the police even with the crackling of gunfire. Farrell wants to call out for help, but all he can muster is a liquidy, choking whisper. He feels himself being dragged by the legs and has no energy left to resist. Messages of fright flash in his mind.

MY GOD WHAT ARE THEY GOING TO DO TO ME? WHERE ARE THEY TAKING ME? JESUS!!! I THINK I'M GOING TO PASS OUT!!!

"The fucker is heavy!" Troy bitches as he grasps the man under the calf and hauls him along with all his might. Marco has the other leg and is pulling like a sled dog. Leaves and twigs are gathering under Farrell's out-stretched limp arms and his bunched up sport's jacket is getting hung-up and snagged.

"Fuck!" Marco says while straining.

The shed is a few yards away. It is made of corrugated

metal and is pitted with rust. Marco stops his part in dragging Farrell and races forward to open the door. Upon doing so, the door almost comes off on its last hinge. Area kids ransacked the small structure over the years. Not much is left except for an overhead fluorescent track light, old car batteries, empty beer cans and some broken bits of tools.

Troy yells out, "Looks really dark in there."

"Take both legs and just get him in here!" Marco orders. He then feels something brush against his hair. It is the pull chain from the overhead light. Marco yanks on it. One of the fluorescent tubes is blackened and burnt out, but the other has a little bit of life left. There are humming and sizzling sounds as the bulb struggles to come on.

"Almost there!" Troy says as he is on the verge of reaching the entrance to the doorway. Marco rejoins Troy, helping him drag Farrell those last few feet into the shed. At that moment, the overhead fluorescent flashes and washes the small cluttered enclosure in a brutal stark light.

"Wow!" exclaims Troy. "This dude looks pretty fucked!"

There on his back, on the dirty floor, Farrell has a crimson froth seeping from the side of his mouth and out one nostril. Sticky bloody autumn leaves dot his body. The knife is still embedded in his chest. With fading but still intense wild eyes, Farrell looks upward at the hovering silhouetted faces of his two assailants and gargles, "I'll – ge – get-you!"

"Yea, what-ever!" Troy laughs nervously.

Leaning down a bit and seething with malicious vengeance, Marco hisses, "Hey Papa, listen to me! I want you to know something before I off you! Your daughter was begging us to fuck her the night she died. But she was such a fat slut we decided to kill her instead!"

Joining in on the mockery, Troy speaks with evil

anxious glee, "Okay! Okay! It's embarrassing, but I'll admit it! I did bang your hog-of-a-daughter a couple of times when we were in rehab! She did suck cock pretty good but her twat smelled like a can of cat food! But I have to go along with my home-boy here, and say that it was more enjoyable to fuckin' duck-tape her head and stick her with a needle!"

Hearing his tormentor's words, Farrell explodes with one last cry, "B-B-Betty!!!"

Viciously, Marco reaches down and works the handle of the knife, digging about with the blade, attempting to twist it. Finally, yanking it free from between the two rib bones, the suction is lost and Farrell's lung completely collapses. It is lucky for the big man that he finally falls unconscious, because Marco is bent on re-enacting an al-Zarqawi al-Qaeda decapitation. The above hanging florescent light suddenly begins to arc and short circuit.

"I want to cut his mother-fucking head off!" announces Marco.

"Holy fucking Christ!" howls Troy with excitement. "You go boy!!!"

In a frenzy, Marco kneels down and quickly begins sawing away under Farrell's' chin. The knife's locking mechanism had been weakened causing the blade to have a loose fit in the plastic handle but the Spyderco is still able to perform its nasty task. Razor sharp serrations rip through skin, muscle and cartilage. There is a sputtering belch as the windpipe is partially transected. With more gurgling, Farrell's body is racked with involuntary spasms followed by pissing and farting. A bright red spurt shoots up as one of the carotids is cut. For a moment, the overhead light flickers out and the interior of the shed is engulfed in pitch darkness.

"What the fuck!?" curses Troy.

Then the light pops back on, Marco's cheeks have been

speckled with red droplets. A rapid pooling of blood is soaking his black jeans as he continues to knee. Marco resumes his sawing but the blade gets caught up on thick tendons and is stopped by cervical bone. Marco thinks, *What the fuck, those heads came off so easy in those Al Qaeda videos!* Marco's hands are slippery and it is hard to keep hold of the knife handle. He almost slices his own fingers.

In an excited tone, Troy speaks from nearby, "Wait! Wait! I want to try something! I just found this on the floor!" He holds up a 5 lb. rusted sledgehammer. Most of the wooden shaft had been broken off.

"What are you going to do with that?" Marco asks, panting with exertion.

Troy replies. "I got one of these off the floor too!" He shows a 4 inch rusted nail. "There's a bunch of these on the ground! I want to bang one into the dude's skull!

A bit annoyed that he could not complete the beheading, Marco wiggles the knife free from the terrible wound and stands up. His black jeans are soggy with blood. Addressing Troy, he quips, "Go ahead. Knock yourself out."

"This is gonna be so sick!" Troy giggles. "Watch this!" He kneels down where his partner had been sawing away, and attempts to position the nail in the middle of the victim's brow, but his bloody hands are too jittery to get that kind of accuracy. Tapping with the head of the small rusted sledgehammer, the entry point is high to the left on Farrell's skull.

"It's starting to go in!" Troy squeals with delight.

With the cracking of bone, a portion of the nail pierces into the fatty squishy tissue of Farrell's defunct frontal lobe.

Troy yells, "That's for trying to choke me, you fucker!"

Sarcastically, Marco says, "I don't think he can hear

you asshole. He's dead."

"True!" laughs Troy. "But you know how I love to vandalize shit. And these last couple days, I'm getting to like fuckin' around with stiffs." He then abruptly, whacks down hard with the head of the small sledgehammer. The nail is not driven in any farther but rather just bends under into a deformed curl. At this moment, the light goes out again, and everything is black.

This time, both Marco and Troy simultaneously say, "Fuck!"

Outside the freezing night wind returns and a swirl of dead leaves pelt the metal shed. The gust comes through the gaps in the door, howling like a Halloween ghost. The light flickers back on. Troy is squatting down and struggling to lift something up from the floor.

"What you doing now?" asks Marco.

Driven in a maddened urgency, Troy is straining to continue to hold up and cradle one of the old dead car batteries. He is not done playing. With a few labored steps, he works himself over to Farrell's body. "Watch this!" Troy says to Marco with breathy speech.

The fluorescent light begins to falter once more, causing a strobe-like effect in the interior of the shed.

"Bombs away!" Troy shouts.

The heavy block drops almost squarely, on the corpse's face. With a hollow thud, the nose is mashed; the right cheekbone caves in, and the front top row of teeth break off and get stuffed to the back of the dead guy's mouth.

Troy cheers, "Cool!" The car battery slides off the ruined face, with a heavy bump to the wet dark floor. Trying again, Troy heaves up the Die-Hard and drops it a second time on Farrell's head.

And a third.

And a fourth.

On the fifth time, Troy nearly suffers some broken toes

as the battery almost lands on his own foot.

"Good thing I have steel-toed workbooks!" Troy huffs. "This is fuckin' tiring! I'm done now."

The overhead light keeps arcing and flashing. Both Marco and Troy are splattered with blood as well as the walls, ceiling and floor.

"Looks like a fuckin' disco in here with red confetti!" Troy says beaming with his face speckled and dripping. His inner maniac was blossoming.

Marco spat, "So you think this fucker is dead enough!"

"Dude!" Troy laughs, "There is no fucking way Humpty Dumpty is going to be put back together again. I never saw brains before. They're pink and mushy! I thought they would be gray!"

"Yea, whatever," Marco replies in an almost pouting manner. "So much for me taking a nice head as a trophy. Let's get out of here; that light is giving me a fucking migraine."

"But hey, bro!" Troy says in an insane, rejoicing tone, "This is our seventh kill! Can you believe it? We're the real deal? I have to admit I was scared shitless that first-time back in the barn. I apologize for being such a pussy, but now!!! Dude, I love the blood! I love breaking and busting people apart like toys! I AM SO HIGH RIGHT NOW!!!"

Cast for a moment in one of the florescent flashes, face sanguine streaked, Marco suddenly gives one of his hideous smiles and nods in agreement.

7:35 p.m. Inside the house, Jesse chose to hide in his mother's upstairs' closet. To him, it seems a bit safer because he is aware that they know the location of his bedroom. Crouching in the corner, he had pulled down a bunch of clothing from the hangers, and is now under a heap of sweatshirts and jeans. Some time ago, he had peaked out the window into the night and witnessed Troy and his friend dragging that guy across the back lawn. He also saw that eerie light pulsating out from around the shed's door.

Oh God, I know they're coming for me next!

Uncontrollably trembling, Jesse tries to stay still but fails. His bare foot comes against something on the floor of the closet. There is a buzzing sound as it is activated.

Fuck! What is it?

The object is his mom's 10-inch pink vibrator.

Twenty-Two

Friday, 5:10 a.m. Dr. Fray suddenly awakes from a nightmare. Sweating and heart thumping, by reflex he reaches out to hug his girlfriend. Her warm, comforting body is not there.

Where are you? Peter panics in his mind.

Shaking away the fog between sleep and full consciousness, he then remembers that she has gone away for a few days to visit her family in Portland, Oregon. Outside his bedroom window, that bitter autumn wind is calling. Peter shudders, alone in his bed in the predawn darkness.

What the hell was I dreaming about?

He tries to remember the actual content of the nightmare but all that he can identify is a lingering feeling of pending doom.

My God, I feel awful!

Tears begin to roll down his cheeks.

Friday, 4:10 pm. Inside the third floor men's bathroom of the On Point Manufacturing Company, Paul Kosakowski had just punched a fist-sized dent in a stall door. An hour ago, 18 full time machinists had been called into the main conference area and informed of a layoff. Their jobs had been cut due to the fallout of the assault rifle ban in Connecticut. Paul had worked for the company for 12 years, which specializes in the fabrication of cheap A.R. parts. Shreds of his pink slip and severance benefit package are scattered about the tiled floor. For a moment, he pauses and sees the reflection of his angry face in the bathroom mirror.

"AAAAAGGGGERRRRR!!!!!" He throws another reverse punch and his image becomes distorted as the mirror spider-glasses.

"AAAAAARRRRRGGGGRRRRRRRR......!!!!!!!!"

Next, he attempts to pull the bathroom sink out of the wall.

Twenty-Three

Friday, 9:41 p.m. The chilling October wind is now joined with a driving downpour. Marco listens to the angry weather as he lies on his back on the motel room bed. The name of the place is the Debonair Motor Lodge. Before sun up this morning, he had Troy drop him off out front. He also made Troy promise that he would go ditch the Camry, Farrell's rental vehicle. Troy had given a thumb's up as he sped away. The vehicle's light blue cloth upholstery had been stained with dark maroon smears.

When first arriving in that pre-dawn hour, Marco, caked with dried blood, walked into the register's office and flashed some hundred dollar bills to the Indian clerk behind the bulletproof glass and got a room key with no questions asked. Marco had chosen the Berlin Turnpike because of its fucked-up reputation. It still has left a few 1950-ish style tiny old motels, which imbue a nostalgic sleaze. They are the kind of places where married car salesmen screw their secretaries, swingers and S&Mers have orgies, and the hopeless rent rooms and commit suicide. The area is also a haven for criminals on the run that need a little breather.

Fuck, I wish I could get some sleep!

Usually the sound of rain would put Marco under but his racing mind would not shut off. He had not slept since Wednesday. For most of Friday, he spent hours staring at the TV, at times falling into a dissociative trance. The satellite service had gone off a half an hour ago due to the bad weather. He has lost the ability to distract himself and there seems to be even a greater flood of adrenaline in his veins as he obsesses for the zillionth time on all the recent madness and the pending ramifications.

How long will it be before that door blows in and I'm swarmed by fucking cops? My luck has to run out soon. I know I should have never trusted Troy enough to hide out with that whore and her son. That fucking little stoner must have ratted us out to the police by now. And how the hell did that whacked-out Charles Bronson wanna-be know we were there? Christ!

Last night, after butchering Farrell, they went back in and searched the house, wanting no witnesses and bent on killing Jesse. They missed checking the upstairs' closet; they had assumed that the kid high-tailed-it down the street.

At the present moment, the only thing Marco is grateful for is that he finally split from Troy. The whole rationale that they should be solo for a while to throw off the authorities was debated. Marco was lying through his teeth when he said that they would meet up in a couple of days to make a new plan.

The rain batters the outside of the motel room.

Never gonna see that asshole again! Marco seethes. *Troy is such a fuckin' spaz, he's probably already in fucking lock-up. I know he thinks he saved my life. So fucking embarrassing! I refuse to owe anybody shit, especially a fucking knucklehead like him. Troy's getting real good at harming people. He gets off on the blood. Never thought the punk-ass had it in him. He can turn on me. It's going to be a one-man show from now on!*

The rain and wind grow louder.

What to do next? Marco perseverates. *I know I need to get my fucking suitcase!*

Going to his Aunt Gina's place to get his stash was attempted yesterday afternoon around 1:30, but Marco got spooked when he saw a large white SUV parked out front. A wad of cash, close to two thousand dollars, is squirreled away in the drug-laden suitcase.

I need to get back in that house and get that suitcase! That cash and that product, that's all I got. But who the fuck was that waiting outside in that mother-fucking Escalade? Undercover cops don't have Cadillac's. That greaser, Vinny, was such a pussy but maybe he really was connected with the mob. They were probably hunting for that fucking lottery ticket! Shit! How the fuck did they know where to track me?

Not having the protection of his lucky suitcase ratcheted-up the prospect of doom. His mind switched channels and he obsessed again about being caught up there on that picket fence, so helpless.

I easily could have gotten shot to fuckin' pieces! It's so fuckin' lame that Troy had to come and rescue my sorry ass!

Feeling what it was like to be prey rather than predator makes Marco shudder.

I can't be making no more fucking mistakes! No more fucking slip-ups! Never again! No more..."

With ever growing paranoia and fear, Marco suddenly bolts from the bed and peeks out the side window through a gap in the blinds. Beads of rain and wet brown leaves obscure the glass. Most of the motel parking lot is dark except for the pale murky glow in the distance from one solitary lamppost. It is hard to count the cars. Wearing only his black t-shirt, a shiver runs up Marco's spine, his penis turtles-up and he feels even more vulnerable.

I'm only staying one night in this fucking place. I got to keep moving. Fuckers could be out there in that parking lot right now, fucking watching and waiting! Tomorrow, I'll sneak back into New Haven and try again to get my suitcase. Then I'll split from this fucking state for goddamn good!

Quickly turning away from the window, he goes into the small bathroom to put back on his underwear and black jeans that had been placed on the radiator to dry. Earlier, he had attempted to wash-up by using the sink. When ringing-out his clothes the water turned brown with all the blood and old piss. Even though he scrubbed himself hard, coagulated flakes remained here and there on his body, in his hair, and he has dried gore embedded under his fingernails. There was no way he would bathe in a regular manner and utilize the shower stall because outside sound would be drowned-out by the running water.

I won't be able to hear' em comin'!

Catching his reflection in the small bathroom mirror, he sees the tattoo of Kali on his chest is no longer indigo blue but rather black. The goddess's glaring three eyes appear more pronounced and ferocious with her new dark face.

Marco pauses and asks aloud, "Fuck, did all that blood on me stain my tattoo black?" He then curses aloud again as he dresses and feels wet coldness on his goose-bump-skin. His underwear and black jeans are still part damp and part soggy.

Whoever comes busting through that door and catches me bare ass, can easily go for my balls! I'll wear these fucking wet clothes! Fuck it! Nobody is going to cut off my nuts.

With revving agitation, he tries the TV again but there is no luck.

"Mother-Fucker!"

Marco's blood shot eyes dart about the small dismal room. There are sudden sensations of claustrophobia.

I've been cooped-up in this fucking place all day and almost all night.

Like a rat conditioned to press a pedal, Marco checks the chain lock on the door and peers out again through the blinds into the dark storminess of the parking lot.

I can't tell if any new vehicles rolled in! I got to re-think things! Maybe they can easily get me in here as easily as they can get me out there! And there ain't no back door in this fucking motel room. I would have to bust out that little window in the bathroom. But what if I got stuck! Shit!

Memories of being caught up on the fence flash again in Marco's mind and he shakes.

Fuck! I can't take this! I got to chance it! I got to get out of here! I'm fucking losing it!

Across from the Debonair in a strip club called Venus Ten. Marco saw it when he first arrived in the morning.

I'll go to the titty bar. Hide in the crowd! I'll fucking do that!

Impulsively, he searches for his blood stained black Converse high-top sneakers and with jittery hands, laces up. Putting on his long black coat, he then scoops up the room-key and shoves it in his pocket. As he reaches for the doorknob, there is a sudden jolt of apprehension.

Marco freezes.

What if they're waiting for me right now, right outside?

There is the sound of his pounding heartbeat in his ears.

"Ah, fuck it!" Marco says aloud and he undoes the bolt chain and swings open the door, expecting pulsing red and blue lights from cop cars or the crack of a gunshot from a hit man.

Come and get me cocksuckers!

There is no living soul in the parking lot but nature does attack.

"Jesus! Wow!"

Marco is slashed with rain and blasting wind. He is chilled to the core as his damp clothes became saturated. Grasping his coat around his body, he struggles as he closes and locks his motel room door. From an aerial view, he is a tiny frantic black figure scampering close to the empty parked cars then quickly zigzagging across the open lot before sprinting across the street and making it into the strip bar.

Sitting in the front vestibule on a stool, the doorman at the Venus Ten is an aging three-hundred-pound biker with a ponytail and a Fu-Manchu mustache. Giving a suspicious once-over, he says to Marco in a rough tone, "What, you don't believe in fuckin' umbrellas?"

Clutching himself and shivering Marco doesn't answer but just seeks warmth.

The bouncer says, "There ain't no cover tonight but make sure ya order something or else you gotta go." He then gestures for Marco to proceed in.

Quickly walking past the biker with squishy wet sneakers, Marco is grateful that he did not have to show any I.D. After going down a small dim hallway, he then enters the main part of the club.

"What the hell?" Marco mumbles to himself.

The place is empty except for a few truckdrivers and a guy with Down's Syndrome and his elderly brother sitting by the stage. A bored female bartender is reading the newspaper.

There's no crowd to hide in. worries Marco. *Hard to keep a low profile!* He nervously scans about. *I can't stay here long!*

On stage is a not-too-young, tall, chunky dancer with a curly red wig and sagging utters. Swaying a bit on the chrome pole, she seems preoccupied and lackluster. She ignores the retarded guy that is waving and trying to get her attention. An hour ago he had used up his six bucks, and she is no longer in the mood in giving him free gawks at her pussy and hemorrhoids.

Marco chooses to sit in the far corner of the stage where there is an exit door. The bartender comes over and he orders a soda. There is no way he is going to drink alcohol. He fears getting drunk and letting his guard down. Tasting the sweet beverage, he suddenly feels a little nauseous. Next comes hunger pangs, and Marco realizes that he has not eaten for almost a full day.

I'm fucking starving!

Over on one of the empty cocktail tables is a half basket of stale peanuts. Marco goes over, snags it and returns to his wet seat. As he greedily shoves the snacks into his mouth, the dancers switch up along with the music. The song Waterfalls by the pop group TLC comes droning through the club's sound system. Flat chested and thin to the point that ribs could be counted, a young black girl stumbles out on stage with bright silver super high platform shoes. She is wearing a cheesy Halloween witch's hat and a small cobweb mesh veil. Large gold-plated hoops hang from each of her earlobes. Making her rounds over to the disinterested truck drivers she does her simulated masturbation routine and picks up a single crumbled dollar bill for her efforts. Knowing to avoid the retarded guy and his white haired brother, she approaches Marco as her last resort.

"Boo," she says with an artificial smile. "Happy Halloween, sweetie pie! My name's Joy. And I'm a naughty witch. Do ya wanna see how naughty I's can be?"

Chewing the last of the snacks, Marco glares up at her with his hostile, dark little eyes, bits of peanuts stuck in his goatee, and his soaked straggly black hair hanging down around his face.

Lordy! Joy thinks to herself. *Dis muthafucker looks evil!*

Marco takes another gulp of cola then sneers "Get lost. I don't like niggers."

Momentarily taken aback, Joy then feels a swell of indignation and has the urge to spit into the customer's face but she keeps it cool. A small stack of cash is by Marco's elbow. Earlier, he had paid for his drink with a fifty-dollar bill and was given change in the form of a twenty and a bunch of singles. Joy had spotted that money -like a vulture coming across road kill. She keeps smiling, which barely masks her hatred, but she is on a mission. Having a hardcore crack-cocaine habit, she once told herself that she would blow every fucker in a Klan rally so long as she got paid.

"Oh, c'mon darling," Joy pouts. "Can't we alls just get along?"

Stiffening in his chair, Marco nervously sucks his teeth.

"Take a look at dis trick," Joy coos, as she lies on her back and spreads her long, ebony bony legs, the big silver shoes hanging off her feet. Pulling her G-string to the side, she makes snapping and popping sounds as she works the muscles of her vagina.

Marco finds himself watching with some mild fascination. It is like discovering a dying jellyfish on the beach. It is also a welcomed diversion to briefly block all the repeating paranoid thoughts in his head.

With a fake moan of desire, Joy says, "A coochie dat talented you knows is gotta rock your world."

Marco flips her a five-dollar bill and she instantly sits up and comes a bit over the small rail in an attempt to rub her small tits in his face. Reflexively, Marco shoves her back with his left hand while his right hand goes into his coat pocket to grasp the Spyderco. She almost falls on her butt.

"Chill baby!" Joy gasps, doing her best not to flip out

and rake his face with her long, artificial metallic blue fingernails. "I's just wanted to say thank ya. Dat's all."

Extremely atypical for Marco, he mumbles the word, "Sorry."

She scoffed up the bills and thinks, *I's bet he's buggin' cause he's usin'!* Joy then asks in a hushed voice, "Hey, do youse get high?"

"Why you ask?" Marco says with a squint.

"Cause we can go party! Dis place is whacked! I ain't stayin'. Da crowd and da money ain't here tonight!"

The idea of returning alone to that motel room filled Marco with dread. Having another person around to help pass those hours before dawn seemed like a sudden blessing.

"Youse got da funds?" Joy asks with building excitement in her voice. The danger of picking up a stranger was all part of the rush. In her tragic young life, she had been raped twice and battered numerous times by johns. Hooking up with some creepy white boy would be just another part of her death wish. Deep in the limbic area of her brain, dopamine is starting to be released causing a building craving to get her smoke-on.

Marco pauses. With his mind racing he attempts to question his judgment and weigh his options. *Should I trust a fucking junky stripper? What am I getting myself into? Women are always fucking trouble! You know that! But on the other hand, whoever the fuck is after me is probably looking for two dudes, not a guy and a female. I could use her as a cover. Plus, I'm going to go fucking over the edge if I spend one more fucking minute alone in that fucking motel room!*

Repeating herself Joy presses, "I says, you got da funds, baby? "

"I'm staying across the way at that shit-hole the Deba-n-or-something. And I got some change. But if you're

237

planning to call up some gangsta porch-monkeys to roll me and get my cash, I'll make sure you don't live long."

Experiencing a jolt of fear as she sees the conviction in Marco's eyes, Joy gives a shaky smile and replies, "No, baby, no. Youse can relax. I's don't want no drama. Youse just let me come to youse room and my pussy will make your dick feel like it's in heaven. All I's want is some bills to go score some rock, dat's all."

180.00 dollars in cash is left. It is money that had been rifled from Farrell's wallet after he was butchered to death. There are also credit cards, but Marco knows the risk of using them.

"Okay," Marco says with one of his sudden ugly smiles. "I'm in room 21." He then thinks to himself, *I don't plan to pay this bitch much!*

Across the way, sitting on the opposite side of the stage, the retarded guy is still waving his arms around in frustration.

Twenty-Four

Friday, 11:40 p.m. The storm is still raging and it is almost witching hour. Marco gets soaked again as he sprints through the downpour. Making it back to the motel room, he peels off his dripping long coat. Shivering and clutching himself, he paces about in apprehension. He starts to have second thoughts about hooking-up with the stripper.

I know this is a fucking bad idea! What was I thinking? Fuck! Fuck! Fuck....

At that moment there comes the sound of rapid knocking. Then from outside there is the muffled cry of Joy's voice. "Quick! Open da fuck up!"

Against the warnings in his head, Marco finds himself undoing the chain bolt and turning the knob. The door flies open and there is a freezing wet bluster as Joy struggles in.

"Goddamn!" she curses, "It's like muthafuckin' Katrina out there!"

Dressed only in a little denim jean outfit and clutching an oversized handbag, Joy is also sopping and chilled to the bone but her hunger to hit that pipe would have made her chance going through a nuclear fallout. Taking a few cautionary steps back after re-bolting the door, Marco looks and sees how the girl is so wired and Jonezin'.

"I's hope you weren't waitin' long, baby?" Joy says with pressured speech. "I's wanted to leave with youse, but dat cracker dat owns da club was being all threatenin' and nasty. Bye, I says, he can go fuck himself and his empty

239

mutherfuckin' cash registers. He's don't knows talent when he sees it! I's go dance someplace else. It don't matters to me! But anyway, baby, enough about my situation! How's about we gets out of dese mutherfuckin' wet clothes and jump in bed and get our groove on. Then youse show me some financial appreciation and I's split and gets what I's really need. All I'm askin' for is two hundred dollars, right? Youse straight with dat?"

Giving a slow nod of agreement, Marco thinks to himself, *This crackhead bitch is so revved that I could toss her fifty dollars and she be out that door like lightening with not the slightest hesitation. But this is not what I planned.* Sounding oddly needy, Marco asks aloud, "Aren't you going to hang around for a while?"

Stepping forward with a desperate wavering grin, Joy replies, "Baby, if youse got da Benjamin's, we's could calls for room service and have some rock or some really fine blow delivered as we's speak. I's knows a nigger who can be right over quicker then mutherfuckin' Domino's. And it mays be rainin' outside but it could be snowin' in here all mutherfuckin' night!"

"I don't know," Marco mutters and in his head he curses himself. *I'm such a fucking fool! This is definitely not the plan! I ain't having any other fucking homey coming here to be in the mix!*

"Maybe a little taste of dis may change your mind, baby." Joy presses up against Marco and with rushing hands starts to tug at his clothes in an attempt to undress him. "Youse pays Mama what she wants, and I'll suck it, fuck it, lick it! Youse understand? I's do anythin'!" She pops the top button of his jeans and yanks down his zipper.

"Woa!" Marco gasps with some surprise and reflexively his body responds. Her rough grip worked his instant hard-on that had sprung out of the flap of his damp, stained underwear. Then he feels her mouth and his balls being cupped as she kneels before him on the rug.

"I'm gonna blow my load!" Marco grimaces.

Instantly, Joy stops and scolds "Hold it, sucker! Youse can't be dat quick!" Standing up, she shoves Marco in the center of the chest and he plops back on the bed. "Now gets those draws off alls da way!" she orders. "Gonna put a jimmie on dat skinny white dick!"

Offended but at the same time really turned-on, Marco kicks off his sneakers and clumsily fights to pull off his soggy black jeans which got caught around one of his ankles. Joy had gone over to her big handbag to dig for some rubbers. Returning next to the bed, she strips bare. Marco is now on his back, naked from the waist down but still wearing his black t-shirt and his tattered, dirty gray socks.

"Just youse remember Crisco, I ain't no skanky ho!" Joy says with breathy hostility, "Use gonna get da pussy of a Nubian princess! And youse better have dat two hundred dollars!" With a snarl she bits and tears open the package to the Trojan with her teeth. Spitting out a piece of plastic wrapper, she takes hold of Marco's painfully rigid slim cock and slips on the condom. Marco works off his t-shirt. Next, she goes for the dominated mounted position. Looking up into her fevered face, Marco sees the loathing and mania in her wild eyes. He also notices that she still has on her large gold electro-plated loop earrings. Rainwater beads her tight cornrows.

Joy looks down at Marco's scrawny milk white chest and the black image of Kali. She exclaims, "That tattoo looks evil! Are youse a mutherfuckin' devil-worshipper?"

"Ignore it!" snarls Marco, "And get to work!"

"Feel dis, white boy!" Joy hisses as she reaches below herself to guide in his sheathed penis. "Youse like dat? Tell me dat ain't da smoothiest, firmiest pussy youse ever had?"

Marco moans. She rides him while tightening and loosening the muscles of her vagina. His hands come to her sides and he feels prominent rib bones under her taunt clammy skin.

"Dat nice? For real, ain't it?" Joy pants. "Black pussy dat good wills make youse change your racist mind."

On the verge of coming, Marco suddenly gets a whiff of a foul smell. It is part sweet, combined with something heavy and sour. The stench causes him to have a flashback of Marsha in the barn and how he tasted her piss as she died. Instantly, he starts to lose his erection.

Joy keeps thrusting and grinding her hips while she purrs, "We's could do dis all fuckin' night, if youse let me call on my cell phone to gets some powder. Wha youse say, honey child?"

The odor is getting stronger and stronger. An extremely high bacteria count is in Joy's vaginal secretions. Marco grimaces and thinks, *she stinks like fucking rotten hamburger!*

Feeling Marco's disappearing erection, Joy rises up a bit and starts riding and pounding harder. There are loud pussy-farts and moist smacking sounds. "Where's youse goin', baby?" Joy asks, "Youse need it faster! Rubber too tight?" His half limp member slips out of her vagina, and he almost suffers a rupture as she thrusts down forcefully with her hips.

"Ouch! Enough! Stop! Get the fuck off!" Marco yells as he bends up forward and shoves with all his might. Falling backwards and to the left, Joy almost goes off the side of the mattress.

"Why youse buggin?" Joy shouts.

Marco looks down at his crotch and sees that he is slick with bright red menstrual blood mixed with yeasty-yellow discharge. The condom is missing from his retracted penis.

"You're fucking raggin' and you reek!" Marco hollers with disgust.

"Sssshit," Joy curses as she stands up near the bed and reaches up inside herself to finger-out the lost rubber. Fishing it out and flicking it away, the bloody condom makes a wet splat as it sticks to the motel room wall.

"Fucking leave now!" roars Marco as he frantically wipes his genitals and pubic hair with a portion of the bedspread.

"Ya, I's will go, faggot!" growls Joy. "But I's still gettin' paid!" She quickly reaches down to Marco's crumbled wet jeans and finds the wad of cash.

"Don't even think about it bitch!" Marco threatens as he springs forward with a clenched fist.

Like a wild cat, Joy viciously lashes out and rakes Marco's bare chest with her long artificial metallic blue fingernails. She also attempts to knee him in his bare dangling balls.

"OWWW! FUCK!" Marco screams as he buckled. His chest feels like it was on fire. Blood runs down from two deep scratches across the tattoo of Kali.

Totally naked but still grasping the money, Joy makes a b-line for the door. Furious, Marco quickly regains himself and does a dash to his long coat that is draped over a chair. Inside one of the pockets is the Spyderco. Almost making it out, Joy twists the doorknob and pushes forward but the chain bolt is still on. There is a blast of freezing wind through the partially open door.

"Lord, help me!" she cries. Her shaking hand with the broken fingernails goes to undo the latch. In the next second, with an ungraceful, long, lunging thrust, the knife gets her in the lower back, puncturing a kidney. An area rich with nerve endings, the searing pain is immense and instantly crippling. Muscle fibers constrict, making a tight seal around a segment of the penetrating steel. Silent screaming follows a gasp as her knees give way and she slides down the inside of the door. Crouching, Marco saws and twists about with the Spyderco, nicking a bit of her vena cava. Yanking the knife free with a spray of red droplets, Marco has not noticed that his own hand was cut from forward slippage when he made the initial stab. Frenzied, he goes back to work with downward pokes and slashes. Quivering with spasms and going into shock, Joy offers no real defense accept a brief rising of her right arm that is promptly lacerated about the triceps, elbow and wrist. Her other hand is still cupping the horrible ragged slit in her lower back. The weakened lock of the Spyderco gives way as the chipped tip of the knife is jabbed into her hard skull. The shark-teeth-like serrations close on Marco's fingers. This time he notices the stimuli of his own cut flesh.

"Fuck! Ouch!" he curses. Quickly, he resets the blade and places the knife under his victim's chin. With vengeful insanity he gloats, "I'm going to cut your head off! I'm going to get my trophy this time!"

There is mercy for Joy Washington because she cannot comprehend her killer's words. She has drifted to that blissful dissociative state right before death. There is no more terror and agony but just a beautiful, clean memory. It is a time before the molestation started. It is a time way before all the drugs. She is five-year's old singing in her Aunt's Baptist choir in North Carolina. A breeze comes through church doors. There is the fresh scent of farmland.

Twenty-Five

Saturday, 7:05 a.m. The remnants of the tropical storm that claimed 18 lives in Cuba had finished its deluge through New England and had moved off shore into the far northern Atlantic. A dawning bright blue autumn sky has returned. Bits of broken branches and soggy fall leaves cover the parking lot of the Debonair. Inside room 21, bright golden sunlight beams through slits in the drawn blinds. Lying flat, supine on the bed, slowly, Marco's eyelids begin to twitch as he proceeds to come out of his slumber. The bad meat stench is even more pungent.

"Fuck," he mutters as he stirs, feeling a throbbing in his cut hand and sharp tenderness from his scratched chest. While stretching out his legs, his bare foot brushes up against something. It is both sticky and hard. Popping fully awake, Marco looks down at the end of the bed and gasps.

"Wow! Jesus!" He says with a startle.

Staring back, Joy's severed head is nested in dark red soaked sheets; one of the large gold plated earrings is still attached to an ear. Both eyes are dull and at half-mast. Her lax jaw creates a sad frown. There is seepage from both her nostrils. Reflexively, Marco kicks out, and the head topples off the bed, thuds, and rolls a short distant on the carpet.

"What the hell!" Marco shakes his own head with some amazement. "Can't fucking believe I slept with that!" As he goes to sit up, he then notices that his entire naked body is smeared and streaked with maroon and brown dried blood. It is as if he is wearing war paint. The inner

245

door and almost all walls of the small motel room are marred with coagulated spatter.

Man, I sure went to town on this bitch! But, I don't fucking remember all of it! I most have gone bat-shit, diced and sliced, then finally passed out! It's like if I smoked fucking Dust and went fucking berserk! I know I have been up straight for too many fucking days! Must have really tweaked! I don't even know what time it is? Fuck! I got to get out of here!

With alarm, he bounds up, but again feels that quick burning sensation near his left nipple. Touching the area, he discovers that one of Joy's artificial metallic blue fingernails is imbedded in his chest. The fingernail is stuck in near the hand of Kali holding the severed head of the demon Raktabija. According to Hindu belief whenever someone tried to kill Raktabija, more demons would spring forth from every drop of its spilled vile blood.

"Shit! Ouch! Fuck!" Marco curses as he pulls out the blue fingernail. There are many other small open wounds and deep scratches on his arms and torso. Being awash with Joy's blood, Marco pauses for a moment and thinks *I hope this fucking ho didn't have anything! Bad enough the rubber came off while she was on the fucking rag.*

Unlucky for Marco it is already too late. While he slept after his frenzied butchering, the Human-Immunodeficiency-Virus was replicating and replicating,

replicating

replicating...

At this moment, it is continuing to spread through his neuro-tissue and other cells. Unknowingly to Joy, she had picked up HIV approximately 2 months ago from unprotected anal sex with a john-on-the-down-low. Her viral load had been very high and she had recently lost a lot of weight. However, Marco's infection occurred not through his urethra but by way of the gashes on his fingers. Last night, as he sawed and worked the knife through her cervical spine there was again a lot more slippage and he kept cutting and nicking himself again and again. His hands had dripped pure bright red with HIV enriched blood from transected enlarged lymph nodes.

Marco shudders for a moment, as he remembers how his junkie mother died of AIDS.

Fuck it! Can't worry about that now!

Suddenly, from outside there is a muffled racket. The motel owner's family is cleaning the debris from the parking lot. Rushing to the window, and peeking out through the blinds, Marco sees Indian teenagers sweeping leaves and picking up twigs and tree limbs. An elderly woman in a sari is pushing a cleaning cart.

"GOT TO GO!" Marco says in a panic. "THE FUCKING DOT HEADS ARE UP!"

In a desperate haste, he finds his black soiled jeans and t-shirt and quickly gets dressed. He swears more, as he has to search a minute to find his soaked Converse sneakers. Marco pauses to wipe his face with a clean part of the bedspread and to bandage his hurt hand with a sock. Unintentionally, he bumps the remote control and the TV pops on without warning. Satellite service is up and running.

With jumpy fright, Marco yelps, "FUCK!"

The happy banter of Good Morning America fills the room. A vertical dried drip of blood obscures a bit of the television screen. Marco then sees Joy's pocketbook by the base of the RCA. Quickly, he forages through it and finds her cell phone. He then gets on his damp coat. Exasperated, he knows there is no way he can leave through the front door without being seen.

I got to chance crawling out that window in the shitter! Fuck!

Moving into the motel room bathroom, Marco

instantly gags and fights hard not to hurl. The stink is powerful and maggot retching. There is a lot more congealing blood but it is mixed with large amounts of loose stool and diarrhea. Joy's headless corpse is in the bathtub, with one of her legs hanging over the side. The Spyderco knife had been left crammed down into a segment of exposed esophagus. Marco slips on the body fluids that had pooled on the dirty tile floor and falls into the tub. For a frantic moment he is partially on top of the squishy body. Catching himself and crawling upward, he stumbles out of the tub, and screams, "ICK!!! A fresh red smear is on his cheek.

Suddenly there comes a jabbing, sharp pain where Joy had scratched his chest before she died. Unfortunately for Marco he had never cared to understand the meaning of his tattoo. Kali is a destroyer of the wicked. Lord Shiva often has to control her vengeful wrath by posing as a corpse. Whenever Kali trips on the body of her fellow deity, it signals her to halt her rampage. Tragically, when Marco tripped on the body of Joy, there is no awakening or stopping of the carnage.

The rattling of the cleaning cart pushed by the old Indian woman from Varanasi is sounding closer out front. Marco rubs his chest for a second then spies the small window above the toilet. Dropping the lid on the bowl, he hops on top, reaches above and frantically works the window latch. It was painted shut. Instantly, fresh crisp air wafts in as he punches out the glass with his hurt hand. Glass shards clink and bounce about. Heaving himself up, he struggles and wiggles.

FUCK, I DON'T WANT TO GET STUCK! FUCK! MOTHERFUCKER, FUCK....!!!

His body is half out, his legs are pumping, and his bloody Converse sneakers leave partial footprints on part of the bathroom wall as he tries to find some traction to push. Out front there is a knock at the door. The old Indian lady can hear the TV. It is on very load. She is not sure if she heard something break inside. She calls out, "Housekeeping! May I come in?"

In the nick of time, Marco squeezes out through the small window like some monstrous little birth.

Twenty-Six

Saturday, 10:40 a.m. Frank cursed old Miss Ferraro for heaving up that garage door and saving his life. Having been rushed by ambulance to St. Rose's E.R., he was placed in intensive care and given 100% pure oxygen to counteract the carbon monoxide in his bloodstream. Once medically stabilized, he was then transferred against his wishes to the hospital's adult inpatient psychiatric unit. The social worker explained to him that he is on a Physician's Emergency Certificate, meaning that the doctor has the right to hold him up to 15 days to determine if he is still a danger to himself.

St. Rose's Behavioral Health unit is an 18 bed locked ward and its general purpose is to provide stabilization and therapy for clients with a wide variety of psychiatric issues. Those with schizophrenia or bi-polar disorder are often admitted to get their anti-psychotics or mood stabilizers readjusted. Waves and waves of human beings in the depths of depression and addiction are common parts of the mix. All walks of life are served here. The gamut could run from a homeless gent found waltzing in traffic and talking to aliens, to a Yale student that slashes her wrists after a bad break-up with her boyfriend, to an insurance salesman with a cocaine problem crashing down from a manic high.

To offer a state of calm, the walls of the unit are painted a soft light blue. There is a TV lounge and day area where group counseling and recreational therapy is offered. Square in the middle of the floor is a nurse's station. It is enclosed in thick protective glass, offering a place of safety for staff in the event a patient gets too uppity.

In an adjacent hallway, there are the patient rooms where Frank is at this very moment. He chose to stay in his bed and not go out in the common areas with all the others. Cocooned in the blankets and moving in and out of a stoned semi-conscious twilight, he wants more Ativan and sleep medication but the nurse denies his request and threatens to lock him out of his room if he continues to isolate himself and not open-up about his stressors. The only thing Frank is grateful for is that he has the right to refuse contact with his family. Voluntarily, he had signed the visitor restriction form. Being a little more lucid, his ruminating thoughts return.

There's no way I can face my sister or my aunt. It won't happen. Never. As soon as I leave here I'm going to go for it again. I'll do it right away before anybody lays eyes on me. If they won't let me go, I'll stay in this friggin' bed until I get the energy to hang myself with a sheet! I wish I could do it now but those pills they give me make me so lazy and groggy. I like 'em. Numbs ya a bit. I want more but now they're gettin' stingy with me like I'm some sorta addict. Pills are sure nice. I wish I could O.D. on 'em. Sleep and just don't wake up. Vinny, are ya listenin'? Did ya make it to heaven? Did ya?

Frank's roommate is a young large, tall white male that keeps pressing Styrofoam coffee cups against his mangled-cauliflower ears in an attempt to keep out the voices. A seeping bandage covers the black stitched infected wound on his left chest. Every so often, Frank's roommate starts babbling and mumbling a series of numbers.

"27, 28, 30, 31, 35, 37"
"27, 28, 30, 31, 35, 37"

"27, 28, 30, 31, 35, 37"

Oh God, that big crazy kid is startin' to recite them numbers again, Frank thinks as he cowers; wrapping the blankets tighter around his body and pretending to be asleep. In the next second, there comes a voice different than his roommate's numerical jabbering. Frank recognizes it in a flash. *Oh no, not her! She's back!*

In the doorway is the social worker, Mrs. Tilly. She is a large, rotund Afro-American woman in her late fifties. Since his arrival to the hospital, she and the attending psychiatrist have been badgering him with questions about his suicide attempt. Frank knew he was causing them a lot of grief because he kept falsely claiming a lapse in memory and that it was too painful to talk because of the burn on his throat.

With a curt command, the social worker calls out, "Mr. Miranda, can you please remove yourself from that bed and come with me, sir."

Frank brings part of the blanket over his head.

"Mr. Miranda!" scolds the social worker. "This is no way to help yourself! I'll say it again, please come with me sir!"

"Jesus," Frank curses. He knows by her tone that this time she means business. *I don't wanna say nothin'! I don't know why I gotta obey her!* But slowly, he pulls the cover down away from his face. *This time around I'm gonna be tough. I'm gonna demand that she release me from this loony bin!*

The Percocet works well when he is still, but as he sits up nothing could fully dull all the agony. A bulky sterile bandage is around his neck. Special dermal patches are taped here and there on his buttocks, thighs and scrotum to address the multiple second and third degree burns from Blaisdale's Zippo. Frank's left hand is still a black and blue swollen mess.

"That's it, Mr. Miranda," Mrs. Tilly coaxes from the doorway. "I can see you are hurting and I thank you for trying."

With a groan Frank rises from the bed, and starts forward with a shuffling gait. His blue Johnny coat is partially opened in the back, exposing some of the injuries on his ass cheeks. Fresh pain suddenly zaps away most of his grogginess.

"Good, Mr. Miranda," says the social worker. "Follow me and we will go speak in private."

Making sure not to make eye contact with anyone in the hallway, Frank slowly follows the woman to a small conference room. Directed to a chair, he has to position himself on his hip because it is too painful to put direct pressure on his burns. The social worker softens her tone a bit more as she witnesses his heightened distress. Sitting across from him, and holding a note pad, she gives a concerned frown. "Mr. Miranda, again I am sorry to see you so uncomfortable, but I need to get some information so we can offer you the proper care. I know I attempted to interview you a few times since your admission and some days have passed and you're still a mystery to us. Here is a paper and a pen so you can write your responses down in case it is still too tender to use your voice."

There is a pause. Frank rasps, "I'll talk." But he is determined in his heart not to self-disclose anything about the recent horror. *I'll take what happened to the grave!*

"Thank you for your effort, Mr. Miranda," replies Mrs. Tilly. "Just tell me if it gets too much. It's quite evident that you experienced some significant trauma. Your sister has given us information about a recent tragedy involving your cousin."

The mention of Vinny's death causes Frank to have a jolting icy ache. He chokes, "W-W-When can I leave here?"

"I don't know, yet. You appear frightened, Mr.

Miranda. Can you describe to me what you're feeling?"

"Frustrated. Being here is no good. Can I leave today?"

Sighing, the social worker says. "As soon as a person is stable, it is time for discharge. We never want to keep anybody here against their will but you had a pretty serious suicide attempt. We are worried about you. Do you still feel that you want to take your life?"

Taken aback, Frank lies, "I feel okay now. I just wanna be home."

"Mr. Miranda, your sister has been quite hysterical and she has been calling the hospital requesting to be by your side. Would you like to rescind the visitor restriction form and have her come in for a family meeting?"

Frank keeps his side-shifting untruthful eyes downcast on the floor, "Ahh, it it's not good for her to see me in a p-p-place like this. I'll have a heart to heart with her on my own when, ahh, I'm out."

"About all those injuries on your body? The medical team is very concerned. Were they self-inflicted? Or did someone hurt you?"

Pause.

"I-I don't know? I don't remember?"

"I see, okay," says the social worker with a sterner tone. "There is also another matter, regarding the police. They also want to talk to you. A detective has left me his card. Would you be willing to chat with them here on the unit?"

Abruptly Frank replies, "No!" with sudden fear. The scorched skin on his throat painfully flares up.

The social worker gives an inquisitive stare and says, "I do want to help you Mr. Miranda. Is there anything you are willing to tell me? Are you in some kind of danger?"

Panicky, Frank winces, coughs, and begs, "There's nothin' to worry about! I-I just wanna go! It was just a stupid mistake. I really wasn't gonna kill myself. Scout's honor! How do I get out of this nut house? Please let me go home? Please!"

"To be discharged from the hospital the treatment team has to deem you safe and there has to be an aftercare plan. Usually a person is connected with some sort of outpatient therapy and a psychiatrist to monitor your anti-depressants. Will you be willing to do future counseling?"

Not fully understanding what the woman is telling him, Frank huffs in desperation, "Sure, whatever. Just tell the doctor to free me."

The social worker keeps prodding, "Okay, but at this moment, if our treatment team could have some sense of what led you to try to kill yourself, the doctor would feel more comfortable in releasing you."

Squirming, Frank realizes that he needs to offer some sort of explanation for his actions. Having been able to lie to Blaisdale in the midst of being tortured, the present interrogation by the social worker would presumably be a piece of cake. With a blend of partial truth and lies he replies, "Okay, I'll-I'll come clean. Ahh, well, I know I wasn't feelin' good for the last couple of days because of money problems. And, and I, ahh, well started drinkin' a lot. And I got all sad. And ahh, really low. So I did somethin' silly with the car in the garage. I wouldn't have done it, if I wasn't drinkin'; I swear to ya."

"Alcohol is one of the most common factors in suicides, Mr. Miranda."

"Ah, guess so."

"How often do you drink?"

"I- I hardy touch the stuff. I'm no drunk. It was just the money situation. I just, ahh, just was tryin' to drown my woes, as they say."

"Can you describe what kind of financial difficulties you were having'?"

"Well, now that I think about it, I sorta jumped the

gun. It was just some credit card debt. No big deal, really. It's gonna be okay."

"Again, can you try to recall why all the burns and bruises?"

Pausing for a moment, Frank replies, "Well, I started up smokin' because all the stress. And, ahh, I was fallin' a lot and passin' out. I probably passed out with a lit cigarette in my hand. Good thing, I didn't burn the house down."

"Has this ever happened before? Have there been other times when you were suicidal?"

"Oh, no, not at all. I'm usually a happy-go-lucky guy. I'm known as the life of the party. "

"I see," says Mrs. Tilly, her non-believing eyes were drilling, "What about the situation with your cousin? Your sister mentioned that you were very close. When did you find out that he was murdered?"

Abruptly, Frank is at a loss for words. He planned to continue with his line of B.S. but the repeated mention of Vinny causes him to fight back a sudden reactive sob. *Oh God. I'm gonna lose it! Oh crap, I'm gonna cry!* Then there is a sensation of nausea.

"Are you okay Mr. Miranda?"

The urge to vomit is strong. Frank sucks in deep and struggles to stand up.

"Where are you going Mr. Miranda?"

Giving a dismissive wave with his uninjured hand, Frank croaks, "My throat's hurtin' again." He then shuffles forward toward the door. Tears are streaming down his face.

"Mr. Miranda, please wait. Can I get you some water? Can you try using the notepad?"

The social worker decides to remain seated and lets him leave the office. She knows that pushing him any more at this moment is probably futile. Shaking her head, she thinks to herself, *This boy is deep into somethin'! He's lyin' and hidin'*. She was aware that his lab results showed a zero blood-alcohol level at time of admission in the ER.

Frank moves down the hallway trembling with a labored gait. Hot spots of pain throb from various parts of his body. One of the psychiatric nurses meets him halfway in the corridor. In an authoritative tone she says, "Mr. Miranda, I know you had a meeting with Mrs. Tilly, but we would like you to now try one of the treatment groups on the unit."

Visibly bothered, Frank responds, "I-I'm not feelin' well. I wanna go back to bed."

"I see you are very upset," quips the nurse, "But it is better to be with others at this time. Staying for hours and hours in that room isolated is not helping your depression. You may go to group or stay out for a while in the day area."

Glancing over the woman's shoulder he sees that his door is closed. Frank thinks.

They probably locked it so I can't go back in and lie down.

"Please attend the therapy session, Mr. Miranda," orders the nurse. "It's the right thing to do at this time. I'll see you later to do a dressing change for your burns."

At that moment the R.N. is redirected away, as a young, bone-thin, tattooed junkie, detoxing from Heroin begins causing a ruckus at the nurse's station, demanding Xanax. Frank absconds to the corner of the day area. Lowering himself down to a chair, resting on his hip, he then hangs his head low and covers his tear streaked face with his hand.

I gotta stop cryin'. They won't let me out if I'm cryin'. Oh, Vinny!

Across the way is the group therapy room. A large glass window offers viewing for on-lookers. Peeking through his trembling fingers, Frank sees the recreational therapist and approximately 12 patients gathered around a long table, doing what appears to be an arts and crafts project.

"What are a bunch of nuts doin' in a kindergarten class," he mumbles with bitterness. "I'll never go in there."

In the next second, the door to the therapy room flies open and a young heavyset female runs out crying in hysterics. A mental health technician rushes up and escorts her away. The girl's wail echoes throughout the unit, sounding haunting. In plain sight through the glass window, it is evident that the recreational therapist is having some sort of verbal discord with another group member. After a few moments, Frank sees a small middle-aged man with slicked-back hair in a blue Johnny-coat emerge into the day area. He is holding a large piece of construction paper. With metered, deliberate stalking steps, he heads right for Frank.

Oh no. Please don't come over here! Frank thinks to himself as he clamps his hand harder in a shield across his brow.

The little man approaches and says, "Are you scared of me?"

Frank doesn't answer but notices that the guy has a strange foreign accent that does not appear to be genuine.

"I said, are you frightened of me?" The man is now standing directly in front of Frank.

With a trembling voice and not looking up, Frank responds, trying to be polite, "No, uh, no. Everything is okay."

With a wicked titter, the man says, "Well, you should be scared. Do you know who I am?"

Glancing up, Frank is unnerved by his tormentor's impish smile and crazed little dark eyes.

"I'm Francis LaBoudy," the man gleams. "Do you see

this bruise on my elbow? I was out causing mayhem with my chauffeur on the highways and got into the most spectacular automobile crash. The authorities locked me in here because I'm too dangerous for the average prison."

Not knowing how to react, Frank just nods.

"Did you notice that chubby harlot that came shrieking out of that group a moment ago?"

Frank gives another nervous nod.

"Let me inform you!" LaBoudy pontificates, "For the last few days she has been boohooing in all the treatment groups about having flashbacks about being raped by her father when she was a child. The little diva was sure sucking up the attention from the moronic counselors and those other dim-witted patients. I surely was going to expire if they gave her one more group hug. My lord, it was so syrupy and sappy. I was almost bored to tears. Well, we were all just in art therapy class. So do you know what I did? Can you guess?"

Cringing, Frank gives a nervous slight shrug.

"I skillfully did her portrait! Observe the expert detailed rendering. I was able to get such superb line quality because I used a very expensive Mont Blanc pen." Snickering with evil grandeur, LaBoudy holds up the large piece of white construction paper. "Take a look! See, I drew her gleefully giving fellatio to her dear old Papa, with an image of Satan in the upper corner applauding her naughty willful behavior!"

Repulsed by the crude pornographic drawing, Frank gulps.

LaBoudy viciously beams, "It is plain as day that the little fat wench has Borderline Personality Disorder. My work of art will surely cause her to scratch and cut herself in despair. Maybe even suicide, if we could be so fortunate. The only thing I will have to endure is more reprimands from the staff for being less than a gentleman!"

Frank grimaces and LaBoudy belts out with an unnerving giggly fit.

I can't stay here! Frank screams internally and he starts to rise from his chair.

"Wait!" LaBoudy barks, abruptly stopping his laughter and dropping his vicious, manic smile. "I didn't dismiss you yet!"

Panicking, Frank halts, not knowing what to do.

"Your dilemma is quite clear to me," LaBoudy says with a haughty tone. "I have seen that look of despair a billion times before. You're hopeless and helpless. Wallowing in the depths of severe clinical depression. Do you want to kill yourself?"

Frank stutters, "I-I just wanna go lay down. I can't talk right now."

"Well, too bad!" snaps LaBoudy, "Your nurse has locked you out of your room. They do that here you know to force you to comply with their foolish treatment program! So, you will have to stay and listen to me. And listen to every word you shall!"

Despite his dread, Frank feels that new awakening anger for a second time. He has a sudden urge to ball up his good hand and strike LaBoudy in the mouth.

"Do you know what patient rights are?" LaBoudy asks.

Frank didn't answer but just looks down at the floor and seethes.

"Listen up, friend." LaBoudy is smiling again. "If a person is no longer suicidal, homicidal, or psychotic, he or she has the right to leave. It is against the law to keep someone locked up after one's head is screwed back on tight. Do you still want to kill yourself, buddy-old-pal? Do you?"

While refusing to answer, Frank is desperate to learn the release route from the ward.

"But of course you're still suicidal!" LaBoudy mocks

with glee. "You give off an aura of doom! But I want to help you. Really, I do. I think it is your right as a human being to choose your own destiny. How dare these fools force you to endure day after day the pain and suffering of this miserable world? Don't you deserve some peace and internal rest? Yes, by all means, my fine sir! So, here is what you are going to do. Are you listening?"

Frank gives a brief acknowledgment by looking up and making eye contact with the strange little evil man, while at same time thinking, *This crackpot may know something. He's right. As soon as I leave here I'll try it again. But this time I'll finish the job. There is no way I wanna be in this terrible world anymore. I can't wait to see ya Vinny! Can't wait!*

"Force a smile, my friend. Wipe those tears," LaBoudy tutors. "Be an actor. Tell them you found Jesus, and that you promise never ever to do something so stupid again as to try taking your own life. Lie to them and say it was just a cry for help, and that you want to see a shrink on an out-patient basis to help you improve your self-esteem and nurture your inner child. State that you are happy to be alive and that you want to live, live, live!!! They will have to release you from here. And as soon as you go home, that day, make sure you find a nice, newly painted light colored wall, start sucking on the barrel of a 12 gauge shot-gun, use your big toe to work the trigger, and, Bang! Let the top of your skull fly off!"

For a second Frank is mesmerized but involuntarily shudders once hearing the description of his own demise.

LaBoudy is laughing again, "Can you imagine how those pathetic do-gooder social workers and holier-than-thou, narcissistic psychiatrists will feel when they learn that you offed yourself? Your brains will be splattered all over the wall, but they'll have egg on their faces. Plus, your family will sue the hospital for negligence and likely get a pretty penny!"

One of the R.N.s finally notices LaBoudy out on the floor, yucking it up with growing volume. She comes out of the nurse's station and bitches, "Francis, how come you are no longer in group? Have you been showing inappropriate behavior?" She then walks up, takes LaBoudy under the elbow and starts escorting him away from Mr. Miranda.

"I want to laugh and live grandly while the world cries" LaBoudy exclaims with his bizarre European accent. He then shoots a look back over his shoulder at Frank and whispers with a hiss, "Remember what I said. Good luck! I hope that in a few days I read your obituary!"

Twenty-Seven

Saturday, 4:20 p.m. Earlier in the day it had been unseasonably balmy with bright blue autumn skies but now the temperature is beginning to drop fast. Shivering and exhausted, Marco has just completed the trek from the Berlin Turnpike back to New Haven. Keeping off the main roads as much as possible and sticking to wooded areas near the highways, proved to be a successful strategy in avoiding detection by the manhunt. At one point he had paused in an attempt to wash the gore off his face by cupping up rainwater from a dirty puddle. Around noon, he had taken a rest in a concrete drainage pipe near an overpass, appearing like some sort of vagabond troll.

How many fuckin' miles did I walk? I can't believe I finally made it!

At the present moment Marco is standing across the street from his Aunt Gina's place. A chilling wind kicks up, causing him to clutch his long black coat tighter around his body but all his gamy clothing continues to be damp, offering no real protection from the cold. Bits and particles of dead leaves are stuck in Marco's dried-blood- encrusted, stringy hair. The soiled sock is still wrapped around his right hand. Unknown to its host, HIV continues to surge, infecting cell after cell at an amazing rate -

replicating

replicating...

Tweaking and paranoid, Marco scans up and down the block. Everything seems quiet. Parked cars align both sides of the street. There is no ominous bright white

Escalade to be seen. His haggard but frantic eyes dart back up to the second floor of his aunt's row house. The last place he hid his suitcase was under his dead little cousin's bed. It contains all the cash and all the drugs while at the same time being his missing shield against harm.

I just need to get in there and get my fucking lucky suitcase and then things will be cool! I'll survive all this shit! I fucking know it! Just got to split to some place where it's mother-fuckin warm! But? Fuck! Wait! Wait! Is now the time to walk in there? Is it really fucking safe? Am I being a fuckin' idiot?

Once again, Marco wildly surveys about, trying to detect anything suspicious.

I don't see no fucking mafia SUV hanging around. But there is a silver car parked down there. Don't think no piss-poor neighbor around here can afford a Chrysler Sebring but who knows? Coast looks sort of clear but I just got a bad vibe! Fuck!!!

The wind carries a chattering swirl of dead leaves up the empty street. There are far away shrieks of kids playing on their bikes. Dogs barking sound in the distance. Marco's heartbeat pounds in his ears. Inadvertently, his uninjured hand touches something smooth and plastic that is in his coat pocket.

I forgot I snagged that fucking strippers cell phone!

Pausing Marco then thinks to himself, *I can call Aunt Gina right now. See if things are on the up and up! I don't think she'll fucking betray me! I'll tell her to just lug down my suitcase and leave it at the back door and I'll be out of her life for fucking ever!*

Flipping open the phone, Marco then hesitates.

But can I really trust her? What about that Escalade? What if they fucking got to her? What if she starts asking me questions about her pussy-ass boyfriend that I capped? Oh, fuck!

Marco also dreads hearing any ranting or crying. Her kindness and concern always greatly disturbed him. At that second, another frigid breeze causes him to be racked with more icy chills. Through clenched teeth, he utters aloud, "Ah, got to do something before I fucking freeze to death!" He starts punching in his aunt's phone number. After a few rings she picks up.

"H-H—hello?"

Instantly, Marco senses danger. Her voice sounds weak and frightened. Pausing, Marco gulps and stammers, "It-it's me. I'm outside. I, ah, just coming by to pick-up my suitcase. Is everything okay?"

There is dead silence on the other end of the phone.

Nervously, Marco asks, "You there?"

Again there is no response.

"Hey, I said are you there?"

Marco then hears sobbing.

Suddenly Gina's shrill voice sounds through the phone. She cries, "RUN!"

With his heart skipping a beat, Marco panics. He turns to book but it is too late. One taser prong hits him in the back of the neck while another strikes directly between his shoulder blades. 50 thousand volts of electricity come sailing through.

"AAAAAAAAAAAAAAAAHHHH!!!!!"

Blaisdale had been watching from a slouched position in the driver's seat of his Chrysler Sebring. Seeing his prey, he had pounced, quickly but quietly exiting the parked car and shooting the Taser at a range of 13 feet away. Squeezing the plastic trigger, he sends more juice. Marco writhes on the ground, snarling and wailing. The zaps keep coming. Bladder control is lost and Marco pisses and soaks his dirty black jeans.

"AAAAAAAGGGGER!!!! SSSSSSSTOP!!! FUCKKK!!!!"

In his frenzied agony, Marco is sure that his upper

trap muscles are about to spasm and constrict so hard that his neck will break. Then suddenly the shocks cease. Lying on his back, he trembles and gasps. There is the sound of footsteps. Looking up in bewilderment, Marco sees a smiling ugly man with bulging eyes towering overhead.

"Gotcha!" Blaisdale says with a tone of vicious triumph.

There then is the crackle of a walkie-talkie. In the next second, the giant White Cadillac Escalade comes tearing around the corner. Marco is roughly turned over on his back. He has no energy left to resist. Blaisdale cuffs him. The backdoor to the SUV swings open. Lifted off the ground, by muscular arms, Marco is thrown inside the vehicle. With the roar of a gunned engine, the Escalade takes off. The abduction is complete in less than two minutes.

Stillness envelops the street. Then the cold wind returns scattering about more dead leaves. A curtain moves in the upstairs window of Aunt Gina's home.

Twenty-Eight

Saturday, 5:16 p.m. Light is fading as evening approaches. It is the first drastic cold snap of the season and there is a long line outside the New Haven Columbus Avenue homeless shelter. The adjacent soup kitchen is now serving chow. Troy mingles and hides among the gathered throng of transients, addicts and alcoholics. He eavesdrops on some old timers bitching about last night's storm. Shivering and stomping his feet in place, Troy cannot wait to get inside. Having to get rid of his grisly splattered pullover and jeans; he had scavenged earlier in the day through a clothing drop box, and scored some beige corduroy high waters and a yellow short-sleeve shirt.

I know I look like a fucking dork! Wish I found a coat! I'm freezing my balls off!

Unwisely, Troy has kept his work boots that are blotted and speckled with dried brown blood.

Just got to get through tonight. Can't wait to hook up with Marco tomorrow. We should split for California. That would be awesome! Maybe meet some porn stars. Hang at the beach all day. Marco should show me more respect since I am now a full-fledged killer! Going to be equals from now on. Fuck yeah!

In the next moment, two New Haven police cruisers start rolling up the street. A sense of tension fills the crowd. The cops get out of their cars and start toward the gathering of homeless folks outside the shelter. More than one person that has been waiting in the chow line immediately falls out and starts walking away. Troy is one of them.

Shit, they're searching for somebody. This ain't good! Got to stay low and get the fuck away from here!

Moving up the avenue and quickly turning on to a city side street, Troy clutches himself, shaking.

What do I do now! It's so fucking cold I can see my breath!

The solution then pops into his mind. It is a true and tried way often used by those living on the fringes of society to quickly find sanctuary in a pinch and to avoid the authorities.

I'll go hide in the hospital tonight! Yea, I should have thought of that before. Get my three hots and a cot!

Troy knows the persuasive words to get admitted. All he has to do is say to the attending psychiatrist in the E.R. that he is suicidal and hearing voices and there is a good chance he will obtain a warm bed on the psych unit.

And the food is better there than at the goddamn shelter!

With hurried steps, Troy heads for St. Roses Hospital.

Twenty-Nine

Saturday, 6:20 p.m. The long corrugated metal doors of the boathouse are slid apart on their tracks to allow the Escalade to roll inside. After the engine is cut, Beef gets out and closes things back up. It has been a long ride. Snarled traffic on 1-95 had delayed their arrival to the Bridgeport docks. More than once, Marco had attempted to kick and struggle while cuffed in the back seat of the SUV. His efforts got him 800,000 volts from a stun-gun baton and repeated beat-downs that resulted in a few spells of unconsciousness. Being blindfolded and gagged with gray duct-tape, Marco has no idea where he is but he does know that he is royally fucked.

I hope they kill me quick!

Beef comes around to the back of the vehicle to haul out the captive. Marco is lifted up onto the muscleman's shoulder and carried like a sack over to a scuffed and scratched wooden stool and plopped down hard.

Who just had me in the air and tossed me? Shit, whoever it is, is big like a fucking ape!

Blaisdale is also now out of the vehicle, stretching his lower back. He says aloud, "Boy, I did not enjoy that trip. Sure tested my last nerve."

Hearing the ex-cop's wicked mocking, Marco's sense of dread bumps up a notch. He thinks, *This fucker sounds like me. All happy to scare the shit out of someone before killing 'em. Gets off on giving pain. But I won't be his bitch! It's fine with me if I just get the chance to bite him. Rip off some flesh and make 'em remember me! But------*

271

I'm so fucking tired. Wiped-out. Can't take much more of those electrical shocks. Felt like a fucking mosquito on a bug-lamp.

A large red blister is on the back of Marco's neck, inflicted by the Taser prong. The super tight handcuffs are cutting off circulation below both wrists. Pain radiates from various contusions and bruises.

I'm fucking cold! Can't stop shivering! I think I smell seawater and motor oil? Where the fuck am I?

Rearing from behind, Beef grips down hard on Marco's quivering shoulders. Blaisdale walks up to his seated captive and roughly starts ripping off the duct-tape strips that had served as a blindfold and gag.

"AAA!!!!" Marco cries out, almost wiggling off the stool. The fresh stimulus is jolting.

Blaisdale chuckles, "Stings a little, huh? Sorry, about that. I think ya just lost a little bit of your five-o'clock shadow." The ex-cop then notices all the specks and blots of dried blood that covers Marco's skin and clothes. He asks, "Wo-wee, what have ya been up to son? You got that special whiff about ya and look like you been out playin' around with someone when they had their veins opened! You like splashin' around in puddles of blood?"

Squinting against the harsh glare of an overhead caged flood lamp, Marco doesn't answer but quickly scans about and assumes he is in some type of garage. Caught in the stark downward beam of light, the rest of the area is obscured mostly in blackness. Off to the left, a bit of reflected glow illuminates some large rusted chains hanging from ceiling beams and a portion of a suspended boat engine. The mixed stench of the tide and petroleum is evident.

Marco then returns his attention to the man with the bulging eyes in the crumpled sport's jacket standing before him.

"Do you know who I am?" Blaisdale grins with excited fury in his bulbous eyes. "I'm the grand inquisitor! And this is the end of your life! What do ya think of that?"

Peering back through his stringy dirty hair that is hanging down in front of his face, Marco hisses, "Fuck you!"

"Now, now," Blaisdale snickers, "Don't feel too bad. You knew you were gonna get caught. If anything, you should have a little sympathy for me. I haven't done a stakeout in awhile. Sittin', crouched down in the front seat of my car, watchin' and waitin' for you to show up, isn't my idea of retirement. Definitely not good for my sciatica. I even had to piss into a water-bottle."

Marco attempts to work up some saliva to spit at the ex-cop, but his mouth is pasty dry and bitter.

Pacing back and forth a bit in front of his seated captive, Blaisdale continues to taunt, "Guess what? I met your Aunt Gina. My gosh, what's the world comin' to? Who could imagine that a woman that attractive would ever go out with a ball-less piece of shit like Vinny. But, I'm the last one to understand broads. Trust me on that! Anyway you should be happy to know, she really didn't wanna give ya up! It was impressive; that skirt really tried to be brave! However, I can't quite figure out why she would wanna save your sorry ass. To me, you seem to be a real dirt bag. But that's beside the point. She had no choice but to fold, cuz I'm a very persuasive individual. After I broke into the house, I had her on the carpet with one hand pressin' on her throat while checkin' her oil with my Glock. I made it really crystal clear to her, that if she ever talked, I would come back, stick my gun back in her twat and pull the trigger. Boy oh, boy did she cry."

At that moment, Marco experiences a rare inkling of remorse for his Aunt. The fleeting tinge of compassion instantly evaporates enveloped by his usual internal rage.

The dude's got bugged out eyes. I wish I wasn't cuffed. I want to poke one out before he offs me!

Blaidale snorts then says, "Well, it's time to get down to business. Hold here; this will only take me a second." Abruptly the ex-cop turns on his heels, moving out of the light, and starts back toward the Escalade.

Where the fuck is he going? Marco thinks. The muscleman still has him by the shoulders. Marco anxiously glances around, feeling the cold wetness in the air. Marco thinks, *They got me here down by the water. That's where I'm going to end up!*

Then there comes the sound of something being dragged across the damp cement floor. Blaisdale comes back into view, pulling along Marco's lucky suitcase.

"Hey, look what I got here." The ex-cop grins. "It's quite the goodie bag!"

Marco's anger kindles up as he sees his prized possession in the hands of another. The suitcase is unzipped and displayed open on the ground. Plucking out a small cartridge box of .25 caliber bullets, Blaisdale rattles it and asks, "When I was at your aunt's place I searched through this entire piece of luggage. Got some rounds here but no gun. Where is it? After ya popped Vinny, did ya throw the piece into the drink?"

Gritting his teeth, Marco glares back but does not reply. The ex-cop was right. The Taurus had been pitched into the lake.

"Hey, it's okay," Blaisdale says with an unnerving pleasant tone. "You can keep a tight lip about that. I was just curious. In all actuality, I couldn't give a flyin' fuck about the gun. But, you know what I'm really here for. Unfortunately, I didn't find the ticket here among all your pharmaceuticals. So, I need you to tell me where it is. But before you answer, did you remember what I said a little while ago?"

Again, Marco kept quiet and seethes.

Blaisdale smirks back and says, "Well, just in case you forgot, I said, tonight is the end of your life. And that is fuckin' definite! But the choice you have is how you exit this wacky world. If you tell me where the lottery ticket is, you get option A. Do you know what option A is? No? Well, let me explain. You got a lot of bundles of smack in this suitcase. I'll work up a nice hot spike and send you down that heroin highway into the great beyond, nice and easy. No pain. No screamin'. So sweet you will mumble thank you before you nod out. How about that? How can ya resist, right?"

Involuntarily, Marco's shivering increases.

With a pumpkin grin, Blaisdale then asks, "But can ya guess what option B is? Can ya? No? Cat still got your tongue? Well, it's kind of hard for me to explain all of it in words. It's better for ya to have a little taste so ya can make the right decision."

The ex-cop looks up at Beef and gives a nod.

The muscleman moves back for a moment to take off his black leather jacket and drop it on the floor. Marco peers over his shoulder and sees the huge bald headed guy, in a white wife-beater and jeans, doing some quick shadow boxing to warm-up. In the next moment, Beef lunges forward and shoves Marco off the stool. Flying forward and landing face down; Marco quickly rolls over onto his back. Still handcuffed, all he can do in defense is to kick up with his legs as the big dude closes in. From a standing position, Beef bends, scoops and catches Marco's right ankle in the crook of his massive arm. He then stomps down forcefully with his black boot into Marco's left inner thigh, overstretching and pinning the lower limb.

"AAAAAAHHHHH!!!!" Marco screams as he feels his groin muscles rip.

"Wow!" Blaisdale comments with excitement. "You

got him like he's a fuckin' wishbone!"

Beef arches his back while cranking on Marco's trapped right leg, pressing his left forearm into his victim's calf muscle. There are more loud wails of agony which vibrate off the metal walls of the garage. Contorting and trashing about, Marco tries to sit up but he is locked in a devastating jiu-jitsu hold where there are no tap-outs or saying uncle. Rupturing of soft tissue and nerve damage is followed by a sudden snapping sound as the fibula fractures.

"AAAHHHOOOOOOO!!!!!" Marco cries, his eyes rolling back in his head.

"Holy shit!" laughs Blaisdale with surprise. "I just heard that! His leg just broke! Nice! Okay, ease up. We got to talk to our boy again."

With disgust, Beef releases his hold, swatting aside his victim's broken leg, and stepping back. Marco groans and squirms on the floor.

"That's a taste of option B!" Blaisdale exclaims, "What do you think of that? Smarts, huh? Trust me, it will only get worse? Now, tell me, where's the fuckin' ticket?"

Curling up on his side, his broken leg bent, Marco gasps and is on the verge of puking.

Motioning again to Beef, Blaisdale barks, "Get 'em off the floor put him back on the stool. I don't want him passin' out!"

Grabbed under the arms, Marco is lifted up by the muscleman and propped back up in a seated position. Quickly, Blaisdale steps forward and gives a backhanded bitch slap.

"Aahh!" responds Marco.

"Start talkin'! Where's the fuckin' lottery ticket!" Blaisdale shouts.

"I never fucking saw it!" Marco gasps.

"Wrong answer!" Blaisdale cracks Marco in the chops,

and kicks at his broken leg.

"Aaaaoooh!!!" cries Marco.

"Hold him tight" Blaisdale says to Beef. "This dirt ball needs some more persuading!" The ex-cop abruptly turns away and goes over to the suitcase to tear open a bag of syringes.

I'm fucked! Shit! Marco screams in his mind.

Uncapping one of the needles with his mouth, Blaisdale comes back and threatens, "See this syringe! Ain't nothin' in it yet! I can do my part of the bargain and send you out, forgettin' about your broken leg or I can stick this in your eye! Now, where's the fuckin' ticket!"

With a string of blood and spit hanging from his split lip, Marco gasps, "I think it got passed off to that other guy!"

"What other guy? That other asshole you been runnin' with? What's his name?"

"It ain't Troy!" Marco shouts back, "It's someone that Vinny knew! Vinny had us stop at some house to get directions to the lake. I think he handed off the ticket there!"

"To who?"

"I don't know! It was some short little fat guy!"

"I don't believe you!"

"It's fucking true!"

"Where's Troy?" Blaisdale points the syringe an inch away from Marco's left eye. "Tell me!"

"He's-he's s-s-suppose to be hiding out at the shelter in New Haven!"

"I bet your lying'!" Blaisdale snarls. "You're tryin' to protect him, aren't ya? Maybe cause you're both queer! Real faggots! In love and all that shit! I deduce that you were planin' to hook up again, cash in the ticket and take off together! Must have had big dreams of fuckin' each other in the ass forever in style! But it ain't gonna happen!

Do you understand that? It's over! You're dying tonight! Now tell me the fuckin' truth! Where's the god damn ticket!!!!?"

"Fuck you," Marco huffs with a mixture of resigned doom and defiance.

"Fuck me? No fuck you dirt bag!" Blaisdale rages at his captive. He then again gestures to Beef and says, "Hold this fucker really good! He's gonna squirm!"

Bending forward while positioned behind Marco, the muscleman tightens his hold around his victim's neck. Instantly stricken with icy terror, Marco squeezes his eyes shut and tries to turn his head. Flooded with sick sexual like power, Blaisdale is thrilled with the opportunity to torture. Internally in his psyche at this moment this is more rewarding for the ex-cop than a billion dollar win at Power Ball. With an excited shaky hand, he attempts to jab the syringe into the Marco's left eye. Managing a few degrees of movement, Marco tucks his chin. The needle misses his eye socket and gouges the side of his nose.

"AOOOWWW!!!"

"Damn it!" Blaisdale curses as he pokes again.

Another miss. The syringe pricks Marco's cheek.

"GERRRRHHHH!!!"

"Hold his head still!" Blaisdale yells in frustration as he begins to frantically jab away. The tip of the needle bends and breaks off as it strikes hard bone above the brow.

"FUCK-OWWWW!!!"

"Shit! Wait!" The ex-cop hollers as he quickly rushes over to the suitcase to retrieve another syringe. Coming back he continues with his sloppy assault.

"GERRR!!! OOWWH!!! AAAAWWHH!!!"

Finally the needle scores two quick hits, piercing the thin flesh of Marco's closed eyelid and puncturing the liquid filled orb.

"AAAGGGERRRRRRRHHH" Marco screams, jerking and kicking out with his good leg catching Blaisdale in the crotch. Beef, despite his weight and strength, has a hard time holding on to his freaking captive. Slipping off the seat, the stool topples over and Marco is pulled upright, off his feet by his neck. A mixture of blood and aquas humor streaks Marco's face from the imploded eyeball and the various pinholes. Puke shoots up into the back of Marco's throat.

"You mutherfucker!" Blaisdale growls and coughs while bent over and holding his nuts. Blaisdale's own rage quickly overcomes the pain and he comes forward again with the intention of burying the syringe into Marco's other eye. Unintentionally, the needle's plunger had been pulled back during the previous attack, drawing in 60 ccs of HIV enriched blood. In an overhand icepick grasp, the ex-cop stabs down with the hypodermic. At that second, Marco flails, twists and bucks in such a manner that Blaisdale misses his intended target. Instead of Marco's right eye, the needle enters deep into the upper muscle of Beef's pumped-up vascular right forearm. Inadvertently, the plunger is pressed by Blaisdale's thumb, injecting the contents of the syringe.

"Ouch! Fuck!" Beef curses, briefly letting go of Marco's neck.

With a shrieking roar, Marco lurches forward on his good leg and goes to bite at Blaisdale's face like a vampire. The ex-cop opens his hands to push back and his left index finger winds up in the inside of Marco's mouth. With mad dog vengeance, side molars gnash the digit.

"AAAAAAAAHH! FUCK!" Blaisdale screams, "STOP! GET HIM OFF ME!!!"

Pulling the syringe out of his arm, Beef rushes forward to regain control of Marco. He quickly slips on the rear naked chokehold. As Blaisdale yanks his hand away from

Marco's mouth, his index finger is partially de-meated.

"OWW!!! I'M FUCKIN' BLEEDIN'!!!" Ex-cop cries, cupping his mangled phalange. "IT FUCKIN' HURTS BAD!!! AOW!!! ENOUGH OF THIS SHIT!!! KILL THIS FUCKER!!!"

Tightening the stranglehold, Beef swelled his own pecs and presses the back of Marco's head forward. The carotid arteries on both sides of Marco's neck are pinched off. Oxygen is restricted to the brain.

"YEA! I SAID KILL'EM!!!" Blaisdale bellows.

Marco feels like he is in a darkening tunnel. Abruptly he goes unconscious and the pain, madness and horror are turned off like a switch.

"MAKE SURE YOU KEEP THAT SLEEPER HOLD ON HIM FOR AWHILE!" The ex-cop shouts. "I WANT HIM DEAD-DEAD!!!"

The muscleman continues to apply the choke then finally let's go as his big arms begin to fatigue. Like a rag-doll, Marco's body flops into a small heap on the cement floor, motionless. Instantly, Blaisdale steps forward and gives some punishing kicks while he rants. "TAKE THAT FUCKER! I'LL STOMP ON EVERY ONE OF YOUR FUCKIN' RIBS! BET YA THINK YOU'RE LUCKY THAT YA BIT ME! WELL NOW YOU'RE DEAD! WHAT DO YA THINK OF THAT! YOU'RE' FUCKIN' DEAD WITH ONLY ONE EYE AND A BROKEN LEG!!! JUST REMEMBER YOU GOT FUCKIN' THE WORST OF IT?"

Breathing heavy, Beef says sarcastically, "The little fucker got it good."

"Screw you asshole!" Blaisdale replies with some embarrassment, "If you would have held him a little tighter this wouldn't have happened like this?"

Rubbing, the needle puncture in his forearm, Beef snaps back, "Yea, well thanks for stickin' me with that fuckin' syringe. I hope this creep didn't have hep C or any other shit."

At the moment, Human-Immunodeficiency-Virus is in muscleman's blood stream on its way to infect neural tissue, lymph nodes and beyond...

Replicating...

Replicating...

Replicating...

"Whatever," Blaisdale huffs while pulling out a white handkerchief from an inside pocket in his sport's jacket. He uses it to wrap his bloody finger.

"Well, what do we do now?" Beef asks.

"Time to cleanup!" Blaisdale barks. "Strip him. I'll check his clothes again. No matter what, ticket or no ticket, we still gotta dispose of the body as planned. Penzetta's boat is outside and is supposed to have plenty of fuel. I'm gonna be the fuckin' skipper and you're gonna be fuckin' Gilligan. Sure as shit, it's goddamn cold out there tonight on that water. Let's make this fuckin' quick cause we got some other people to find."

Bitching under his breath, Beef reaches down and takes hold of Marco by the ankles and starts to drag him across the cement floor. He stops then starts stripping the body. Blaisdale sifts through Marco's wet, reeking clothes but he knows his search is futile.

"The kid's got a cool tattoo on his chest," says Beef, peering down at Marco's twisted bloodied and dirty body.

"Yea, and a pathetically small dick," balks Blaisdale. "Now, you can start by packin' our boy here into that oil drum. Hop to it!"

Nearby in the darkness is a large black oil barrel with an open top. Patches of orange corrosion spot the metal. The interior of the container is still slick with residual petroleum gunk. Marco's limp naked body folds at the waist as it is lifted up and stuffed into the barrel. Roughly, Beef grabs Marco's fractured left leg that is sticking out of the top, gives it a bend and presses it down. A rubber mallet is used to bang tight the lid.

Saturday 9:05 p.m. In total freezing darkness, Marco's one good eye flickers as he momentary regains consciousness. Unfortunately, he has survived the chokehold to wake-up in a different type of nightmare. Moments ago, up on the surface of the water in the cold moonless night, Beef had pushed the barrel off the back of the boat. The oil drum is now spinning and turning end-over-end as it makes its descent toward the bottom of Long Island Sound. Racked with nauseating vertigo, choking on petrol fumes, Marco bites into his tongue as searing-icy jets of salt water shoot into the interior of the barrel. Folded in half with both knees crushing against his chest, it is hard to scream, hard to breathe. Helpless in a horrific state of sensory overload, Marco has a flashback of being held down and sodomized in juvie-hall by three older Spanish kids. Then there are glimpses of his drunken dad punching mom in the breast, followed by other quick murky memories of being paralyzed with dread while being left alone in a play-pen, with fecal smeared toys.

Like a can of condensed rage and agony, the oil drum sinks deeper and deeper into the frigid blackness. The last thought Marco has before he drowns is of Marsha's dead face.

Thirty

Sunday, 10:21 a.m. Paul Kosakowski slowly begins to awake, prodded by the shrill ring of a telephone. His small efficiency apartment is dark and dank with the shades closed. Almost an entire case worth of empty beer cans are strewn about along with depleted bottles of Old Grand Dad and Yukon Jack. The drinking started on Friday after being escorted off company property by security and told if he returned he would be arrested. Saturday consisted of staying shut in and existing in an intoxicated blur punctuated by explosive verbal tirades, episodes of dry-firing Mr. Whoop-Ass, and painfully masturbating with his gay porno magazine.

The phone keeps ringing.

Continuing to lay there, belly-up on the dirty carpet, Kosakowski sniffs the air and smells shit. During his bender, he had been incontinent and had a case of the trots. Wearing only a pair of soiled boxers, his patsy white legs are smeared brown.

The ringing appears only to get louder.

Alcohol induced swollen meninges, causes a brutal pounding in his head.

"Fuck," groans Kosakowski as he swats out with a clumsy hand toward the phone on the cluttered coffee table. The receiver is knocked off the cradle and a frantic distant voice is heard coming through the line.

"Mr. Kosakowski, are you there? Mr. Kosakowski? This is Ms. Murphy, R.N. supervisor, at Pleasant-Health Nursing Home. Hello, is anyone there?"

With an abrupt sensation of dread, Paul rolls up on to his shoulder and reaches forward to grasp the phone. Bringing it to his ear, he stutters, "W-w-what?"

"Is this Mr. Kosakowski?"

"Y-y-yea?"

"Sir, we have been attempting to make contact for the last hour. I'm sorry to inform you that your brother, Ronald, appears to have had a stroke. He has been rushed to St Rose's Hospital."

"Is-is this a dream?" Paul asks with a trembling voice.

"No, sir. This is real. Your brother is in critical condition."

The call is instantly cut off as Kosakowski yanks out the cord and throws the receiver across the room. With a roar of lament, rebounding in the dim stank, the last bit of foundation in his life has crumbled.

Thirty-One

Sunday, 4:05 p.m. The attending resident in the emergency room was sort of green and had bought Troy's line of bullshit about hearing voices and having suicidal thoughts. Safe for the time being, Troy is now in a blue johnnie-coat, lounging in the day area of Saint Rose's inpatient behavioral health unit. Attempting to read a magazine, he is waiting for the dinner cart. Sitting nearby is a 79-year-old Hispanic gentleman originally from Puerto Rico with a long history of disorganized schizophrenia. The recent onset of dementia overshadowed his prevailing symptoms of psychosis. Reportedly, Mr. Ruiz had been brought in after being discovered living in total squalor and eating raw chicken. Earlier, Troy had stolen a dessert off the old man's lunch tray.

Troy thinks, *I'll get some more chow. Take another shower. Rest up here tonight. And in the morning, I'll tell the doctor, the social worker and those asshole nurses, that I'm fucking signing out against medical advice. I hope Marco won't be late tomorrow; I don't want to be hanging out in front of that shelter for too long.*

An hour ago, Troy had been offered Seroquel. Cheeking the anti-psychotic medication, he then went into the bathroom and spat the pills into his palm. Later, he hid them under his mattress. The plan is to take along the stash of meds upon discharge from the hospital. Troy knows that any kind of pill, even if it did not induce a high, still has a street value. *I can sell a junkie any kind of shit.*

285

He had tried to weasel some Xanax but the nurses were tough on giving out benzos.

At the present moment, Troy watches in mild amusement as a large young male with a bald head comes shuffling down the hall, mumbling numbers, drooling, and covering his ears. The big kid is being followed and taunted by another patient. They both are in johnnie-coats. The tormenter is a small guy with slicked-back hair and a weird foreign accent.

"Come on Mr. Ritchie, my good sir!" the tormentor coaxes, "Take your hands off your ears and listen to me. I want you to twist and rip off your remaining nipple! If you don't try, I assure you, the voices will only get more nasty and profane."

Troy laughs.

The small man with his riveting beady eyes instantly locks in on Troy and gives a flirtatious smirk. He then glances back up at Warren and says, "Good-bye Mr. Ritchie, you gigantic mathematical ignoramus! I leave you in your lunacy! I most make haste and go to a kindred spirit that I spy sitting nearby."

Warren Ritchie mutters back with a vacant unblinking gaze, "27, 28, 30, 31, 35, 37"

Abandoning his victim, the little man starts sashaying toward Troy. He calls out, "Hello there. I know something about you."

"Ah, I'm not in the mood to talk right now," Troy snaps back. He then thinks to himself, *This nut-job talks weird. Sounds like some foreign faggot.*

Glaring and coming forward, the little man replies, "Listen to what I have to say. It is a matter of importance to you and your destiny. I was eavesdropping next to the nursing station. Those fat hens were talking about you. They say you should not be here and that you're malingering. Faking hearing voices. Is it true? Are you just hiding out? I notice that you have a lot of cuts on your hands? How did you get those? Were you in fisticuffs? Are you a bad boy on the run?"

Irritated and suddenly unnerved, Troy responds, "What? Hey. Huh? Whatever. Fuck the nurses. And why don't you mind your own business!"

"Do you know who I am?" the little man asks.

"No," Troy snorts.

"I'm Francis LaBoudy."

"Well, okay, Francis" Troy says with sarcasm. "Why don't you go scamper along and go watch TV or something."

"I can't," LaBoudy says with indignation. "They have restricted my viewing rights. Accused me of breaking unit rules by repeatedly turning on programs that are considered too disturbing to the client population on this unit. Yesterday, they caught me watching my favorite A&E rerun on the subject of serial killers. You know, someday the media will do a docudrama on my life? Do you know why? Do you?"

Troy sighs and just rolls his eyes.

"Because, I'm like you," LaBoudy exclaims. "I'm a bad boy, too! I'm not insane like these other worthless inbreeds on this ward. I'm just a free thinker who is going to make the world pay for underestimating my ability to cause destruction and bedlam!"

Smirking Troy quips, "So you're an evil genius or something?"

"Yes!" beams LaBoudy. "Yes! Very good insight my young friend." LaBoudy then brandishes the Mont Blanc and says, "Do you see this? Do you know what this is?"

At that second, Troy is taken aback as he sees the creepy little man uncap the fountain pen, revealing the pointy metal tip.

"This is a very expensive writing implement. It belongs

287

to a psychologist. I stole it off his desk right before his eyes. Every night I have to sign it back in for safe keeping at the nursing station. I journal with it! I draw with it! But now, I'm going to do something else with it that will change our destinies forever!" LaBoudy quickly snatches the magazine out of Troy's hand.

"Hey, what the fuck," Troy curses with annoyance.

In a frantic scribble, LaBoudy writes on the cover of the magazine. He then thrusts it back at Troy, saying "Here! You may have this!"

Troy looks down at what is scrawled. There on the front cover of TIME, midst the graphics and topography advertising the feature story on Sarah Palin, is a handwritten phone number.

"Have no hesitation to call me!" LaBoudy says with breathy excitement. "Tomorrow, I'm going to be discharged from this madhouse. I'm seeking another bad boy to conspire with to make the world cry while we laugh! My chauffeur is named Chester. We can come and retrieve you at any time, any place!"

Despite the recent rampage of murder, Troy is more skeeved-out at this moment than when he was manhandling all those dead bodies. He thinks, *This little crazy dude gives me the fuckin' willies!*

"So will you promise to call that number when you leave here?" asks LaBoudy with an almost lustful plea.

"Sure, you bet," Troy replies with a placating tone.

"Hail Satan!" LaBoudy cheers, clapping with joy.

At that second, Troy feels his heart skip a beat as he peers pass LaBoudy and sees another patient shuffling by the day area. The man is in hospital garb and has a bandaged neck. Despite all the facial bruising, Troy is still able to recognize the individual. *It's that guy that Vinny stopped to meet up with! Holy shit!*

"Who are you ogling?" whines LaBoudy, sounding

instantly jealous, while turning to see the person of interest.

For a fleeting instant, Frank's tired, pain-ridden eyes connect with Troy's stare.

"Oh, ignore him!" LaBoudy protests. "He's just some poor old sack that I psychologically programmed to kill himself. It's all rather boring. Now, let's just talk about you and me and our future mission to cause mayhem."

"Why's that guy here?" Troy mutters to himself. "It don't make sense?" He then thinks, *Maybe the mob sent him here to get me! Maybe he's also faking being nuts and all injured, so later he can murder me in the shower or something. Fuck! This sucks!*

Frank lumbers on down the hallway like a zombie.

Troy then begins to doubt himself, *It can't be him! It's just a look alike! Must mean I'm getting paranoid! If I stay any longer in this fuckin' loony bin I'll probably see fuckin' Elvis next!*

"Hello! Hello! Bad boy one to bad boy two, you're spacing on me!" LaBoudy bitches, losing his European accent. "I demand your undivided attention! Do you understand me?"

With a flash of homicidal rage, Troy looks back at LaBoudy and snarls "Get the fuck away from me!"

And this time, it is LaBoudy that gets the willies.

Old Mr. Ruiz starts laughing and making loud squawks like a barnyard rooster.

Thirty-Two

Monday, 9:41 a.m. It is another bright, crisp autumn morning in New Haven. The yellow cab is weaving through traffic on its way from Saint Rose's Hospital to the Elm City Behavioral Outpatient Program. In the back seat of the taxi, awkwardly positioned on one hip, Frank is taciturn with a flat affect, but internally his mind races like a blender as he contemplates his own mortality.

What do I do? God! What do I do? What? What? What? ....

The ward's inpatient psychiatric staff was leery about discharging Mr. Miranda even though he stated that he was no longer suicidal. It did not take a Ph.D. to see that the man was lying. Unfortunately, the cold hard fact that prompted his abrupt discharge was a lack of medical insurance. A bill of $1800 dollars had already accumulated. A hasty appointment with Dr. Fray was arranged. Outpatient services were much cheaper. Given a cab pass, Frank was on his way to the clinic for further behavioral health treatment.

I wanna tell the driver to pull over and let me out on the street! Should I do it? I wonder if I don't show up at that clinic, will they call the cops? Christ!

A big fear for Frank is the police. Before leaving, the social worker stressed to him that after his meeting with the psychologist in the morning, he should then make contact with the authorities in the afternoon. A detective from the homicide division had left his card for a second time and was requesting that Mr. Miranda show up downtown for questioning, ASAP.

Geez, they're all breathing down my neck!

Frank's thoughts then return back to that lanky young guy on the unit with the cut hands and the wild blue eyes.

So spooky! I swear he looked like one of the punks that night with poor Vinny!

Wish the police would go interrogate him! Mother Mary of God, I don't know what to do? Saint Jude help me!

The yellow cab continues through the busy commercial congestion. Leaning his head on the cool glass of the back window, Frank is disgusted with himself for doubting his own initial plan of re-attempting suicide. An hour ago, he had even called his sister and lied, saying that he was being discharged from the hospital tomorrow. If she knew that he was out at this moment, he is certain that she would be by his side all protective and smothering.

Why am I askin' God and all the others for help? I know what I got to do! I shouldn't be losin' my nerve! Can't be no coward! Gotta stick to joinin' up with Vinny before the day is done. Can't have no family, no shrink, no police screwin' things up!

With his troubled mind in overdrive, Frank then recalls how at age 12 his mother and aunts came to him and told him that his father had died in an automobile accident.

I knew then and I know now that it was no friggin' accident! There were no other cars involved. They lied! He didn't fall asleep at the wheel! Damn it; I never believed that story they tried to sell me as a kid! The truth is, he had enough just like me and decided to end it! Took his Buick and plowed into a bridge abutment. Simple as that! He killed himself!

Memories flash in Frank's brain of his dad's face, flat, pale, and void of joy. The old superstitious Italian relatives would gossip and say he was cursed, stricken by "male-occhio," the evil eye. In reality it was nature, genetics and physiology that were the culprits. Both father and son were prone to low testosterone and serotonin levels that led to chronic dysthymia and bouts of severe, major, depression.

The church says if you commit suicide you go to hell. Frank questions in his head. *Is it true? Will I see pops? And I know Vinny can't be no angel.*

The taxi turns down another street and is almost at the clinic. Frank's trembling hand slides into his front pocket and his fingertips rub against the thin square piece of paper. Upon discharge from the hospital, the mental health worker had given him back his belongings, which included his brown tattered trousers. His shirt was missing but had been replaced with a gray sweater from the ward's charity clothing bank. Choosing to wear the same pants again he was surprised to discover the lottery ticket.

It's like an evil bad luck charm. Can't get rid of the thing.

Strangely, Frank gives a bitter smile as he feels the blackened holes in the fabric next to the front pocket.

That bastard cop almost accidentally torched three million dollars when he was burning me with that lighter. If he only knew how close he came, ha.

The Elm City Behavioral Health clinic looms up on the right and the cab comes to a stop in front of the building.

"We're here," says the young Jamaican driver.

Frank mutters "Thanks," and exits the taxi with achy, labored movement. The cold fresh air is shocking but seems to instantly soothe all the healing burns and bruises. He no longer has that bulky bandage on his throat. It has been replaced with a smaller sterile-strip. Clutching his gray sweater, while apprehensively standing there on the sidewalk, Frank nervously eyes the brick façade of the clinic with all its graffiti.

The taxi just pulled away. Do I make a run for it now? Should I go inside and just make a show of it, then bolt?

At that moment a squad car starts to turn down the street on patrol. Last week, Dr. Fray had asked the clinic's administrative staff to request increase police presence since Kosakowski's truck had been vandalized. Seeing the approaching cop cruiser, Frank panics and thinks, *Oh, no! Are they lookin' for me?* With hurried steps, he slips inside the clinic.

Being Monday, the lobby and waiting area are packed. There are a lot of Hispanic women with crying children. A security guard prompts Frank to go up to the front to register. Doing as he is told, Frank goes ahead. The young stressed out receptionist behind the counter, quickly takes down his name and tells him to go find a seat and that he will be called when the clinician is ready to see him. Looking over her shoulder, Frank sees a man in a rumpled tweed jacket, hastily pulling out files from a metal cabinet. Their eyes meet for a moment. Despite being in a hurry, the man takes a second to give a brief nod and a faint welcoming smile. Instantly, both men pick up the vibe that they have something in common, a certain desperation.

"Please go sit down, Mr. Miranda." The receptionist scolds.

Quickly, Frank moves away, feeling embarrassed. A part of him wants to leave at this very moment but he wonders if the police are still outside on the street. Racked with indecision, he spots an empty chair and goes over and lowers himself down.

Seated nearby, Rhonda Butkus is purposely wearing a short sleeve blouse so everyone can see her newly self-inflicted scratches that run up and down both forearms. She is waiting for her appointment with Dr. Fray. Since her lover-boy Troy took off she has gone into a tailspin, not eating, not bathing, and not sleeping. Her suicidal ideation was rampant. Upon seeing Frank, she lets out an attention-getting loud sob.

"Oh, God," Frank says in alarm. "Are you okay?"

Rubbing her scratched arms, Rhonda sighs, "I'll never be okay."

Taken-aback, Frank is lost for words. He then utters, "Sorry to hear that."

"I want to die!" Rhonda announces in a provocative manner.

Muddled in his own chaos, Frank again is unsure how to respond to the woman's comments. He then decides to ask, "Isn't this place gonna help ya?"

Rhonda huffs, "Yea right! You see that guy over there, with the messy hair?" She points to the man that is continuing to gather his files behind the receptionist. "That's my psychologist, Dr. Fray. He tries to help but it's a lost cause. Do you know why?"

Frank shrugs.

"Because I'm cursed," Rhonda says. "The doctor says I got borderline personality disorder but I don't believe it. I was just born under a bad sign and I will just be fucked over for the rest of my life or until I kill myself. And the one person I really loved just took off on me."

With his anxiety level ramping up even more, Frank is shocked how this woman, could easily broadcast her despair to a stranger. He needs to leave. It is all too hard to tolerate. But he does feel sorry for her.

This gal is so bad off. We both got the same kind of feelin's about life.

Frank stands up to go but then has an impulsive thought. Reaching into the front pocket of his brown tattered pants, he pulls out the lottery ticket. "Here," he says, offering out the small square slip of paper. "Take this. Maybe this will help ya make a fresh start."

Plucking the ticket from his hand, Rhonda looks at it and snorts, "Yea, thanks. That's what I got, a one and a million chance in life."

"No," Frank says pensively. "Go check the numbers. You'll be really surprised. Just promise me to wait a couple of months before cashin' it in."

Perplexed, Rhonda peers back at Frank and says, "I don't like jokes. And by the way, what happened to your neck?"

Not answering Frank quickly turns and heads toward the exit, wondering if he just did the woman more harm than good.

Thirty-Three

Monday, 11:17 a.m. Having signed out against medical advice from the hospital an hour ago, Troy hoofed it back to the Columbus Avenue homeless shelter. He now waits for Marco

Where the fuck is he? He's supposed to be here by now! What the fuck?

Wired and pacing out in front of the shelter, Troy is dressed again in his yellow short sleeve shirt, beige corduroy high waters, and dried blood splattered steel-toed work boots. This time, he really doesn't feel the cold because he had impulsively traded some Seroquel for a couple hits of crack-cocaine. With excess dopamine flooding the synapses of his neurocircuitry, Troy's thoughts zoom.

Fuck, wow! After all these days of killing people, I forgot to get high. Maybe, I should go back into that alley over there and hit that pipe again! That old nigger in there shouldn't be stingy or I'll give him a smack down and take all his shit for myself!

Others start gathering on the street, wanting to be early when the nearby soup kitchen opens for lunch.

Hey, wait! What the fuck am I thinking? Troy tries to calm himself down while frantically running his hands through his hair. *Can't have no drama! Can't bring attention to myself. Damn, where the hell is Marco, that fucker? But one more smoke can't do any harm while I wait. Right? Maybe I got something left to barter.*

Searching the pockets of his corduroys, Troy takes out

the discharge forms from the hospital.

"That's not what I'm looking for!" Troy mutters. "Fuck, where's that other folded stuff? Oh, got it! Good!"

Before leaving the hospital, Troy had torn off the front cover of the Time Magazine he had been flipping through and had used it to wrap up the medication he had stashed. There is one Seroquel tablet left. Chasing the cocaine high, Troy makes a b-line and returns into that darkened side alley

A few moments pass and a large white Cadillac Escalade shows up on the street. It is doing another slow drive-by. The vehicle had been prowling around the area since early morning. A greater number of homeless people are now on the block waiting for the chow line to be formed. In the next second, Jessie Butkus, wearing a tattered jean jacket decorated with multiple rock n' roll band patches, comes peddling up on his black Huffy. His mother Rhonda, being in another suicidal blue funk had refused to buy any groceries despite having plenty of food stamps. It was common behavior for her. More than once, Jesse had utilized this soup kitchen when he was starving or just had the munchies.

"Hey you, kid," says a gruff voice as the window lowers on the giant white SUV. The vehicle eases to a stop.

Pausing on his bike, Jesse looks up and sees a mean looking bald guy peering back down from the driver's side.

"Know anybody around here named, Troy?" asks Beef.

Hit with fear, Jesse gulps and rapidly peddles away, crossing over to the other sidewalk. The Escalade begins to roll on. With his heart fluttering like that of a scared bunny, Jesse stops and watches as the SUV disappears down the street. In the next moment, there comes the sound of coughing and hacking from the side alley. Emerging from the darkened passageway, while kicking at empty beer cans, Troy bumps right into Jesse.

"You!" Troy shouts; his eyes are crazy and watery. There is a growing blister on his lower lip after just burning his mouth on a hot four-inch segment of car antenna that was a makeshift stem for the crack pipe. His throat is raw. He has also just boosted some drags of Wet. Troy rasps, "Why the fuck are you here?"

In a panic, Jesse tries to flee, but Troy grabs hold of the Huffy's handlebars.

"Answer me, you little bitch!" Troy screams and bugs-out. "Are you trying to set me up? Did you call the cops on me? I saw that fucking Escalade when I peeked out from back there? Who the fuck was that?"

Unable to control his tears of terror, Jesse cries, "I don't know! I don't know! I swear, just let me go!"

"Why are you here? Fucking tell me!"

"I just came down to get some food!"

"You lie!"

"No, I swear to God! My mom hasn't cashed her welfare check yet!"

"Did she look in the shed yet?"

Sobbing and trembling, Jesse gasps, "No. She doesn't know anything. Nobody has gone in there."

Coughing up junk from his lungs, Troy feels an ever growing paranoia fueled by the Phencyclidine and cocaine. He thinks, *I got to get off this street! Can't be around here no more, Marco can go fuck himself! I got to go hide some place! I got to get some money!*

"Come on Troy, just let me go!" Jesse begs. "I promise not to snitch! I won't tell anybody nothing! I promise!"

Troy gives a vicious, angry grin and speaks at hyper-speed, "Things are different, now! Cause you're my new partner in crime, little man! Thanks for keeping a tight-lip on that mutilated fucker in the shed. Now, let's go home together and see your mommy. Peddle slow cause I'm going to jog right next to you. I got to burn off some of this crack and embalming fluid! They're fucking better than Red Bull, a 12 ounce Monster, a Starbucks Venti and a fucking case of 5-Hour Energy!!! YEA BABY!!! LET's GO LITTLE MAN!!!"

Thirty-Four

Monday, 12:00 Noon. Frank gets off the public bus and with slowed labored steps heads home. His plan is to sneak back into the garage, take off with the Lincoln and die like his father.

I should have tried crashin' the first time around rather than usin' the engine fumes.

Making sure to avoid the prying eyes of old Miss Ferraro, Frank comes upon his property from the backward. Nearby, a small white cement statue of the Blessed Mary on a half-shell stands as a sentinel amidst an overgrown rock garden. Dead fall leaves crunch underfoot. A sudden sense of apprehension hits Frank but he pushes himself forward. The house is unnervingly dark and still from the outside. Frank assumes that nobody is home and that his sister is still staying with Aunt Theresa. There is no need to use the hidden key under the patio block because the busted lock on the backdoor has not been repaired. Slowly and quietly, Frank goes inside.

I got to do this quick. I can't get cold feet.

Earlier, after absconding from the Elm City Behavioral Health clinic, Frank had taken the bus route that made a stop at Gulf Beach in Milford. There, while walking on the cold beautiful shore, he took an hour to savor for the last time one of the few things that gave him a true sense of joy. Looking out on Long Island Sound and Charles Island, he wept for a while then was bestowed with a sense of peaceful resolve as he felt the sunlight on his face and smelled the salt air. There were neither aches nor cramps in any part of his body, not even his stomach.

12:18 p.m. At the present moment, as he moves down the back hallway of his house, he tries not to look at the family photos hanging on the wall.

I know my sister and aunt are gonna suffer even more if I die but what am I supposed to do? Even if I went into a witness protection program, I still can't live with all these bad things in my head. I wonder if that shrink with the messy hair could have helped me. He had kind eyes.

Seeing the kitchen again is jolting. There is the old peeling yellow linoleum floor, all the hanging pots and pans, the picture of Jesus in the corner. Instantly memories flash of good meals, Vinny telling his funny grandiose stories at the table, and the smell of sis's red sauce.

We had some good times here.

Frank then looks out the window near the sink and gasps. There in the distance is the silver Chrysler Sebring parked out on the street. Next, there comes the sound of rapid, pouncing footsteps.

"Hey, about time, cocksucker! Nice to see ya again." Blaisdale roars as he bursts into the kitchen from the front living room, pointing his Glock model 30. His left hand is wrapped in a dried bloody handkerchief. He still has on the same crumpled sports jacket.

Trembling, Frank winces and expects to feel a bullet.

"Sit down!" Blaisdale shouts.

Impulsively obeying the ex-cop's command, Frank lowers himself down on to a chair at the kitchen table.

"I heard you were in the hospital," sneers Blaisdale as he continues to stand and point his gun. "Feelin' better? Sorry I didn't send ya any flowers."

Grimacing, Frank thinks to himself, *I hope he pulls the*

trigger and gets this over with! I can't stand hearin' his voice!

"Well, well," Blaisdale suddenly sighs, "You know, you surprised me; I beat ya and burnt ya and ya still held out on me. Impressive. Gives new meanin' to wanting to be a millionaire. But it ain't gonna happen. Do you understand that? I could torture you some more but I don't know if that will really work. I need that ticket. I haven't slept in days and I think I need surgery on my thumb. Enough is enough. Will you just come clean and hand it over? Life will be so much fuckin' easier."

"I don't have it," mumbles Frank, covering his face with his quivering hands.

"Okay asshole, you can continue to lie like a fuckin' little snake but I want ya to hear me out. I went around your aunt's house again. I saw your sister out in the driveway. Sort of a short fat Italian girl with a big fuckin' nose. Definitely not a looker but I bet she cooks really good. Probably goes to church a lot and is the kind that has a crush on a faggot priest. Am I right?"

Not answering, Frank feels a building dread.

Blaisdale gives one of his sick grins and glares. "I won't waste my time in torturing you but I could torture her. How about we give your sister a call right now and have her come over? After I break her nose, would you like to watch as I strip her naked and give her a Brazilian wax job with my lighter? A fat Italian girl like that is sure to have a lot of thick, black, curly pussy hair. If I light her big bush on fire, both you and I will be smellin' roastin' fish. Pee-yew! "

Deep inside Frank, red-hot anger awakens.

Taunting, the ex-cop continues, "Then I'll take a broom handle and give her a hysterectomy. I'm sure you would like to see that."

Frank still has his hands over his face but he is

trembling with more rage than fear.

Then in an odd moment of self-introspection Blaisdale drops his vicious smile and ponders aloud, "Do you know what I just realized? I'm mad at women. All my life I wanted a girlfriend or a wife but broads were always repulsed by me. More than once, women called me ugly. They hate my eyes. Even my mother, who was a fuckin' drunk, said I was homely. And because of that, I think I will really enjoy torturing your sister. It will be my revenge against all the cunts in the world."

"Okay, enough," Frank mutters. Hatred burns inside.

"Okay, what?" snaps the ex-cop.

Pause.

"Okay, I'll take ya to get the ticket. Just don't touch my sister."

"I won't touch that fat virgin so long as I get what I want! Now where the fuck is the ticket?" Blaisdale's blue bulging eyes seem to grow larger.

Frank swallows hard and lies, "It's in a safe deposit box in a town nearby."

"You are gonna fuckin' take me there, right now!" orders Blaisdale.

"I'll drive," says Frank with a sudden calmness in his voice.

Thirty-Five

Monday, 12:45 p.m. The flow of vehicles on I-95 is moving at a steady clip. Tightly grasping the steering wheel of big maroon Lincoln Continental, Frank intently stares ahead as he drives faster and faster. Blaisdale is in the front passenger seat. The Glock is out on his lap. Both men are not wearing their seatbelts.

"So where exactly is this safe deposit box?" Blaisdale asks with excitement. "What town?"

"Ah, Milford," Frank lies again. "At a local bank." His foot presses harder on the accelerator.

"Okay," Blaisdale smiles. "We just gotta get over the Q Bridge. The traffic is not too bad."

Desperately Frank prays that his plan will not fail.

"Don't look so glum." The ex-cop says, sounding unnerving friendly. "This will all be over soon. I have to say I like your car." He runs his hand along the dark leather upholstery. "These old Lincolns are beautiful. What year is it?"

"84," mumbles Frank.

"Nice. Like to have one of these myself." Blaisdale points to the stereo cassette in the dash. "Do ya got any Sinatra? Old blue eyes must sound perfect playin' in this car. You know they say he was a moody fuck. The world's greatest singer but never really happy. Supposedly he was manic-depressive. What do ya think of that?"

Frank doesn't answer. It is the moment of truth. Coming up on the right is a large parked, orange D.O.T. Mac truck.

Crossing from the left lane, Frank floors the gas pedal. The big V-8 surges and the Lincoln speeds up to over 90 miles per hour.

"Hey, slow down," Blaisdale says with concern. "Why ya drivin' so fast?"

"This is for killin' Vinny!" Frank glances over at the ex-cop with an expression of utter, molten vengeance.

"FUCK!!!" Blaisdale screams in terror. He tries to reach out and get hold of the wheel but it is too late. "NO!!!!"

The Lincoln plows into the back of the truck. Being a late model automobile there are no airbags. Frank's leg bones and pelvis fracture and deform as the engine block comes hurling back into the car cabin. With the cracking of his sternum and the splintering of his ribs, his aorta busts as the steering wheel embeds into his chest. The impact and force are so great that there is no time to feel any agony. All that registers are brief flashes of memories. Images of the beach, Charles Island and Long Island Sound play one last time in Frank's mind. Then there is final peace.

With a great burst of flying glass, Blaisdale rockets out of the front windshield. Looking like a stunt man shot out of a cannon, his body sails in the air and strikes high up on the back gate of the Mac truck. In a shower of clinking shards and limp like a rag-doll, he then bounces back, landing on the roof of the wrecked Lincoln. There is the blowing of horns and the slamming of brakes as the nearby traffic reacts to the horrific collision. Miraculously, Blaisdale is still alive. In shock, his big blue eyes are bulging wider than ever, staring up at the clear autumn sky. Lying sprawled, belly up on the top of the smoldering vehicle, he fades in and out of consciousness. There is no recognition of pain related to the jagged piece of glistening humorous poking out of the upper sleeve of his sports coat. He tries to move but it is impossible. Only a few strands of his spinal cord are left intact at the fragmented second cervical vertebrae.

Thirty-Six

Monday, 12:55 p.m. Jesse stays outside on the stoop and is too afraid to go into the house. The two awful possibilities would be either violence or mom and Troy would make-up and start fucking. With his nerves on edge, Jesse wants to chill so he chances smoking outside in plain view. Taking out a little baggy of weed from his jean jacket, he twists up a joint with the last bit of rolling paper.

This is so uncool. My mom is in there with a friggin' psycho killer and she is probably gonna blow him.

Breathing in the bud, Jesse tries not to think about the corpse in the shed. During the last couple of days, he attempted to convince himself that the murder never happened despite the growing odor. Getting high a lot helped block things out but when he fell asleep he was stricken with nightmares.

From inside the house, Rhonda's screams of jubilation can be heard. She is bouncing up and down and hugging Troy while the two stand in the dirty kitchen.

"It's a miracle! I knew you would come back! Our lives are gonna change forever!"

Troy pushes her away with a sense of disgust even though he is the one drenched with sweat. He asks in a panting threatening tone, "So have you cashed your welfare check yet? I need some money!"

"Honey, don't you ever have to worry about money again! We have been blessed by an angel. This morning, I was at the clinic feeling all suicidal because you were gone, and this little sad fella comes by, who I thought at first was a nut, and gives me a lottery ticket. I was about to toss it but he seemed so fucking sincere. So I left the clinic and went to the supermarket and had one of the cashiers run the ticket through the lottery machine. And guess what?"

Looking dumbstruck and hostile, Troy doesn't say anything back.

"WINNER!!!" shouts Rhonda with euphoria. She holds the ticket up in front of Troy's perplexed face.

"Bullshit," he gasps.

"No darling, it's true! Three and a half million fuckin' dollars! I couldn't believe it myself at first either but here look!" Rhonda shows the verification slip with the list of winning numbers.

Immediately Troy snatches the ticket from her hand and checks it for himself. "Fuck," he utters, feeling his head swoon. "This has to be some kind of setup."

"No, sweetie!" begs Rhonda. "You have to believe me! It's all good! Our lives have been so rough, God just decided to have some pity on us and give us some good fortune. We just gotta go to the lottery claim center in Newington, present the ticket and the people there will write us out a big ass check!"

"What did the guy look like that gave you the ticket?" Troy asks with a tremble in his voice.

"He was just sad. I remember he seemed really bruised up and had something wrong with his throat."

Troy feels icy cold.

Rhonda continues, "The only thing he said about the ticket was to wait a couple of weeks before cashing it in. I got no clue why."

Abruptly, Troy sticks the ticket into the front pocket of his corduroys and starts to pace while running his hands nervously through his damp hair. Already paranoid from all the crack-cocaine and PCP, his thoughts race, *This is a fucking trap! I know it! The mobs playing with me!*

Wonder if they already whacked Marco. But I can't believe I got 3.5 million dollars fucking sitting in my goddamn pants. This is too good to be true! Got to figure somehow to chance claiming it without getting caught! Fuck! I got to think! What I'm going to do? Fuck!

"It's okay baby!" pleads Rhonda. "You can have the ticket. Just promise me that we will be together forever. We'll be so rich. And we'll make love every day in the hot tub in the mansion. And don't worry about Jesse. I know he would just cramp our style. We won't even tell him about it. We'll just take off on him!"

Looking back at the woman with mistrust, Troy worries in his head, *Maybe the mob got to her! Maybe she's in on it!*

Rhonda brings up her scarred, scratched arms in another attempt to embrace. She coos, "Come on sweetie, relax. You look so tense. I brought groceries. How about I cook you a nice meal, then later on we'll 69."

With a quick sneer, Troy steps back from Rhonda and pushes away her arms.

"Don't do that!" Rhonda whines. "I can't take you rejecting me! If you take off on me again, I won't just cut myself; I may really end it for real! If I committed suicide because you broke my heart, how would that make you feel, Baby?"

Impulsively, Troy reaches out and grabs the jar of Ragu on the kitchen counter and uses it to smash Rhonda on the side of the head. There is an explosion of spaghetti sauce and glass. Rhonda is knocked out on impact. Dropping to the floor, blood streams from a large laceration on her left temple but it's hard to discern what is gore and what is marinara.

"Fuck!" curses Troy in pain. He had cut his hand again. There are shards in his palm. Lifting up his right foot, he places his big work boot on the woman's throat.

Giving a quick hop, he attempts to stand on one leg, driving downward with his bodyweight. There is a popping sound as the cartilage of Rhonda's trachea collapses.

"Yea, that worked!" Troy exclaims.

Gurgling, Rhonda is next dragged by her feet over to the cellar door near the pantry. With some jostling and shoving, Troy sends her body tumbling down the stairs into the darkened basement. The cellar door is shut with a loud bang.

"Well, that's done!" Troy says sounding winded. Red sauce is splattered all over his yellow short-sleeve shirt and beige corduroys. It is in his hair and it speckles his face and bare arms. Troy says aloud, "I smell like a fucking pizza!" Pacing again, Troy's mind is in overdrive, *Well, what the fuck do I do now? What's next? What? Shit!*

There are some faint knocking sounds coming from the cellar as Rhonda convulses. Troy fails to notice. He walks back and forth in the kitchen like a caged tiger. His big boots leave spaghetti sauce footprints on the grimy white tile floor.

Got to think! I need to get to that lottery place in Newington. We're talking over three million dollars here! I got to chance claiming it! That much money is worth the fucking risk! But I know this is all fucking crazy! I know they're fucking watching me! Fuck! I really can't decide!

Up and down in the small kitchen Troy continues to pace. He then slaps his forehead, *Maybe I could send someone else in there to claim the ticket for me! Yea! That's it! Somebody who knows nothing about nothing. But who? Fuck! Who?*

At that moment the sweet stench of cannabis wafts in the room from outdoors.

"Jesse!" Troy shouts aloud with the proverbial light bulb going on over his head. He then thinks, *Yes! The kid will be perfect! He's like a fucking sorry little puppy! If*

someone's waiting there, let him take the fucking bullet!
But if the coast is clear, I'll be scooping up that money
and fucking heading for Disney Land!

The present need to obtain a ride to the lottery
headquarters is the next part of the plan to be solved. Troy
slaps his head again and remembers the folded up Time
magazine cover in his back pocket. Frantically Troy starts
digging for it. He gets it out! He unfolds it! There written
in black ink from the Mont Blanc fountain pen is Francis
LaBoudy's phone number scrawled across the photo of
Sarah Palin's face.

Thirty-Seven

Monday, 1:49 p.m. The battered and dented white Ford Tempo is stuck in a massive traffic jam on I-95. Miles up ahead, emergency crews are handling the fatal crash involving the Lincoln Continental and D.O.T. Mac truck. Both sides of the interstate are closed down to allow the Life Star helicopter to land and airlift out the victim with the broken neck.

"I can't fucking believe this shit!" curses Troy has he keeps fidgeting in the back seat of the Tempo. "Why ain't we fucking moving?"

Sitting in the front passenger side is Francis LaBoudy, dressed in a crisp white shirt and gray trousers. His thin black hair is slicked tight to his skull with extra Vitalis. The Mont Blanc pen is in his breast pocket. With his head cocked around, he keeps staring at Troy with ecstatic desire. LaBoudy purrs, "Oh, I can see you are like a chained beast, waiting to break free and tear at the world! I'm just so delighted that you called. We're all just a gang of bad boys out on the loose!"

Troy is so repulsed by LaBoudy that he is tempted to punch the creepy little man in the face. It is a hard urge to control but the prospect of all that money produces some restraint. In his racing mind, Troy thinks, *I'll kill everybody in this fucking car later! I just got to wait until the ticket is cashed in!* Shifting his attention back to Jesse, Troy says in a pressured, breathy tone, "So do you want to go over the plan again? You better not fuck it up! Remember, you're just going to walk into the lottery headquarters and show them that ticket I have been letting you hold." Troy reaches out and nervously pats the front pocket of Jesse's jean jacket. "Ask for a lump sum check. Grab it and run back outside. We'll be waiting for you out in the parking lot. After that, we'll fucking floor it all the way to the nearest bank, cash it in and be fucking rich!"

Wringing his hands, LaBoudy giggles with excitement, "Oh, this seems so daring!"

Cramped in the back seat, next to Troy, Jesse is pale and lost in another world full of sickening fear and hopelessness. It is hard to move because the rear passenger door, on the driver's side had been bowed in during the past accident. A sheet of opaque plastic has been taped up to cover the shattered window. Bits of glass still glisten on the floor mats.

"Did you hear what I said? Are you fucking listening to me!" Troy barks at Jesse. "You look like you're going to fucking cry!"

With a quivering lower lip, Jesse asks, "Did you kill my mom?"

Troy is taken aback. There is a pause. Huffing, Troy then stutters, "Wha-wha-what the fuck are you talking about? I told you, she was tired. She didn't want to come along! I think she had her fucking period. She wanted to take a nap!"

Gulping, Jesse questions further, "Then why are you all covered with blood?"

"What?" Troy snaps. He then looks down at his yellow shirt and beige corduroys and realizes he is still blotched with red splatter. "Ah, fuck!" Troy says with some embarrassment, "This isn't blood! It's fucking tomato sauce!"

LaBoudy has a puzzled look on his face as he thinks; *I've been trying to ignore the stains on Troy's clothes. I dare not tell him I can't stand the sight of blood. I hope it is tomato sauce!*

"I like tomato sauce and macaroni," chimes in Chester as he sits behind the wheel.

Raw and irritated, Troy, responds, "I can't believe we have a fucking retard driving this car!"

"Don't call me a retard! That's not nice! I'm handicapped!" says Chester.

"Yea, then why do you got that weird haircut?" bickers Troy. "Looks like someone used a bowl on your head when they gave you a snip! Only retards get haircuts like that!"

"You're a bad person," pouts Chester. "I shouldn't be givin' you a ride."

"Be quiet, Chester" reprimands LaBoudy. "You're a chauffeur and chauffeurs are not supposed to talk back to the guests."

Uncomfortable in his oversized, green winter coat, Chester whines, "My sister is gonna be mad. She said I couldn't have you in the car anymore, Francis, cuz you made me get into an accident!"

"I said hush-up!" snaps LaBoudy

Troy grits his teeth and internally he boils, *Rain Man, the faggot and this little pothead next to me are all going to die! Can't fucking wait to strangle 'em all!* Raking his hands through his hair, Troy bitches aloud again, "God, why isn't this fucking traffic moving! "

Behind the Ford Tempo, off in the distance, there comes the angry blaring of a horn.

Trembling, Jesse shuts his eyes to fight back the tears. Like a parasite, the Lotto ticket rests in darkness in the front pocket of his jean jacket.

Monday, 1:55 p.m. The large black Dodge Ram with the busted driver side window is about an eighth of a mile back behind the Ford Tempo. Paul Kosakowski palm-heals the horn again and sends out another loud blast. Dripping with sweat, he has on a soaked white t-shirt and desert camouflage pants. His fury is an atomic bomb about to mushroom cloud. Earlier in the morning his brother was finally pulled off life support following another massive stroke. It was the last straw following Friday's pink slip. The wrecking ball is swinging and Mr. Whoop-Ass, along with 18, 30 round magazines are stacked on the front passenger seat of the truck. Paul also brought along his short Samurai Tanto sword. Kosakowski's plan entails finding his ex-wife Peggy and her new Dominican boyfriend and shooting them full of holes until they are unrecognizable. Numerous ex-co-workers and the factory supervisor are also on today's death list. However, his first intended target is Dr. Peter Fray. Pounding the dashboard, Kosakowski blurts aloud, "I'm just gonna quickly stop by his office and rush upstairs and empty a full mag into his face! TEACH YOU TO FUCKIN' INFRINGE WITH MY GOD GIVEN RIGHT TO BEAR ARMS!!!"

The horn of the Dodge truck blasts again.

"Wonder if its fuckin' road construction up ahead?" Kosakowski steams like a pressure cooker. "I always hated the Department of Transportation in this fuckin state. Fuckin' corrupt bastards! Always takin' fuckin' kickbacks for slow shoddy work. Bunch of union slackers getting' fuckin' paid for draggin-it on the fuckin' job! Cheatin' us fuckin' taxpayers! I THINK I'LL GO SHOOT TWO OF THEM RIGHT NOW!!!"

The rampage could no longer wait. Impulsively, Kosakowski puts the truck in park and takes hold of the AK-47 along with an extra 30 round magazine. Exiting the Dodge Ram, he starts forward between the two lines of stuck traffic. Most people in their vehicles never notice the enraged fat guy with the assault rifle walking past. They are either zoned out listening to the radio, daydreaming or bitching on their cell-phones. A few do see the gunman and are frozen with disbelief.

Moving further and further ahead, Kosakowski suddenly stops and utters in astonishment. "License plate number DPR-163!" In his unwell, monstrous mind he then thinks, *I can't fuckin' believe it! I wonder if these are the same wise-ass pricks? The car looks kind of banged up though. I don't know, but I gotta kill somethin'!*

Chester turns as the muzzle of the AK-47 taps tauntingly on the driver side window. In the next second with flashing eardrum-popping crackle, there comes a jerky horizontal torrent of 7.62x39 caliber rounds. Glass pulverizes and fragments, showering the air. A red mist materializes and hovers for a moment as Chester's head comes apart. Bullets zip past LaBoudy, blowing out the opposite side passenger window, punching through the door panel. In the back seat, Troy is stricken immobile for a couple of beats, then some internal survival mechanism kicks in, and he finds himself bolting out of the car.

"IT'S A FUCKING HITMAN!!!!" Troy screams in terror as he sprints.

Kosakowski fires across the roof of the Ford as his fleeing target tries to make it over to the embankment. One of Troy's big work boots gets tangled in the steel cable of the guardrail. Hot shiny brass shell casings eject with rapid mechanical power, flying and tumbling. The majority of the 18 round burst misses, however, one bullet gouges Troy's right elbow while another enters just above his right hip and exits out his lower left abdomen.

"YEA!!!" Kosakowski shouts with homicidal glee.

Instantly, Troy drops out of view as his lanky body topples, long limbs flopping. He bounces and rolls down the grassy slope. Kosakowski is unsure if he scored a kill because his prey had vanished so quickly from his line of fire. The spent rounds clink and roll around on the asphalt. The AK's magazine is empty.

"HELP!!!!!!
AAAAAAAAAAAAAAAAAAAAAHHHH!!!!!!!!!!!!!!!"
LaBoudy is wailing but cannot hear the volume of his own voice because his eardrums had ruptured from the roar of gunfire. Still sitting in the front passenger seat of the Tempo, it appears that he is gravely injured and bleeding but miraculously he has been spared any lethal wounds. The blood and fatty pink brain pudding that is splattered all over Francis' face, white shirt, and gray trousers are from his chauffeur. Slumped dead behind the wheel, Chester's head is misshapen like a smashed pumpkin. A large fissure runs up from a blackened ragged crater where his nose had been, to the top of his forehead, giving the ghastly appearance that his face is cracked in half. A lifeless eyeball hangs down where there was once a cheekbone. Almost his entire occipital lobe has been hollowed out.

"EEEEEEEEEEEEEEEEEEEEEEEECK!!!!!!!!!!!!!"
Freaked by all the gore, LaBoudy continues with his high-pitched whine of horror. A large dark ink stain continues to grow on the front of his bloodied white shirt. During the initial shooting, a round had come dangerously close as it grazed LaBoudy's chest and splintered the Mont Blanc pen in his breast pocket. Finally, noticing that his own right thumb had been shot off, Francis faints like a teenage waif.

In the back of the Tempo, Jesse is too frozen to make even the slightest stir. Being small, he had been able to stuff himself down off the seat, his face pressed against the floor mats. Glass glistens in his hair. A small wet, jagged piece of Chester's skull had landed and gotten stuck down the collar of his jean jacket. The loud blasts of the AK have also affected Jesse's hearing. Temporarily deaf, and with his eyes squeezed tightly closed, he wonders if he is dead.

Monday, 2:14 p.m. Connecticut State Trooper

Brenda Mitchell is the closest by when the call comes in regarding shots being fired. With lights flashing, she tries to make her way up the breakdown lane but motorists have gotten out of their cars and are fleeing in a panic. Others are mulling about asking those running for information. A tearful heavy-set soccer mom steps in front of the path of the approaching police cruiser, pointing and signaling that the danger is straight ahead. With the siren on, Officer Mitchell speeds forward, her heart thumping. What she sees next makes her have that sudden feeling of ice in her veins. She gasps, "Oh my God, it can't be him! OH GOD, IT IS!!!!"

Kosakowski is standing next to the White Ford Tempo, trying to desperately remove the empty mag from his assault rifle. His plan is to send a few more rounds into the car before moving on with his killing spree. Juiced with a tsunami of adrenaline, his fine motor dexterity has been lost, and he cannot get his fingers to work the magazine extractor. *Fuck, why won't this mag free up?!!!*

With the blare of the siren and oscillating blue and white beams, the police cruiser screeches to a halt on the left side shoulder of the highway. Officer Mitchell rushes out of her vehicle and takes a semi crouched position behind the front wheel-well. The Sig P220 shakes in her hands. Her voice is trembling as she shouts out, "P-P-Paul, drop the fucking rifle now!"

With his ears still ringing, all external noise seems distant and muffled like hearing music underwater. The flashing lights from the police car finally jar Kosakowski from his tunnel vision and make him aware that he is under threat. At that moment the empty magazine from the AK-47 finally releases, falls, and clatters on the ground.

"For Christ's sake, Paul!" screams Officer Mitchell "I said drop the goddamn weapon!"

It is then that Kosakowski makes the startling realization that the female state trooper who is pointing a gun at him is his ex-sister in-law. Robotically, he reaches down to the oversized side pocket on the right leg of his camouflage pants to retrieve the second AK-47 magazine.

"I WILL BLOW THIS LESBIAN CUNT BITCH IN HALF!!!!" He proclaims.

Inside the Ford Tempo, LaBoudy abruptly regains consciousness and wretches. Looking like some type of gruesome tie-dye, watery puke is now added to the red splatter and black ink that soaks the front of his white shirt. After spitting-up, LaBoudy starts again with his high pitched wailing as he rocks and clutches his hurt hand. "HHHHHHHHHHHHELP!!!! HHHHHHHHHHELP!!!"

Kosakowski is able to slam home the fresh magazine and starts to raise the barrel of the assault rifle.

"DON'T DO IT YOU ASSHOLE!!!" Officer Mitchell pleads for the last time but it is to no avail. As the muzzle of Mr. Whoop-Ass is pointed in her direction she fires away with her pistol. A volley of .45 caliber HST hollow-points strike Kosakowski in various parts of his hulking anatomy. The first group of slugs hit him low. One grazes his right inner thigh. Shot two zips through his crotch turning his left nut into goo and making a furrow in his left ass cheek as it blows out the back of his pants. Another drills in right above his navel, expanding in his tallow and guts, losing energy and stopping in his body only after it splinters a lumbar vertebra. Hollow-point number four also hits at center mass but goes on a diagonal course puncturing his stomach and liver and leaving his torso near the right seventh rib with a quarter-coin-sized exit wound. Coming up on his toes, Kosakowski then buckles at the waist while his finger keeps continuously squeezing the assault rifle's trigger. AK-47 rounds stitch the backside panel of the police cruiser and pop a rear tire. A few of the wild 7.62 X 39 caliber rounds travel across the way to the south bound lane shattering the window of a Subaru and catching a gawkier in the jaw and sending teeth flying along with an ejaculation of blood.

Still in the front passenger seat of the Ford Tempo, LaBoudy continues with his soprano distress call, "HELP! HHHHHHHHHHHHHHELP!!!"

Officer Brenda Mitchell continues to blast away with her Sig Sauer.

As Kosakowski folds forward, a .45 HST nips his left upper arm. Another pings and bends the assault rifle's trigger guard. While still another hollow-point enters above his left collar bone and goes on a downward trajectory through his lung, piercing through the top of his heart and coming to a stall in the left ventricle. Kosakowski continues to descend face first toward the asphalt, into blackness, into oblivion.

Suddenly inside the Ford Tempo, LaBoudy instantly ceases his distressful bawling. A stray round from Officer Mitchell's gun had entered the car and caught Francis in the left temple. A bright red geyser pumps out from the bullet hole in the side of his head and sprays the already sanguine dashboard. For the little creepy man that did not like blood, he is now drenched in it upon death.

The slide of the Sig P220 is in a retracted position, indicating that all eight shots have been fired. A stinging whiff of cordite comes and goes just like the fading echo of gunfire. Sorrowful silence follows but it is only momentary as the sound of approaching sirens can be heard from a distance. Trembling and lowering her empty pistol, Officer Mitchell, whispers "Oh, Jesus." Tears brim up in her eyes.

Kosakowski is dead, lying face down in a heap on top of his rifle. A dark pool is growing out from underneath him on the pavement. The wrecking ball has been stopped.

Monday, 2:37 p.m. Troy keeps fading in and out of consciousness; decaying autumn leaves cover his eyes and twigs poke his face. When awake, he can hear the clamor of sirens and the crackle of police car radios coming from far above. Desperately, he wants to call out for help but all he can manage is soft wheezing and a wet gurgle. Having rolled down the 18-foot embankment into a thick hedge of brambles, none of the emergency crew up top on the highway are aware of his existence. They fail to notice the blood trail that marks the nearby slope behind the stretch of guardrails.

More time passes.

It is colder and Troy is already shivering uncontrollably as he teeters on the verge of going into full-blown shock. His right arm is numb from the elbow joint down while his left hand is useless due to a fractured wrist that occurred during the fall.

Suddenly a news chopper passes overhead.

"H—h-elp!" Troy gasps. Attempting to move his legs, he suddenly experiences hot searing agony that almost causes him to black out once again.

Fuck! This fucking hurts! I can't take it!

Earlier, when the AK-47 round ripped through his lower midsection it had yawed pushing out a segment of viscera from an exit wound that consists of a three-inch tear on the left side of his belly. Presently ensnared in a clump of bushes, a loop of his duodenum is entangled around a branch of prickers. Every time Troy stirs, a little bit more of his intestine is pulled out from his body.

I smell shit! Troy thinks to himself. *I'm going to puke!*

The stench of his open bowel is becoming overpowering. Essence continues to soak the damp black ground.

I'm fucking freezing! I can't get up! I'm fucking trapped! Oh, no! Oh no!!! NO!!!

The quaking and horrible icy feeling is growing by the second. His blood pressure is plummeting. Before Troy dies, he has flashbacks of being a child in foster care, tied with belts and locked in a closet with the lights turned off.

Don't lock me in here!
Don't lock me in here!
I can't move!
It's too dark!
NO!!!

Back then nobody knew how to control the little hyper boy who liked to break stuff. When they finally let him out of the closet, he was so crazed he just destroyed more things.

Thirty-Eight

Monday, 3:18 p.m. A code red trauma alert has been called for Saint Rose's E.R. Life Star had already choppered in Blaisdale. There are three dead-on-arrivals from the shooting spree on the highway. Jesse is brought in by ambulance. After an initial examination in triage, it is determined that the kid has no physical injuries but is placed on watch for shock. In a small observation room with a drawn curtain, Jesse's clothes are removed. He is re-dressed in a johnnie coat and covered with blankets. Bits of glass are still in his hair along with crusties of dried blood. A young Hispanic nurses aide is seated at the side of his gurney. She reaches out and holds his clammy hand.

"Can I get you anything?" she asks with genuine compassion.

Looking back with wide eyes full of bewilderment, Jesse does not answer right away. He then whispers, "Can I see my jean jacket for a second?"

"What? Your jacket?"

"Yea."

The aide is hesitant because she knows his clothes are soiled with blood and already bagged in plastic and put away in a locker. She replies, "Your stuff may be kind of dirty. Also I think the EMTs may have cut your clothes up a bit when they went to do their thing."

Taking a hard swallow, Jesse begs softly, "I don't care about my pants and shirt. I just want to see my jean jacket. Please!"

After another pause, the young girl smiles and sighs,

"Okay, I'll be right back. Just use the call light if suddenly you don't feel well."

Jesse gives a nod and returns his head to the pillow. Left alone in the small observation room, the sounds of chaos coming from outside in the hallway seems to grow louder. There are shouted commands from an E.R. doc, the beeping of monitors, and the screams of the injured.

My hearing is working again. Jesse thinks. *I was sure that I went deaf. God, please let that chick find my jacket. I really need what's in those pockets. Please! Please! I'm really praying to you this time God! C'mon!"*

A few more moments pass.

Finally, the aide returns, holding up the jean jacket. She is wearing Latex gloves. There are blood splatter stains on the fabric.

"Yeah. Cool!" Jesse says with some energy as he sits up on the gurney.

"Here," the aide says. "You can have it for a bit. But they'll probably make me lock it back up again."

Jesse greedily takes the jacket.

"Do you need anything else?" The girl asks. "Do you want some juice?"

Jesse does not look up nor answer the aide as he burrows with his hands into the jacket pockets.

"I said do you want something to drink? Your lips look really dry."

"What? Yea, whatever! Sure," Jesse snaps with some irritability. "You can go. I want to be alone for a while. I'm okay!"

Dropping her smile, the aide replies, "I'll get you your juice. But I need to come back and stay with you because you're still on observation. I don't want to get in trouble. This is my first day on the job."

Again Jesse does not reply but continues to search his jacket. The young girl departs from the room.

"Yes!" Jesse gasps with relief. In this time of distress, there is only one thing he deems as a shining beacon of good fortune. He pulls it out. There, in his trembling hands is a plastic baggy with a little bit of leftover weed. He retrieves a Bic lighter from a different pocket.

Thank you Jesus! Jesse cheers internally. *You don't know how bad I need to smoke a joint at this moment! Man, I can't fuckin' believe what I just went through!*

Jesse then frantically searches the jacket again for rolling papers.

"Shit!" He curses, "I think I'm out!"

At this second, Jesse's fingertip touches and finds the small square piece of paper stowed away in the front breast pocket of the jean jacket. Earlier, when Troy was babbling about claiming a lottery ticket, Jesse did not believe a word that was being said. He assumed that his nemesis was just insane.

Jesse removes the Lotto ticket from the jacket pocket. A dried brown-red fingerprint has slightly marred some of the numbers but the sequence is still legible. It reads 27, 28, 30, 31, 35, 37. Jesse is clueless regarding its value. His only concern at the moment is to feel a nice calming buzz as quickly as possible. Sprinkling out a line of marijuana onto the lottery ticket, he rolls it up into a sloppy little joint.

"Come on! Come on!" Jesse says anxiously.

It takes three shaky flicks at the Bic to produce a flame. The joint ignites with a flash of fire. Instantly there is the sweet stink of burning cannabis. Jesse sucks in like it is his last dying breath.

Time to kill the pain. He thinks.

The paper burns up too fast and little smoldering embers of pot fall to the floor along with the promise of 3.5 million dollars.

Finally, the parasite is dead.

In the next moment, the young aide returns with the juice.

"Hey!" she scolds with anger, "You can't smoke in here!"

Jesse instantly breaks down with a long wrenching sob.

Thirty-Nine

August, nine months later.

Friday, 3:16 p.m. Connecticut Department of Transportation workers while removing brush near the interstate find a human skeleton, with the bones of the feet still inside a pair of big moldy steel-toed work boots. The only remaining bit of flesh left is a dried piece of black intestinal jerky wrapped around a brittle thorn branch.

Friday, 3:17 p.m. Retired Bridgeport Detective Donald Blaisdale dies from pneumonia, complications from his C-2 spinal cord injury. Some of the nursing aides working at the physical rehabilitation facility had cruelly referred to him "as just another angry head." Before expiring, he spent his days and months hooked up to a respiration vent. He wept a lot but could only scream aloud in his mind.

Friday 3:18 p.m. In downtown New Haven, Dr. Fray has taken the afternoon off to meet his fiancé at an artsy coffee bar. He waits in line by the counter. Nearby there is a newspaper rack and he eyes the headlines. A sensational top story is plastered on the front cover of the Elm City Register involving the recent murder suicide of alleged organized crime figure Sal Penzetta. Reportedly an ex-employee and semi-pro MMA fighter, a Mr. Anthony Amato, had beaten and choked the gangster to death before committing suicide. Sources close to the case expressed that Mr. Amato, was infuriated after being fired by Mr. Penzetta. Reportedly, Mr. Penzetta had been quoted as saying he did not want any gays working in his organization. A sister of Mr. Amato did report that her brother was recently diagnosed as HIV positive and had become emotionally troubled.

Dr. Fray turns his gaze away from the news rack. He cannot tolerate reading any more about tragedy and death. The last year was horrific. Today is a good day. Jesse Butkus had come to the clinic earlier in the morning for a therapy session and expressed feeling stable since joining a faith-based recovery program. Peter sees promise in the kid despite the heavy PTSD.

Hope he makes it.

The line of customers at the coffee bar is growing shorter. In the back, behind the counter, there is a large young guy with a five-o'clock shadow, dressed in a green apron, struggling to fold up a vegetarian tofu wrap. He seems a bit clumsy at the task. Peter squints and thinks to himself, *He looks familiar. Where do I know that face?*

A female employee comes to the big fellow's assistance. The girl is short and chunky with blue hair and a pierced eyebrow. Peter notices how she presses her body flirtatiously up against her coworker. The psychologist surmises that the two are dating and his assumption is correct. It is a blossoming workplace romance. With glee, the girl has been bragging to her punk rock pals that her new boyfriend only has one nipple.

For Warren Ritchie this is the happiest time in his life. The new medications are sort of working and the voices and paranoia are at bay. The ability to tolerate a job in a public setting is a grand achievement. To hold a girl in his arms and to experience tenderness is ethereal.

Friday, 3:33 p.m. Kali is not on a rampage today.

A Departing Public Service Announcement
From the author

According to the National Board of Psychiatry, two out of every five Americans will have some sort of mental illness some time in their life. It could be your neighbor, co-worker, a relative, a spouse, your child, or you, the reader of this book.

Adios!

Thank you for reading.
Please review this book. Reviews help others find New
Pulp Press and inspire us to keep providing these
marvelous tales.

If you would like to be put on our email list to receive
updates on new releases, contests, and promotions, please
go to NewPulpPress.com and sign up.

About The Author

In his youth, he took soil home from Dudleytown, Connecticut and was scolded by Mrs. Warren. As a man, he traveled abroad and walked the Killing Fields of Cambodia and the grounds of Auschwitz, Poland. At a Luxor temple in Egypt, he was shown the remnants of an al Qaeda terror attack. Bullet holes from AK-47s marred the ancient stones. Recently, Mr. Cervo was told by clairvoyant mediums that he is being infected by a hoard of raging entities dwelling in his dirt cellar..

NewPulpPress.com